S0-ARO-657

"I know you," he said softly. "You're a DaCosta jaguar . . ." His voice trailed off, and Jaden was surprised at the level of violence she sensed beneath the surface. There was a darkness inside him that was lethal. A shiver rolled over her skin as she gazed at him.

"You've got to be joking. Was I that forgettable?"

The air around him shimmered, and before she could blink an eye, Julian was at her back, his arm across her chest as he pulled her in tight to his body. What the hell had happened to him? *She* was the warrior, not he.

"I know who you are." His breath was hot against her neck. His heart beat heavy against her ribs.

His hand slowly slid down her skin until it rested against the soft flesh that pulsed at the base of her neck. The beat was fast, and Jaden tried desperately to keep her jaguar at bay. Her skin was on fire, aching. It felt as if she were being ripped in two.

"You're a DaCosta," he said. "Convince me I shouldn't just snap your neck and be done with it."

By Juliana Stone

His Darkest Salvation
His Darkest Embrace
His Darkest Hunger

His Darkest
SALVATION

JULIANA STONE

AVON
An Imprint of HarperCollinsPublishers

This is a work of fiction. Names, characters, places, and incidents are products of the author's imagination or are used fictitiously and are not to be construed as real. Any resemblance to actual events, locales, organizations, or persons, living or dead, is entirely coincidental.

AVON BOOKS
An Imprint of HarperCollins*Publishers*
10 East 53rd Street
New York, New York 10022-5299

Copyright © 2011 by Juliana Stone
ISBN 978-0-06-202263-9
www.avonromance.com

First Avon Books mass market printing: August 2011

Avon Trademark Reg. U.S. Pat. Off. and in Other Countries, Marca Registrada, Hecho en U.S.A.
HarperCollins® is a registered trademark of HarperCollins Publishers.

Printed in the U.S.A.

10 9 8 7 6 5 4 3 2 1

*This book is dedicated to my mom, Miss Millie,
and my dad, Stevie B. None of us has the power
to choose our parents. There is no store to shop
in, no catalogue for the top models. I'm cool with
that 'cause I lucked out and hit the jackpot. I love
you both more than you know.*

acknowledgments

There are so many people involved in this process, and they need to be thanked. It truly is a team effort.

Laura and Esi, again the keepers of my dreams. Thanks for being there and helping when I need it. Pam, you rock the publicity department and introduced me to Steri-fab. New York was so much fun, thanks for the opportunity to come hang in your awesome city. I look forward to a return visit!

All the wonderful authors who write for HarperCollins, especially those on our paranormal loop who are always keen to answer questions, offer support, and give advice. You're all incredibly cool, talented, smart ladies, and I'm humbled to be included in your group.

Amanda Vyne, you're the best. That is all.

Elisabeth Naughton did a quick read for me as I was about to panic, thanks for being there in a pinch.

I want to thank everyone at HarperCollins who worked on this book, there are a ton I don't know by name, but please rest assured everything you do is so appreciated. Tom, once again thanks for giving me a smokin' cover. Adrienne, you are one cool lady, and, well, you love Bruce.

Friends and family for your support and enthusiasm, especially Terre, Crystal, Tracy, Shelli, The Mudslides, The Sirens and Scribes, and Aunt Wendy.

Finally, a quick thank-you to the readers who've e-mailed and brightened my day, with your kind words and love for my jaguars. Please don't stop. Ever ☺

Last but not least, special thanks to Andrew, Kristen, and Jacob, just because you all belong to me.

His Darkest
SALVATION

Prologue

The light had given way to an unprecedented darkness: a flash of heat, a taste of sulfur, then nothing but fire.

The pain was constant. It drifted over his skin like black mist, sliding across flesh and caressing every inch of it, full of an evil that both fed upon and nourished him.

It sustained a need that grew stronger every day he was in this hellhole.

And it *was* hell, of that there was no question.

At the edge of Julian Castille's vision a shape lingered, drifting, out of focus, ethereal. Watching . . . waiting, until it was time. Then she would carefully slice into his chest, peel back a piece of skin, and resume her position.

To wait once more.

For the day he'd finally break.

Chapter 1

Six Months Later

Jaden DaCosta knew she was in trouble about ten seconds before the door opened.

It was in the air she dragged deep into her lungs and the electricity that ran along with it, pulsing, burning, as it slid down.

She whipped her head around, eyes scanning with quick, cool precision, and dove behind the sofa just as a click echoed into the darkened penthouse.

Her heart slowed automatically, and she relaxed her limbs, calling the shadows to her as she slid forward on her belly. Fingers felt along her waist to cradle the edge of the charmed dagger there, and her senses sharpened as the animal inside awakened.

The door swung open slowly, sweeping across cool tiles and allowing a thin beam of light to fall into the dim interior. She saw a shadow reflected on the floor as long moments passed. It was impressive, and she gritted her teeth in anticipation.

And then he was there, striding into the room as if he owned the place.

Jaden gripped the dagger tightly. She inhaled the stench of otherworld, yet it was somehow different, already fading fast.

The intruder paused, his tall frame humming with an energy that was unlike any she'd ever come across. There was a familiarity to it that tugged at something deep inside her.

As he kicked the door shut, she watched in silence, wincing at the harsh echo as it slammed back against the frame.

The man held still for a few moments, then his head turned slowly. He paused, his nostrils flared. Her breath caught at the back of her throat. Would he be able to smell her through the charm that masked her scent?

Who the hell is he? What the hell is he?

The stranger relaxed a bit and rotated his neck, running his hands through thick hair that hung in waves to his shoulders. Power clung to him, gripping his tall form hungrily, electrifying the air.

It was tinged with a darkness that was hard to read.

After a few moments, he headed toward the kitchen, and the fridge door swung open at his command. Jaden could have saved him the bother. She'd already checked it out, and no one had been inside the penthouse since Julian Castille had pulled a Copperfield and disappeared into thin air. The food was either moldy, dated, or dried up.

The shrill echo of a cell phone pierced the silence, and she bit her tongue as her body jerked. The coppery taste of blood flooded her mouth, and her eyes narrowed as the stranger answered the call.

"Yeah." His voice was low, husky. He straightened, running a hand along the back of his neck as he rolled his shoulders and listened. Jaden strained to hear, but even with her enhanced senses, she couldn't pick up anything.

"I just got in." He sounded weary, and she inched forward slowly to get a better look but froze as he turned once more and headed toward her hiding place, stopping a few feet away.

There was something about the man that called to her, and Jaden was finding it harder to remain calm and undetected.

She studied his profile, her gaze running over the aristocratic nose, high cheekbones, and a mouth that, even from this angle, was to die for.

Inside, the cat erupted, and she broke out in a sweat as her skin began to burn and itch. The tattoos along the side of her neck became inflamed, the nerves pinched and sensitive.

Son of a bitch! It couldn't be . . .

"It's bearable," he said as he ran his hand over his chest. He nodded in answer to whatever was being said on the other end before whispering harshly, "Don't worry, I'm ready. Tomorrow we hunt."

He threw the cell phone onto the sofa where it landed with a thud. Jaden's heart was pounding so hard it was a miracle he couldn't hear it.

Julian Castille back from the Twilight Zone? *Was it possible? Had the bastard managed to survive whatever the hell he'd disappeared into?*

She ignored the rush of heat that rippled over her flesh as she struggled to keep it together. The man who'd haunted her dreams for the last three years stood not more than a few feet away, very much alive, when she'd thought him dead.

As much as Jaden loathed him, deep inside her soul the jaguar was singing, wanting nothing more than to mate. To

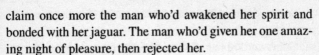

claim once more the man who'd awakened her spirit and bonded with her jaguar. The man who'd given her one amazing night of pleasure, then rejected her.

How pathetic.

Jaden's cheeks stung with a sharp slap of humiliation as she recalled the look of disgust that had crossed his face when he'd realized what she was.

No one had ever made her feel like that before. Like dirt. Like less than dirt.

So many questions crowded her head, but she pushed them away so she could concentrate. Something was off. This wasn't the Julian Castille she remembered. Nope. Back in the day, he'd been total *GQ,* hot for sure, but polished and boardroom ready. This man? He was edgy, dark—the word *sinister* came to mind.

She watched as he crossed to his bedroom and paused in the entrance, his head cocked to the side for a moment. He then padded over to the large bed just beyond and stripped the shirt from his body before slipping the jeans from his hips.

Jaden's mouth went dry. She couldn't take her eyes from him as he stood there, tall, fierce, buck naked with nothing but moonbeams through the window caressing his taut, powerful frame. He'd packed on some serious muscle since she'd last seen him.

She bit her lips once more to stifle the groan that now sat inside her mouth. Her jaguar was chomping at the bit, wanting out, and a wave of dizziness rippled through her skull.

Heat erupted between her legs, which only infuriated her more. *How the hell can he do this to me? After all this time?*

She closed her eyes, wanting nothing more than for him to disappear.

"If you want, I can bend over and give you a real treat."

The words slid out into the space between them, and

Jaden's eyes flew open, her hand going for the knife as adrenaline kicked in.

But it was too late. A flash of white teeth and a shimmering blur of air rushed at her. Jaden barely had time to roll to the side, and she jackknifed her body, landing in a crouch, with the dagger held in front of her.

Only to feel the heat of him at her back.

Fuck!

She reacted instinctively and swung her hips to the side, kicking her right leg out, intending to drop him hard. But it was she who took a tumble as large hands gripped her shoulders and spun her around like a top until she ended up on her back, splayed out like a total loser.

The knife clattered across the tiles, teasing her from several feet away. Jaden clenched her teeth and fought the urge to curse a torrent of foulness. She'd just pulled a total newbie move and had no one but herself to blame.

Julian stood over her, and, slowly, her eyes moved up his long frame, skipping over the impressive display of manhood, up his taut belly until she saw a sight that was immediately sobering.

Jaden swallowed heavily and couldn't look away from the macabre display of scars that crisscrossed his chest in perfect precision just under his left pectoral. They looked raw and painful.

"Didn't anyone teach you it's impolite to stare?"

Jaden's eyes jerked up to rest upon a face that was every bit as arresting as she remembered, if not more so.

Even in the dim light, she saw the flare that lit up his golden eyes, eerily so, yet the smile that fell over his mouth didn't reach them. A shiver ran over her body.

Julian Castille was not the person she remembered. At all.

"I'm sorry . . . I . . . ." she began, and actually blushed

as she stammered like an idiot in front of him. "I didn't expect . . ."

"To find me in my own home?" Julian took a step back, and Jaden carefully got to her feet. She eyed him warily.

"Where have you been?" she asked as she moved closer to where her dagger had fallen.

Julian's eyes narrowed. "I know you," he said softly.

Jaden's eyebrows arched, and harsh laughter fell from her lips as she snorted. "Ya think?" she asked sarcastically. *Christ, is he brain-damaged?*

He regarded her in silence, and a sliver of *something* flickered in the depths of his eyes but quickly disappeared as his lips thinned.

"You're a DaCosta jaguar. You were there in Belize just before . . ." His voice trailed off, and Jaden was surprised at the level of violence she sensed beneath the surface. There was a darkness inside him that was lethal. A shiver rolled over her skin as she gazed at him.

But then his words sank in, and her anger exploded. He honestly had no memory of their past? Of what they'd shared together?

"You've got to be joking," she whispered harshly, more to herself than anything. "You really don't remember who I am? Was I that forgettable?"

The air around him shimmered, and before she could blink an eye, Julian was at her back, his arm across her chest as he pulled her in tight to his body.

She had no time to react and dazedly wondered what the hell had happened to him. *She* was the warrior, not he. Yet it seemed he'd ingested a bit of superhero dust wherever the hell he'd been.

"I know who you are." His breath was hot against her neck. "Jaden DaCosta."

She began to struggle, but even with her superior strength, he was too strong. Several moments later she gave up, her breaths falling in pants as she tried to calm herself.

His heart beat heavy against her ribs, the rhythm steady, and the heat of him scorched her flesh.

"Why are you here?" he whispered, his breath warm against her neck as he nudged the mess of hair that lay there with his nose. Small bursts of electricity fell across her skin, and she shivered, pissed that she had no control over her body.

"Where have you been for the last six months?" she asked in response, barely able to get the words out from between her tight lips.

His hand slid along her jaw, and he gripped her hard, his fingers digging in until he drew a whimper from her.

"Lady, you don't want to know where I've been. Not really. So why don't we stop playing this game, and you tell me why a DaCosta jaguar is holed up in my place." She felt his fingers dig in a little more. "And no lies. I've not had the pleasure of kicking anyone's ass in a long time and really don't give a shit if the ass is"—he ground his groin against her backside—"nicely rounded."

Jaden's mind whirled, calculating every angle possible. Could she trust him?

"I'm looking for something," she muttered, as her mind frantically processed all of her options.

"Yeah, well, aren't we all."

Shit. She had no idea what she should do. Julian Castille had never figured into her plans for the night.

His hand slowly slid down her skin until it rested against the soft flesh that pulsed at the base of her neck. The beat was fast, and Jaden desperately tried to keep her jaguar at bay.

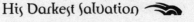

Her skin was on fire, aching. It felt as if she were being ripped in two.

"You're a DaCosta. Convince me I shouldn't just snap your neck and be done with it."

Something in the air changed, darkness slithered around them, and she began to shiver as it clung to him and bled into her. His energy was empowered with strange nuances. It was potent, strong, and rippled along her skin until she felt nauseated.

Could she trust him? Did she have a choice?

"You didn't seem to care about *that* three years ago."

Jaden winced as her thoughts slipped from between her lips, a soft whisper, but vocalized nonetheless.

He stilled, and she tried to ignore the hard planes of his body as he gripped her even tighter.

"Three years ago doesn't count anymore." His voice was soft at her ear, in total contrast to the tense feel of his body. "If I'd known you were DaCosta then, I'd never have touched you."

He does remember.

Humiliation scorched her cheeks with heat, and Jaden sought a place of calm. His words ripped into her harder than she'd like to admit. The man had been an invisible part of her life for longer than she cared to admit, and she'd been nothing more than the biggest mistake he'd ever made.

His hand slid from her neck, trailing a line of fire downward until he rested his large palm against her heaving chest. Her nipples were hard, and she flinched as his fingers passed over them.

Julian's mouth was near her ear, and his breath sent tingles of energy across her skin as he spoke, his voice low and sensual. "But it's a different world today, and right now you could be the devil's bitch for all I care."

Jaden's pulse quickened even more, and her eyes widened as his left hand traveled down to her hip, where he gripped her hard. The unmistakable feel of his hard cock dug into her back, and the throb between her legs was unbearable.

What the hell is wrong with me? She should be kicking his ass but good instead of dancing on the edge. This game would not end well for her.

"It's been too long, Jaden."

Her tongue caught between her teeth as her name fell from his lips. The way he said it sent waves of pleasure rolling through her. It wasn't fair. She wanted to hang her head in shame at the betrayal of her body.

He tipped her head up until it rested against his chest, and their eyes met as he looked down at her. Long moments passed, and the only sound heard was their heavy breathing.

He smiled, but there was a cruelty in the depths of his eyes that gave her pause and put her instantly on edge. "Yeah, way too long," he said roughly. "You'll do."

Then his mouth was upon hers, open, hot, and demanding.

In that moment, nothing existed but the two of them. And even though it was all wrong and dark and humiliating, deep inside, the cat began to purr.

Chapter 2

Julian kissed her long and hard, brutally invading the softness beneath him with a ferocity that should have surprised him but didn't. Not anymore.

His body slid against hers, and he felt an edge of darkness begin to circle his brain. It was a seductive, exhilarating feeling that he welcomed wholly. He knew the woman he held had no warm feelings for him whatsoever. He didn't care.

He'd felt nothing but pain and torment for so long that the sensations sliding over his skin were exquisite torture.

His body hardened even more as she moaned into his mouth, and he turned her until she was flush against his chest. Jaden DaCosta. Jaguar shifter. She'd been the last face he'd seen in the jungle before the lights went out; it couldn't be a coincidence that she was here. *Now.*

The same night he blasted back into the human realm.

Pain ripped along his damaged, torn skin, and he hissed

as fire lashed across his flesh. It was all good, though. It meant that he was alive.

The cloaking charm melted as her passion rose to the fore, allowing her natural scent to color the air. He took it deep into his lungs, savoring the unique scent.

She ripped her lips from his and gazed up into his eyes. He'd forgotten how velvety hers were, like soft black liquid in huge round pools of glass.

"I hate you," she whispered hoarsely, her mouth open slightly as her tongue played along the edges of her teeth.

"Yeah," Julian said softly. "I can see that." He held her gaze, enjoying the confusion, passion, and yes, anger that lit the dark depths.

Her cheeks flushed a deep color, and she began to struggle in his embrace. She was strong, which wasn't surprising, and though he could have easily kept her pinned to his body, he let her go.

Maybe a quick fuck wasn't such a good thing. It wasn't like he had time for complications. And she'd be a major one. There were other ways to relieve the pressure he felt down below.

He watched her closely, his gaze running along the beautiful lines of her face, the soft golden skin, dark eyes and brows, and the long, thick hair that, when loose, hung to just above her ass. It was a detail he remembered with clarity.

She was magnificent.

But she was a DaCosta nonetheless and not to be trusted, especially now, when the stakes were so freaking high.

His hand went to the damaged skin on his chest, as memories rushed through him in hard flashes, but it was the dark ones he focused on. The black holes full of emptiness and pain. They fed him in a way nothing else could.

Cormac and Azaiel.

They were at the heart of the poison that was slowly seeping into the human realm. They were the enemy. They were also his road to salvation.

If I don't find them . . . Julian looked away and banished those thoughts.

"What the hell happened to you?" she asked carefully, haltingly, as if she were having trouble forming her words.

He let Jaden back away. It was the smart thing to do. He needed to focus on the task at hand. Sex was something that wasn't part of the equation.

The air around her shimmered, and small tufts of mist hung lazily in the air. She was close to the change, her jaguar was excited.

It fed the animal inside him, and he clenched his teeth as he considered his options.

He could take her down in less than a second, snap her neck, and toss her body out the window. Call it a night. No one would know.

Or he could play things out. Was she working with her family? Was she rogue?

He sensed no immediate danger. Maybe it was sheer arrogance on his part, but Julian truly felt she meant him no harm. *Even though she hates me.* He snorted at the thought.

"I'm gonna take a shower." He turned from her and walked toward his room. "Then we'll talk."

Julian felt the weight of her stare at his back, and a ghost of a smile flickered across his face as he stepped into the bathroom. Seconds later, it was filled with steaming-hot water, and he stepped under the spray, letting the heavenly wetness slide across his skin.

It was the simplest of pleasures and one he'd not enjoyed for a very long time. As the warmth spread along his tall frame, caressing the hardness between his legs, he rested his head against the tiles and willed his body to relax.

He couldn't believe he was out, that he'd been pulled from the bowels of hell.

All thoughts of pleasure fled, and a muscle worked its way across his jaw as he clenched his teeth tightly. He thought once more of the shadowy figure who'd held the instrument of pain in her hands. Of how she'd sliced and diced until she'd reached the part of him that was sacred.

And then had methodically ripped half of his soul out of his body.

Even now, the pain pounded away inside him, the half-empty hole ragged and raw. It agitated the jaguar, filling his mind with all kinds of madness. He'd lived with it for six months and would continue to deal. He had no choice.

Julian let the spray wash over him for a good long time, his thoughts centered on the woman he'd found in his home. Three years ago, he'd seduced her, *screwed her,* then left like a coward. At the time he'd had no idea who she was, but the fact that she'd been a shifter had been enough to make him run.

Julian shook his head. Yeah, nothing was the same. There was a time when he'd hated anything to do with his shifter heritage, and now he embraced it with a savage need.

His world had indeed come full circle.

Five minutes later, he left the bedroom, dressed in jeans, T-shirt, and the heavy boots he'd arrived in.

The shower had invigorated him, and his head was clear. He ran his hands through the damp thick waves, pushing his hair back as his golden eyes swept the room.

She was where he'd left her. Arms crossed over her chest,

legs spread as she looked out the window over the darkened city below. The dagger lay at her feet.

He crossed the floor silently until he was inches from her body and studied her closely as she turned her head to the side.

"Long shower," she said, and looked away.

He saw her face reflected in the glass. She'd lost a bit of weight since he'd last seen her. The blush of youth had given way to adulthood. It showed in her cheeks, but the end result was toned and lean. She wore formfitting black clothes and kick-ass boots.

She'd let her hair out from the band that had confined it earlier and it flowed, just as he remembered, down to the soft swell of her butt.

She really was a beautiful woman.

"If you want, I can bend over and give you a real treat." The sarcasm that laced her words was thick, and Julian smiled as their eyes met in the window.

"If you bent over right now you'd be giving me more than a treat," he said, "and I'd have to do something about it."

He watched as her eyes fell to his crotch, and his teeth flashed white at the look of disgust that passed over her features.

"Can we skip this?" She whirled around. "The whole banter thing? 'Cause we're not buddies, and I'm not in the mood for games. I need to be somewhere."

"Be somewhere?" Julian's eyes narrowed. "You got some other penthouse to break into?"

"No, asshole, I was only hitting you tonight."

Julian took a step closer to her. "Well hell"—he stood with his arms stretched out fully—"hit me."

Jaden's face darkened. "You're still an arrogant son of a bitch who doesn't have the balls for someone like me," she snapped. "There will be no *hitting* between us. Again. Ever."

Julian watched the flurry of emotions that crossed her face. Her chest strained against thin fabric as she inhaled a ragged breath and pushed a long strand of hair behind her ear. The soft curve of her neck stood out in stark contrast to the silken black, and he imagined his fingers twined into the luxurious waves.

It was then that he spied the tats along her neck, and inside, his jaguar began to make noise. She was not *just* a shifter. The woman before him was a jaguar warrior—rare for a female, and that meant she was mated. The warrior tats on females only materialized *after* sex with the person she'd claimed as hers.

For some reason, that information left a bad taste in his mouth, the kind that lingered, and he frowned heavily.

"Why are you here?" he asked, watching closely for any hint of deceit.

Jaden pursed her lips, and he could see the indecision in her eyes. His own kept straying to the tattoos on the side of her neck, and when her hair fell forward once more and covered them, he couldn't say he was sorry.

Where the hell was her mate? Christ, if she belonged to him, he'd never let her screw off into the night, *hitting* homes that housed dangerous sons of bitches like himself.

"There's been chatter that something big is gonna hit the fan sooner rather than later. Like nasty big." Jaden began to tap her foot impatiently and moved across the room, her long legs full of grace and stealth. "Everyone's looking for the portal, and I thought . . ." She sighed heavily and turned toward him. "I don't know what I thought. Some information fell into my lap, and I acted on it."

"What information?"

Jaden eyed him warily and bit her lip. She was clearly

uneasy. "Let's just say your name popped up. I thought maybe there was something here that had been overlooked, so tonight I hopped on the jet and flew up from Mexico."

Julian cocked his head as the ever-present darkness inside him shifted. It left him edgy, aggressive. This could not be a coincidence. He fucking hated being nothing more than a chess piece to be moved about until someone with power yelled, "Checkmate."

"I don't suppose you brought the portal back with you?" she asked pointedly as she clenched her fists at her sides.

He considered dismissing her outright but instead shook his head, no.

"Are you going to tell me where you've been?" she asked.

"In hell."

The words were simple, his tone harsh, and she winced as they slid from between his lips.

She opened her mouth to speak but then closed it, running a hand along her temple wearily.

"Who called you?" she asked abruptly, her dark eyes wary. "Earlier tonight on the cell."

"Declan," he answered. Julian had no need to lie.

"The sorcerer is alive, too?" She looked shocked. "Do Jaxon and the others know you're back?"

"Not yet." Julian answered.

He moved closer to her and nailed her with *a don't fuck with me* look. "Are you working with your family?" There it was. The question that he most wanted answered.

Jaden's eyes widened slightly, and he heard her heart beating fast against her chest. The color in her cheeks darkened once more, yet it only enhanced the golden tone of her skin. He fought the urge to pull her to him, just so he could touch her softness and inhale her fragrant odor.

It had been so long.

"No." Her voice was low and husky. "I've done everything in my power to stop them, to find the portal and destroy it." She looked away. "I'm ashamed to say we share the same DNA."

He was about to answer, but his body froze. Every instinct inside him screamed "attack," and he growled softly. Something was out there, beyond the glass, on the balcony that ran the length of his penthouse.

He rushed toward Jaden, his body a blur. A look of surprise flickered over her features, then he was on her, taking her down as the large pane of glass shattered, erupting into deadly projectiles that rained down into his home.

He felt the familiar burn creep over his skin, his animal wanting out, and time stopped as he stared down into her eyes. Something passed between them, and in that moment, they were in perfect harmony.

She went for the dagger as he rolled off, clearing the way, and her aim was both accurate and deadly. The dagger flew in silence, slicing through the air near his cheek as it sailed behind him.

A loud grunt was heard, and he was on his feet in time to see a body fall to the floor. The dagger was embedded deep into the skull, between the eyes, cutting through bone and brain tissue.

It twitched violently, then stilled as an obnoxious odor leaked from the wound. Filthy, stinking, *dead* demon.

Jaden bent down and cursed as she kicked the prone body. "Goddamn it! Must there always be drama?" she yelled. Her anger and frustration boiled over into a string of profanities that at any other time Julian would have found both impressive and nasty.

Except, he had no time to congratulate her on her choice of vocabulary as he was staring at a huge problem.

"Shit," Jaden whispered as she straightened and stood beside him, the dagger back in her hands and dripping blackened liquid.

Six nasty demons slipped through the shattered window, bringing with them the stench of otherworld.

Six demons against two jaguars.

Julian looked down at the woman beside him and snarled, glorifying in the dark energy that had just blown in. It fed him in a way nothing else could.

"You ready to rock and roll?" he asked harshly.

"Hell yeah," Jaden answered as she squared her shoulders. The air around her body began to shimmer as her jaguar made noise. "But let's make this quick."

She ducked as one of them flew at her.

"I don't want to miss the Buffy marathon that starts at midnight."

Chapter 3

Jaden leapt over the sofa, hissing in pain, as droplets of the demon's blood burned into her skin. She swept the dagger across the fabric, cleaning it as she flew over, and twisted her body so that she landed to face the two demons that broke away from the others.

Her skin was on fire with the need to change, and mist was already crawling up her legs.

One of the demons followed her lead and jumped over the sofa, his stench seeping into her nostrils. The dude had some serious hygiene problems.

He landed in front of her, mouth agape and dripping saliva everywhere.

"Christ, you boys don't exactly win the prize for best-looking," she snarled as she charged forward and leapt up at him. The demon met her in the air, and they slammed together with such force that her breath was knocked from her body.

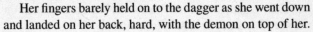

Her fingers barely held on to the dagger as she went down and landed on her back, hard, with the demon on top of her.

He stared down at her, smiled viciously as he licked his serrated teeth. "You jaguars are weak, pathetic creatures," he said.

Jaden wrinkled her nose. "Yeah? Buddy, you're strong. I'll give you that." She tightened her grip on the dagger and prayed that the charm still carried enough power to inflict damage. "But body odor isn't something to be proud of."

She hissed loudly and swiped the dagger up toward the demon's throat. He grabbed her hand just in time. and the two of them struggled for the blade. The demon rose from the ground and brought her up with him, as she poured all of her strength into her grip.

He laughed, and inside, her jaguar erupted into a fury. Jaden's eyes flashed, and she lashed out with her right leg, kicking hard and fast.

When in doubt, aim for the junk.

The monster roared in pain as she connected with his demon jewels, and she yanked the dagger from his hand. He lunged toward her, blind with fury, and Jaden used every bit of strength she had as she arced the weapon in a perfect line. It was a large dagger, razor-sharp.

The change was already falling over her frame as the demon fell at her feet, his cleanly severed head landing a few inches away.

Bones popped and elongated, muscles stretched, and a thick black pelt rippled along her flesh as her jaguar burst from inside. Her clothes were ripped to shreds as the large cat erupted from her body, and they fell in pieces at her feet.

Jaden growled loudly, her mouth open and panting as she reveled in the power of her animal. The cat heard the sounds of battle, of Julian and the others, but she concentrated on the suddenly wary demon in front of her.

He glanced down at his fallen comrade and began clacking his teeth in a strange sort of sequence, moving his head slowly. The *clack, clack, clack,* was raw, ragged, and she circled as the demon began to change.

Jaden had seen this before. She knew if the demon had time to morph into his true form, she was pretty much screwed.

Her hind legs dug in, and she jumped up onto the sofa, using it to propel herself upward. Her claws were fully extended as she attacked the demon. He was beginning to stretch. His human shape began to morph and distort while his colors changed from flesh tone to a shit brown green.

She hit him at shoulder height and ignored the pain as his arms went around her body, crushing her to him tightly. He roared loudly as her claws dug in, and when he bit into her shoulder, the pain was immediate and intense. Jaden had never felt anything like it.

Liquid fire burned across her shoulder.

She held on and clawed her way upward, loosening his grip, and with relief she felt his mouth give way as she zeroed in on her target.

Jaden growled loudly as she anchored her body and dug in. She opened her jaws as wide as they could go, then clamped down on his skull. Her large incisors went deep, ripping into bone and tissue, and she fought the urge to let go as the taste of the demon flooded her mouth.

He screamed in pain and began to twist violently. Jaden held on; she could not let him win. Her shoulder was on fire and she feared the demon's poison would be too strong for her.

Her vision blurred, and a wave of dizziness fell over her,

but still she gripped hard. The demon moaned loudly and began to wobble as he struggled to stay upright, and, with a loud crash, the beast fell forward, pinning Jaden beneath his heavy weight.

She released her hold and fought the red haze that danced in front of her eyes. The pain had spread from her shoulders across her back, and it felt like a thousand tiny teeth were slowly peeling back layers of her skin, from the inside out.

The demon was a deadweight, and she struggled to get out from beneath him, feeling instant relief when the monster was thrown from her body. She hissed and tried to scramble to her feet, her mind darkened with both fear and fury.

She turned, bared her teeth, her great tail sweeping back and forth, but it was Julian who knelt before her. She relaxed somewhat, panting heavily as she surveyed the carnage in the room.

Six demons dead.

The ancient magick of her people took hold, and she clenched her teeth as the change rolled over her body. It was quick but painful, and as her human form took over, the thick glossy pelt sliding from her skin, she groaned loudly and fell back to the floor.

"The bastard bit me," she said hoarsely, wincing as the fire continued to spread.

"Lie still," Julian whispered.

She rested her head along the cool tiles, hearing nothing but his breathing and the heavy beating of their hearts. His hands felt along her shoulder.

"You're lucky. His teeth aren't meant to rip through heavy fur. They didn't penetrate too deep."

"Yeah, that's what I was thinking," she managed to get out. "This is only phantom pain."

Julian knelt beside her, and she tensed as his hands continued down her body to rest at her hip. She was totally nude, and it made her feel that much more vulnerable.

"It still doesn't negate the severity."

Jaden's heart sank. What he said was true.

"It means you have a few hours more than most would." His words were matter-of-fact, his tone colorless.

She hissed loudly and turned her dull eyes to him. "Nice to see you haven't lost your charm, Castille."

She struggled to get up and slapped his hand away when he would have helped her.

"Make yourself useful and get me something to wear," she whispered hoarsely as she knelt, bent over and cradling her chest.

The poison made her nauseous, and she so didn't want to heave on his feet even though it would serve the bastard right. She panted softly, concentrating on the sounds, the rhythm, and eventually the nausea faded.

When he returned with a pair of trackies and a T-shirt, she snatched them from him.

"I don't need an audience."

The words slipped through tight teeth, and she watched from hooded eyes as Julian turned away from her. She stood on shaky legs and, with great effort, managed to get the shirt over her head, then slipped the gray track pants up over her hips. They were huge, and she fumbled as she tried to tie the waist.

She felt sweat break out along her skin, small rivulets of water that were tinged with the scent of poison. *Shit, this is not good.*

"Here, let me."

Jaden wanted to refuse his help, but, truthfully, she just didn't have the strength. She felt his fingers, warm against her tummy, and as he quickly hiked the pants up and secured them, her head fell against his chest.

Her tongue was thick, the acrid taste from the demon strong. "Water," she whispered softly.

Julian's body was high on adrenaline and the beast inside him was agitated something fierce. The smell of blood was in the air—both Jaden's and the dead otherworlders that littered his home.

He looked down at the woman who rested against him and tried to block the conflicting emotions that struggled inside him. His mind was a chaotic mess, but it was the dark thoughts that held sway. They were always the strongest.

His first thought was to leave. Grab his shit and go.

Declan was waiting for him, and every minute counted. That had been drilled into their heads. They had maybe a week—if they were lucky—to find the portal and destroy it. If not, the alternative wasn't something he wanted to dwell on.

Jaden DaCosta didn't figure into his plans. Even now, he could smell the poison as it infiltrated her cells. Soon, it would hit her major organs, and she'd be a goner anyway. A waste of time.

"*Water*," she whispered against him.

Julian clenched his teeth. He'd like to say he was shocked at the calculating, coldness of his mind. But he wasn't. He was forever damaged, and after spending six months in hell, how could it be any other way? The hole inside him was a reminder of what he'd lost, what had been ripped from him. It was a burn that was constant, and it wouldn't let him rest.

And yet Julian was afraid that even if he was successful and completed his mission, he'd never be whole again.

He feared the half of his soul that was still intact had been poisoned by the steady diet of darkness from which he'd fed.

He sighed harshly. Angry that he'd been back less than an hour, and things were already fucked up.

He glanced around his home and knew there wasn't much time. He'd been liberated from his hellish prison but it seemed the demon underworld was determined to drag him back.

Though liberated might be an overstatement. It's not like his release came without consequence if he was unsuccessful in his mission. There would be repercussions.

Deadly repercussions.

Jaden groaned and tipped her head up, dragging him from his thoughts to focus on her once more.

She'd been fucking amazing.

Her dark eyes were dulled with pain, and she moistened her lips in an effort to speak more clearly.

"I need to get to the plane," she managed to get out.

Julian leaned her back against the counter and grabbed a glass of water, helping her drink as much of the liquid as she could.

His mind was circling the entire time, but the images of her in battle touched what little bit of humanity there was left inside him. As she struggled to stand upright, clad in his oversized T-shirt and his track pants, he knew he could never leave her here to die with the filth that littered his home.

She should be with someone when it happened.

"Where can I take you?" he asked, trying not to notice the tilt of her neck or the vibrant tattoos that shimmered along the skin there.

Her eyes narrowed slightly, and she pushed away from the counter. It cost her, the effort it took, and the grunt that escaped her lips echoed into the quiet.

"Forget it. I don't need your help." Her face whitened as she clenched her teeth. "I'll get there on my own."

She took a step, then another, and admiration rifled through him as he watched her slowly make her way to the door.

Something tugged at him, and he took a step forward. Fuck! He had no time for this shit. He was supposed to meet Declan in the morning. The clock was ticking for the both of them.

"It's been a slice, Castille. Thanks for nothing."

Jaden yanked the door open, letting in the soft light from outside, and he saw the bloody footprints that followed along behind her. Shattered glass was everywhere, and while he had his boots on, she was barefoot.

Again he hesitated, pissed off at himself, knowing in another lifetime he'd never contemplate abandoning someone who was in need of help. Except this wasn't another lifetime ago. This was the here and now, and he wasn't whole.

She disappeared from view, and he blew out hot air as he quickly grabbed the cell phone he'd thrown on the sofa. The headless body of the demon Jaden had slaughtered lay before him, mocking his inability to act.

He took one more look around the penthouse and cursed loudly before following Jaden's lead. He caught up with her at his private elevator. She was leaning against the wall, her breaths raspy.

He stopped beside her and, as the doors slid open, grabbed her up into his arms. She struggled but was substantially weaker than only a few minutes before and eventually became still.

Julian entered the code that would take him to his private garage and settled back as the lift descended rapidly.

Her hair wrapped around him, the long silky strands flowing loose as her head rested in the crook of his arm.

"Where can I take you?" he asked again, his voice gruff as the doors slid open to reveal his private collection of cars. He strode toward the large black SUV parked in the far corner, ignoring the BMW, the shiny Mercedes and the collection of Harleys.

"My private jet," she managed to whisper.

She curled into a ball as he slid her into the passenger side, and, minutes later, Julian was backing the large vehicle from its spot. The truck hadn't been used in nearly a year, but the mechanic he paid to maintain his vehicles had done an excellent job.

He cruised along the darkened streets of DC, and when the cell phone rang, he picked up quickly.

"Castille." The hoarse voice belonged to Declan O'Hara.

"You sound like shit," Julian answered as he sped along the highway that led to a private airstrip outside of town. He'd managed to get that much info from Jaden before she passed out.

"You have any visitors?" Declan asked.

Julian's lips thinned. "A couple."

He continued to navigate the roads, his senses still aflame from the threat of danger that lurked beyond the darkness.

"Yeah, me too. I have a feeling our little vacation from hell ain't exactly gonna be restful." The heavy sarcasm was noted.

"I've got Jaden DaCosta with me."

Long moments of silence greeted his words. Julian exited the highway and headed toward the private tarmac at the small airport. He saw several jets in the distance, but the black-and-gold one screamed DaCosta.

"You still there?" he asked as he turned to the left and drove through security with no issues at all. He shook his head. Had 9/11 not taught them anything?

"Yeah, I'm just trying to shake the whole déjà vu thing.

Wasn't too long ago your brother called me about finding Libby. No offense, but life pretty much went to hell after that. Like literally." The Irishman paused, and Julian could hear the wheels turning.

"She dead?"

"Not yet." Julian's voice was dry, and he glanced toward the unconscious woman. Though that would change. Very soon.

"Again, the déjà vu thing. Care to explain?"

Julian pulled up alongside the large plane. "No. I'll talk to you tomorrow."

"Just don't—"

But Declan's words were lost as Julian pocketed the cell. He exited the truck and opened the passenger-side door. Jaden's eyes flickered open, and she grimaced as his arms slipped underneath her body once more.

They were glassy, and her pupils were so large her eyes appeared to be solid black pools of velvet. He admired her strength but didn't know how much longer she could last.

The jet was running, and the steps were lowered. It was adorned with the DaCosta crest, which was woven underneath, NIGHT SKY RESORT AND CASINO. He vaguely recalled something about hotels in Mexico and the DaCostas.

Carefully, he made his way up and ducked his tall frame through the narrow entrance. His senses rode the wind, and as far as he could tell, he was alone; but he knew that didn't mean a thing.

He proceeded with caution, expecting the worst.

The jet was large, luxurious, and surprisingly tasteful in both décor and furnishings. Gently, he laid Jaden on the nearest chaise, propping her head against a soft cushion.

"In the cupboard," Jaden whispered, her voice so faint he barely heard her. She motioned toward a large bank of cabinets that lined the far side of the cabin, and he looked at her, not understanding.

"Antidote," she managed. "Hurry."

Antidote? Since when?

Julian hesitated, and she glared up at him, wincing in pain as she rasped, "Are you *trying* to kill me?"

He crossed over to the cupboards, yanked them open, and was taken aback at the interesting array of weaponry displayed. Several firearms were stored there, as well as daggers, and an interesting-looking bow. He spied a container of vials and grabbed one. The shelves were labeled with some long weird word that he didn't understand, but underneath it one stood out boldly and it was one that he did know, DEMON.

He ripped the cap off and returned to Jaden, feeling that spark of respect and admiration jump again as he watched her struggle to a sitting position. The woman had balls. He'd give her that.

He held it to her lips, and as her fingers intertwined with his, and she gulped the potion, he couldn't ignore the emotion that pummeled his chest. He didn't know what the hell it was, but it felt so much better than what he'd been used to for the last while—pain and *nothing*.

"Thank you," she whispered, as her head collapsed against the cushion. Her long, elegant neck was fully exposed, and as her breathing returned to normal, he was fascinated by the clan tattoos that crept up her skin.

They were beautiful, exotic, and his hands found their way to her flesh without thought.

Electricity tingled along the edges of his fingers as he traced the lines that shimmered beneath her skin. Slowly, he made his way down and paused at the base of her neck, relishing the feel of her pulse now that it was beating strong and steady.

A soft gasp escaped from her lips, and he looked at her, surprised to see her eyes regarding his, their dark depths clear and shiny.

"Demon antidote," he said dryly. "Since when?"

"It cost me a fortune, but my science team finally managed to get it right."

His eyes wandered over her face, to land on the full lips. His fingers followed where his eyes had traveled, and when they traced the outline of her mouth, he reveled in the softness.

"Move away from her, or I will put a bullet clean through the back of your skull."

They both turned, startled by the words that slid from the darkness, and Julian felt his animal begin to burn beneath his chest as two men walked from shadow to light.

One he vaguely remembered, a tall, lean, blond man— Skye Knightly's brother, Finn. He was an eagle knight. The other, he knew quite well, and his jaguar erupted painfully as he leapt to his feet.

Nico.

"I'm not joking, Castille. Give me one good reason why I shouldn't take you out right now."

"I could give you a hundred, in alphabetical order if you like," Julian retorted, his words tinged heavily with sarcasm.

"Nico, enough," Jaden rasped as she stood up, her legs still a little shaky.

The warrior growled and took a step toward them. "There's no way we can be sure he's not compromised."

Julian laughed at that. The asshole had no clue. He was way beyond contaminated.

"You will not touch him," Jaden growled, surprising Julian by stepping past him and squaring her shoulders.

"Give me one good reason why?" Nico snarled.

"Because," she said as she pushed her way past them, "he belongs to me." She disappeared into the darkness beyond, leaving only her words trailing behind.

Julian stared after her. "I belong to no one."

"Oh really?" she shot back, her voice stronger, deeper. "Where the hell did you think these warrior tattoos came from Castille? An immaculate conjugal?" She laughed.

He opened his mouth to speak, but her voice sliced through the dark, effectively silencing him.

"I've had them for three years, Castille. You do the math."

Chapter 4

Jaden closed the door and leaned against the cool surface.
Her chest felt tight, but as the seconds ticked by, the iron
band loosened and she was able to breathe normally.

What the hell had she just done? Why on earth did she
spill to Julian about their bond? It wasn't like he gave a shit.
It wasn't like she *wanted* him to give a shit. She was doing
just fine without him.

She pushed away angrily, pissed at herself and her lack of
control. A shower would clear her head.

Her shoulder was killing her, but the antidote was working. She felt the pain receding as the poison slowly left her
system. Underneath her feet, the jet hummed, its energy vibrating with a subtlety that tickled her bare flesh. She knew
they'd be wheels up within the hour.

Julian Castille would be long gone.

She grimaced as she slid out of the oversized T-shirt he'd
given her. She could smell him, his tangy, earthy scent teas-

ing her nostrils. It had been months since he'd worn it, yet it still called to her.

For a jaguar, smell was a powerful thing, more potent than visual memories. She hated that his scent tortured her, riding her hard with a sense of unfulfilled need.

It was an ache she'd come to know well, but she'd deal. She'd been doing just fine without the bastard for the last three years.

Her hands fell to the waistband of the pants that she wore, and she was about to drop them when the door crashed open behind her. Nico's angry growl echoed into her quarters, but it was not he who stood inches from her.

"What the fuck did that mean?" Julian's furious words ripped into her. "We're mated? I don't want you," he began, "we can't . . ."

Jaden cocked her head to the side. "No shit," she whispered hoarsely, as his words swept across her like physical blows. She knew they had no future, but still . . . to hear his denial, his dislike, was like a kick to the gut.

She felt his anger. It was in the coldness of his voice and the subtle vibrations that lingered in the air. Inside, her jaguar stirred, and her skin began to burn as she clenched her teeth tightly.

"I am going to enjoy throwing your ass off this plane." Nico's threat was met with harsh laughter.

"You could try," Julian answered.

"Leave us, Nico," she said quietly, and held her breath. The warrior was a wild card at best, and she didn't have time to referee the two of them.

She felt the chilled air against her back and fought the urge to grab the newly discarded T-shirt. She was naked from the waist up and was suddenly very much aware of the fact. Her nipples puckered into hard pebbles, a reaction to the cold, and she crossed her arms over her chest, glad the men were behind her.

"We leave in ten minutes," Nico said, his voice angry, barely controlled.

Jaden winced as the door slammed shut. Lately, the warrior had become more than a little protective of her. She would never claim him, and his attitude wasn't good for either one of them.

She forced a calm over her body, one that she wasn't feeling, and walked to the closet that held her clothes. She felt Julian's gaze upon her back, knew that he watched her closely. She pulled the door open, loosened the tie at her waist, and let the trackies fall to the floor.

She heard Julian hiss as he exhaled loudly. Her heart began to beat heavily inside her, and she felt the electricity in the air begin to tingle, jumping over her bare flesh in small pulses.

She grabbed a robe, slipped it over her shoulders, and took a few moments to tie it properly before she turned to him.

His eyes were dark, the irises' bleeding into gold until they glittered dangerously. They bored into her with an intensity that left no doubt as to what he was feeling.

Julian Castille was in a dark place, and his anger was focused solely on her.

What fucking nerve.

"Are you going to explain to me how a DaCosta jaguar is mated to a Castille?" His tone was harsh. "On what planet is that even possible?"

"Apparently on ours," she snapped back.

He raked his hands through the thick mess of hair atop his head. "How in the hell did this happen?"

She arched her eyebrow. "For Christ sakes, Castille, do you really need me to explain the fine details? Did Daddy never explain the birds and the bees and the warrior mating rituals?"

"You don't get it!" he exploded, and he moved so fast, she felt the wind against her cheek as he stood in front of her. Jaden was startled at his speed but held her ground, her dark eyes meeting his boldly.

"There will never be anything between us," he spit out. "I will not accept your claim."

Jaden smiled and shook her head, swallowing the bitterness that hung in the back of her throat. "Don't worry about it. You made that more than clear three years ago." She nodded. "Move back. You're crowding me."

Julian bared his teeth. He was on edge, the strange darkness that clung to him rising to the fore. It agitated her cat something fierce, and she trembled slightly at the force of it.

"I mean it," she said forcefully. "Back off."

His hand reached out, and, inside, everything stilled. She could hear her heart beating heavily against her chest, felt the pace quicken as warning bells began to explode.

Her breath hitched, and her mouth went dry as his fingers settled over her clan tattoos. She felt them, burning beneath his touch. Another chunk of humiliation to add to her armor of shame.

"So beautiful," he whispered harshly.

Jaden flinched at his tone.

"So deceptive."

She wanted to rip his hand from her flesh but refused to let him know how affected she was by his touch. Instead, she smiled up at him and let her tongue run along her lips.

"I'm also the best piece of ass you'll never have again."

His breathing changed, slowed, and the air around them stilled. Jaden's heart leapt crazily, and a wave of dizziness circled her brain. She was dancing with the devil, and that was always a dangerous game.

His hand moved up from her neck to grip her jaw. She refused to look away, though the cold glint in his eye left her stomach tight, nauseous. He looked like he wanted to strangle her.

"You do not want to mess with me." He smiled, a cold slash of white. "I'm not anything like what you remember."

No shit.

His anger and dislike were meaty, tangible. Jaden kept her face blank, but inside she fought the bleakness that lay there.

His lips thinned as he spoke. "Our meeting three years ago was no accident. You will tell me what your agenda is."

He leaned close to her, and Jaden closed her eyes as his scent slid over her flesh, caressing her skin. "If I'm satisfied with your answer, I might let you live."

Her eyes flew open at that, and her flesh burned as a wave of anger hit her hard.

"Take your hands off me," she said carefully.

His grip tightened as he smiled down at her, a cruel bent to his lips.

"I could snap your neck right now if I so chose."

She was hot, on the cusp of change.

"You could try." Jaden's words were stilted, her mouth dry. "But you won't." She sensed his thin control.

He arched an eyebrow and brought her closer to him, so close that she could see the tiny veins of his eyes. Her skin was burning, the animal inside enraged at his blatant show of force.

She wanted to punch him in the face, break his aristocratic nose.

She wanted to feel his lips on hers, taste the warmth and eat the danger that clung to him.

"Don't be so sure, little cat." His breath was warm against her flesh, and as it slid across her skin, she ached inside. "You have no idea what I am." His voice lowered. "What I've become."

"Well, one thing is the same." She inhaled a cleansing breath. "You're still an ass of epic proportions."

Jaden snapped her head back and brought her knee up into the softness between his legs. At the same time, she jabbed him hard, right above his heart, where she knew his skin was tender. Damaged.

His grip loosened, and she was away from him in a flash, a blur of long silky hair.

He didn't make a sound though his dark eyes stalked her from across the room. His mouth was tight. She knew he was in pain, but she was cool with that.

He totally fucking deserved it.

Yet an image of his raw, ragged flesh flashed in front of her eyes, and she swallowed thickly, hating the small sliver of remorse that slid through her. Her robe was gaping, and she angrily drew the ends tight together, hissing at the sly tilt that tugged at the corner of his mouth.

Underneath her feet, the jet's engines rumbled.

Suddenly, she felt defeated. Tired of all the bullshit.

"Look, I don't have time for this crap because seriously, this is way bigger than the two of us." Jaden ran her fingers through the loose hair that fell around her shoulders, and she shook her head. "I'm tired, Julian, and pretty much fed up."

"Join the fucking club," he snarled. He was seriously pissed off.

She opened her mouth to retort but then closed it as she

studied him in silence for several seconds. When she did finally speak, her voice was muted, raspy.

"I meant what I said. Our mating means nothing." Jaden ignored the hard clutch at her chest, the way her belly twisted in pain. "A cosmic fuck-you, really, and nothing more."

"You think this is natural? That we're mated?" His voice was cold, his eyes flat.

"I don't know what it is, but like I said, it means squat." She flicked a long piece of hair behind her back and shrugged her shoulders. "So I'll never have children. I'm cool with that."

He laughed as his eyes slowly traveled the length of her body. "You think to live a life of celibacy?"

She nailed him with a direct stare, her eyebrows raised. "You're an arrogant son of a bitch," she said, laughing at his insinuation. "Seriously? You think that after I've had you, there would be no one else? I didn't say that. I just said that since I'll never let you touch me again, a pack of kiddies isn't in my future."

"Because a female warrior can only have children with her mate." His voice was low, rumbling, as understanding crept into his eyes. He glared at her.

"Don't worry about me. When my itch needs scratching, I've got plenty of options that don't include you."

"Like Nico?" he spit out.

His words surprised her, but she took care to stay neutral. Julian didn't like the fact that she might be having sex with Nico. Interesting.

"He's one of many." The lie slipped out, blatant and sharp. She turned from him. "I don't give a rat's ass whether you believe me or not, but I didn't *seduce* you three years ago." She laughed a dry harsh sound. "In fact, if I recall correctly, you stalked me like the animal you are and pretty much dragged me back to your room."

At his snort, she felt her anger triple.

"You screwed me, then made no effort to hide the fact that what I was . . . *what I am* . . . totally disgusted you." She exhaled softly. "So get the fuck over yourself, Castille. I wouldn't want you if you were the last man on earth." She shrugged. "Which, given our situation, just might become the case."

"I don't trust you."

"Well, that's something we have in common." She nodded toward the shower. "Look, we're wheels up in like, five, and I need to wash the demon stench from my skin. So if you don't mind . . ."

She turned from him and stopped as his voice slashed across her, his fury barely contained.

"But I do mind."

She felt the heat of him at her back though he was careful not to touch her.

"My chain is being yanked, and I'm not liking that one bit."

She hesitated, her heart beating a meticulous rhythm as she composed herself. "We're all being played somehow, but that's not what's important. The portal needs to be destroyed, or we can kiss life as we know it good-bye."

She reached for the bathroom door. "*That* is what I know. I will find it, and nothing will stand in my way." Her head cocked to the side. "Not even an arrogant prick back from the dead."

Jaden closed the bathroom door behind her and released a long, torturous breath. *Christ.* Julian Castille was a complication she so didn't need.

The robe slipped from her body, and she stepped into the shower, letting the water soothe her heated, frustrated self. She stood there for a good long while before grabbing the soap and cleaning the last remnants of demon from her flesh.

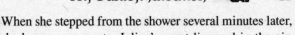

When she stepped from the shower several minutes later, her bedroom was empty. Julian's scent lingered in the air, and she wrinkled her nose as she quickly dressed.

He probably couldn't get off the plane fast enough.

She slipped her feet into a pair of soft slippers, wincing as the tender flesh rubbed against the fabric, and toweled the dampness from her hair before heading back to the main cabin.

The tone and feel of the engines had changed, and she knew they were ready to head back to Mexico. Her gaze wandered the cabin until they landed on the men in her unit.

Nico sat facing her, his body tense and his features cold. He'd shown up at her resort one day six months ago, not long after she'd returned from Belize. She'd not asked why he'd decided to take a break from his self-imposed exile, but the warrior was willing to do whatever it took to defeat O'Hara. Over the past several months, they'd formed a solid, tight unit, and had run several successful missions for PATU.

Jaden sighed. Things were never easy with the jaguar. He carried a lot of baggage, but his spirit and strength more than made up for his somewhat cranky attitude. She ignored him, knowing that when he was angry, the best thing to do was steer clear.

Finn nodded, his vivid blue eyes striking as they bored into her. "Castille is looking a little worse for wear."

Finn Knightly had been sent her way from Jaxon's unit in Canada. After the shit that had gone down in Belize, Jaxon Castille had been made aware of her undercover status. She ran her own operation but had helped out on several occasions when Jaxon had requested it.

"I don't think he was holidaying anywhere we'd want to be," she answered quietly.

Nico snorted loudly, but they both ignored him.

"He give anything up?" Finn arched a brow as he looked up at her.

"No. If he knows where the portal is, he wasn't sharing." Jaden exhaled slowly. "Did your contacts have any information?"

Finn shook his head. "Same old. The chatter is loud, shit is gonna hit soon, but no one seems to know where or when." He smiled up at her though the weariness that clung to him shadowed his features. "No rest for the wicked."

"No," she murmured, "there won't be rest for any of us until this is finished." She nodded. "Contact Jaxon at PATU when we get back and see what he's got. Fill him in on our status." She paused, and whispered softly, "He should know that his brother lives."

"Will do." Finn settled into his seat and looked away. The eagle shifter had always been somewhat aloof; they were, after all, natural enemies, but lately it had been worse.

Things had changed, the game had progressed. They all knew the end was near. Jaden slipped into her chair and exhaled loudly. She just wanted it to be over.

"Buckle up, we're due to taxi to the runway in one minute."

Her pilot's voice drifted through the speakers, and she secured the lap belt as she turned to the window. Outside, the vast darkness that blanketed the area looked beautiful as the lights of the city sparkled like diamonds. How deceptive, she thought. She knew what the darkness hid, what evil was out there watching and waiting for the chance to infect her world.

As she settled into her seat her insides twisted. An ominous feeling of dread pressed into her. The tide had turned. She could feel it.

Julian and Declan were back, by what means she didn't

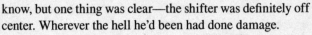

know, but one thing was clear—the shifter was definitely off center. Wherever the hell he'd been had done damage.

There was no way she could trust him. Besides, the man could barely look at her. She clenched her teeth until her jaw ached and as she stared at her reflection in the glass, she made a vow *to not care.*

There was no time for soft feelings and regret. She had a mission to accomplish, and no one was getting between her and the portal.

Not even the man she called mate.

Chapter 5

Humid air swept across cool tiles and pulled at a melancholy anchored deep within, one that was long forgotten. Julian stopped and let the memory of it, the *feel* of it, wash over him.

The scent of the jungle tantalized his nose, caressed his skin, and slid over him. He felt it, the mystery and magic that lay in the surrounding area, and his jaguar chomped at the bit, wanting nothing more than to shed the cloak of humanity that held him back.

He'd been back in Mexico for several hours and had just arrived at the Night Sky Casino and Resort. The place was impressive, to say the least, covering several miles of prime coastland deep within the heart of the Mayan Riviera. It was a virtual paradise on earth.

He snorted. Yeah, the DaCosta crime family had done a bang-up job building one of the premier luxury resorts in the area. His eyes narrowed. Blood money. The family was rank

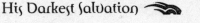

to the core and this . . . this place of beauty and tranquility was nothing more than a big fucking hoax.

Like the shades that had lingered below in the filth of the demon realm, with their phantom skin. None of it was real.

His gaze strayed to the hordes of new arrivals, and he felt disgust. Business was good.

He tipped his driver and grabbed the small bag he'd brought along for the trip, before entering the main lobby area. Within seconds, he knew where every security camera was located and was careful to stay out of their line of sight as he made his way over to the bar just beyond reception.

The place was busy, but he had no problem grabbing a spot at the bar and ordered a double whiskey while he waited.

As he let the amber liquid burn down his throat, his mind wandered back to the one face that had haunted him for the last twenty-four hours. Jaden DaCosta.

He exhaled sharply and ordered another drink, ignoring the interest from the blonde who sat a few feet away.

His thoughts darkened, and he frowned. He didn't know what Jaden's agenda was, but he sure as hell didn't believe one word that fell from her lips. How could he? She was a DaCosta.

Nervous energy had him itching to leave, but he forced himself to relax. He needed to keep a cool head.

After he'd left the jet and driven back to his condo, his mind had been all over the place, but one thing had become clear. Jaden was the key to everything. It was no accident they'd met three years earlier. He didn't believe that for one second.

Just as it was no accident that she'd been at his place the night he returned to the human realm. She'd also been in the jungle the night he'd been banished to hell. As far as he was concerned, she was up to her ass in the entire mess. He needed answers, and he needed them yesterday.

His eyes drifted back to the lobby, over to a young couple waiting to check in. Their children laughed and played hide-and-seek while they held on to each other and watched, their faces full of love.

They had no fucking clue what walked the earth and what waited beneath. He gritted his teeth and drained the glass.

No fucking clue at all.

"I'll buy you another."

Julian turned to the blonde. She'd moved closer and was smiling at him. Her eyes were unnaturally green, her generous breasts on display, pert and firm. Her overlarge lips were wet as she ran her tongue over them in an open invitation for a quick fuck.

She was all kinds of plastic.

His sensitive nostrils flared. He smelled her interest.

He smiled at her, then glanced up at the clock perched above the bar. It was early. He had more than enough time to ease the ache that had taken hold the night before.

She moved closer and signaled to the bartender.

"Two more of what he's drinking."

Christ, even her voice was controlled, the accent in her words uncomfortable, as if she were trying desperately to be something other than what she was. The woman was the total opposite of Jaden.

A vision of the dark-eyed witch burned behind his eyes. She'd been magnificent fighting the demons, and as he let his mind settle on an image of her, with her hair flying everywhere in the heat of battle, he was instantly hard. The blonde giggled as she slid up against him.

"You ready to go, tiger?" She opened her mouth and

laughed. A practiced line to be sure. "I have an hour before the bus arrives."

Julian looked down at her, and even though his body was aching and unfulfilled, he knew she wouldn't cut it. There was no way in hell the woman could satisfy what he needed.

She wouldn't even come close.

Julian stared down into the empty tumbler and frowned viciously. He was pissed off. He had no time for this shit. No time for complications.

No time for emotion. He much preferred the blank canvas that had draped his soul for the last six months.

"My name is—"

"I don't give a flying fuck if your name is Cleopatra; it ain't gonna happen." The words were ripped from his throat, and it gave him perverse pleasure to watch her green eyes fade, her smile fall.

"Are you for real?" she retorted, embarrassed, confused, as her long lacquered nails fluffed the blond strands of hair that fell around her shoulders. She looked around as if afraid they'd been overheard.

Julian couldn't explain the fury, the rage that flushed through him. It left him panting as he struggled to control the darkness that sank into his head.

"Lady," he whispered hoarsely, "you should go."

"You're an asshole."

"He's been called worse."

They both turned as Declan O'Hara slid up against the bar. "He wouldn't be any good anyways." The tall Irishman smiled at the blonde and winked. "Trust me, he hasn't had sex in a seriously long time; I doubt he'd last more than two minutes."

The woman's mouth fell open, and she stuttered, but no

words came from within. She shook her head and turned on her heel, disappearing into the crowd within seconds.

"Nice," Declan murmured.

Julian scowled and pushed away from the bar. "What took so long? Thought you were going to meet me at the airport."

Declan's eyes narrowed though he kept a smile pasted to his face. He ordered a cold beer.

"I had a visitor."

"More demons?"

"Nope."

Silence fell between them as Julian stared at the sorcerer. He was tight-lipped and tense.

"You gonna elaborate?"

Declan grabbed the coldie from the bartender and took a long, hard swig. "Ana."

Julian let that information settle a bit. The vampire was not someone the two of them discussed. Not once in all the time they'd been trapped in hell had Ana been mentioned.

But Julian knew how deeply Declan's feelings ran.

"Didn't take long for her to hunt you down," he said carefully.

Declan finished his beer. "Pretty easy to do considering Jaden contacted PATU and gave them a heads-up."

PATU. Paranormal Anti-terrorist Unit.

It was the government agency run by Julian's brother Jaxon and one that Declan had belonged to up until six months ago. Technically, he supposed the Irishman was still a part of the elite unit, but the both of them knew their journey had been altered dramatically the day they'd left the human realm.

"Jaden contacted her?" He was full of disbelief.

"Yeah; apparently she's one of the good guys."

Julian snorted. "Sure she is."

Declan shrugged his shoulders. "I'm just the messenger. Ana said she's been working under the umbrella of PATU covertly for years."

Julian ignored his words.

"How are they?" Julian asked. "My brothers. Did Jagger make it out of the jungle with Skye?"

"Yeah. They're good . . ." Declan's voice trailed off. "They're all good. Normal and fucking peachy-keen."

The two men stared at each other. *Normal* was not a word they'd ever be able to use again.

Julian clenched his teeth and let the wave of pain that sat upon his chest ride over him. The tangle of scars burned, pulsated. It was a constant reminder of what he'd lost. Most of the time, he was able to ignore it; but sometimes, like now, the burn was much too intense.

If he let it, it would surely drive him mad.

"And Ana?" he asked softly.

Declan carefully placed the empty bottle on the bar. "The same."

Julian watched the sorcerer closely, knowing the conversation was over.

"You boys want another?" The bartender drew his attention; Julian shook his head and followed Declan back into the lobby.

His heart rate slowed as his animal gathered tight. He let his senses fly, but as far as he could tell, there wasn't a hint of otherworld; nor was there any sign of the DaCostas.

"You sure this is a good idea?" Declan sounded doubtful. "I was kinda liking the idea of working this alone. You know, Butch and Sundance, Starsky and Hutch. . . . Bonnie and Clyde." He laughed softly at Julian's dark look. "Of course, you'd be Bonnie."

Julian sighed and shook out his tight limbs. Declan had never lost his sense of humor; Julian just didn't find anything funny anymore.

"I'm not sure about anything other than the fact she wants the portal as badly as we do." He continued to study everyone and everything. "We don't have a lot of time, and she may be the easiest way for us to get our hands on the danm thing."

"She's not gonna want to work with you."

Julian smiled darkly, a flash of white against the deep tan of his face. "Well, that would take all the fun out of it now, wouldn't it?"

Declan rolled his shoulders and exhaled softly. "All right, let's do this."

"You got your cloaking charm handy?" He didn't want his prey to sense a Castille jaguar in their midst. He nodded toward the security cameras. "I don't feel the presence of any DaCostas, but Nico is around here somewhere and the eagle shifter, too."

Declan smiled rakishly, winking at several women who walked by the two of them, their hips swaying suggestively. "Piece of cake."

Julian felt a tingle of energy slide over his skin and looked at Declan in surprise. He was still smiling at the women, but Julian sensed his concentration and saw how his hands were loose at his sides, though the fingers were flared.

The sorcerer's powers had tripled with their time spent in darkness, but it had been fed by something pungent, evil, and he knew Declan was living too close to the edge. They both were.

One wrong move, and the two of them could be lost forever. The lure from the darkside was incredible, intoxicating. Totally Darth Vader.

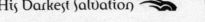

The energy tickled his flesh as they moved through the throng of tourists still waiting to check in.

"So, we got a plan?" Declan asked.

Julian shook his head. "Hell, no."

"Good to know," Declan answered.

They headed toward reception, bypassing a long line. The young woman behind the counter began to protest, but Julian cut her off with a smile, feeling nothing as she melted beneath his gaze.

She smiled, hesitantly, her young face shy. "Sir, you can't—"

"Jaden DaCosta is expecting us. Can you tell me where her room is located?"

Surprise fell across the young woman's features. "Um, sorry we're not allowed to give out that information."

Julian watched her closely, saw her eyes shift toward the elevator at the extreme right. It was nondescript, set away from the large bank of them grouped closer to reception.

"I can call her if you like."

"No, that's fine. I have her number." He turned abruptly, instantly dismissing the woman.

He nodded toward the single door, his eyes catching the security camera above and, for the first time, the large man who had been half-hidden by a huge palm tree.

"That gives us access to her."

Declan nodded. "Yeah, but all I can see is the freaking Neanderthal between us and the door."

"Don't worry about him."

Declan snorted. "You gonna invite him to tea?"

Julian moved away. "Nope. Don't drink the stuff."

Declan on his heels, he approached the security guard, the energy inside him gathering deep in his gut. His heart began to beat faster, his jaguar no longer content to be still.

The guard moved toward them, his hulking frame blocking the elevator with no problem at all. He was built like a goddamn tank.

The two of them stopped, and Julian smiled harshly as the scent of otherworld drifted on the breeze. The man was a shifter. He was jaguar, and as his eyes passed over the clan tattoos on his arm, he knew the man was a warrior. Not DaCosta, but dangerous nonetheless.

The hulk's eyes narrowed, and his lips peeled back into a grimace that was supposed to be a smile.

"You two gentlemen lost?" He nodded toward the bank of elevators several feet away. "This is private, you need to back away."

Declan smiled. "Dude, what's that on your arm? Christ that is the ugliest fucking tattoo I've ever seen." Declan looked at Julian, who was staring silently at the warrior. "And I've seen some ugly-ass tattoos. Shit, hope you didn't spend heavy on it."

Julian felt the guard's anger and tensed as the mountain of flesh flexed his arms and rolled his neck. "I suggest you move away before I—"

"Before you what? Kick my ass?" Declan sneered.

The guard growled, his tone low and menacing. Declan's glee at the guard's anger was a little too reckless for Julian's liking. He didn't want to attract any attention.

"I don't think so." Declan continued to taunt as he moved in closer, drawing the warrior's attention. They were now hidden behind the massive palm tree. "An overlarge tattooed fairy has no chance at my ass." He laughed as the guard flexed his hands. "Besides, I'm thinking you'd like it just a little too much."

Declan's inference regarding the warriors sexuality was apparently the last straw. On cue, the hulk lunged, but Julian's hand shot out at the same time that Declan threw an energy pulse. His fist blurred as it connected, hard, with the shifter's temple, and it was followed by another quick jab to his throat.

The warrior stumbled, suddenly fighting for air, and Julian moved quickly to subdue him, his large hand pressing against the guard's windpipe as he held him still.

Within seconds, the large man was unconscious.

"Get the door." Julian nodded, but Declan was already on it, his hand hovering above the control panel, energy sizzling from his fingers.

It slid open silently, and, seconds later, they were safely inside, along with the deadweight of the warrior at their feet.

There was only one button, and Julian pressed it while Declan took care of the security camera. If anyone was watching, they might see a blur, a ripple in the air.

Magick came in handy at the trickiest of times.

The lift rose in silence, and as the seconds ticked by, the energy inside Julian darkened. His thoughts continued to center on the woman who had managed to make his miserable existence even more of a spectacular failure.

Jaden DaCosta claimed they were mated. That he was responsible for the warrior tattoos adorning her flesh. Fucking ironic, he thought, and a DaCosta no less.

When the doors finally parted, his body was tense, the muscles bunched good and tight.

Jaden's soft scent lingered in the air, teasing him with its exotic flavor, and he exhaled harshly in an effort to ban it from his nose.

Julian squared his shoulders and shook his arms until they hung loose at his sides. He stepped into her lair, proceeding slowly, with Declan right behind him.

The penthouse suite was simple, elegant, with a bank of

windows that ran the entire length of the room, letting in the beauty of the Mayan countryside. Outside, the sun was high, its warmth caressing his skin as he stepped into the center of the large room.

He knew right away the place was empty. There were no energy signatures, no indication of life.

He relaxed a bit and walked over to a simple table with several pictures on display.

Jaden's laughing face stared up at him, and he cocked his head as he studied them closely. Most were of Jaden and a woman who appeared to be an older version of the shifter. Her mother maybe?

The woman looked sad, something about her eyes was haunted, but Jaden looked unaware, happy and incredibly young.

A few were recent, but there were none of Jakobi, her father, or any of the brothers.

Declan joined him. "You gotta admit the woman is one fine piece of ass."

Julian tensed at the crude words yet remained quiet. His eyes glanced back at the pictures. There was no question as to her beauty, but the blood that ran through her body was tainted.

"She's nothing more than a means to an end. She will help us whether she wants to or not."

Declan shrugged and turned away. "So, what now?"

Julian smiled harshly as he focused on a picture of Jaden, her lean body barely covered by a bikini.

He exhaled slowly and glanced up at the Irishman.

"We wait."

Chapter 6

"Where's Tank?" Nico's harsh tone grabbed her attention as Jaden accepted a folder from one of her staff members. She turned toward the elevator that led to her private suite.

It had been a long morning. She'd been hard at work for hours. Running a huge resort was not for the faint of heart. Coupled with her secret duties, lack of sleep was something she'd learned to deal with early on.

And she was definitely tired. Jaden was not quite back to full strength and had only slept a few hours on the jet, if that. Demon poison usually took a few days to dissipate fully, and she was still feeling the aftereffects.

She pursed her lips together tightly. *What now?*

Night Sky Resort and Casino was her baby, the one good thing in her life, and running it, as well as being the head of her own special branch of PATU, was tiring at the best of times.

Her senses flared as her eyes swept the entire lobby. Tank, her shifter guard, was always at the elevator, and his absence spelled trouble. She felt her muscles bunch instantly, felt them tighten in anticipation.

"Miss DaCosta?"

"Yes," she answered as she continued to scan the immediate area. Nico had already moved from her side and was halfway to the elevator.

"There was a man asking for you. I thought you'd want to know."

She looked at the girl sharply. "Did he leave a name?"

"No, he said you were expecting him."

Jaden glanced back at the elevator. This was not good.

"Thanks," she said softly, and turned away.

She joined Nico, who stood near the large palm tree that hid the elevator. The warrior was tense, the corded muscles in his neck a testament to the state of mind he was in.

"Something's off," he spit out, his eyes flat and black as his nostrils flared wildly. "Tank would never leave his post unless it was covered."

Jaden felt a whisper of energy in the air, an echo of something frenetic, something dark. No one had ever been bold enough to attack her within the resort, but times were changing, and the stakes were so much higher.

She should have seen this coming. She'd been leading a double life for the past several years, and borrowed time eventually expired. If anyone in her family or any of their nasty alliances discovered she worked covertly for PATU, she'd have a bull's-eye tattooed on her ass for the rest of her life.

Maybe her time was up.

She looked at Nico. "Call Security and alert Finn; we'll need an overhead search just to be on the safe side."

She moved toward the private lift and was reaching for the control panel when Nico grabbed her arm, his grip firm, his tone harsh.

"What the hell do you think you're doing?"

Jaden glanced down at his hand on her flesh and suppressed the quick anger that scratched below the surface. Christ but she was getting tired of his attitude lately. She needed no one's protection.

"Nico, you need to back away." Her words were low, controlled, but the tension between them rose sharply.

The shifter took a step closer, and she looked up into his eyes, feeling a snag of remorse as she caught a glimpse of the pain that lingered there. She knew his history, knew the damage that lived inside him, and, because of that, she would tread carefully.

"I don't need the caveman routine, seriously, I'm a big girl. You know I'm more than capable of taking care of myself. I'm a warrior, same as you." If his overprotective attitude continued, she was going to have to make some difficult decisions.

Nico's grip held firm. Why was he making this hard?

"I'm not Bella," she said softly, the hint of danger in her tone not to be missed. "So I suggest you remove your hand and remember who and what I am."

The mention of the woman's name was enough, and Nico wrenched his hand from hers, a snarl falling from his lips.

Bella was his mate—*had been his mate*—she'd been lost to him several years earlier. Jaden wasn't privy to all the details, but what little she did know broke her heart. The warrior had never recovered from his loss.

Nico took a step back and glared at her. "I will accompany you up to your suite."

His tone brooked no argument. She nodded before reaching for the panel again and scanned her hand over the laser pad. A subtle trace of energy rushed along her fingers, a remnant of someone, or something, that shouldn't be there. She had state-of-the-art security, and it would take a lot to breach it.

Jaden tensed as her hand dropped. Something was definitely up.

The door slid back silently while Nico called Security and ordered a sweep of the entire grounds. She kept an elite guard that would be able to run the command discreetly, mixing with the human populace and able to remain hidden in plain sight.

Her eyes skimmed over the humans who milled about the lobby of her resort. They had no clue of the danger or the monsters that lived amongst them, and she would do everything in her power to make sure it stayed that way.

The elevator seemed to take forever, and by the time it slid back and allowed them entrance to her suite, her nerves were humming.

An eerie quiet fell upon her, its whisper thick and unnatural. There was no energy in the air, no hint of intruders, living or dead. But the fact that she sensed absolutely nothing had her internal alarm shrieking.

It felt like she'd slipped inside a black hole, as if everything had been wiped clean. It was unnatural and reeked of otherworld. *Dark arts.* Her eyes scanned the immediate area, but nothing was out of place. She looked at Nico, and he nodded before moving toward the left.

Inside, her jaguar shifted, and she felt the burn ripple across her flesh. She kept the temperature in her suite cool, but that did nothing to alleviate the heat suffusing her skin. The room looked untouched, and though there was no indication that things were amiss, everything inside her screamed danger.

She scented the air, but again nothing, and as she slowly made her way down the hall to her bedroom, she was careful not to make a sound.

She passed the small study where she kept a personal office, yet it was empty, in darkness, and she continued along until she reached her bedroom.

Soft light fell from the windows that ate up the entire left side of the space, the beams cutting through gloom in a flickering array of gold. Outside, azure water beckoned, and farther in the distance, the outlying jungle cradled its beach.

This was her own private view of the land she loved with all her heart, and it pissed her off that someone had dared trespass in her domain.

She kept her heartbeat steady, calm, though every instinct inside her prepared for battle. Her feet were bare of the sandals she'd worn, and they hung from her fingers as she carefully made her way into the room.

Her bed showed not a wrinkle, the maid had obviously been, and she slipped toward the small alcove that housed her large walk-in closets.

The silence hurt her ears; it weighed upon her like a physical blow, and she grimaced at the weird sensation. A slight tremor hung in the air, a foreign vibration that was somehow familiar to her.

She paused at the entrance to her closet, and even though she tried to keep calm, she felt the blood inside her veins thicken and rush through her body. Her skin was itchy, hot, and as the tattoos began to tingle along the side of her neck, she stopped, her focus shifting to the shadows that clung to the corners.

Someone was there.

Adrenaline spiked inside, she felt the power gather and pulse. Jaden pretended to turn and exit, then at the last second whirled around, the stiletto-heeled sandals hurtling through the air like deadly missiles.

She ducked as a curse fell from the darkness, and the sharp heels flew back at her, to land with a thud against the wall where her head had been seconds earlier.

"I would have guessed you too old for hide-and-seek, Castille," she said as she retrieved her sandals and tossed them aside.

She took a step back and watched as the tall shifter fell from shadow. He looked surprised, his handsome face scowling, the eyes glittering dangerously.

She tapped the side of her neck. "The tattoos will always know you, no matter how strong the cloaking charm." She hated the fact that her heart pounded crazily inside her and that the flesh of her cheeks darkened in reaction to the sight of him.

"What the hell are you doing here?" *Damn, why do I sound out of breath?*

The gold of his eyes receded into twin black holes of intensity, and the clench of his jaw attested to his inner feelings. He made no attempt to hide his dislike of her.

"How the hell did you breach my security? Tank alone should have given you major problems, but the elevator doors are activated by select signatures only."

Power clung to the man like the scent of a lover; she felt the thickness of it in the air. But it was tainted.

It should have repulsed her. It didn't. Instead, it fed something that answered in kind, and she shifted, uncomfortable and angry.

He moved toward her but she refused to budge. When he

stood inches from her body, she looked up at him, her actions measured, precise, while inside, her jaguar scratched, wanting out.

"Apparently your security measures are subpar."

Was that anger in his voice?

"I had no problem at all." He glared at her. "It was much too easy."

Angry and accusatory. Where the hell did he get off?

Jaden swallowed hard, her throat dry. Damn, but she needed a drink.

She regarded the warrior in silence and shook her head. "Why are you here?" she asked again, not interested in the how, only wanting to know his reason.

He smiled, yet his eyes remained cold, flat. His hand swept upward, and though she tried to remain still, she flinched as his fingers fell across her cheek. The spark of energy that sizzled along her flesh awakened a need so intense that, for a second, everything blurred. Her animal was all kinds of agitated, and a hiss escaped from between her lips.

She yanked her head to the side and pushed him away, a low growl vibrating from deep within her chest.

"Stay the fuck away from me, Castille," she bit out, furious at her reaction, "and answer the question."

He cocked his head, an arrogant tilt, and said nothing.

Jaden clenched her hands and took a step toward him once more, visualizing her fist connecting with the perfect lines of his nose. It would give her great pleasure to break the fucking thing, and she flexed her fingers at the thought.

"I came for you."

She blinked in surprise and shook her head. "Excuse me?"

The smile left him, and the way his eyes glittered had her gut twisting hard. There was no more pretending. Julian

Castille was seriously damaged, and the predatory gleam that flickered briefly had her hackles up instantly.

The man was freaking insane if he thought she was going anywhere with him. He was on the edge, and she had enough to deal with.

"It's simple really," he began, his tone conversational as if they were buddies, friends. "You and I have something in common."

Her eyes narrowed. What the hell was he getting at? "The only thing we have in common is our mutual dislike for each other and a fondness for whiskey, but we're not going there . . . again."

"We both want the portal."

For a moment, Jaden was speechless. The portal?

"Ah no"—she shook her head—"no, no, no." Was he on drugs? "I am so not going there with you," she retorted, as her mind worked furiously, trying to figure out his angle.

"You *will* go there with me"—Julian bared his teeth—"or else."

"Do not threaten me, Castille." Jaden was so angry she could barely get the words out. *The fucking nerve.* "I am not someone you want as an enemy."

"I will get my hands on the portal, Jaden." He dismissed her as if she were nothing more than a nuisance and moved away from her. "I'd prefer it sooner rather than later."

Fury rushed through her, hot and sharp. She pushed it back, knowing she could not let him get to her. She needed a cool head.

She watched as his hand crept up to his chest, and an image of his scarred, damaged skin flashed in her mind. What the hell had happened to him?

"So," she began carefully as she put more distance between them; her mouth seemed to work better the farther away she was. "You want to work together to retrieve the portal?" It was hard to keep the sarcasm from her voice, and she watched as he arched a perfect eyebrow and cocked his head.

"You will help me."

Unbelievable.

His arrogance left her mouth agape, but he was already walking away from her before she could answer.

"You're one hell of a prick," she yelled at him, willing him to stop, and she swore loudly as he kept walking. Her face tightened, and her eyes narrowed into dark slits of anger. "Hey dickhead, I'm talking to you! Give me one good reason why I should help you?"

He stopped abruptly, and she nearly ran into his back. His body was hot. She felt the heat scorch the air.

He turned around, and she retreated a step, her chest heaving as she struggled to calm herself. His muscled frame was draped in casual cotton, the light-colored fabric a foil against his tanned skin. The open collar drew her gaze to the pulse that beat strong and steady at his throat, and she swallowed thickly, her mouth suddenly dry.

His long legs were encased in faded jeans, the kind that hung low; so low, in fact, that she could see the taut skin of his belly as he lifted his arm and ruffled the hair at his neck. Even though Mexico was hot as sin, his feet were encased in the same pair of boots he'd worn the night before. The man was seriously hot. Too bad he was such an asshole.

"You done?"

Her eyes jerked back up to his. "Done?"

"Checking me out. I thought you saw enough last night, but hell, if we have time—"

"Fuck you, Castille."

"Seems to me you already did," he whispered softly, the tone of his voice dangerous like dark chocolate.

Her arm flew out as the anger inside her erupted. She felt the power of her jaguar gather and aimed her fist for his nose. But he grabbed her just above the wrist before she made contact and twisted until a whimper eventually fell from her lips.

Small spurts of air escaped from between her lips as her chest heaved. She tried to pull away, but he refused to let her go.

"I don't have time for games. If the portal is not found . . . if Cormac is not stopped, all hell will break loose in the human realm, and, trust me, if that happens, I will be the least of your worries. There will be such madness, chaos, and pain . . ." His voice trailed off, and Jaden's gut twisted as fear began to grow.

Deep within the recesses of his eyes, something flickered, something haunted. She swallowed heavily, and whispered, "Let me go."

He held her for several long moments, his eyes never leaving hers, then gently withdrew his hand.

She stood there, rubbing her throbbing wrist as her mind whirled into a thousand directions. Julian Castille had not been vacationing in Club Med for the last six months. He'd been someplace dark, twisted. He knew what was coming.

But could she work with him?

A loud crash echoed into the silence, and she jumped.

"What the—?" Jaden pushed past Julian and was down the hall in seconds, her mind and body on red alert.

She reached the main room and froze, her eyes staring at the scene in disbelief. Anger, hot and instant, burned her, and she shook her head as her jaguar protested loudly.

"Motherfu—"

"Shit, that's not very ladylike."

Her words were cut off, and she glared at Declan O'Hara as he stood surrounded by the smashed remnants of a large piece of pottery. The air shimmered around him, a barrier of magick, and Nico circled him warily, growls and hisses falling from him.

The warrior had shed his human skin and flicked his long tail in agitation as he continued to circle the sorcerer.

"You wanna call off your kitty?" Declan flashed a smile, yet his eyes, too, were as hard as Julian's, full of darkness and secrets. "I'd hate to have to singe his fur, but if need be, I'll fry his ass."

Jaden ignored the sorcerer and walked toward them, her hand reaching for the large jaguar. "Nico, be still."

The cat barked twice and hissed, but moved between her and Declan as she knelt amongst the mess. She stared down at the ruined pottery for several long seconds. Her breath fell in ragged swells as she fought to control her emotion. The ceremonial jug had been a gift from her mother, Sophia, an ancient treasure from a long ago time, and the only link she had to her mother's family.

It was worth a small fortune, but to Jaden, that paled in comparison to what it had meant to her mother. What it meant to *her*.

She shook her head, vaguely heard Nico hiss as she carefully picked up a large piece and turned it over in her hands, her long fingers caressing it lovingly. Her heart contracted, and her chest tightened, full of sorrow as she eyed the shards.

The energy in the room shifted, and she looked up at Declan as he let the barrier fall. She tried to cloak her true feelings but wasn't successful.

"I'm sorry," he said simply. There, deep within the recesses of his eyes, she saw a spark of compassion. It lightened his features briefly, then disappeared.

Weariness, bone-chilling and dense, swept over her, and she sighed softly as she began to gather the pieces together. She sensed Julian at her side the same time Nico's growl warned her.

"You will not touch these," she whispered roughly, hating the thought of anyone other than herself holding the pieces that meant so much.

He stood back, and she went about her task with careful precision. Long moments of silence accompanied her, and when she was done, she stared down at the pile. Her heart broke. She knew it was beyond fixable.

Just as her world would be if Cormac was successful. They needed to find the portal and destroy it immediately, or every loss she'd suffered would be for nothing. Every sacrifice she'd made would have been in vain.

She stood quickly and shook the sadness from her mind. There was no time for pity. She could deal with that later, when she was alone.

She looked up at Julian. "I agree that we can accomplish the task much more efficiently working together than apart, but I'll only do it on one condition."

Nico growled loudly, and she glanced at the animal in warning as mist crawled along his limbs.

Julian nodded slowly. "And what would that be?"

"You need to share everything. For us to work together, some kind of trust needs to be established. I need to know where you've been, what you went through." She paused and glared at Declan. "What your endgame is because I sure as hell don't believe it's all about puppies and rainbows. You have an ulterior motive, and I want to know what it is."

The dark energy that slid along Julian's skin vibrated, and her breath caught as she felt the caress of his power.

Julian glanced at Declan and nodded. "I'll tell you what you need to know when . . ." His voice drifted off and he arched an eyebrow.

"When what?" she mimicked, irritated at his superior attitude. She was going to have to break that real quick.

Julian nodded toward Nico, who now stood in his human form a few feet away and snarled.

"When your boyfriend puts on some clothes and leaves us alone."

Chapter 7

It took a considerable amount of energy to control the darkness that tickled along the edge of Julian's mind. And it was fierce . . . the need he felt to crush Nico in such a way that maximum pain would be involved.

The warrior stood proudly, his naked body a testament to his hard past. His skin glistened with sweat, and the heavy muscles were adorned by several jagged battle scars.

Nico bared his teeth and took a step toward him as Julian clenched his hands, a vicious smile sweeping across his face.

"You will show her respect, Castille," Nico snarled.

"Respect needs to be earned," he said silkily, "then kept." Julian nodded, his voice matter-of-fact, "something you know firsthand, no? Crazy Nico, isn't that what they call you?" He stood loosely, with his hands at his sides, waiting for the warrior to strike.

"For fuck sakes, I don't have time for this." Jaden turned to him, her chest heaving and skin flush with heat. His eyes ran over her, and his gut tightened as she licked her lips and exhaled.

"You need to shut your mouth because I'm this"—she pinched her fingers in his face—"close to kicking your ass but good."

Damn but she was fearless.

"I think I might enjoy that," he whispered, surprised to find his thoughts falling from his lips so readily. His words were soft, meant only for her ears, and her skin darkened in response. It gave him perverse pleasure to know he was the cause of it.

"Move away from her," Nico growled, and Julian glanced at the warrior, hating the way he looked at Jaden as if he owned her.

"You couldn't protect your woman. What makes you think you can do any better with Jaden?"

Nico's face whitened, and the air stilled, thinning, as if it were sucked away into a black hole of nothingness. It was a low blow, and he knew it, but Julian didn't give a flying fuck. Truthfully, he just wanted to hurt, spread that lovely sensation wherever the hell he could.

They should all experience the hole that was inside him.

His eyes fell back to Jaden's, and he snarled before turning away.

"You're an asshole," she spit at him.

"Yeah, that's the second time he's been called that today," Declan interjected, his tone light. Ever the comedian.

Jaden snapped, "You don't get to talk to me, not after what you've done." She shot a look of such loathing toward the sorcerer that Declan closed his mouth and remained silent.

Declan glanced at Julian, his face screwed up into a caricature of *what the fuck?*

Julian looked down at the pile of clay and instinctively knew the piece had meant a lot to Jaden.

"Nico, take Cormac's spawn down to the hub; I'll be along in a bit."

Nico's eyes never left Julian's. The warrior flexed his muscles yet remained silent. Julian saw the pain there; it was something he recognized and knew intimately.

He fucking lived with it every day.

He cracked a smile and raised his chin in invitation. He sensed the jaguar was on the cusp, and Julian stood lightly, ready for battle. Inside, he felt his animal stretch, the power within him flex, and he reveled in the sensation.

It told him that he was still alive even if part of him was cold and dead.

"Nico, he's not worth it," Jaden said softly as she moved toward the warrior. She put her hand on him, and Julian's skin burned with a need that was foreign.

"It's all right, I'll be fine. I need you to contact Finn and get him down there, too." She glanced back to Julian, her eyes narrow, her lips thin with anger. "Castille and I need a few minutes."

Nico remained quiet but didn't move. The air was charged with things unsaid, acts undone, yet the woman between them pleaded for calm.

"Nico, please," Jaden said softly, "I don't have time for posturing. Just go."

Julian studied the way the warrior looked at Jaden, and it took a lot for him to remain still. Nico wanted her or, at the very least, wanted to protect her.

But she's mine.

The thought slid through his mind, and he paused, surprised. *What the hell was that about?* The woman meant nothing to him.

Julian sighed wearily, suddenly tired of it all, and nodded to Declan. "Go with him, I'll be there as soon as Jaden and I . . . have a conversation."

"If you touch her in any way that's inappropriate, I will kill you," Nico rasped.

"You could try," Julian began as he turned from the warrior, "but I'm way ahead of you since half of me is already dead."

As he spoke, he felt a whisper of regret for a life unlived, a chance that was never to be. He'd never be whole again, would never be free of the pain, both physical and emotional, unless he accomplished what was required.

And even then, the odds were a total crapshoot.

"Go, Nico." Jaden's soft whisper and her obvious affection for the other jaguar grated on his nerves. He felt fingers of tension work their way across his jaw as he clenched his teeth together tightly.

Jaden whispered something to Nico, too low for even his ears to hear, and though he pretended to turn from them, he would have given anything to know what she'd said to calm the warrior. A promise from a lover? A reward for good behavior?

The jaguar was seriously pussy whipped if he was gonna let sex rule his actions, but then again, Jaden DaCosta was a damn fine piece of ass. He should know. He'd tasted her on a long-ago evening, not unlike the one that was fast approaching.

His eyes swept the length of the room, taking in the magnificent view that the endless wall of glass afforded, and he studied the waning sun as it began to descend lower into the sky.

He heard the elevator doors open.

"Dude, I need a drink. You think we can hit the bar on

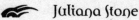

the way down?" Declan's voice drifted back to him as did Nico's answering growl. Julian shook his head, wondering how the sorcerer could remain so flip in the face of such darkness and death. He supposed it was how he dealt with the pile of shit that was his life. The same pile of shit Julian needed to dig out from under.

He watched as Jaden crossed the room and opened a cupboard that was located near the window. He saw her reflection in the glass, and it afforded him a chance to study her without her knowledge. Her lean body was covered in a simple skirt and blouse, both professional yet feminine. Her generous breasts strained against the thin fabric, and his gaze lingered.

Her hair was pinned loosely, and as she turned, her tattoos glistened vibrantly. He found himself fascinated by the luminescent quality, the exotic design.

She grabbed a glass and threw some ice into it before pausing. "You need a drink? 'Cause I sure as hell do."

"Whiskey, over ice," he answered without thinking. He turned back to face her and let his eyes drift over her body once more. Her feet were bare, the toenails painted bright pink.

His eyes lingered there, on the feminine arch and delicate lines.

"Some things haven't changed," she said softly, and, for a moment, he was clueless as to her meaning. He shook his head slightly, more than a little pissed at how easily she was able to distract him.

She raised his glass, and the sound of the ice tinkling against the tumbler echoed loudly between the two of them.

"Everything has changed," he retorted, not liking the sensations she seemed to pull so easily from him.

"Whiskey," she said. "It's what you were drinking that night . . ."

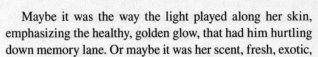

Maybe it was the way the light played along her skin, emphasizing the healthy, golden glow, that had him hurtling down memory lane. Or maybe it was her scent, fresh, exotic, and wholly feminine.

Whatever it was, suddenly things shifted, like reality had taken a vacation, and he saw her as she'd been three years earlier, younger, fuller, and so passionate that she'd taken his breath away.

She walked toward him, and he sensed her jaguar scratching just below the surface.

Her clan tattoos seemed to move along her skin, and the sudden urge to run his tongue along them, to taste them, pulled at him.

Hard.

Julian clenched his teeth and frowned darkly as he accepted the glass from her. She smiled, a sly lift to her mouth, and turned away, letting her long hair down as she did so, the thick waves slipping from the clip to caress her bare shoulders and fall nearly to her ass.

"Don't play this game with me," he said harshly, before draining half the glass in one gulp.

Jaden laughed softly, leaned against a sofa, and raised her glass to him before letting the liquid slide down her throat. His eyes were drawn to the delicate lines there, to the muscles that moved slowly as she finished the entire contents of her glass.

The energy in the air changed. It was now electrified, potent. She licked her lips and stared at him, her dark eyes glistening.

"I don't play games, Castille." She shrugged and returned to the cupboard, pouring another generous amount into her glass. "I've no time for that shit, so why don't you come clean, and we can move on."

She turned back to him, but he remained silent. "Let's face it, the sooner we end this, the sooner we can forget—"

"Forget what?" he asked softly, and his body moved in a blur of energy and power until he stood inches from her. He felt the heat of her skin, saw the blush of warmth along her cheeks, and the powerful clawing inside him increased tenfold.

"Us . . . forget that we ever met," she whispered.

He wanted her. As insane as that was, he couldn't deny the fact.

His body began to hum with an energy long forgotten, and he inhaled sharply as a myriad of sensations spread across his flesh, caressing the raw scars that lay there.

"Move back, Castille." Jaden's voice was low, rough, and he studied her eyes closely, watching the irises darken and swell until they were deep pools of inky black velvet.

Her small nose twitched, and her tongue darted out to run along her top lip quickly. He followed the action and found himself bending down.

He would have one more taste.

"Don't," she said softly, and he paused. His mouth hovered just above hers, with only the caress of her breath between them.

Julian closed his eyes and breathed in her seductive scent. He felt her hand against his chest, there where he was damaged, and his eyes flew open as they connected.

She shook her head. "We don't even like each other so this, this . . . whatever it is we're feeling is unnatural." She pushed at him, harder, and he let her go as the pain along his flesh twisted and burned.

He grimaced as the wave rolled over him and exhaled slowly, his eyes never leaving hers.

"Lady, I'm probably the most unnatural thing you'll come across, and trust me, we don't have to like each other to fuck. In fact, considering the world is heading for the shitter, the whole 'no strings' thing suits me fine."

His eyes narrowed, and he flashed a smile at her. "Hell, if you're sharing your goods with Nico, why can't you at least give it up for your mate?"

She looked startled at his crudeness, and hissed, "If you need to relieve tension that bad, I suggest you take a long shower and go it alone or hang at the bar because I'll never let you touch me again."

Jaden pushed away, and he let her go, not really sure why he was goading her so. He only knew that getting a reaction out of her made him feel alive somehow.

She slammed her empty tumbler onto the counter and whirled around. Her face was dark, the finely arched eyebrows drawn together as she stared at him, tight-lipped. He knew she was pissed. Actually, the woman was beyond pissed and closing in on furious.

"I can't work with you if you're going to be an asshole." She shook her head violently. "There's too much at stake."

Her eyes nailed him with an intensity that quieted the demons inside him, at least for the time being.

"We can't do this . . . play this game. There's no time, so let's establish a few things." Jaden pushed away from the counter and began to pace in front of the window. Behind her, long bands of red and gold stretched across the sky as the sun began to set. It painted fire across the water.

"Let's forget everything that happened three years ago. None of it matters anymore."

"The tattoos along the side of your neck tell me otherwise," Julian retorted, not liking her tone or the way she was looking at him.

"Trust me, Castille. They mean nothing." Her eyes nailed him.

Liar.

"What does matter is that we find the portal, and by we, I mean myself and a bunch of people, including your brothers."

At the mention of his brothers, Julian stilled. "I hear you've gotten tight with them."

She nodded and turned to stare out at the landscape below. "I've been working covertly for PATU for the past several years. I started out as an independent, working exclusively to bring down the DaCostas. But a few years ago, I was given command of my own team. They're housed here at the resort."

She turned to him abruptly. "Your brother Jaxon was in the dark about my work until after Belize. You know, when you, Declan, Cormac, and Azaiel pulled the big vanishing act." She stared at him for several long moments, and Julian tried to block the images from his mind, but it seemed today was the day for trekking down memory lane.

The scars on his chest began to burn and pulsate, and he tasted sulfur inside his mouth and smelled fear. It left him feeling nauseous, drained. He dragged his hands through his hair and exhaled loudly.

Shit, I need another drink.

"Where were you?" she asked softly. She must have felt his need because she grabbed the decanter of whiskey and walked back to him, pouring another generous amount into his glass.

Julian downed it greedily, letting the fire slide down his throat as he took a few more seconds to compose himself.

"We were in the darkest place you can imagine." He opened his eyes, but it wasn't the sunset, or the cool tones of the room, or even Jaden that he saw. Once more he was surrounded by the stench and evil of the underworld. He was ashamed to say that fear rippled along his flesh like a conduit, spreading anxiety along with it.

He couldn't articulate what he was feeling and turned from her, angry that she'd led him down this path. Even if he could, he wouldn't share his pain with her . . . a DaCosta. He'd rather she feel it.

Her family was a catalyst for every fucking thing that he'd gone through in the past six months. The fact that he was half-dead? With half his soul missing? That was all on them.

"We were in hell," he said harshly, watching her reflection in the window. "And not figuratively. It was the real deal."

Jaden took a step toward him, then stopped, as if she thought better of it. You should stay far away from me, Julian's mind whispered.

"Where are Cormac and Azaiel?" she asked hesitantly.

"If I knew that, I wouldn't be wasting my time here with you." Julian no longer tried to control the darkness that slid over his skin though he knew there would be a price.

Funny how the dark side felt good until you dipped your toe in.

He felt a sliver of admiration as she stood up to him, her eyes flashing with anger. "How did you get out? Your charm leave you, so Lucifer blasted your ass out of there?" Her words dripped sarcasm.

Julian snorted. "I never had the pleasure of meeting the son of a bitch, though if you talk to Declan, I think his story might be different." He shook his head. "I don't know who or what pulled us out of there." The lie slipped from his tongue, and he continued with ease. "What I do know is that the portal, that fucking disc that the eagle knights protected, is key. I need to find it, and if I can manage to kick Cor-

mac's ass while I'm at it"—he rotated his neck and smiled wickedly—"then bring it on."

"Who's pulling your strings?" she asked softly, her lips pursed into a concentrated line. "Sorry if I don't believe you're doing this out of the goodness of your heart."

The woman did not give up.

He opened his mouth to retort, but an alarm sounded, followed by a disembodied voice that fell from the security device located near the elevator doors.

"Jaden? It's Finn."

She tossed a don't-move look his way before answering.

"Go ahead." He watched as she crossed the room and leaned over the com unit.

"We've got a situation you need to be aware of."

"What now?" She threw her hands into the air, not bothering to hide her annoyance. "Declan O'Hara is nothing more than an overgrown child. He's not that hard to manage."

"Sorry, but this has nothing to do with the sorcerer. It's your family."

Julian was at her side in an instant. She kept her face averted, her breathing was calm. Yet her fingers were white as she clutched the com unit. He could smell her fear. It oozed from her pores in waves.

She was a warrior, a woman who was more than capable of looking after herself in intense situations. Hell, he'd seen her take out two demons the night before and live through the poison one had infected her with.

She was terrified. What the hell was up?

"Who?" she asked sharply.

"Your father's car just arrived. You've got maybe five minutes."

"Fuck," Jaden whispered hoarsely.

"Yeah," Finn answered. "You need to get rid of the Castille shifter or . . ."

Jaden bowed her head. "He knows something's up. The bastard's internal radar is freaky. Do what you can to delay him, get staff on it right away."

"Already in play."

"And for Christ sakes, keep O'Hara under wraps."

She exhaled loudly and turned around. Her eyes were bleak, dead serious as she looked up at him.

"Nothing you went through will compare to what will happen if my father finds you here."

"I doubt that," Julian answered frankly, while inside the jaguar began to make noise, as if sensing the closeness of his enemy.

Jaden snorted. "You don't understand. My father eats demons for breakfast." She looked outside. "Its dinnertime, and he'll be hungry."

Chapter 8

Jaden nearly choked on the dread that sat in her throat. The feeling was awful but she forced it away while her mind circled fast. Her hot skin was suddenly cold, clammy, and her belly rolled as she walked away from Julian, narrowly missing the jagged pottery on the floor. Her feet were still tender from the night before, but she'd rather walk a mile over broken glass than face her father right now.

Yet, as in keeping with her week so far, the general direction down into the crap hole would continue.

She was just so tired of it all, the double life that she led; some days it was hard to keep it all straight in her head. Was she secret agent girl working for the greater good? Or the spoiled rich kid with daddy issues who was plotting to take over the world?

"You must stay hidden," she mumbled, as her mind continued to whirl. She pointed toward the large balcony that ran the length of her suite. "There, you can make it up to the roof."

"I'm not a pimply-faced kid afraid to meet Father," Julian retorted, his tone flat, his arms loose and ready for battle. "I won't run like a coward."

"I'm not asking you to run," she said, exasperated. Did he mean to continually annoy her? Was everything to be a fight?

"I'm asking you to listen"—she paused for a second to gather her thoughts—"and listen carefully."

Something in her tone must have penetrated his thick skull. Though he rolled his shoulders and looked uninterested in what she had to say, she had his attention.

"My father cannot find a Castille shifter here, in my home. He'll go ape-shit, and believe me, on a good day he's not a nice man." Her voice broke, and she ignored the way his eyes narrowed, the way his mouth parted as he stared at her. He must love seeing her like this.

"I've given everything in order to bring him down. To make him pay for all the fucking shit and evil crap that he's . . . you've no idea . . ." Her voice trailed into a whisper. " . . . of the things that he's done."

"Enlighten me," Julian retorted, a hint of sarcasm coloring his words. "I'm all ears."

Jaden gritted her teeth as a wave of nervous energy rolled through her. "I don't have time to share the wonders of my childhood, and we're so close to ending it all . . . I won't let you screw it up." She exhaled a ragged breath. "You need to listen to me."

Finn's voice interrupted once more, and she jumped. "Jaden, he's in the lobby. O'Hara is concerned about the cloaking charm on Castille. He seems surprised that you were able to sense him. He also says you need to let Tank out."

"Tank?" she asked, a frown pulling at her mouth as she looked to Julian.

"Yeah, apparently they hogtied him and stuffed him in the closet."

"Nice." Her eyes were now shooting bullets at Julian. "Tell Declan not to worry about the cloaking charm, it's working fine. And let's go dark, no more transmissions. I'll be down as soon as I can." She looked at Julian and pointed toward the glass.

"Please," she whispered, hating that she had to beg the one man she hated almost as much as her father.

"How can you be sure he won't detect my scent?" he asked quietly, his manner suddenly dead serious.

A strangled noise escaped her lips. She so didn't have time for 101 questions.

She rubbed her neck impatiently. "The only reason I knew you were here was because of the tattoos. They burn when you're around." Her eyes looked away quickly. "It's the whole mating thing. We're connected on a level that even I don't understand." She nodded and ran to the door. "Trust me, O'Hara's magick is strong. Jakobi won't know you're here unless you screw up."

Yeah, keep telling yourself that.

Sweat broke out along her forehead, and she wiped it away impatiently. Julian looked like he might protest, but she was ready to knock him on his ass if he did so.

His mouth lifted into a smile, and she clenched her hands into fists as she took a step toward him. But at the last moment he surprised her and slipped by, his tangy scent tickling inside her nostrils before he disappeared into the gathering dusk.

The air left her lungs in a wild gasp, and Jaden whirled around, grabbing the second glass off the table, the one Julian's fingers had been all over, and she tossed it into the trash behind the bar. She'd just smoothed her wild mass of hair around her shoulders when the elevator door slid back, and Jakobi DaCosta entered her suite.

As if he owned the fucking place.

He was followed by a large warrior, Benicio, one of his elite guard. The jaguar warrior ignored her and stood to the side, maintaining a respectful distance between himself and Jakobi.

Hatred awakened inside her as she smiled at her father, her face tight and unnatural. For a moment it shadowed the fear that was also present, but then the walls in the room shrank, and the air that she dragged into her lungs thinned.

It felt like he'd sucked the life out of her home in less than five seconds. She had to give it to him; that was some kind of record.

Her father was a tall man, with sleek, predatory lines. His powerful frame was draped in expensive Italian, Brioni, if she wasn't mistaken. He'd always had a love of the finer things in life, and the empire he'd built on the backs of innocents went a long way in supporting his endeavors.

Night Sky Resort and Casino was her baby, though, the one thing his evil had not been able to penetrate. A gift from her mother, and one Jaden would protect until the day she died.

He looked at her closely, and his nostrils flared subtly. For a second, she stopped breathing. Did he sense Julian?

But then his gaze fell upon the broken pottery at his feet, and he grimaced. He kicked at it dispassionately, daring to scuff the leather shoes that he wore, then slowly walked around it, crunching several small remnants into nothing more than dust as he did so.

"I was never fond of that piece," he said, and smiled, though the cruel depths of his eyes never changed. "Your mother's taste left a lot to be desired." The silver in his hair glistened eerily, creating a striking foil to his darkly tanned skin. "I suggest you call a porter immediately."

Jaden nodded but kept her distance. Things had been this way for many, many years now . . . hard, unyielding, and complicated.

"You seem on edge, my pet," he murmured silkily as he stopped a few inches from her. He knew she hated the endearment, so he made a point of using it every chance he got.

Alarm bells sounded but on the outside she remained calm.

"What can I do for you, Jakobi?" The slight tremor in her voice couldn't be hidden, and she watched a slow smile spread across his face.

He loved it. The power he had over his children. The fear that he inspired.

He pursed his lips. "Can a father not visit his offspring without having a reason?"

Jaden exhaled softly. *What game is he playing now?*

"Would you like a drink?" she asked politely, changing the subject.

His nostrils flared once more, his eyes narrowed. "You've already indulged, whiskey from the smell of it." His voice held a hint of distaste. In his mind, a lady should never develop a taste for hard liquor. Wine was a much more refined spirit.

But, of course, she was no lady.

Jaden turned from him, filled with the need to do something, and grabbed her glass, hoping he couldn't see how her fingers shook as she reached for the crystal decanter.

"Have you spoken to your brothers lately?" His voice was flat, cold, and, just like that, any shred of civility vanished. The pretending was over.

She paused, took a few moments to carefully pour herself a drink, then turned back to him.

His eyes were dead. There was nothing there, at least nothing that was good anyway.

"I talked to Degas several days ago, why?" Degas was the eldest DaCosta sibling, and the most like her father. He was a man filled with darkness, who lived on the edge of sanity, always striving for their father's approval. He'd just never clued in to the fact it was never going to happen.

Their father cared about no one but himself and the image he wanted them all to project.

"He feels you've been distracted of late." A slight hint of *pissed off* was present in her father's voice.

Her vision blurred, and her belly rolled, but Jaden smiled tightly. She'd been playing a double role for so long that her reactions were always spot on.

"Distracted?" She laughed softly. "He's full of crap. Degas is always looking for a way to push me out of the picture."

Her father remained silent, and she didn't like the way he was staring at her, like he knew something. Inside, her heart fluttered, and though she tried to keep the blush of heat from her skin, she felt her cheeks redden as he continued to stare at her.

The tattoos on the side of her neck began to burn, and it took everything inside her to keep from glancing back at the balcony. If Julian was there, all would be lost.

"You're so like your mother," Jakobi whispered as he walked toward her. She cringed, an automatic reaction to his proximity, and hated the way his mouth lifted into the merest whisper of a smile.

It wasn't real, of course, and only amplified his distaste for her.

She recovered quickly. Fear fed the sadistic soul that lived inside him, and she'd rather he starve tonight.

He stood not more than two inches from her and she held on to the glass in her hand so tightly that her fingers ached. She heard the air wheezing inside her lungs as her heart rate continued to accelerate.

Damn his sarcastic, arrogant ass. Jakobi knew what he did to her. Why the fuck did she even try?

"Your mother was a whore, too." His hands reached for the clan tattoos along the side of her neck, and she sensed his anger now. It was in the thin bent to his lips, the eerie glow that lit his eyes from behind.

"You are the shame I cannot hide."

Jaden swallowed thickly but couldn't move away. Though his words should have bounced off her like rubber, they didn't. Even after all this time, they still hurt.

The ache inside her chest tightened as she gazed into his face, fighting the need for him to understand. She was pathetic.

"That you would take a mate yet remain unattached is both unnatural and sinful."

She flinched at the look of disgust that pinched his features. He would never let it go. "Father, he wasn't for me," she managed to get out.

He snarled, and the air around him blurred as he drew his hand high and slapped her, *hard,* across the cheek. Jaden's head snapped back as pain ripped across her flesh. Blood gushed inside her mouth, the coppery taste flooding her tongue, inflaming her senses.

"Stupid, weak woman. Your path was set, the only thing you needed to do was choose wisely. It should have been one of our own, and now . . ." He spit at her though his voice never deviated from a flat tone. "You're damaged goods . . . nothing more than a whore who plays in her resort, fucking anything that moves."

She cringed at his crude words, hating the way they ripped into her soul.

Would there ever come a time when his words would only be flesh wounds and not cut so deep?

Benicio watched silently, several feet away, and her cheeks darkened, flooded with the heat of her shame, as the warrior smirked. Inside, the cat began to scratch at the surface, pulling at her painfully in an effort to get out and act upon her rage. For a second, the air around her blurred, heavy with magick and mist that crawled up her legs.

"Do not think to attack me, little cub." His whisper was deadly, and she knew his threats were real. She'd seen him in action before. The man was ruthless.

Jaden hung her head and flinched as she felt his breath against her forehead. Her father continued to speak, yet she couldn't understand his words. Her mind went blank, leaving only a visual behind. Of a long-ago time, before her father's heart had been blackened.

To a time when his touch had been gentle and his gaze warm.

She blinked rapidly, trying to banish the memories. They were much too painful, filled with of a lifetime of losses.

When his hand dug into her chin and forced her head up, she remained silent, though the jaguar raged against her chest.

"The only reason you still live is because you hold some value to me. Remember that."

He shoved her away, and she stumbled but quickly regained her balance.

"Why are you here?" she asked, proud that she managed to keep her voice even though inside the ghost of a little girl wailed.

"To keep you on track, focused."

She watched her father warily as he walked toward the balcony, and the fear inside her spiked as adrenaline kicked in. Her cheek throbbed, but she ignored the pain.

"You don't have to worry. I know what is expected of me."

She needed to keep him inside.

"Do you?" he asked softly, his dark gaze sweeping across her as if she were nothing more than a nuisance.

He reached for the whiskey decanter and held it aloft, watching the amber liquid swish against the cool glass.

"What were you doing in Washington?"

How the hell did he find that out?

She glanced at Benicio once more, but the warrior was focused elsewhere, his massive body leaning against the wall. He looked bored, but then he'd seen their family drama played out so many times, they'd not covered anything new.

She rubbed her cheek and felt the swelling of skin along the curve.

"You should put some ice on that," Jakobi said, smiling softly as if they were sharing a secret. "But before you do, tell me about your trip."

Jaden stared at her father for several long moments and took the plunge. There was no use in lying.

"A little bird told me that Julian Castille was back from the dead."

Surprise flickered deep within the depths of Jakobi's eyes. It flared to a bright red, then was gone. He was an expert at keeping his cool.

"I decided to check it out," she continued as she walked the few feet to the side cupboard and retrieved her glass of whiskey. She downed the remnants of it and turned back to him. "The little bird was wrong . . . as far as I could tell."

Plant the seed and keep them occupied. She knew this info would drive her father crazy.

Her father's eyes narrowed, and his lips tightened. "Where did you get that intel?"

Good question, she thought.

Jaden shrugged her shoulders and ignored the tightness that swept across them as she set down her empty glass. She needed one helluva massage to rid her body of the dark energy that was tying her up in knots.

"A conversation with a man at the bar a few nights back. He got loaded, I got some information," she answered truthfully. "Doesn't matter though, the intel didn't pan out."

"Interesting," he said, more to himself than anyone else. "Benicio, call the driver." He nodded to her, his eyes narrowing. "Clean yourself up and for God's sake let out your plaything. I can smell his fear from here."

Alarm rifled through Jaden, but she relaxed when she realized he must have sensed Tank. She, too, could smell his fear though it was overshadowed by embarrassment.

Her father walked toward the elevator and paused as the doors slid open, his profile sharp against the lit interior.

"You will stay the course, little pet, or the consequences will be swift and hard. The portal is our only agenda. It's the key to everything."

He walked past Benicio, entered the lift, and turned, his eyes piercing as they focused on her. "Kragen Black has requested a meeting. You will take it. He's here and is expecting you for dinner. Dress well for him and do whatever you must to secure his allegiance."

Jaden nodded but remained silent, trying to keep the disgust she felt to herself. He had called her a whore, spoken of his shame, but was the first one to pass her off as nothing more than a prostitute when the situation presented itself.

"If I sense a hint of betrayal, I will kill you."

I love you too, Daddy. The little girl voice rushed through her brain, and she shook her head slightly, pushing back at memory lane until there was nothing but heavy silence.

The doors slid shut, and Jaden felt her energy leave in a rush.

Her teeth began to chatter, and she wrapped her arms around her body, trying to seek what little bit of comfort she could. But she was empty, tapped out, and as she closed her eyes, a single solitary tear escaped and slowly made its way down her face.

It slipped over the swelling flesh where her father had struck her, and she wiped it away angrily, relishing the pain that rippled along her skin as she touched the tender area.

Pain was good. It gave her something to focus on instead of the pile of shit her life had become. And the pile was getting larger every day . . . so big that it was becoming a physical entity.

At night, when she was alone in bed, it would press against her chest, hold tight, and drown her in sweat and fear. Not so much fear of the unknown or of dying, but the loneliness, the absolute knowledge that she had no one else.

Not really. Nico and the others were there for her when she needed them, but none of them *belonged* to her.

That ship had passed and left her a long time ago. Three years to be exact.

You gotta stop thinking about the future.

The doors to the balcony slid open behind her, and she exhaled slowly. She was no longer alone. Guess it would have been too much to ask for Julian to just straight up disappear.

"I see Daddy Dearest has some anger-management issues."

Her mortification was now complete. Obviously, Julian had watched the entire exchange. Every painful detail.

"Cheap entertainment here at Night Sky Resort," she tossed at him lightly, glad the tremors that bounced around inside her didn't find their way out vocally.

She didn't turn around, even when she felt the heat of him at her back. In fact, she found herself weakening, her flesh aching for a warm body.

An image flashed in her mind, of his arms wrapped around her tightly, providing the comfort and strength she needed.

She felt herself waver, her feet barely able to hold her body upright.

"Your father might be a total fucking jerk, but he's right about one thing."

Jaden cocked her head to the side, feeling the moment leave in a rush. "And that is?" she asked quietly.

"You should put some ice on that."

Chapter 9

Julian watched as Jaden's shoulders slumped, and he winced at the harshness of his words, but really, what else could she expect from him?

And yet there was something sad about a woman of such strength and determination cut to the bone by the asshole who was her father.

Something flared inside him, a small sliver of emotion, and he clenched his hands tightly at his sides, fighting the urge to reach for her.

That was a line he wouldn't be crossing.

The silence in the room was sharp, it pulled at his ears. Inside his mind, the beast continued to howl in frustration, burning him with anxiety. His jaguar scratched beneath the surface, enraged. It had taken every ounce of control he possessed to remain on the balcony when Jakobi had attacked Jaden.

He shouldn't care. So she had family issues, so what? It wasn't like his own upbringing had been a bed of fucking roses.

You were never beaten.

He shook his head in an effort to banish the voice that was trying to break through. The other half of his soul perhaps?

He grimaced and took a step back, squashing the warm fuzzies before they had a chance to sprout.

He had no time for it.

He watched as she gathered herself together and walked toward the kitchen. She retrieved some ice from the fridge and threw it in a plastic baggie. Her skin was flushed with heat and emotion, even as her teeth still chattered.

She took a few moments, then headed to the com unit, leaning against the wall as she pressed the button.

"Finn, you there?"

"Yeah, just watching your dear old dad exit the resort. I'm guessing you made it through without getting your head ripped off?"

Her chin trembled slightly, and Julian felt uncomfortable watching, glad when a curtain of hair fell against her cheek and hid her face from his view.

"What's a few bruises amongst family?" she retorted.

Silence greeted her words.

"Hell, Jaden I'm sorry—"

She cut him off before he could continue. "No worries, where's Nico?"

"What about Castille?" Nico's voice drifted from the com unit, his voice gruff and forced.

Jaden turned slightly, her eyes meeting Julian's dispassionately. "He's still alive if that's what you're asking."

A grunt sounded loudly, Nico's answer, and Julian's eyes narrowed as Jaden straightened and pushed away from the wall.

"I'll send him down, but I have a change of plans. Kragen Black is here, I'm meeting him for dinner. Apparently he wants to talk."

"Jaden, I don't want you anywhere near him," Nico warned, but she cut him off before Julian could hear any more.

Who was Kragen, and why did the name sound so familiar? And why the hell did it burn his ass that Nico cared so much?

"I'll be fine. Jakobi thinks he wants to align himself with the DaCostas. Maybe he does, but I'll do my best to see if he knows anything about Cormac's whereabouts and intentions."

"Jaden—"

"Nico, enough. The meeting is here. I'll be fine."

She flipped off the com, effectively cutting off the torrent of curses that fell from Nico's mouth and turned toward Julian.

She kept her eyes averted, placed the ice against her skin, then walked toward her bedroom.

"Don't leave this suite, Castille. When I'm done, we'll talk, and for Christ sakes can you let please let Tank out."

She disappeared from sight, and the air rushed from his lungs. He'd not realized he'd been holding his breath until the wave of dizziness followed.

Julian hated the tightness that pulled at his gut. Hated the way things were no longer cut-and-dried but blurred and fucking crazy. When he'd been in hell, there had been some sort of order to things.

It had been real simple. The bitch in the corner, her knife, pain, then more pain. That was it.

Julian much preferred the darkness and pain. At least he knew where he stood. But none of this made sense to him. Funny how feelings muddied the water, made things so much more complicated. It was probably good that half his soul was missing; it made it easier to push back when his emotions started making noise.

Like now.

Jaden was a DaCosta, the enemy. She was also, apparently, his mate. She was strong, a jaguar warrior, yet she let her father beat her, made no effort to protect herself.

He began to pace the length of the room, his nostrils flaring in disgust as Jakobi's scent wafted over him. It was tinged with violence, and he could still smell Jaden's blood as well.

It only served to agitate him even more.

He crossed to the closet that was located near the kitchen and yanked the door open, ignoring the strangled growl that gurgled in the back of Tank's mouth. The jaguar warrior was furious.

He quickly untied his feet, stood back to allow him room to leave, then followed the large guard back to the elevator.

He refused to untie Tank's hands, however, and pointed to the lift with a smile. "Jaden says you need to be a good kitty cat and go back to your post." He winked. "But this time don't fuck up."

Tank stared back at him, his eyes fierce and filled with anger.

"Go back to your post, Tank, I'll talk to you later." Jaden's voice drifted back toward them from down the hall, and the warrior threw Julian another nasty glance before disappearing from sight.

He heard the shower start and decided he needed to do something rather than think of her naked and wet. She might be a DaCosta, but that didn't negate the fact that she was achingly beautiful.

His eyes fell upon the broken pottery that was now scattered across the floor. He quickly crossed to the kitchen, searching through her cupboards until he found a large container. Carefully, he retrieved the pieces, noticing the intricate carvings and exotic markings that adorned them. They were Aztec, he recognized that much, and very old from the looks of it.

Once he'd placed all the pieces into the container, he swept up the remnants of the ones that were not usable and tossed them into the garbage.

He yanked her fridge open and snorted. It was nearly as pathetic as his had been: a half loaf of bread, some eggs, and a carton of milk. He grabbed the milk and gulped the cold liquid heartily, washing away the whiskey as he did so.

He finished it and tossed the empty container into the garbage before striding over to the balcony once more. He slid the door back and stepped into the lush, tropical air.

Instantly, he felt his animal relax as the cooling breeze off the water ruffled his hair. Night was falling fast, and her far-reaching fingers would blanket the area within the hour.

He closed his eyes and inhaled deeply, letting his nostrils grab the myriad of scents that drifted up toward him. He smelled the underbelly of the jungle, the rich earth and tangled foliage. The salt that lay beneath the water, the sand that met it on the shore . . . the smell of sex from the couple below.

All of it rushed at him, exhilarating his mind and body and filling him with a need to act. To do something.

His jaguar burned and itched, and his eyes were lit with an eerie fire as they flew open. He began to pant and leaned over the balcony to stare at the ground below.

Could he make it?

"It's a long drop, but I've done it."

He stilled as her voice caressed the breeze. Uncanny how the woman could read his mind.

Julian turned back from the edge, to stare at a vision that could only mean trouble and heartache.

Trouble he could handle, and as for the heartache, well, since his was defective, he wasn't too worried about that either. He could enjoy whatever the hell it was they shared, with no strings.

Not that she'd let him, but still.

Her hair was loose, just the way he liked it, the long damp tendrils falling in silken waves behind her shoulders. A lot of her golden skin was on display; the low-plunging neckline of the dress she wore left nothing to the imagination. It barely covered her breasts, and with a slit the size of Niagara Falls up the side, a good expanse of her legs could be seen.

Her clan tattoos glistened, and he was mesmerized by them. Fire ripped through him as his eyes drank in the exotic markings, etchings that declared her taken.

And his mouth went dry as he heard a whisper of insanity inside his head. *Mine.*

He took a step toward her but paused as she arched an eyebrow and spoke. "I see you like the dress, and since I know you can barely stand to be in the same room with me, my job is done." She smiled bitterly. "Apparently, I play the part of Daddy's little whore well."

She looked down at the floor, stretched out a long lean calf, as if admiring the sandals that cupped her feet. But he caught sight of the pain that shimmered in her eyes and the way her lips trembled. "I'm going for dinner. You can either have room service or go down to the hub. Declan is there along with the rest of my team. They'll be expecting you."

She glanced up, and he had to admire the steely core at the center of the woman. Gone was any form of weakness, her mouth set in a determined line, her expression blank.

His eyes sought hers, then drifted to the discolored flesh of her cheek. It was slightly swollen and would be a bitch of a bruise in the morning, but none of it detracted from her beauty.

Hell, the woman could have two black eyes and sport missing teeth, but she'd still have that something, that thing no one else possessed. The kind of charisma that turned heads, held interest.

"Who's Kragen?" he asked gruffly.

"Why do you care?" she shot back.

Good question. He shouldn't care. At all. As his eyes slowly ran the length of her once more, he felt a prickle of anger. Seriously, what was it about her that affected him so?

He should be hunting for Cormac and Azaiel instead of standing here worried about some mystery man she was going to screw.

"Lady, I don't give a shit who you're fucking tonight, but if this Kragen has anything to do with the portal, I need to know."

She flinched at his words, but he didn't care. Hell, it was the truth, wasn't it? Jaden stared at him hard, her eyes glittering through the gloom.

"Kragen is a sorcerer, one with a known affiliation to Cormac. I've been trying to find out where the bastard is holed up, and right now, Kragen is my only lead." She turned around, and his eyes fell to the gentle swell of her butt. Christ but her ass was delicious.

Yeah, good job staying focused.

"Your father seems pretty convinced you're loyal to the

DaCostas. You sure you're not looking on his behalf?" he asked, his eyes never leaving her backside.

She paused and cocked her head to the side. Damn, but her profile was as hot as any other angle. "Of course that's what he believes, but no, definitely not." She moistened her lips, and his eyes were drawn to them. "This is the last time you will question my intentions, are we clear?"

In that moment, Julian knew she meant what she said. There was clarity there, an intent that could not be mistaken.

He said nothing but nodded.

"Good, if all goes well, Kragen will have the information that I need."

The woman was a major distraction, and the fact that he'd tasted her once didn't count in his favor. He wished he'd never laid a hand on her. Images from that night skirted the edges of his mind, entangled limbs, lean, naked lines, and an arched back that made his mouth water. The need to touch her again was becoming hard to resist.

His groin tightened, his skin burned.

"Hopefully, I won't have to fuck him to find out."

He missed the sarcasm in her words. Hell, the only word he'd heard was *fuck,* and a red haze swam before his eyes.

Anger exploded within his chest as her words sunk in, but she'd already exited the balcony and was halfway to the elevator doors before he caught up with her.

Julian grabbed her arm, felt the heat of her flesh beneath his fingers, and his heart pounded in tandem to the fury that was suddenly raging beneath his skin.

"Take your hand off me, Castille."

It took a few seconds for him to dial down the roaring in his ears and focus on the woman that he held.

"I mean it. Don't make me kick your ass in a dress, especially this one." Her eyes flashed. "I wouldn't want the girls to fall out."

His eyes fell to her heaving chest. Her nipples strained against the silky black fabric, their soft roundness barely covered. It irritated the crap out of him that he should care so much. *Notice* so much.

The sharp lines of her collarbone drew his attention, and his gaze traveled up to the tattoos that were etched into her golden skin. He hissed as they shimmered, and his hands held firm though she tried to break his grip.

He couldn't help himself as he felt his inner caveman stir. The clan tattoos were there because of him—as much as he didn't want it, that was the reality. They were markings that proclaimed the woman taken, spoken for. His.

"They don't mean anything," she whispered softly, a slight tremor to her voice.

Was she a fucking mind reader now?

Lines were blurring all of a sudden, lines that he didn't want to cross. But it seemed the bastard he'd become in the last six months didn't care jack shit for rules of any kind. He was beyond being a gentleman.

He yanked on her arm hard and pulled her close until the softness of her curves hugged his frame. Her long lines fit perfectly into the hard valley of his body, as if she were meant for him.

He groaned as her scent drifted in the air, and a longing sparked inside him that rippled over his flesh painfully. Nothing had changed in three years.

Nothing and *everything*.

The scars along his chest burned as the jaguar became agitated. His eyes drank in soft golden skin, lips that were full and candy red, hair that beckoned to be touched. Her body moved against his, fucking Jezebel that she was, and the need inside him grew—as did his cock.

He felt himself harden and closed his eyes as the sensation of her body against his flooded nerve endings long denied.

He could smell her arousal, it was there, subtle, beckoning, and he groaned as his eyes flew open.

Twin pools of liquid velvet glistened as her eyes stared up at him. The color was high on her cheeks, and he felt her heart rate increase.

He could take her. Right now. He knew this.

An image of his body thrusting deep into hers flashed before his eyes, vivid Technicolor grade A porn. It burned through him with an intensity that left him struggling to breathe, and he closed his eyes, visualizing once more her breasts, generous and swollen with need, long, tangled hair flying everywhere, and her body writhing atop his as she'd ridden him hard.

Would he ever forget that night? He'd thought about it often enough. Deep within the bowels of hell, when the darkest of shit was falling on his head, she'd gotten him through.

Fucking Christ, but the woman drove him nuts. A DaCosta jaguar.

Her lips were parted, and the white of her teeth could be seen as she panted, the small breaths falling rapidly from between her lips.

His hand slowly slid along her thigh until the silk of her dress parted, and he felt the warmth of her flesh beneath his fingers.

"Don't." She shook her head, but he didn't hear her, his eyes focused on her mouth and the way she bit, then sucked on her bottom lip as his hand continued along her flesh.

He cupped her ass, reveling in the feel of her toned flesh, and his large hand splayed across the curves, fingers caressing as he pulled her into him even more. He hissed when he realized there was no barrier there, no thin scrap of fabric protecting the treasure that lay between her legs.

Shit, the woman was commando. As hot as that image was, and his mind was certainly focused on her silky ass, it was pretty much overshadowed by an intense jolt of fury. The thought that she would go out in public, to dinner with another man in such a way made his body shudder in anger.

But, then, why wouldn't she? She was on a mission tonight. The woman was sex on legs, this he knew from experience. She was more than willing to put out in order to get what she wanted. He'd obviously been a target three years ago no matter what she claimed. In the world they inhabited, there was no such thing as coincidence.

He snarled savagely, and his right hand held her secure as his other reached around to cup the hot juncture between her legs. Her eyes deepened and a groan fell from between her lips as she pushed against his chest.

"Please," she whispered softly.

Julian felt the dampness there, the welcoming warmth as her legs parted for him, and he lowered his head, teeth bared as his passion exploded.

"Please?" he whispered hoarsely. "Babe, you don't need to beg."

And then he took what he wanted, his mouth claiming hers even as she started to protest once more.

Her softness opened for him, his mouth eating her words as he plunged his tongue into the warm, wetness within. She tasted like sin, just as he remembered, and she shuddered against him, whimpering as his fingers sought the hot button buried within her slick folds.

The darkness that crept along the edges of his mi... tinued to grow, and he felt a punishing thirst awaken ins... him. He felt the need to mark her once more, to inflict his will upon her in such a way that she'd never forget to whom she belonged.

As the crazy thoughts continued to circle his brain, he deepened the kiss, taking, tasting, what was his. She moaned into his mouth, and his right hand crept up along her back, up to her neck, until he buried his fingers within the softness of her hair.

He held her head in place as his mouth continued to drink from the softness of her lips, and when she opened fully beneath him, when her tongue welcomed his with equal fervor, and she ground her hotness beneath his fingers, he saw red.

He felt as if he were coming apart. His insides quaked, running hot and cold all at once, and the pain that ripped across his chest only added to the exquisite torture.

"Oh God," she whispered into his mouth. "I can't . . . not with you."

Her spoken words startled him, as did the intensity, the *need,* and he pulled back, welcoming the coolness that ran across his lips as the heat of her left him.

Ragged breaths fell from between his lips as his eyes focused on the swollen red of hers. They stared at each other, long and hard, and she squirmed against him as his confused emotions pounded him. What the hell did all of this mean?

What did he want it to mean?

She exhaled slowly, and the passion melted from her eyes, her face going blank as she stilled beneath his touch. She pushed against him, and he let her go, not really understanding what had just happened.

The pain inside him tripled, fire lashing against his chest

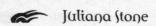

as he watched her walk away from him, her hands smoothing the lines of her dress and pushing the mass of hair behind her shoulders.

She pressed the elevator button, and the doors slid open silently.

"Thanks," she said softly.

Julian arched an eyebrow and answered. "For what?" he said harshly, barely able to get the words out.

She stepped inside and turned to face him with a smile though her eyes flashed a furious glint. "I can skip dinner and head directly for dessert." Her hands slowly ran over her still-erect nipples, and Julian hissed, feeling a pull deep in his cock as she did so.

"Hopefully, Kragen will be enough to satisfy, but I have a feeling he's a little too vanilla for my tastes." Her meaning brought such darkness to his mind that Julian growled, welcoming the burn as it rippled along his flesh.

The doors started to close.

"I might have to search out some dark chocolate."

He lunged forward, a snarl falling from his lips, but the doors closed before he could get to her.

Julian growled loudly as he stood there, legs spread, hands clenched to his sides, sporting the most painful hard-on he'd ever had.

He began to pace, a furious need inside him banishing all else from his mind, and as the cool night breeze drifted in from the balcony, he paused. The night air calmed him somewhat, the sounds and smells of the land and surrounding sea deeply embedded in his psyche.

The sudden urge to shed his skin and run wild called to him, and he grabbed at his clothes.

Seconds later, he stood crouched upon the railing of Jaden's balcony as he stared down into the darkness below.

The path that ran along the back of the building was the cobblestones lit by a soft lamp several feet away.

Deep throngs of mist crawled along his body, the heavy magick caressing hard lines as he stood and spread out his arms. Inside his soul, where the ravaged half still lived, his jaguar growled in delight, eager to run.

Eager to hunt.

Moonlight fell in soft beams from above and was the only witness as Julian jumped. His body flew through the air, twisting gracefully as bones popped and elongated, the magick caressing every inch of him as he hurtled toward the ground.

He'd flown from the balcony a man, but it was a powerful jaguar that landed easily on all fours to the left of the path, deep in the soft foliage that was there.

The great cat stood still for several seconds, scenting the wind until he found the one he was looking for.

And then the golden jaguar slid into the night, its dark rosettes bleeding into the dusk before it disappeared entirely.

Chapter 10

"Jaden DaCosta."

She didn't like the way her name fell from Kragen Black's lips. Like liquid honey, as if he had the right to be so intimate. "You're looking a little tense," he continued with a smile. The silver-gray eyes that stared at her were unsettling.

Jaden nodded to Kragen and stood back as he pulled out a chair for her. His hand fell to her shoulder, and she kept her smile firmly in place as his breath warmed the side of her neck.

He was much too forward, which pissed her off, but she'd play the game. Her father didn't have to worry; she'd do whatever it took to achieve *her* agenda.

"I'll do my best to help you forget about your worries." His tone was silky smooth, confident.

She slipped from his touch and held her hands steady as the urge to rip into his flesh tore at her fingers. She felt the burn beneath her nails but settled into the chair calmly.

They were alone, seated at her private table several feet away from the main dining area, nestled into an alcove on the terrace. It afforded a certain amount of privacy, without making her feel detached from the activity in the main room.

As she smiled at Kragen she couldn't help but think she'd love to be detached right now, separated from the mess that had become her life.

"It's been a hell of a day," she replied, accepting a glass of red wine from Paulo, her manager.

"I can see that."

He nodded, and her hand grazed the sore area of her cheek as she turned from him, willing the shame that would surely stain her flesh away.

She took a sip, felt the liquid slowly pass over her taste buds, and fought the urge to guzzle it down like water.

She needed to keep a cool head, but that was going to be hard considering that every single nerve ending in her body was on fire. Kragen's eyes slowly drifted over her and rested for several long seconds on her breasts.

Why the hell did I wear this dress?

Because you wanted Julian to see you in it.

Even now she felt her sensitive nipples ache as they strained against the thin fabric that barely covered them. Her breasts felt engorged, and an image of Julian, suckling at them, tugging on the turgid peaks flashed through her mind. She stifled a groan as the erotic pictures continued to play, struggling to block them out.

She loosened her tight shoulders, rolled her neck, and crossed her legs, an effort to alleviate the throbbing that was constant between them, but the action only inflamed the sensation, and she gritted her teeth.

Good timing, she thought. Yep, perfect week to be on

the cusp and nearly in heat. The yearning deep within was compounded by the fact that Julian was nearby. Even now, his scent clung to her. It was inside her and was enough to drive a girl insane.

She raised her glass, nodded to Kragen, and tossed the rest of the wine down her throat.

Christ, I need an hour alone with my vibrator. She was on the verge of losing control and totally pissed at herself.

"Care to share the details?" Kragen asked softly, like they were friends . . . or something.

"Not particularly," she replied, glad that her voice had at least returned to normal even as her thoughts continued to focus on Julian.

She should have kneed the bastard in the balls, cut, and run.

Kragen's eyes narrowed as a predatory smile swept over his handsome face. She supposed some women found the weird color of his eyes attractive, but to her it screamed otherworld.

Skye had warned her about Kragen. Finn's sister had had dealings with him before. The sorcerer was a bastard of the highest order but handsome as all hell. He was used to getting what he wanted.

"A toast then." He lifted his glass, which was nearly full, and as Paulo swiftly refilled hers, he smiled. "To an unforgettable evening."

She held her glass high and finished it in two gulps. Daddy should see his little whore now, she thought, dressed to kill and guzzling wine like it was grape juice.

Real fucking ladylike.

She exhaled slowly and forced herself to relax. She needed to keep the big picture in mind and forget about Julian, her father . . . all of it. Her eyes fell on Kragen. To-

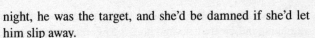

night, he was the target, and she'd be damned if she'd let him slip away.

"What do you feel like? Have you had a chance to read the menu?" she asked softly.

Kragen leaned back in his chair, totally relaxed. Confident. "What do you suggest? I'm feeling the need for something exotic and can't decide." He took a sip of his wine, his focus entirely on her, "I'd love to taste . . . everything."

Small bursts of energy flew from his fingers. They began to shimmer, wafting into the air like petals of mist. Her eyes followed them in surprise as they fell over her skin with the delicate touch of soft feathers.

Her surprise soon turned to anger, and she gasped as an odd sensation crawled along with them. It felt as if tiny fingers were running along her flesh, between her breasts and across her nipples.

Bastard! She felt her cheeks darken. If she was to be manhandled, it wouldn't be by these means.

She was not playing this game.

She leaned forward, smiled wickedly, her leg stretching out underneath the table, and placed her stiletto-encased foot between his legs. She applied just enough pressure to make her point, and his eyes widened as the air around him stilled.

"Don't pull that freaky mojo crap with me because I won't hesitate to impale my heel all the way up your dick. Are we clear?"

The sensations stopped immediately as Kragen's eyes narrowed. He studied her for a few seconds, then whispered softly, "Understood."

"Wonderful," she said. "Let's order 'cause I'm starved."

She signaled Paulo and proceeded to order for them both. Steaks, rice, and steamed vegetables.

Kragen took another sip of his wine, his eyes never leaving hers, and cleared his mouth. "You gonna remove your foot anytime soon?"

She laughed softly, dug in a tad more, then let her foot fall. "You're not what I expected."

"Oh?" She grabbed a piece of warm bread from the basket and settled back. "Disappointed?"

"Not at all. I'd heard that the DaCostas were somewhat . . ."

"Stale? Old-world?"

He stuffed a good-size portion of bread in his mouth and chewed slowly before answering. "Bloodthirsty and cutthroat."

His eyes ran the length of her once more, and a grin fell across his mouth, but he was more dismissive than anything. "You seem neither though you have spunk."

His mistake.

"Spunk?" Jaden nearly showered Kragen with wine as she snorted. "Spunk will get you bitch slapped, my friend, and cutthroat"—she winked at him—"will get your balls worked over by six-inch heels." Jaden shook her head. "Never forget who and what I am."

"I don't think you'd be on anyone's forgettable list," Kragen retorted dryly. His eyes glittered as he stared at her intently.

Her jaguar stirred and she was glad that Paulo chose that moment to refill their wineglasses. She was edgy, riding on the cusp of something reckless, and in her world, that could prove dangerous.

So she sipped her wine, mentally rearranged herself, and a half an hour later, when Paulo served their meal, she was in control.

They ate, made polite small talk, each skirting the issue

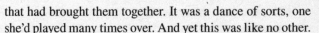

that had brought them together. It was a dance of sorts, one she'd played many times over. And yet this was like no other.

Jaden was headed toward an end that she could not predict. An unknown, and that was utterly terrifying.

The fragile rhythm of the earth was crying out as darkness slowly embedded itself deep within her soul. The frenetic energy that slithered through the jungle bled death and destruction into everything it touched.

And it wasn't just here in her small sliver of the world. PATU was responding to calls on every continent. They couldn't train new operatives fast enough. Demon activity was up more than 50 percent in just six months. Hell, up until a few months ago, she'd never laid eyes on one. Now she was a goddamn expert.

Otherworld crime was on the rise, with vamps, shifters, and magicks making more noise than ever. Old rules were being broken, lines crossed, and alliances built.

It wouldn't be long before the otherworld came crashing down upon the human realm.

She looked past Kragen out into the night and let the warm whisper of air caress her heated cheeks. It tugged at her hair and she closed her eyes as long strands snaked out to ride the wind.

The breeze was fresh, tangy, and she inhaled deeply. It fed the sorrow that burned in her chest, and her muscles tightened painfully.

God, it would be wonderful to go to sleep and wake up in another time and place. One that didn't suck as much as right now.

If Cormac was successful in locating the portal, they were all screwed. He'd unleash such legions of darkness upon the human realm that the world would never recover.

The goddamn underbelly of hell.

Julian had been there. He knew what was coming.
Forget about Castille.

She toyed with her food, not really listening to whatever the hell was falling from Kragen's lips. Christ, the man talked more than Robin Williams on crack. She forced the last piece of steak past her throat and washed it down with the rest of her wine.

"—don't you think?"

"What?" she asked as she rested her hands on the table.

Kragen frowned, and his tone was irritated. "I was just asking—"

She cut him off before he could continue because she really didn't give a damn. Enough of the bull; it was time to party.

"Where's Cormac?"

Kragen cocked an eyebrow, surprised.

"You *do* know where he is, correct?"

Kragen settled back in his chair, his freaky eyes luminous, reflecting the light from the candle on their table. His entire demeanor changed instantly.

Jaden took notice and sat up straighter, realizing the sorcerer had been playing her as well. The darkness that scratched below the surface of his skin bled through. The man was dangerous, and she couldn't forget that.

"I feel like dessert." The words were pure silk. The air had changed, and she felt a shift in the energy. "Something tasty and smooth."

Her animal stirred once more, and her heart beat faster.

Why not walk on the wild side? Besides, it wasn't like she could get anything accomplished here in the restaurant.

She stood in one fluid movement, smiling to herself as his eyes fell to her breasts. She leaned over the table, enjoying the game. Knowing if she moved to the right, he'd get a peek at the dusky tips that were still hard, aching, and unfulfilled.

"Something sweet?" she whispered softly.

It was amazing what a great rack could accomplish. It could reduce the most dangerous man to a pile of putty if used properly.

"We can continue our meeting in a more . . . private situation," she said, then tossed her hair back, exhaling as she did so.

A soft breeze rippled across her skin, teasing the hot flesh, and suddenly she was filled with a need so intense her skin burned hot, like she'd been dipped in a fire. Everything blurred for a moment, and she stumbled briefly, regaining her balance just as fast.

Her eyes swept across the terrace, out toward the darkness, and she paused. Something was there, watching. The weird sensation lingered, then evaporated in the breeze.

"Are you all right?" Kragen asked politely though his eyes were focused on her breasts. Too bad the girls didn't know how to speak. He'd have a heart attack for sure if they could answer.

He stood swiftly, and she sensed his arousal. The signals were loud and clear. The sorcerer wanted to screw.

Jaden hissed softly. "Follow me."

Thanks to Julian Castille, so did she.

She looked back at Kragen and crooked her finger, smiling as a hungry glint lit his eyes. His body was tall, lean but muscular, and there was no denying that the man was attractive.

She felt her belly tighten in anticipation, wondering if he could ease the ache that had erupted between her thighs.

Maybe she could have her cake and eat it, too. Have her itch scratched and gather the information she needed.

"Thank you, Paulo," she murmured politely as she strode past her manager. She knew Kragen was not far behind and led him from the restaurant, taking the path that led toward the gardens.

Cool mist crept along the ground, slithering across manicured grass like long fingers of smoke. The gardens were deserted, dark. Her guests usually kept to the well-lit paths, and that was one reason she'd designed the large area to be free of light.

She could come here and be alone.

Kragen caught up to her, she felt his hand at her back, heard the rhythm of his breathing escalate as he touched her. It was almost too easy.

She resisted his touch and turned to the right, taking a path that led toward a grouping of large palm trees. At first glance, they seemed a solid wall, but she slipped through and into a clearing, her very own secret garden.

A waterfall trickled in the corner, its sound musical, calming. Any other night it would have sung to her, but this night, with all that hung over her head, she heard nothing.

She turned to Kragen, and the two of them stared at each other in silence. Was she out of her ever-loving mind? Had her judgment gone on vacation? Or was she playing Daddy's little whore a little too close to the bone?

She ached inside, and it wasn't going away. In fact, the need was growing stronger, impairing her judgment.

Could she seriously have sex with him? Would it do any good? Alleviate the craving that clawed at her incessantly?

Only Julian.

She snarled and pushed thoughts of the jaguar from her mind, ignoring the ferocious desire that tugged at her. Slowly, her hands crept along her hips, up toward her chest until she grazed the hard nipples that sat below silk.

Her lips parted as pain shot through her belly, sitting low and heavy until it liquefied and filtered into the hot juncture between her legs. She fought the urge to put her hand there, all of a sudden not sure what it was that she wanted, or needed.

Kragen lifted his hands, held them palm up, and seconds later, the small area was lit with an eerie glow.

His face was dark, hidden in shadow, and a trickle of apprehension ran along her spine. Her animal burned beneath her skin, sensing things were off.

"You are the hottest thing I've seen in a long time," he muttered as he took a step closer.

"Where's Cormac?" she asked softly, the anxiety slowly fading as she focused on the matter at hand.

The goddamn vibrator was looking more and more attractive, so the sooner she got this over with, the sooner she could snuggle down with the blue dolphin.

Kragen walked toward her, a true predator, and stood inches from her body. His hand reached for her, but she stepped back, just out of reach. He frowned, and she felt his energy change once more.

She would have to move quickly.

"Does he still have the fallen with him? What can you tell me about Azaiel? Are they working together?"

Kragen arched an eyebrow, and he paused before answering, his freaky eyes glowing. "Azaiel is tied to the jaguars and eagles, you should know this stuff." His tone was dismissive. "It's not my fault you've lost touch with your history, your culture."

Jaden frowned. She knew squat about Azaiel really, only what Skye had been told. That the fallen angel had been betrayed eons ago by a woman, Toniella. That only he had the power to destroy the portal.

Azaiel was the rock star in this whole mess.

"Let's talk business later, shall we?"

There was a cruel lift to his mouth, but she let him move closer, let his hand slide along her jaw until he cupped her head.

"Tell me more of Toniella. Who was she? What happened to her after Azaiel was banished to hell?"

Kragen laughed and shook his head. "I'm not a history teacher. If you want to better understand the dynamics of what is going on, you should look to the past. You'd be surprised at the answers you can find."

His eyes were half-closed, and though Jaden let him believe he was in control, she was already growing weary of the game.

"Why did you want this meeting?" she asked.

Truthfully, she was more than a little puzzled. With Cormac off the grid, and the portal seeming to have disappeared, all bets were off. New alliances were being drawn up every day. Drawn, then broken. Such was the way of it with the otherworld. Loyalty was a bitch that no one believed in.

"I'm into self-preservation and just testing the waters. Curious as to where the DaCosta jaguars stand in this whole mess."

"We want the portal." I want the portal, she thought.

"Don't we all?" he answered though his focus was on her lips.

He tried to pull her closer, but she resisted. "Cormac has gone rogue; he can't be trusted. Once the portal is opened, he'll be after all our asses. He's not exactly the sharing type."

She let a smile fall across her tight lips. "We need to work together, so when the tide turns, we come out on top, no?"

Kragen studied her closely but didn't answer.

She rubbed against him, her voice husky. "So why don't you tell me where he is, and we can get on with it."

"That's a secret I'm not sure I'm ready to share yet," he whispered softly.

Jaden pushed away, feeling little bolts of energy ride over her flesh as she did so. She was pissed but needed to keep a cool head.

"You indicated that you had information. We all want to get our hands on the portal, and I can help you." She blew a strand of hair from her face as she faced him.

She was going to have to get physical. She could feel it.

"Lady, there's only one way you can help me right now, and it has nothing to do with Cormac."

Jaden ran her tongue along her teeth, ignoring the hum of energy that slithered over her hot skin. Her hair was damp and clung to her shoulders, and the tattoos along her neck were irritated. They burned like hell.

"Really?" she purred softly, welcoming the dance that was about to begin. She had way too much pent-up energy, and a good asskicking was the perfect way to expend it.

He grabbed her shoulders, and his eyes glittered dangerously as he spoke. His energy was black, thick, and repugnant. "You've been nothing but a cock-tease the entire evening, and now it's time to collect."

She let him pull his body along hers, gritted her teeth as he lowered his head, and when he would have claimed her mouth, she head butted him.

Hard.

He cursed loudly, but his arms kept her pinned as a grimace crept across his features. "Like to play rough?"

She smiled up at him. "I told you earlier not to forget who and what I am." She dug her nails in deep. They were razor-sharp and cut him quickly.

"I am going to enjoy breaking you," he whispered hoarsely, and the air shimmered around him as the heat was sucked away and replaced with a blast of cold.

Jaden's power erupted from deep in her gut, and she hissed loudly as she stomped a six-inch heel into the top of his foot. She laughed as she felt it break through leather, and when he drew his arm back and swung it forward, she grabbed it, held it in place, and grinned at the surprise that rolled over his features.

She jabbed him hard in the gut, her long nails piercing skin, then she spun around, putting several feet between them in an instant. She'd moved fast, her body a blur of dark hair and long limbs.

"Let's try this again," she spit. "Where the hell is Cormac?" She held her hands loose and ready, her legs wide, pushing the boundaries of the silky material as it strained against her flesh.

She watched him warily as his eyes gave her the once-over and made no effort to hide her disgust. To think she'd considered, even briefly, using him for sex. It spoke of desperation, and in that instant, she hated Julian Castille for everything he'd done to her. Even if it wasn't his choice.

She was gonna have to become a nun. She thought of the blue vibrator. Or invest in a lot of batteries.

"You really are quite magnificent." Kragen took a step toward her. "I was telling you the truth. I have no idea where Cormac is holed up. He's gone dark over the last few months, and from what I can tell, paranoid as all hell."

He shrugged and ran his hands through the hair atop his head. "He's waiting."

"For what?" Jaden let that information run through her mind. He knew more than he was letting on. She was sure of it.

"He's gathering his forces, preparing for when the shit hits."

"And when he sends out the call, will you answer?"

The sorcerer shook his head and shrugged. "At this point, my only concern is taking care of my own ass. I have no idea how things are going to shake out." He pinned her with a direct stare. "O'Hara is one helluva powerful mage. I don't think you know what you're up against. You'd best tread carefully. I'd hate to see your lovely ass served up on a platter at one of his parties."

"We are committed to the cause," the lie slipped from her mouth easily, "but we don't trust Cormac."

"Lady, you've no idea . . ." Kragen looked away and for the first time Jaden saw fear shadow his face. That had all kinds of alarm bells banging inside her.

"I need to find him," she said firmly, "and will do whatever it takes to accomplish that."

He laughed. "Including screwing total strangers?" He leered at her. "Your father pretty much offered you up for free. A taste of DaCosta meat is what I was after."

The glow from his hands flashed bright, then disappeared, leaving her temporarily blinded.

"I'm not leaving until I get it."

A burst of energy hit Jaden in the chest, throwing her off balance. Kragen was there in an instant, his arms going around hers, pinning her tightly. Inside her jaguar burned, welcoming the violence, feeding upon it.

"This is going to be fun," she whispered softly, her body stilling as her power gathered inside.

"Yeah," Kragen whispered at her neck, "that's what I was thinking." Her skin crawled as his heat swept across her, and her cat recoiled instantly.

"Wouldn't have it any other way," she ground out. "A good asskicking gets the blood moving."

"Right," he whispered.

She felt a pull on her limbs, some invisible force tugging at her hands, and she flexed her fingers as heat seared across the skin.

Son of a bitch! The pain was incredible as it roared across her palms.

"The only ass that's gonna get kicked is yours, but I promise, I'll be gentle." His voice was hoarse, and she could tell the thought of violence excited him.

"Fuck you, Kragen."

His voice was thick, colored with need, and she grimaced as she felt the hard length of him press into her back.

"Yeah, that's what I was hoping for."

Chapter 11

Jesus Christ, were all men cut from the same cloth? Did they all think with their dicks?

She gritted her teeth as a fresh wave of anger swept over her, hot, pulsing, feeding the strength inside and agitating her jaguar into a frenzy. Kragen was gonna learn the hard way it wasn't smart to corner a cat.

He was breathing hard behind her as he attempted to pin her tight to his body, but she arched her back and slammed her foot onto his once more. His yelp of pain made her smile.

"Fucking bitch."

She smiled to herself as she used every bit of strength she possessed to break his grip. The bastard was strong, but his strength paled next to that of an enraged jaguar.

She whirled around, her arms flying wide, but he threw an energy pulse at her. The force of it knocked her in the chest hard, another burst of searing heat to join the flames that still licked at her hands.

She doubled over, breathing heavily as her eyes frantically searched for a weapon, anything that she could use. Her palms were on fire, but she ignored it, her muscles bunching together tightly as her jaguar continued to make noise.

Kragen rushed her, and she sidestepped at the last minute, twisting her body, throwing her hips into the air as she did so.

Her legs arced upward, and she knocked the sorcerer in the back as he went by and sent him flying. Damn ninjas had nothing on her.

A smile cracked her mouth open wide as her body began to shift, her energy exploding. The mist was already clawing its way up her legs, and she reveled in the ancient magick that took hold.

She rolled to the side, bones popping as fur rippled over her flesh. Seconds later, her dress was in tatters, and she barked a warning as she emerged from the mist to face her enemy.

Her long tail swung back lazily, flicking the air and catching the eye of the sorcerer. Kragen was breathing heavily, his face a dark mask of hatred, and Jaden wondered how she'd ever thought him handsome.

"I'd love to see your sorry ass locked up in a zoo somewhere."

She ignored the taunt and moved forward, her movements slow, precise. Kragen was frantically weaving a spell in the air, and she knew she didn't have much time.

She was about to pounce, her paws digging into the earth beneath her, when a blur whipped by, a golden mix of fur and snarls.

A large spotted jaguar took Kragen down, *hard*, the great cat swiping his paw savagely across the man's face.

Kragen emitted a god-awful sound and began to struggle. The jaguar swiped once more, and he was still.

The spotted cat made a keening noise, deep from its gut as it turned from the sorcerer and stared at her, its golden eyes burning with a madness that gave her pause.

She called the mist to her once more, her eyes never leaving his, letting her anger push her through as the change took hold. Kragen belonged to her, no one else.

Seconds later, she stood in human form, her body tight and humming with an energy that had every single nerve ending on fire.

"Goddamn it, Castille, I don't need your help," she spit at him. "I had him on my own."

She walked toward the downed sorcerer, well aware of the jaguar as it stared at her, studied the naked lines of her body. The cat slowly moved away giving her room, and she bent over Kragen. His flesh had been cut, a gash across the cheek that put her bruises to shame. Blood was flowing freely, but his chest rose and fell. He wasn't dead, thank goodness, only out cold.

She'd have Nico take him to the hub, and they could interrogate him. Kragen Black would answer their questions one way or another.

The jaguar made a weird sound from behind her, one that pulled deep in her belly, and she shivered as it slid up over her skin, teasing the tattoos along her flesh.

She heard the jaguar panting softly, felt the shift in energy, and tried her best to ignore him as she scooped up the remnants of her dress. The black silk was pretty much in tatters, and she sighed heavily as she fingered the soft fabric. Damn, but she'd done a bang-up job in totally ruining the Cavelli original.

She looked to the side. *Where in hell are my Jimmy Choos?*

"Are you out of your goddamn mind?" Julian's voice was low, but there was no mistaking his anger. "He could have raped you. Or worse."

"I was in no danger. Trust me, I've handled lots worse than that asshole."

"I'll bet you have."

"What the hell does that mean?" She turned to him, the tatters of her dress forgotten as they fell from her fingers. Why did she let him get under her skin like that?

He didn't answer.

Julian stood several feet away, his tall form half-hidden by the shifting shadows the wind produced. She'd seen all of him the night before, but still, the sight of his hard, muscled frame made her mouth go dry.

The man was walking perfection. An amazing blend of *GQ* looks with the predatory danger of an animal.

It was wrong. For her to want him as she did . . . all of it.

He hissed, and his chest rose and fell as he continued to stare at her from the darkness.

"Why are you here?" she asked again, curious really, as to why he felt the need to follow, to stalk, someone he didn't care for. "Are you trying to prove something? Some weird, alpha control thing? None of that shit will work on me."

"Lady, I don't need to prove anything to you. I want the portal. End of story. You're the part of the equation I'm not sure of."

Her nostrils flared madly, and she took a few steps toward him. "For the last time, you will not question my loyalty or actions." She was livid. "If you want my help, accept the fact that we're on the same side or get your ass away from here."

"So defensive," he whispered. Julian took the remaining steps between them until they were but inches apart.

Her heart pounded against her chest, the beat heavy and

strong. It kept time with the madness that danced along the edges of her clan tattoos, the energy biting, thrilling.

She was tall but felt inadequate next to his six-foot-four-inch frame. Damn but she wished her Jimmys were still attached to her feet.

He changed the subject. "I hate to point out that Kragen had you exactly where he wanted."

"And where would that be?" she asked cheekily, the words dripping in sarcasm.

"Between his legs."

She snarled, and her hand flew up, but he caught her fist before she could do any damage, while his other arm grabbed her around the shoulder and held her still. His fingers dug in, but she refused to acknowledge the pain and glared up at him.

"You don't want to do that," he whispered dangerously.

"You have no idea what I want to do to you." She tried to pull away, but he refused to let her go; instead, he jerked her close, and she inhaled sharply as her nipples grazed his hard flesh.

She felt a blush creep up her cheeks as his teeth flashed white, cutting through the gloom. His lips were firm, open slightly, and she fought the insane desire to grab them, claim them as hers once more.

She knew how amazing they felt as they slid along skin.

"I've a pretty good idea," he answered, his long lashes sweeping downward as he gazed at her hard, aching nipples. "Always the little whore, no?" He laughed harshly and nodded behind them. "Magick man not enough for you?"

He bent his head, and, for a second, she was afraid he would kiss her, and she'd never have control over the emotions and urges that were ripping through her relentlessly.

She felt liquid heat pool deep within the softness between

her legs and wanted to lash out at the irony. That she should feel such overwhelming desire for a man who thought she was no more than a common prostitute.

She tried to arch away, but he held her firm, and his mouth settled near the hollow in her neck, allowing her a moment of relief. But only a moment, and she shuddered as his warm breath spread shivers of energy across her heated flesh.

He inhaled a deep breath and sniffed along her collarbone, his hands tightening against hers painfully, but she didn't care.

Inside her body, everything had melted into liquid fire. Her jaguar burned beneath her flesh, wanting the man she'd claimed years earlier.

He continued to slowly move back up the side of her neck until his lips were next to her ear. "Or have you already had dessert?" The energy in the air changed then, as did the tone of Julian's voice.

His tongue licked along the small juncture between her ear and her neck, and she couldn't stop the groan that fell from her lips. She shook her head slowly, hating the way he made her feel. The lack of control he pulled from her.

"Did you fuck him?" he asked abruptly. He was hard and ground his erection against her belly, his hand loosening its grip on her shoulder as he slowly dragged his large palm downward against her butt and held her tight.

Her nostrils flared as she looked up into the glittering depths of his eyes. "Take your hands off my ass." Her voice was low, the words precise.

His eyes narrowed, his lips were tight. "Did you?" he asked once more. "Spread your legs for that piece of filth?"

"What if I did?" she answered, her own anger rising to the fore.

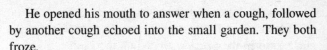

He opened his mouth to answer when a cough, followed by another cough echoed into the small garden. They both froze.

Shit. They had company.

Jaden peered around Julian and spied both Finn and Declan. Finn looked away, but Declan grinned at her, winking as he did so.

Could this night get any worse?

"We were just . . ." she began. "I was just . . ." She bit back a curse. Her jumbled mind was making her sound like a freaking idiot. "Kragen needs to be taken to the hub for interrogation."

Julian didn't move, and for that, she was grateful. It was bad enough for one of her men to find her in such a ridiculous position, but damned if Declan O'Hara was going to get a peek at her naked bits.

Declan's grin widened. "Where is he?"

Jaden frowned, not understanding. "What do you mean?" She looked up at Julian but his eyes were focused behind her, his expression thunderous.

She glanced back and hissed as she shook her head.

Kragen was gone.

"How in the hell?" The words slipped out of her and she winced at the stupidity they represented. "He was right here," she finished lamely.

"Probably used a simple cloaking charm. If you two were"—Declan cleared his throat, obviously enjoying the show—"otherwise occupied, it would have been easy for him to sneak away unnoticed."

Julian glared at her, his eyes flat, his lips pulled back in a snarl. He cocked his head to the side. "Can it, O'Hara."

She looked away as silence fell between them all.

Awkward didn't even come close to cutting it.

"Where's Nico?" she asked hesitantly, but before anyone could answer, the warrior strode into the garden, his arms clasped around a dazed-looking Kragen Black.

His eyes swept over the scene, and he stopped abruptly.

"What the hell is going on?" he asked, his eyes flashing with accusatory zeal as they locked onto hers. "This is how you conduct an investigation?"

Julian turned though his body still blocked her nudity from the men. "Take the sorcerer down for interrogation."

Nico blew out a hot breath, loudly. "You do not give me orders, Castille."

"No, but I do." Jaden spoke quietly. "Take him down, Nico. That is all."

Nico glared at her, and though the hard lines of his face were set in stone, she saw the disappointment that shadowed his eyes. It cut her deep inside, and Jaden shook her head, hating the way Castille had managed to come between her and the team in only twenty-four hours.

She opened her mouth to speak, but Nico turned abruptly and left, dragging a protesting Kragen with him. Finn glanced her way, his eyes somber, and turned to follow in his wake.

Great. Now she felt like absolute shit.

Declan arched an eyebrow. "I'll leave you two kids alone to, uh, do whatever it was you were doing."

Jaden watched him disappear into the darkness.

She didn't know what to say, how to feel. Nothing felt right. Her eyes shot bullets at Julian's back. When it came to the jaguar, she didn't know jack shit.

He turned abruptly, and the breath caught in the back of her throat at the feral look that haunted the golden depths. Slowly, her eyes swept across features carved from stone, lips that she knew from experience gave great pleasure, until she rested once more on the scars that marred the otherwise perfect flesh.

"This isn't gonna work," he said, and she looked up in surprise. "What the hell was I thinking?" His eyes flattened to that dull color she'd grown to dislike, and all expression fled his face. "I can barely stand to be around you."

She'd like to say that his words meant nothing, but that would have been a lie. They cut her deeply, and she felt the prick of tears sting the backs of her eyes as she stood like an idiot, staring up at him.

Julian turned from her and slipped into the darkness, disappearing as quickly as he'd come.

She sniffled and gave herself a mental shake. Enough of this crap. It should have been *her* leaving after dropping a line like that.

Jaden clenched her teeth and spying her heels by the bench in the corner, grabbed them. She shivered as the damp air caressed her softness.

"Azaiel is tied to the jaguars and eagles, you should know this stuff. It's not my fault you've lost touch with your history, your culture."

The sorcerer's words echoed inside her head, circling around and around as she flirted with the excitement they brought.

The bastard was right.

In order to hunt Azaiel and Cormac, she needed to understand every little detail about the portal and its connection to the fallen. She needed to go back to where it all began.

She left the garden and kept to the shadows, intent on grabbing a towel from the pool area before heading up to her suite.

There was only one place that she could find the answers she needed—The Temple of the Warriors.

Only problem was, it was buried under the ruins of Templo Mayor, guarded by ancient magick. Dark, powerful shit. The kind that wouldn't take lightly to her poking around and disturbing history.

A thrill shot through her at the thought, and she smiled to herself. She felt like she had purpose again, like she wasn't spinning her wheels.

Jaden slipped through the back entrance to her building. Tank didn't flinch at her state of undress. Being a shifter, he understood. He moved aside and cleared his throat.

"Miss DaCosta," he began, but Jaden shook her head and disappeared inside her private lift.

"Castille is a bastard. Just don't let it happen again." The door slid shut before the jaguar warrior could respond, but her mind was already moving forward toward a plan of action.

Tomorrow, she would head out and find The Temple of the Warriors, located deep within the ruins of Templo Mayor. She'd go alone. If this was a wild-goose chase, she didn't want to waste her team's time. There were a million and one things they needed to focus on.

More importantly, there was no way in hell she wanted Julian Castille along for the ride.

Chapter 12

Hours later, as dawn's welcoming rays split the darkened sky into fragments of light, a large jaguar emerged from the jungle. The rhythms of the earth had changed subtly, and the huge animal paused, its powerful body still as it scented the air. The cat barked once, its dark rosettes glistening against the golden coat as mist swept along the ground toward it.

The jaguar moved once more, its steps slow and precise as it disappeared into the fog, only to reappear several seconds later in human form.

Julian Castille was fatigued. He'd been running for what seemed like hours, and as he turned his face to the warmth of the sun's first caress, he closed his eyes and exhaled slowly.

His thoughts, as always, turned to the one person who somehow managed to get under his skin in such a way that it drove him crazy.

Jaden made him lose focus. She resurrected feelings and

emotions deep within that he hadn't the strength or tools to deal with. Mass confusion rained down upon him when she was in the picture, tugging at the small thread of humanity that still existed within.

It was painful, and he didn't like it one bit; nor did he have time for it.

His eyes flew open, and he moved toward the resort. He was done. He'd find Declan, and they'd cut and run. He didn't need her to find the portal. What the hell had he been thinking?

He slid through the silent resort unnoticed, avoiding the odd tourist up in time to welcome the morning properly. He circled around back of the main building, growling softly as he passed the secret garden.

Minutes later, he took a run at the wall beside Jaden's balcony and quickly leapt upward, his hands and feet gripping the side of the building as he began to climb. He made quick work of it, a soft sheen of sweat covering his frame as he swung over the railing and dropped into a crouch.

His muscles bunched tightly, but he held his hands loose, his stance rock solid and ready to take a hit.

But there was nothing. Only silence.

He exhaled, the breath whistling between his lips, surprised she'd not taken the opportunity to pounce, inflict some sort of damage.

He would have.

But, then, maybe he didn't haunt her mind the way she did his. Maybe she didn't give a rat's ass whether he returned or not. Which was fine. After all, he was leaving.

His clothes were strewn where he'd left them, and he dressed quickly, the soft denim and cotton T-shirt damp from the early-morning dew. His shoes went on last, and he slipped into her suite, careful not to make a sound.

Julian paused and scented the air, his nostrils flaring as her subtle, exotic scent wafted through him.

Damn, but does she have to smell so good?

He glanced down the hall toward her bedroom as he crossed to the elevator. Julian had no clue where the hub was, but he was pretty sure he'd be able to convince Tank to show him the way.

He clenched his hands at the thought and flexed his arms in anticipation. He pressed the button located beside the com unit, but once more his eyes turned back toward her bedroom.

Something didn't feel right.

The doors slid open, rolling back silently, yet he didn't take that step. His entire frame hummed with the need to act, but, instead, he turned and walked down the hall.

He cursed the voice of reason that echoed inside his head as he moved forward. The one that told him he needed to find the portal and not waste time on Jaden DaCosta.

And yet, he couldn't help himself, even as the skin beneath his left pectoral burned relentlessly.

He ignored the pain and kept on.

He crept into her room and felt the air deflate from his lungs, an anticlimactic whoosh. He knew the place was empty before he saw the bed. It hadn't been turned down and didn't look as if she'd slept in it.

His thoughts turned to Nico. Was that where she'd fled? Julian frowned, not liking the thought of Jaden and the warrior together, but it was the most plausible scenario.

She'd been hot the night before, on the cusp of coming into heat. Her scent had been intoxicating. Even now he felt it, pulling deep in his gut—the need to take her, to mark her as his and plant his seed deep within.

Nico had felt it, too.

Hell, he was pretty sure every male who'd come in contact with her had felt the pull of her sexuality.

Julian shook his head savagely. He shouldn't care. She should be able to tame the desire that lived inside her with whomever she chose. He turned from her bed.

He had more important things to worry about, like saving the world. *Saving his soul.*

His eyes circled the room once more, and he moved toward the bed. Several photos were displayed on a side table and caught his attention. They were photos of Jaden with people he didn't recognize. Some looked to be staff members, others were faces he didn't know or care about.

His fingers ran along the top of the ebony surface and he slid the drawer open. He pushed aside papers, a brush, passport, and stilled as he felt the hard edges of another picture frame.

Carefully he withdrew the shot.

He blinked, then frowned. The picture was of a couple and their children. Jakobi he recognized instantly, and his breath caught at the woman in his arms. It was Jaden, yet not. Obviously, her mother.

They were younger, happy, and the five boys and small girl who stared up at them adoringly, were postcard perfect.

His finger caressed the moment snatched from time so long ago. What the hell had happened to the DaCosta family? How had they become splintered, distant, with a father who was nothing more than a sadistic son of a bitch and a mother who . . .

His eyebrows furled as he realized he had no clue of the whereabouts of Jaden's mother.

The flickering light of a computer caught his eye, and he crossed to her desk quickly. He tapped the keypad, but he was locked out. She'd password protected the damn thing.

He should go, yet he stared at the blank screen, a frown furling his features. Quickly, he typed in the words, *DaCosta, Jaguar, Portal*, but nothing happened. His fingers hesitated, and he shrugged, typing in *Castille*. Again, nothing.

What the hell am I doing? He typed *Julian* and smiled as the screen flickered and came to life.

He hit history and quickly scanned the pages, noticing several phrases over and over. *Eagle knights. Jaguar warriors. The Temple of the Warriors.*

Back in the day, before this whole mess had invaded his life, Julian had been quite the student of history. He knew of this temple, of its purported secrets.

He also knew of its power and the ancient magick that surrounded it. He was puzzled. What the hell did she want with the Temple? What could she possibly find there? It was full of nothing more than old relics and echoes of a long-ago past when great warriors walked the earth.

He exited her screen and closed the program. He had no time for puzzles.

Jaden DaCosta wasn't his concern. The portal was what he needed to focus on. Time was not on their side. Cormac was out there somewhere with Azaiel, and if the portal wasn't found, all bets were off. The human realm would fall into darkness.

His sacrifice would have been for nothing.

His face creased as his lips pulled back in a feral snarl. Over his fucking ass would he let that happen—he'd die trying to stop it—no one should experience the holiday he'd had in hell.

The elevator doors were still wide open and Julian disappeared inside. He spared not a glance back. He no longer cared.

He rode the mechanical lift in silence and when it opened, he shot out, his hands fisting into hard weapons as he pounced on Tank. The shifter never had a chance, and he pinned the jaguar to the wall.

"Where are Nico and the eagle?" he asked, enjoying the power he held. He pressed his fist into Tank's larynx, watching his eyes bulge as the man struggled for air.

Slowly, he relaxed his grip. "I could end you right now," he whispered hoarsely as he struggled with the need, the desire, to inflict more pain.

The clarity through which he saw things wavered, like the color and essence of the world had receded. A film of gray passed before his eyes, and he hissed at the odd sensation as he felt the darkness within him stir.

He saw fear sweep across the jaguar's face and knew that the man had glimpsed a sliver of what lived inside him. Or rather, of what no longer existed.

He felt nothing as the man continued to struggle, his words wheezy as he managed to spit them out from between tight lips.

"You are unnatural. You have the strength of a great warrior, yet . . ." His eyes fell to the flesh of his neck. "You do not carry the tattoos."

"Yeah, so I'm not a fan of LA Ink, doesn't mean I won't kick your ass but good if you don't tell me where I can find Declan." His grip tightened, and the shifter struggled as his airway became nearly nonexistent.

"What are you?" Tank managed to wheeze.

Julian leaned close, barely able to control the violence that he felt. "Trust me, my friend, you don't want to see what lies beneath my flesh."

He pushed Tank away, watching dispassionately as the man inhaled deep gulps of air. Julian rolled his shoulders and widened his stance, aware that a crowd had gathered. "Shall we give them a show, or you gonna point me in the right direction?"

The shifter stared at him, labored breaths falling from his lips as he rubbed the raw flesh at his neck. Beads of sweat seeped from Tank's pores, small rivulets sliding across his face as the large man stared at Julian, his eyes full of hate. And indecision.

The large shifter grunted, and Julian watched him carefully, noting the shift in his eyes and the way he shuffled his feet nervously.

This sad excuse is what Jaden had guarding her home? Un-fucking-believable.

He saw Security running from across the pool area, their radios echoing into the still-quiet morning.

He looked at Tank. "Your call, buddy."

Tank cursed and nodded toward a stairwell that was located near the lobby and barely managed to speak. "That takes you to the lower level. Once down there, you'll find your way. Just use your nose."

Julian turned without another word and seconds later disappeared through the heavy glass doors, smiling as the heard the excited shouts of Security and tourists.

Nothing like a little chaos to feed the soul and start the morning off right.

The sounds disappeared almost immediately as he jogged to the bottom. A large conference room was off to his right, as well as a business center. Both were empty, and he quickly made his way down the hallway to his left.

Declan had been down this way in the last while. He wrinkled his nose; Nico as well.

Jaden's scent, however, was fast fading. He only caught small snatches of it. It was an elusive trail that led his feet toward a small alcove. Directly in front of him was a door. It was unassuming, and he tried the handle, shocked when it opened with ease.

He stepped through and was immediately greeted by a young woman.

"Can I help you, sir?"

She was otherworld. He smelled the tinge of magick that coated her flesh, and saw the glitter of it in her eyes as she smiled at him.

She was the first line of defense from what he could tell, and though she appeared almost frail, with her pale skin and jet-black hair, he knew that she held power. It vibrated in the air, subtle pulses of energy that told him she was not to be messed with.

His thoughts turned to Tank, and he frowned. Seemed as if Jaden cared more about protecting "the hub" than she did about her own safety.

"I'm looking for Nico and the eagle shifter." Julian cracked a smile though his features remained tight.

She didn't bat an eye but held his gaze for several long moments.

"They've been expecting you, Julian."

She lifted her hands and made several quick motions in the air as Julian watched in surprise. The wall behind her began to shimmer, to pulsate, and, seconds later, it disappeared altogether, allowing him to see "the hub."

He nodded to the woman as she stepped aside to allow him entrance.

This indeed was an entirely different world. Totally *Mission Impossible.* A huge bank of monitors lined the wall in front of him, sending live feeds from all over the world. In front of each sat an operative, furiously tapping away at a console.

Some of the images were harsh. Interrogations taking

place by brutal means, yet his eyes passed over them without thought. That was nothing compared to what had been dished out below.

The bitch with the dagger had seen to that.

The energy was frenetic, one tinged with violence, and he scented the air. He knew that the sorcerer Kragen was somewhere down here. Hopefully, out of his mind in pain.

He snarled. Served the bastard right. He only wished he'd been given a chance to work him over. Julian shook out his tight limbs. It was early yet. There was time.

He proceeded deeper into the hub, his long legs gliding over the cool tiles in silence. Everyone here was otherworld. There were vamps, magicks, shifters of all kinds. Each and every one of them was busy, focused.

He glanced up at the huge screen that dominated the entire area. A picture of Cormac stared down at him.

He felt his gut tighten and exhaled roughly, taking a few seconds to calm his mind. He glanced around one more time but didn't recognize a soul. They were definitely government operatives. Everything about them screamed order. Purpose. Mission.

The exact opposite of the chaos that dwelled within his mind.

He'd never once visited his brother at PATU. Hell, up until several months before, he'd never known of its existence. He'd been total white collar, living in a world filled with boardrooms, private jets, beautiful women, and endless meetings.

Blue Heaven Industries, the company his father had built and one he'd taken to the next level, seemed like a lifetime ago. He was not the same man. A bittersweet smile cracked his cool facade. There was no going back.

An image of his mother floated in front of his eyes, and

his chest tightened. God, he missed her quiet strength. Did she know he was alive? Did his father bemoan the fact that all three of his sons had been pulled deep into the legacy they'd been born to?

Ironic really. Both he and his father had long denied the jaguar heritage that pulsed through their veins. As a young man, he'd never matured into a warrior; the clan tattoos that marked his younger brothers as such never appeared on his flesh.

To him it had been a blessing, and he'd carried on, the perfect candidate to take over his father's company.

But everything had changed when he'd answered his brother Jaxon's call for help. Being back in the Belizean jungle had changed him in ways he'd not expected.

Living in hell for the last six months had completed the metamorphosis and made him what he was now. A freak-of-nature shifter with half a soul who'd fed on the darkness of the underworld to survive.

Not the type you'd want to bring home to Mama.

As his eyes traveled around the room, he thought of Jaden. Of how he'd rejected her three years earlier because of what she was. And wonder of wonders, he felt shame wash over him. It startled him, that sliver of emotion, and he stopped abruptly.

"Where the hell have you been?"

Declan's voice intruded on his thoughts, and he forced the unfamiliar feelings away as he glanced at the sorcerer, surprised that Declan had been able to sneak up on him so easily.

He couldn't afford a walk down memory lane. In his world, emotion was a weakness that would get you killed.

"I needed to clear my head."

"You need to hit that fine piece of ass and get it the fuck over with."

Julian glared at the sorcerer but remained quiet.

"Just sayin'. Why didn't you tell me you guys were mated? That you have a history together?"

"It doesn't mean anything," Julian retorted, angry that the Irishman thought he would even entertain a discussion about the jaguar.

"Yeah, keep telling yourself that." Declan looked away, and muttered, "You Castille boys are all the same. You have no fucking clue."

Julian took a step toward Declan, and whispered softly, "Jaden DaCosta is not someone we will discuss."

Declan rolled his eyes and smiled, a nasty *fuck-you* grin. "You look like shit," he declared. His tone was light, a direct contrast to the cold, dead glint in his eyes.

"I could say the same," Julian replied.

"Breaking someone who has dipped their toes into the dark arts isn't exactly a restful way to spend the night."

That sparked his interest. "What did you learn?"

A muscle worked its way sharply across Declan's cheek as he clenched his teeth. "Nothing."

Julian's eyes swept the entire area. "Where is he? Let me have a shot at him." Julian grinned at the thought of inflicting pain on the asshole whose hands had been all over Jaden.

Declan ran his hand through the thick hair atop his head before releasing a long sigh.

"Ain't gonna happen, sport."

Damn, but he hated it when Declan called him that. He arched an eyebrow and glared at the sorcerer. "And that would be because?"

Declan paused, then spoke quietly. "The bastard is dead."

Julian felt his frustration rise and clenched his hands together tightly. "Dead," he ground out.

"As a fucking doornail," Declan answered.

Julian glared at the sorcerer, not impressed with his attempt at humor. Declan's attention was diverted, and they both turned as Finn nodded at them.

"You see Jaden?" the eagle shifter asked.

Julian shook his head but remained silent.

Finn swore under his breath before turning to an operative at the station nearest him. "Max, track her down. I've already tried her cell, and she's not in her suite."

"Will do, sir."

"What's up?" Julian asked, his curiosity piqued. The atmosphere had changed, the air lit with an energy that sizzled along the room, touching them all.

Finn sighed and rubbed the back of his neck. "We've got a situation in Mexico City."

Alarm shot through Julian. Templo Mayor was in the heart of Mexico City.

"What kind of situation?" he asked gruffly.

"The demon kind," Nico answered. The jaguar emerged from a room down the way, and Julian's already tense shoulders tightened even more.

"Where?" he asked.

Nico ignored him, and Julian glared at the shifter.

"We locate Jaden yet?" Nico asked Finn.

"Where the hell is this demon shit happening?" he asked once more as he took a step toward the jaguar.

Nico snarled, and the air shimmered between the two of them. All Julian could visualize was slowly ripping each and every limb from the other jaguar's body.

"Boys, let's settle down, shall we?" Declan stepped in

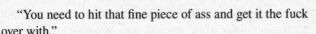

"You need to hit that fine piece of ass and get it the fuck over with."

Julian glared at the sorcerer but remained quiet.

"Just sayin'. Why didn't you tell me you guys were mated? That you have a history together?"

"It doesn't mean anything," Julian retorted, angry that the Irishman thought he would even entertain a discussion about the jaguar.

"Yeah, keep telling yourself that." Declan looked away, and muttered, "You Castille boys are all the same. You have no fucking clue."

Julian took a step toward Declan, and whispered softly, "Jaden DaCosta is not someone we will discuss."

Declan rolled his eyes and smiled, a nasty *fuck-you* grin. "You look like shit," he declared. His tone was light, a direct contrast to the cold, dead glint in his eyes.

"I could say the same," Julian replied.

"Breaking someone who has dipped their toes into the dark arts isn't exactly a restful way to spend the night."

That sparked his interest. "What did you learn?"

A muscle worked its way sharply across Declan's cheek as he clenched his teeth. "Nothing."

Julian's eyes swept the entire area. "Where is he? Let me have a shot at him." Julian grinned at the thought of inflicting pain on the asshole whose hands had been all over Jaden.

Declan ran his hand through the thick hair atop his head before releasing a long sigh.

"Ain't gonna happen, sport."

Damn, but he hated it when Declan called him that. He arched an eyebrow and glared at the sorcerer. "And that would be because?"

Declan paused, then spoke quietly. "The bastard is dead."

Julian felt his frustration rise and clenched his hands together tightly. "Dead," he ground out.

"As a fucking doornail," Declan answered.

Julian glared at the sorcerer, not impressed with his attempt at humor. Declan's attention was diverted, and they both turned as Finn nodded at them.

"You see Jaden?" the eagle shifter asked.

Julian shook his head but remained silent.

Finn swore under his breath before turning to an operative at the station nearest him. "Max, track her down. I've already tried her cell, and she's not in her suite."

"Will do, sir."

"What's up?" Julian asked, his curiosity piqued. The atmosphere had changed, the air lit with an energy that sizzled along the room, touching them all.

Finn sighed and rubbed the back of his neck. "We've got a situation in Mexico City."

Alarm shot through Julian. Templo Mayor was in the heart of Mexico City.

"What kind of situation?" he asked gruffly.

"The demon kind," Nico answered. The jaguar emerged from a room down the way, and Julian's already tense shoulders tightened even more.

"Where?" he asked.

Nico ignored him, and Julian glared at the shifter.

"We locate Jaden yet?" Nico asked Finn.

"Where the hell is this demon shit happening?" he asked once more as he took a step toward the jaguar.

Nico snarled, and the air shimmered between the two of them. All Julian could visualize was slowly ripping each and every limb from the other jaguar's body.

"Boys, let's settle down, shall we?" Declan stepped in

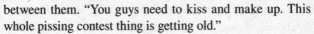

between them. "You guys need to kiss and make up. This whole pissing contest thing is getting old."

Declan glanced toward him, his eyes focused, yet Julian sensed the bleakness that lingered there. "We've got a problem that needs solving, remember? I don't have to remind you of the consequence . . . ticktock and all that." Declan turned to Nico. "So, you gonna spill?"

"Templo Mayor," Finn answered instead.

"What did you say?" Julian rasped, though really, he didn't need the eagle shifter to repeat himself. He'd heard his words clear as day.

Son of a fucking bitch. Only Jaden would head straight toward trouble.

"We've intercepted a few transmissions that lead us to believe something is going to go down, and the entire zone has gone hot in the last few hours." The eagle shifter shrugged his shoulders. "We're not sure why, but we should send a team to check it out. I wanted to run it by Jaden, but she's not around."

Finn nodded to the operative, Max. "Try Tank again and see if he knows where Jaden is."

"Don't bother," Julian answered as he nodded to Declan. "We need to vamoose."

"You are not in charge of our team," Nico rasped.

Julian paused and took a moment to center the anger that was flush in his system. He and Nico were going to have it out. Just not today. "I don't give a shit about your team. Jaden's not in her suite."

"And you know this because?" Nico's voice was low, but the bitterness hung in the air.

Julian glared at the shifter. "By my guess, she left just after midnight for Mexico City, and if we hurry, we might be able to get there before she gets her ass kicked."

Nico's eyes widened, and his instant concern pissed Julian off. It was totally unreasonable, but he wasn't in a reasonable state of mind.

"It's a nice piece of ass, no? Be a shame for it to be damaged in any way." He turned and headed toward the exit, smiling as he heard Nico's enraged snarl follow his words.

Declan fell into step beside him. "Tell me again how this whole mating thing doesn't matter?"

Julian ignored him, and the smile soon faded as his mind went dark.

"And why we're wasting time sniffing after Jaden when we should be focusing our efforts on finding the portal?"

"She is tied to the portal," Julian stated. An hour earlier, he had been ready to go his separate way, but his gut told him the path he needed to follow led to Jaden. He'd been a ruthless businessman and had learned one thing early on. Always follow your gut instinct.

Jaden DaCosta had a way of finding trouble. She'd better hope he was able to find *her*.

In one piece.

Chapter 13

Jaden grabbed her bag and slid from the truck, stretching out stiff muscles as she did so. She'd driven like a maniac, had made the trip in just under twenty hours. The private jet would have been so much easier, but she didn't want her father or anyone on the team to know where she'd gone. So she'd paid cash for a rental in Playa Del Carmen and driven straight to Mexico City.

She stifled a yawn. Though she was a creature of the night, the lack of sleep over the last few days was starting to catch up to her.

The cool wind that swept across the street felt wonderful, refreshing, and she let it play along her flesh as she stared at the huge structure not far from her.

Templo Mayor.

The ruin was in the heart of Mexico City, and she felt the enormity of its power as she stood in the dark, staring at it. Moonbeams fell upon the stone, touching the surface in an eerie glow. Even from several hundred yards out, she was humbled and impressed by the magnificence of the structure.

This had been the seat of power for the Aztecs hundreds of years ago. Their culture and that of the Mayan were intimately connected to her people, to that of the eagle knights.

They'd worshipped her ancestors. Emulated their fierceness and wore their likeness in battle.

Sadness rolled over Jaden as she moved forward. Time rolled on and was harsh, her deep-reaching claws destroying even the greatest of civilizations. Such was the way of things.

Humanity had always managed to survive, to reinvent, and to adapt. And yet how long would luck be on their side? Jaden had a bad feeling about what was coming and wasn't sure they'd survive an assault from hell.

She slipped between the shadows and moved silently through the gloom. Security was sparse, and she slid by them with ease. If they only knew what they guarded, what power lay deep within the ruins.

Templo Mayor had been built back in the 1300s. It had gone through several reincarnations, due to both structural issues and war. At the end of the Aztec reign, the Spanish had destroyed it, then built their city over top of it. And here it had lain, silent in its grave, until a city worker had discovered a valuable piece of history.

Her people would have been content to let the temple rest in peace, but excavation had begun in earnest, and a large part of the temple had been unearthed over the past thirty years.

Now, it was a major attraction in the city, drawing thousands of visitors from all over the globe. They came to get a taste of history, to view the grandeur that had been such a part of the Aztec culture.

And yet they hadn't a clue as to the secrets hidden deep within. Of what they could unleash.

"Hey, lady, it's dangerous out here. Why you walking the streets alone?"

The voice slid at her from the darkness, and Jaden turned. A tall man leaned against the crumbling walls, his demeanor casual, but there was something about him that immediately set her on edge.

Where the hell had he come from? She should have been able to pick up on his presence before now. Something wasn't right.

"Don't worry about me, I'm good," she replied carefully, trying to read him. But he was blank, like there was nothing there. She rotated her neck slowly, feeling the crack that released a bit of tension and narrowed her eyes, never taking them from him.

She had a bad feeling that the dude was otherworld.

Okay, she thought, let the games begin.

"Sure you don't want some company?"

She stretched her fingers out, letting them hang loose, and scented the wind as she did so. As far as she could tell, he was alone. There was a guard several hundred feet away, but he was busy chatting up a couple of young women.

It was good that he was distracted.

She smiled and looked at the man. There'd be no witnesses.

"I don't normally talk to strangers so . . ." She kept her voice light and turned from him though she was very aware when he pushed away from the stone wall and headed in her direction.

"I don't think you understand," he began, and the hair on the back of her neck electrified as his voice modulated, thickened, like he was talking in layers of sound.

He was definitely otherworld. And not the good kind. She had a nagging suspicion that the dude was demon and had some sort of cloaking charm that hid his nasty-ass scent.

"I said I'm good, back off."

She clenched her teeth, her muscles tight, and slid her hand inside the bag. Her charmed dagger was freshly shot up with all sorts of shit, courtesy of Tess, and she smiled viciously.

Kicking some random demon's ass was a great way to start off the night.

"Good might be overstating," he whispered, and she felt the air shimmer at her back. "As of now, I think you're fucked."

His hand was on her back, but she was ready and dropped to the ground, spinning her leg out as she whirled around.

She connected with his body and grinned as he went down, his face smashing into the stone beneath them as a string of foulness erupted from his mouth.

She was on him in a flash, her knee digging into his back as she struggled to hold him still. Jaden was strong, but even her enhanced strength barely kept the demon beneath her.

"Watch your mouth, or I might be inclined to wash it out with soap."

He continued to struggle, and the cloaking charm melted away fast as his demon scent bled through. She could now see the gray mist that clung to him.

"I am gonna enjoy killing you," he said, his voice doing the weird-vibration thing again, "slowly."

"Oh please, you know how many times I've heard that same line?" she retorted. "It's getting old."

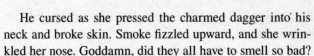

He cursed as she pressed the charmed dagger into his neck and broke skin. Smoke fizzled upward, and she wrinkled her nose. Goddamn, did they all have to smell so bad? Was that a prerequisite to being demon?

He snarled and pushed against the ground, nearly unseating her, but she held on, grabbing a hunk of his hair as she did so.

She was careful to keep the dagger pressed into his skin and hoped like hell it had enough juice to prevent the asshole from changing into his true form.

He began to struggle in earnest, and she pitched forward and backward but held on.

"Why are you hanging around Templo Mayor?" she asked softly, her voice dangerously low.

"Why are you?" he shot back.

She snorted, not believing his arrogance.

"In case you hadn't noticed, dickhead, I've got the knife, so I'm asking the questions."

He made a weird gurgling sound, and she grinned as she stuck the knife in deeper, twisting it slightly as she did so.

He began to spew obscenities, then a bunch of crap came out of his mouth that she didn't understand. Ancient words. Demon speak from down below.

She let go of his head and slammed her fist into the base of his skull. His nose broke beneath the force as it smashed into the stone once more. She smiled at the squeal of pain that fell from his lips.

"Holy crap, spare me the drama will you? I'm kinda in a rush." She felt winded, and it was all she could do to keep the bastard contained.

He stopped moving, and he relaxed beneath her. In the distance, voices echoed on the wind, and she glanced behind her. The security guard and the girls who surrounded him were looking in their direction.

She concentrated with all her might and coaxed the shadows toward her. If she could just have a few more minutes, she was certain she'd be able to dispose of the piece of crap she sat on, with none the wiser.

"I'll make you a deal," the demon began, but she cut him off before he could go any further.

She leaned down, and whispered near his ear, "I don't play that game with the likes of you." She paused. "My rules are simple. You answer my questions, and I let you live."

Jaden twisted the dagger for good measure and felt nothing as he grunted in pain.

"Let's try this one more time. Why are you here?"

The demon laughed. She felt the vibrations running through his body as he did so. "It was a nice night for a walk, until this bitch showed up and . . ."

Cheeky asshole!

She grabbed him by the neck, digging her claws into his skin until she elicited another scream of pain. Her jaguar burned beneath her flesh, and Jaden's breaths fell in small spurts as adrenaline kicked in.

The voices were becoming louder, and she knew her time was nearly up.

She pressed harder, using her legs to hold the bastard still. "One more chance or I cut your head off and leave it as a sacrifice to Huitzilopochtli. I have a feeling it's been a long while since he fed."

"Your god of war lies in prison, weak and pathetic." The demon was shaking badly beneath her. "We're everywhere. Life in this realm will darken and change, and one day my brothers will be liberated from the bowels of the earth."

Shouts rang out, and Jaden knew she had to act fast. The shadows were slipping from her skin. She didn't have the skill to hold them in place for long periods of time.

"Where is O'Hara?"

"Cormac is a fool. He'll not remain hidden long. He cannot double-cross Lilith and live, but the others . . ."

"The others? What the hell do you mean?"

"We're looking for them everywhere. They can't escape us."

The demon began to laugh, and as his voice deepened, she felt his energy shift. A series of clicking noises erupted from deep within him. He was trying to change into his true form, but with the dagger spreading poison throughout his system, he was having difficulty.

She knew there was nothing more to gain from him.

She closed her eyes and unleashed her power. Her hands yanked hard on his hair, she pulled him toward her, and, with one quick stroke, severed his head from his body.

Jaden jumped back quickly and tossed the head as black liquid spewed everywhere. She'd been burned by the nasty stuff before and had no plans to experience that again.

The remains began to smolder and break down as an ungodly stench drifted up her nasal passage.

She ran, disregarding the shouts to stop, and knew by the time the security guard reached the demon there would be nothing left but a puddle of crap. The poison would work quickly to dissolve the demon flesh.

Tess had done a great job.

Her animal was enraged, wanting out, but Jaden tapped into the power of her jaguar, and her legs flew over the terrain. The darkness swallowed her whole, and moments later, she stood before the ruin, the demon and security officers left far behind.

She slowed, staying close to the shadows, and paused as she came upon a stone wall of skulls. They looked eerie in the darkness, the shadows that played upon them sinister and she shivered slightly as she moved forward.

She knew there was a tunnel that led to the unearthed portion of The House of the Eagles, which was part of the temple. She needed to gain access to what lay beneath—because it was there, in the very heart of these ruins, that Toni-ella had charmed the fallen, Azaiel, from the upper realm.

It was there that he'd made the portal, there that he'd been cursed. And it was there that she was hoping to find answers, anything that would help her not only to find the elusive duo but to destroy them both when she did.

She slipped inside the tunnel, avoiding security, and it wasn't long before she stood inside one of two adjoining ancient rooms. Her eyes allowed her to see clearly at night, but even she was having problems so far below the surface. The shadows were different here. They were menacing.

Jaden grabbed a flashlight from her bag and felt the enormity of history unfold before her eyes as she gazed around. It was impressive.

Two large statues guarded the far wall. They were amazing replicas of eagle knights, and as she slowly walked toward them, she felt her heart begin to accelerate. She felt a presence, like she was being watched.

She shined the light onto the faces of the statues and hissed softly as they came into focus. The eyes looked real, and the effect was freaky.

Jaden stilled, letting her senses fly out once more as she scented the air; but as far as she could tell, there was no one there.

She was alone, yet she knew that she wasn't. The ancient magick that inhabited this place was potent, and she knew she needed to tread lightly. One wrong move, and her ass would be fried.

Cool, damp air licked at her heated flesh, and she shivered as she gazed upon the walls before her. Intricate, beautifully done etchings of eagles and nature were abundant, and she shook her head at their beauty. It was incredible, really, that these people, the Aztecs, had been so bloodthirsty in battle yet so refined and talented when it came to the arts.

But enough of that.

She sidled up to the walls, walking along low-slung benches as she eyed the interior closely. Her hands fell along the cool stone, and she felt the vibration of power that lived deep within.

She walked the entire area, twice, and stopped in frustration. As far as she could see, there was no way to get to what was below. She knew the sacred temple was there. Hundreds of years earlier, the jaguar warriors had hunted and killed the eagle knights, because of their knowledge. They'd made a point of knowing every detail about the shifters.

It was a dark time in her world. A time when several of the jaguar clans had fragmented off into the darkness. She hung her head in shame and felt a wave of anger rush through her. The DaCostas had aided in the bloodletting, and it was only by the strength of Skye Knightly's family that the portal had remained hidden.

Safe.

Until Cormac O'Hara.

The son of a bitch had ruined everything.

Jaden shook her limbs out and pushed all thoughts of Cormac and the portal away. She needed to concentrate and find her way inside, or she was no further ahead than she'd been last week.

She wracked her brain for several long moments and

cursed softly as she circled the room once more. She should have brought Finn with her. The eagle knight would surely have more knowledge than she.

Tiredly, she rubbed her temples and tried to shrug off the weariness that crept into her bones. Maybe she'd been at this too long. Maybe it was time to accept that her brain was dead, and she was fast losing focus.

She turned back toward the entrance and was about to take a step forward when a whisper caressed her cheek like the faintest touch of a feather. Her flesh erupted in goose bumps, and she stilled as her heart beat once more in earnest.

A touch at her hand made her jump, and the flashlight went flying, sending a distorted array of light to dance across the walls in a macabre display of shadow.

She whirled around, but there was no one there.

Jaden exhaled slowly as she forced her heart rate to steady, and she shifted her energy, welcoming the flood of power from her jaguar as the burn rushed over her skin.

The ghosts hidden in the shadows were powerful indeed, and she felt malice in the air as she stood there, light on her feet and ready to rumble.

"Show yourself," she whispered hoarsely. "I don't have a lot of time." She snorted. "What with the end of the world and all that."

"What is a jaguar doing in our sacred house?"

The whispered words were stronger now, cracking inside her skull and reverberating around the room. She winced at the sensation, like someone was speaking underwater, and turned in a circle, grabbing the dagger once more as she did so.

"Stupid cat. You think that will stop me?"

A tingling flash of energy hit her on the back, and Jaden

stopped. Her breaths fell in pants, the sounds sharp, as her lungs expanded to force them out. Her chest felt tight, but it was all good. Her body was primed for battle.

She rolled her shoulders and turned around.

And that was when everything went dark.

Chapter 14

It was like a sheet of obsidian had been pulled over her eyes. Suddenly, Jaden was off balance, her equilibrium gone. She couldn't see a thing and bit down hard as a wall of panic threatened.

When the smash to her face came, she had no chance to react or to defend herself because she couldn't fucking see.

She went flying backward and barely held on to the dagger as she hit one of the stone benches, *hard*. She was winded for a few seconds and groaned as pain exploded along her frame. The pain vibrated out from her shoulder, and spread along her bones as they absorbed the brunt of the impact.

Her shoulder was still tender from the demon bite only two nights earlier, but she ignored it as she rolled to the side. Another flash of heat blasted the bench where her head had just been, and stone erupted into deadly shards that flew everywhere.

"How dare you darken the door of our sacred temple?" The voice was incredibly angry, and Jaden was beginning to think she'd made one hell of a mistake in coming alone.

She shook her head in an effort to clear the shadows from her eyes as she sharpened her senses, trying to figure out where the invisible man was.

"Technically, I'm not in your sacred temple, though I'll be honest, I wouldn't mind a point in the right direction."

She felt a whisper of energy in the air and jackknifed her body, but wasn't able to evade the hit entirely. This time the asshole did manage to connect with her face, and pain erupted along her cheekbone as her head snapped back. Blood spurted inside her mouth, the coppery taste spilling over her tongue in a rush that enraged her animal.

She growled loudly, enjoying the fire of power that erupted from deep within her gut as she snarled.

Son of a fucking bitch! The bastard wasn't playing.

She whirled around and ducked just as a flash of heat came at her. She felt a ripple of energy as it passed by, inches from her limbs, and twisted her body into an arc.

She was successful in avoiding the hit and moved fast, her speed and strength pushing her forward. But she skidded to an abrupt halt, barely able to keep her balance, as she spied the entity that stood several feet away.

Shit! Her bad luck wasn't improving any as she eyed the tall creature that stood between her and the entrance. His massive frame effectively blocked her only means of escape.

The shadows fell rapidly from his form, and she took a step back as the full range of his power became apparent to her. This was no regular eagle knight.

Her eyes strayed to the large statues that stood tall and silent. He was nothing like them.

His power was palpable.

And at the moment, she happened to be the focus of every scrap of his dark energy.

Jaden's jaguar itched beneath her flesh, and she felt her canines break skin, her nails elongate, as her animal began to make noise. She forced it back. Now was not the time. She needed to keep a cool head.

The man who stood before her was not wholly corporeal, yet his power was such that she had a nagging suspicion he was of a much higher order. Like near the top.

"I am Nanauatl. Do not trifle with me, Jaguar."

Jaden swallowed tightly but held his gaze. Okay, so he was *at* the top.

Unbelievable.

Only she would get trapped inside an eagle temple with Nanauatl, their sun god.

Bet Castille would love to see this.

The thought snuck into her head, and she grimaced. How the hell did he manage to intrude on her thoughts, even now, when she was about to get her ass kicked.

Jaden forced the image of Julian from her mind and exhaled slowly, wincing, as pain lashed across her cheekbone.

The blood inside her mouth had stopped flowing, and she spit out the last remnants, hesitating as she heard him make a harsh noise.

Her mind was racing, searching for a way out. Would the sun god listen to her? She decided it was worth a try to play nice.

"Look, I'm sorry if coming here is a big no-no, I mean, me being a jaguar and all, but seriously, I've got a good reason." She paused, encouraged at his silence. "Surely you know what's going on out there. The darkness that's invading the human realm needs to be stopped, and I'm thinking the answers are here someplace."

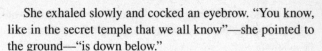

She exhaled slowly and cocked an eyebrow. "You know, like in the secret temple that we all know"—she pointed to the ground—"is down below."

Nanauatl's eyes narrowed, and an unholy light emanated from deep within his body. The effect was eerie, and the incandescent shimmer made him more sinister and definitely more threatening.

He shook his head. "It is your people, *your kind* who orchestrated all of this. You hunted my warriors mercilessly, killing them when they were at their weakest, when the sun was in hiding. All in an effort to steal the portal for your own ill gains." His voice began to resonate, and his anger was an invisible force that hurtled through the air at her. Jaden opened her mouth to reply, but then closed it. What the hell could she say? He was right.

"If humanity fails to recover from the darkness that will most surely overtake them, the jaguar warriors will be solely responsible."

A spark of anger erupted inside Jaden, and she took a step forward. She so wasn't willing to take the blame for everything.

"It wasn't a jaguar who tempted Azaiel from the upper realm but one of your own."

He hissed at her impertinence, his eyes blazing, his face a macabre grimace of fury. "You will not speak his name!" the sun god bellowed, but Jaden rushed on, needing to speak the truth and make him understand.

"Azaiel made the portal for the betrayer, and she would have used it to destroy the earth." Jaden paused, chest heaving. "That has nothing to do with the jaguars; that is all on you."

Nanauatl roared his anger and hissed as fire burned through his eyes. The temperature inside the chamber rose quickly, and Jaden struggled to breathe as the intensity of it infiltrated her pores, sending scorching flames across her flesh.

"I will kill you," he snarled, showing an even row of deadly, serrated teeth.

"Again with the killing." Jaden's eyes searched in vain, but she couldn't see a way around him. "Seems these days I'm either going to get killed or fucked."

If she launched her body upward and twisted just so, she might have a chance to clear the temple.

A flash of light, or rather, a shift in the shadows caught her attention. She stilled, her eyes watching the sun god warily.

"I suppose both are possible." The sun god ignored her words. Jaden took a step back while her belly ached from the tight muscles that pulled at her abdomen.

An eerie glow began to slowly build. Something was happening, and the hair on the back of her neck tingled.

That was never a good sign. She just might be screwed.

Jaden swallowed slowly and cleared her mind, her stance loose and ready to fight. And she'd be fighting, of that there was no doubt. She just hoped she'd be giving more than receiving.

Shadows pulsated against the stone walls, the eerie glow now resembling some kind of otherworld aurora borealis. The shimmering beams of light slithered along the dark surface, invading every nook and cranny and spreading the energy of Nanauatl over the sacred etchings.

The etchings of eagle knights.

Jaden balanced on the balls of her feet, not really believing what she was seeing, and she'd seen some weird-ass shit in the last few months.

But the shifting shadows and light began to hum, to

vibrate, and she opened her mouth in astonishment as the eagle knights that had been encased in rock began to move and take form.

"Motherfu . . ." she whispered, ignoring the soft laughter that fell from the sun god's lips as he interrupted her train of thought.

"There is no way one jaguar warrior can stand against my eagle knights."

"But I thought . . ."

Nanauatl interrupted her once more, and she glared at him as he returned her look with a ghostly smile of his own. "In the human realm, my warriors are at full strength when the kiss of the sun touches their flesh." His eyes glowed a feral red. "But these knights are unlike any you will ever meet."

The heat of his words flickered across her skin like a physical blow. Which she supposed it was; he was, after all, literally breathing fire.

Jaden squared her shoulders, and though she hoped she appeared fierce, she had her doubts that even she was that good of an actress. In front of her, standing in a loosely connected semicircle, were seven full-fledged eagle knights.

They were tall, even the lone woman included in the bunch, and on a good day, with her fancy Jimmy Choos for added height, Jaden might come up to their chins.

Panic nipped at her gut, and she ignored the nausea that was having one hell of a party deep within. She needed to think, or quite simply, she'd most likely not see another sunrise.

"Well, shit, this hardly seems fair does it?"

Nanauatl arched an eyebrow, the tilt of his chin and line of his jaw aristocratic and condescending.

"You don't care that the human realm is about to go the

way of Armageddon?" she continued as she moved to the right. "Does their fate not matter?"

"I only care about guarding that which is mine." His tone was cold, dead.

She reached down quickly, grabbed a large rock that lay at her feet, and whipped it at the female knight. The stone landed with a thud against the far wall. It had passed through her body, and Jaden glared at the bitch as the eagle knight laughed, the sound cutting through air like shattered glass.

The eagle knights were not wholly corporeal, the same as Nanauatl, and she studied them closely, looking for some sort of weakness.

But how could you fight something that had no essence? Nothing to inflict pain upon? No freaking head to cut off?

Her jaw ached from tension, and she struggled to relax. She knew they had no such problem. They would kick her butt around like a sorry-ass soccer ball.

Nanauatl's mouth turned up into a smile. He wasn't fooled by her bravado. Christ, her fear hung in the air like bad perfume.

Most of the knights stared at her in silence, their faces devoid of emotion other than the glimmer of light that shone from their eyes. But a few, including the woman, smiled at her wickedly.

It was a smile of anticipation.

Jaden clutched the charmed dagger at her side.

This was like a bad scene from *Star Wars*. Where the hell was her Obi Wan Kenobi? She was fighting the freaking Phantom Menace.

"Don't you care?" she tried once more. "About what is seeping into the human realm? About stopping the evil before it has a chance to take root and grow?"

Nanauatl leveled his gaze upon her, and Jaden felt the full

force of his power. She winced, her eyes protesting, as the light that shone from within him nearly blinded her.

"I will feed upon the flesh of the jaguar." He looked to his knights and smiled. "*That* is all."

They moved forward, and, instinctively, Jaden stepped back, her heart lurching as the back of her legs connected with another low-slung stone bench. She had nowhere and no room in which to run.

Her eyes methodically searched once more, but she knew it was no use. She blew out a breath and cracked her neck as she rotated her head and rolled her shoulders.

She grasped the charmed dagger in her hands, not sure if anything that Tess had done to the damn thing would work against what she faced; but at this point, it was pretty much all she had.

One of the phantom warriors rushed her, and she jumped up onto the bench, propelling herself forward into the air. She twisted as she gained height, her arm arcing downward as she catapulted overtop the knight. She sliced downward and nearly dropped the dagger at the sensation that crawled over her skin as her hand passed through whatever the hell it was that made up his body.

She landed inches from the line of scrimmage and moved to the side as instinct took over, barely missing the energy bolt that was thrown her way. She heard an unearthly howl rip through the room as the eagle knight behind her shouted his rage.

Silence fell between all of them, and time slowed down, ticking by in long seconds that felt more like minutes.

Jaden's lungs expanded as she exhaled, and the beat of her heart was like a drummer on meth, wild and crazy.

Her long hair clung to her skin, and she angrily shoved it away, her chest heaving as she tried to focus. The dude behind her made a weird series of grunting noises, and she shifted slightly, keeping him in her peripheral vision.

It was then that a realization hit her. She would most likely die here.

Stunned, Jaden faltered and nearly dropped her weapon.

Such sorrow and sadness rifled through her that she was momentarily paralyzed. It was like a fist of pain had reached inside and grabbed her heart, squeezing until she couldn't breathe.

Nanauatl shook his head, and laughter erupted from deep within his chest. It echoed around the stone walls like a macabre symphony, each note jarring and off-key.

"You should be very afraid, little jaguar. We will cut you to pieces and eat every last delicious morsel of your body." He looked at the phantom knights and grinned wickedly. "It's been much too long since we've had a sacrificial ceremony."

Jaden shook her head but remained silent even as her ending flashed before her eyes. She wasn't afraid of dying. In fact, for a jaguar warrior, to die in battle was the ultimate honor.

The pain that ripped through her was for all things lost and those that were no longer fixable. For the evil that had infiltrated her family and turned her father and brothers into monsters. For a mother who had long ago perished.

She felt tears prick the corner of her eyes, their heat stinging against her skin as an image of Julian shimmered in front of her.

She laughed, a hysterical outburst. God help her, but she couldn't stop. She knew by the expressions on the eagles' faces, that she'd shocked them.

Score one for team jaguar.

To think that Julian Castille would be the last memory

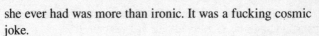

she ever had was more than ironic. It was a fucking cosmic joke.

She gripped the dagger as the laughter inside her dried up.

Nanauatl stared at her hard, and she felt the whisper of death caress her cheek as a shiver crossed over her flesh. The eagle that she'd flown over advanced once more, and the six remaining started to chant. Ancient Aztec words fell from their lips as their voices blended, thickened with power.

The sun god stood back and watched, his entire body now emitting light as he fed upon the energy in the room.

Maybe he was the key? Chop off the head, and the rest would fall? Even though she knew that wasn't literally an option, maybe there was still a way to do damage.

There was only one way to find out.

Jaden bunched her power into a tight fist that sat in her chest and flooded her limbs. Her legs were shaking with the need to act, and she screamed her warrior battle cry as she flew toward them.

She knew the lone knight was at her back, but she was fixated on their leader. It was her only hope.

She threw her body into the air, sideways, twisting as her legs ran up the wall. She tried to arch her back, to once more propel herself over the line of knights, but, sadly, it was anticipated, and she was sent flying.

Pain ripped along her rib cage, and nausea pushed up from her gut as the strange sensation edged along her flesh. Their touch was like poison, and as she rolled to the side, she literally saw stars from the force of the hit.

But she was up in an instant, ignoring the pain and the enemies that surrounded her. Jaden's only focus was their leader, and as she felt the creepy touch of one of them at her back, she arced her arm around, and heard a hiss as the dagger passed through whatever the hell he was.

And yet it was too late. The entire game was over before it had begun.

Nanauatl's hand slammed into her chest and she screamed as fire ripped across her flesh. The phantom knight behind her pinned her arms to her sides, and she thought she was going to toss her cookies as the intensity of his touch sent every single nerve ending into agony.

"I do admire your need to fight, little jaguar." The sun god stood inches from her, yet the pain that had settled along her back took away much of her focus. Her eyes dimmed, and she struggled to hold on. She called upon her animal, even knowing that she couldn't shift.

A haze of red clouded her vision, and she snarled as Nanauatl grinned down at her. His mouth thinned, and his voice deepened as his hand reached for her.

She could do nothing to avoid it and ceased struggling. There was no point.

She looked up at him, her body on fire, and she was surprised that she was able to speak.

"You had a chance to make things right," she managed to get out. "To get over your small-minded vendetta and help humanity."

His breath was flames across her face, but she refused to look away, and when his hand closed around her neck, she stilled.

"I care not what happens outside these walls," he whispered. "Not anymore."

Jaden closed her eyes, fighting the tears of helplessness that hung at the back of them. His fingers dug in deeper, spreading his special brand of pain along the flesh there, and she yelped as it burned bright.

Inside her body, the jaguar erupted in anger. She felt the flood of power once more, infusing her cells with such a rush that she reacted instantly, yelling her warrior cry as she jerked her arms and began to struggle in earnest.

Nanauatl gripped her hard and yanked her upward until he held her in the air like a puppet, her limbs moving erratically as the dagger fell from her fingers.

Deep, guttural sounds escaped from between her lips, and as a red haze infiltrated her vision, she met his eyes one last time. She felt shame at her weakness and sadness for an end that would come much too soon.

A realization came to her. Was there really honor in such a death? One that would leave so many things unfinished? She gritted her teeth and prepared herself, pushing the despair from her mind.

And she knew the bastard would enjoy her death immensely.

Chapter 15

Julian knelt, his nose wrinkling at the otherworld stench that hung in the air. He grimaced and looked up at Declan. The entire area was rank with it.

"A fresh kill," Declan observed, his eyes scanning the area around them. "She's definitely here."

Julian stood quickly. He was anxious, on edge, and his animal clawed beneath his skin. He wasn't used to feeling, and much preferred the cold wall of nothing he'd enjoyed over the last six months.

He rolled his tense shoulders, his eyes slowly sweeping the area as he did so. They'd made damn good time, all things considered. The jet had been a no-go. Jakobi was still in the area, and it would have been a red flag. They'd cut some time by driving to La Corone, and from there, they'd chartered a small flight.

It was eerily quiet. He glanced down at his feet once more. They might be too late.

Finn and Nico came jogging up from the other side of the ruins. Julian ignored the warrior and focused on the eagle knight.

"Any sign of Cracker?" They'd contacted Jaxon and learned the operative had been dispatched the day before, when the first reports of demon activity had surfaced.

His conversation with his brother had been short and to the point. There'd been no time to fill Jaxon in about his whereabouts over the past six months. That would have to wait. It had been enough to hear his voice and to know that Libby and Logan were safe, as were Jagger and Skye.

The tall blond man glanced at the goop that lay in clumps along the ground before meeting his gaze.

"No."

Nico grunted, and Julian arched an eyebrow. "Care to share?" he asked, though he ignored the warrior and spoke to the eagle. He felt the other jaguar's glare, and it pleased him to know that he was irritating him, even if only in this one small manner.

Finn smiled wryly and shook his head. "It's freaky quiet. We caught a security guard partying it up with two ladies; but other than that, nothing."

"Are we going to sit here all night or are we going to find Jaden?" Nico exploded. "She's here. I can smell her."

Julian turned his attention to the warrior, his golden eyes dark, his mouth set into a hard line. He felt his beast stir once more, and the urge to pound his fist into the jaguar's face was heavy. He took a step toward him, growling as he did so.

Nico's tone was possessive and touched on something inside Julian he didn't care to explore; however, he couldn't help the way it made him feel.

"She's mine."

The words bounced around his brain, and he didn't realize he'd spoken them aloud until Nico's eyes widened in surprise, and the warrior snarled. "She belongs to no one."

Julian clenched his fists together as the burn continued to rip along his flesh. The edge of his mind was dark, corroded, and the pure unbridled rage he felt at that moment fed his soul hungrily.

Nico lunged at him, the tall warrior ferocious as his own anger boiled over. He leapt into the air, but Julian was ready, his stance wide, a feral grin falling over his face.

His scars pulsated in rapid, sharp bursts, as they did whenever emotion took over, but he welcomed the pain. It meant that he was still somewhat alive.

And yet, the hit never came. Nico was pulled from the air like a puppet and slammed into the stone wall that was several feet away.

"You boys done playing?" Declan asked softly. The sorcerer stood casually off to side, looking like he was bored as hell. But Julian knew better.

Declan O'Hara was as damaged as he, and the dark, flat eyes that stared at him were but two shades above dead.

Nico snarled, kicking his feet as he bellowed in rage. Declan tossed him an easy smile, though his eyes remained fixed, cold. He arched an eyebrow, slowly walked toward them and, with a flick of his wrist, released the hold he'd had over the jaguar.

Nico's body slowly slid to the ground, and he landed lightly on his feet, his face screwed up something nasty, pissed that he'd been bested.

And by a magick no less.

Declan spit into the ground and glanced at the warrior. "Oops." His eyes swung back to Julian's, and the two men stared at each other. No one would ever understand what they'd gone through.

"Don't worry, it's nothing personal." Declan's eyes lowered, and he studied his fingernails, buffing them against the leg of his pants as if he had all the time in the world. "Seriously, a by-product of my vacation in hell. A little bit of extra mojo."

Nico was breathing hard, both from the ferocity of his emotions and the bottled-up rage that left his limbs trembling.

Julian could relate. He was barely able to keep it together.

"You're just like your father," Nico rasped.

Declan stilled, and, for a second, his true self was revealed. The air around him charged with electricity, and Julian smiled as the power surged forth. It danced upon the air, crackling and stinging their flesh.

Everything went quiet, like the sound had been peeled back, leaving a layer of thick white noise ringing in their ears.

Declan's face was devoid of emotion, but Julian knew how close he was riding the edge. Hell, he was right there with him.

Declan opened his mouth and was about to speak when a scream rent the night air. It was full-bodied and powerful, and it sang to the dead part of his soul.

It was the jaguar warrior battle cry.

It echoed on the night wind, then died, leaving the four of them in silence. The white noise disappeared abruptly, and everything came crashing back . . . the cool evening, the dark energy, and the need he felt to get to Jaden.

Julian whirled around and flew through the darkness as he ran toward the ruins.

Low-lying fog crept along the ground, mixing with the gray and the dark until the entire area was enveloped in a wall of forbidding mist.

They definitely weren't alone.

Julian slowed as he passed a wall of skulls, his nostrils flaring as Jaden's scent reached him. She was near. He could feel it.

"She's definitely in the temple, the outer sanctum." Finn spoke quietly, his manner grave. "I have no idea how she made it inside, or else I would have searched there first."

"What do you mean?" Julian asked harshly.

"The wards that protect the temple are strong, only an eagle can gain access unless . . ."

"Unless what?" Declan stepped forward, his face was tight and his hands were clenched into fists at his sides.

"Someone let her in," Finn said softly. "We need to hurry."

They followed the eagle knight, moving forward as a unit, paying no mind to the scent of danger. It was dark, cloying, and stank of otherworld.

Julian glanced at Declan. It was an odor they knew too well. A shiver raced across his flesh as an eerie groan drifted across the breeze.

The bastards sounded hungry.

They approached a man-made tunnel with caution, and as soon as they were swallowed by its damp entry, Julian's otherworld radar went into overdrive. The energy down here was thick, menacing. It mingled with Jaden's scent, and that alone enraged his animal to the point that his skin itched and burned.

Another scream filled the tunnel, and the pain across his chest tripled at the sound. The four of them erupted into a chamber, and the sight that greeted him stopped him cold.

An eerie glow caressed the damp stone walls, enabling

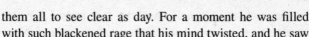

them all to see clear as day. For a moment he was filled with such blackened rage that his mind twisted, and he saw everything through a thick haze of red.

Deep red. *Blood red.*

The blood of whatever, or *whoever* the fuck it was that held Jaden like a rag doll.

He was aware of creatures, phantomlike beings that stood just behind Jaden, but it was the large asshole who gripped her by the neck that had all his attention.

Mist crawled up his legs as his body changed. His bones popped, and golden fur rippled along his flesh as the ancient magick took hold.

"Time to party, boys." He heard Declan's words echo in his brain and was vaguely aware that Nico was transforming as well, but his only thought was to get to Jaden.

The entity that held her turned eerie eyes toward them, and he sensed the madness that lay there as he shook the woman that he held.

Jaden's toes dangled several feet above the ground, and her hands hung loose at her sides.

Was she dead?

He barked loudly and the power of his jaguar flooded him as his hind legs bunched tightly. He sprang forward with a roar and leapt into the air, his heavy, powerful frame carrying him forward with ease.

Julian snarled in pain as his body slammed into them. The man was not wholly corporeal in this plane of existence, yet, there was solid matter to him. It burned, an incredible flash of heat that enveloped his entire body as they connected.

Jaden was another story. He hit her hard but was able to shake her loose from the monster's grip, and the two of them tumbled to the ground.

Nico was right behind him, the tall, powerful jaguar zipping by as he confronted whatever the hell these things were. An energy blast flew over top of his head, courtesy of Declan, and Julian positioned his body over Jaden's limp form as his mind methodically processed the entire scene.

Declan was weaving a spell into the air, his hands making intricate patterns as energy flew from him in sporadic bursts. He was protected, a ward already in place, safe to do whatever the hell it was he was doing.

Finn, however, seemed frozen, his face set with disbelief.

And the tall man in front of him, the leader it seemed, ignored them all, his eyes focused solely on Julian.

"How perfect," he said, and Julian shook his head as the man's weird amplified voice hung in the air between them. "The little bitch has a mate."

Julian snarled and faced him, his long tail waving back and forth as he prepared to fight. He'd tear the bastard apart before he let him touch the woman on the ground.

Behind him, a painful growl was torn from Nico, but Julian refused to turn around, though he was aware that Finn sprang into action as he swept by them in an effort to aid the other warrior.

Julian crouched low to the ground as he moved in front of Jaden, positioning his body in such a way that she was protected.

"You silly, pathetic animals. You know not what you deal with." The creature smiled wickedly and showed off a healthy set of razor-sharp teeth.

Julian's mind went still, and he pushed everything away, concentrating solely on the thing in front of him.

He bunched his powerful legs together, prepared to strike once more, and felt a rush of adrenaline kick in as he pushed off with a mighty shove.

The blackness inside him rose to the fore, and the dark power that lingered there exploded as he flew through the air, his jaws open wide.

His target's arrogance soon vanished as Julian once more crashed into him, this time prepared for the shock of pain. His claws dug in, clinging to the weird feel of him, and he ignored the fire that spread along his body as the man's arms closed around him.

He staggered back—his enemy—his legs nearly buckling under the weight and pressure of the large spotted jaguar. The two of them clung together in a macabre dance, and Julian snarled, exposing his deadly canines.

He strained against the man's hold, his eyes focused on his head and neck. The need to crush and destroy was so strong in him that all else faded away.

The scent that rolled off him was definitely otherworld, but it was unlike anything Julian had come across in the last year.

"Brave little cat, aren't you?" the man spit out, smiling sharply, though he grunted at the effort it took for him to contain the jaguar. "I will crush you, then eat the heart of your mate."

Julian snapped his jaw wider and threw his weight at him full force. The two of them struggled for several long seconds, each trying to best the other in a game of pure brute strength.

The man dug his fingers into Julian's side and Julian grunted in pain as the phantom's fingers penetrated fur to rip into his flesh. Julian twisted sharply, feeling a keen sense of satisfaction when his claws sunk in farther and he was able to push until they both crashed to the hard ground.

Julian landed on top, but the man was able to hold him off, and the jaguar's deadly canines were not getting any

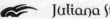

closer to his opponent's jugular. A groan from behind caught his attention.

Jaden? He stilled for but a second, yet it was enough for his enemy to shift and throw him off.

Julian rolled to the side, his powerful paws digging in and propelling him forward once more, but the man was no longer there.

A loud blast bounced off the walls and he looked toward the entrance in shock. Smoke and dust nearly choked him as the ceiling near the doorway crumbled downward, forming a large pile of crap that blocked the only way out.

The tall man grinned back at him, licked his lips, and snarled. "Now we get down to business."

Julian's powerful body was still. Declan looked like he was in a trance, his fingers feverishly weaving symbols into the air as sparks of energy flew from them.

Another groan sounded to the side of him, soft and feminine. He chanced a quick glance and felt relief at the sight of Jaden sitting up. She looked dazed, but when her eyes connected with his, something sparked deep within their depths. An understanding.

She rolled to the side and jumped to her feet, a long deadly dagger clutched in her hands.

Nico roared behind him, and Finn's cry of rage followed; they were pretty much cornered by the shadelike creatures.

Julian kept his eyes on the leader and slowly backed up until his body was next to that of his woman. He felt her warmth, heard the beating of her heart, and when her hand fell to the fur at his neck, for that one second, the pain, the anger . . . everything that was mad inside him faded away.

"Well, my eagle knights, looks like our evening has been enriched in ways we'd never expected."

Julian's instinct was to attack, but the hand on his shoul-

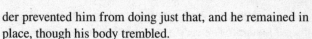

der prevented him from doing just that, and he remained in place, though his body trembled.

"Just wait," Jaden whispered. "Declan is up to something."

Julian's mouth hung open, harsh pants falling from within, his canines exposed and deadly. He forced himself into somewhat of a state of calm. He needed to be smart.

He stared at the man before him. Who the hell was he?

"He's Nanauatl, the eagles' sun god."

Jaden's voice whispered close to his ear. It was eerie, how much the woman anticipated his every move and thought.

The sun god stared down at him, his superior attitude plainly evident in the arch of his brow, the smile that tugged at the corner of his mouth.

He snorted and looked behind them, and as his expression changed subtly, Julian moved against Jaden, pushing her slightly to the side so that he could better view the entire scene.

Nico hissed viciously, spitting and growling at the crew who had him cornered, while Finn stood tall and met the gaze of their leader with a calm that surprised Julian.

He had no fear, and Julian felt a spark of admiration for the eagle knight as the powerful shifter came forward, passed the two of them and stopped just in front of the leader.

"You are one of us," Nanauatl whispered hoarsely, his nostrils flaring as he bent forward slightly. "A Knightly no less."

"I am Finn, son of Michael, brother to Skye," he answered solemnly.

"It is your family who lost the portal." The sun god's eyebrows closed together, his expression fierce as his face darkened. "Your line has grown weak." He nodded to the rest of them, a snarl ripped from his throat as his eyes passed over

Julian and Jaden. "And now you consort with the likes of them? Jaguars? The very people who've hunted our own for these last centuries? Our enemy?"

Nanauatl took another step, but Finn remained silent though Julian observed the clenched hands at his sides. He knew that the eagle knight was no match for any of them, without the strength he drew from the sun—he couldn't shift, and his power was diminished—but it didn't keep him from the fight.

Finn had honor.

"Who let you loose?" Finn asked abruptly. "I thought you were cursed to spend eternity etched in stone."

The sun god roared his displeasure as did his followers. Julian eyed them cautiously and noticed that Nico had been able to move closer to his position. The shadelike warriors were focused on the drama being played out between Finn and Nanauatl.

If the jaguars were going to make some kind of move, it would have to be soon. Jaden's warm hand dug into him once more as she knelt beside him. He noticed, for the first time, more bruising along her cheek and her neck. Blood ran from both her nose and her mouth, and he fought the urge to rub his head against her.

She looked at him, her large eyes dark as the night sky, and he thought they softened a bit. "Why is it every time we get together, I end up all bloody and shit?"

Julian growled softly and stilled as she grabbed him close, her scent invading his nostrils and pulling such savage need from him, that he barked and tried to back away.

She held fast, ignoring his action, and whispered hoarsely, "We need to get to Declan . . ." She pushed at him hard. "Now!" She glanced at Nico before pushing away and

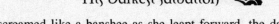

screamed like a banshee as she leapt forward, the dagger raised in front of her as if it were a shield.

Julian froze, for just a second, his mind not believing what he was seeing. Jaden twisted in the air, yelling at Finn to run, as she arced gracefully her face set in a feral grin.

"Hey asshole," she yelled, "eat this."

Declan shot a bolt of energy at Jaden, and it enveloped the dagger, burning an intricate series of etchings into the metal. The sorcerer shouted, "Julian, now!" It kick-started him into action.

His feet dug in, but he snarled as pain lanced across his back end. He whipped his head around, canines exposed and deadly. One of the shadelike creatures grinned at him, but then Nico ripped into the side of its neck, and though no real damage was done, the eagle knight faltered enough that Julian was able to escape.

Julian whirled back and glanced up, his heart nearly beating out of his chest as Jaden sailed through the air, end over end. Her arm was extended and the dagger sliced through Nanauatl, eliciting such a roar of pain and anger that the walls shook from the force of it.

She landed on the other side with a jarring jolt, and Julian was there in an instant, avoiding a blow from the sun god as he streaked by. Finn leapt in front of him, took the hit, and went flying from the force of it.

A great rumbling began underneath their feet and Declan's eyes burned a savage red as he held his hands aloft, glistening symbols dancing on the air in a strangely beautiful arrangement.

The phantom eagle knights bellowed as they tried to run past their sun god, but an invisible wall held them back.

The air was rank with dark energy. It rolled off Declan in

waves, and Julian didn't care to know what he'd tapped into in order to gain such power.

"Finn!" Jaden shouted, and she would have moved past Julian, but he held her still, his massive body shoved against hers even as she pounded her fist into his side.

"Get the hell out of my way," she screamed. "He's one of my men!"

Mist crawled along his body, and as the earth continued to groan beneath him, he let the magick take hold and pushed her toward Declan as his body shifted, the jaguar falling from his skin as his human form took over.

He ran toward the fallen man. Nico was there, and the two of them grabbed the eagle shifter as an incredible ripping sound sliced through the air. It was a sharp, keening noise, like nails raking along glass, and he shook his head as it pounded against his brain.

They reached Declan just as a massive hole opened beneath them, and the world fell away.

Chapter 16

Jaden came awake with a start.

At first she was disoriented, then slowly her mind cleared, and she became aware of a few things. One: it was cold, damp, and the air was stale, full of the smell of ancient earth. Two: there was a complete and utter lack of noise, which was eerie. And three: her body was pressed tight against a hard-bodied male.

The scent that flowed into her lungs was Julian's. She lay across his chest and felt each and every breath that he took. They were slow, measured, and even though she couldn't see his face, she was pretty sure he was unconscious.

To be truthful, she had no clue where she was or how long she'd been there. The last thing she remembered was the floor opening up and falling through, like a crazed Alice in Wonderland.

Except she was no Alice, and it wasn't a rabbit hole she'd slipped down.

Her head lay against Julian's shoulder. She carefully moved her body and rolled to the side, her back slamming up against cold stone. A wave of dizziness washed over her, and she paused as her body struggled to orientate itself.

She was able to see clearly. A wash of golden light made it possible, and though she couldn't find the source, she was grateful.

Her eyes swept toward Julian, and her heart rate increased as she rested them on his face. He looked younger and so much more vulnerable. An image of him as a younger man rushed into her mind and pulled bittersweet strings.

She didn't like this, these feelings the jaguar brought out in her.

Satisfied that he was all right, suffering from nothing more than a bump on the head, she raised herself on her elbows and turned away from him, but not before catching sight of the magnificence of his hard body. *Sweet Jesus, but does he have to look so incredible?*

She cleared her throat, rolled up onto her knees, and slowly looked around. The chamber that they were in was small, and she could see that part of it had caved in. There was nothing out of the ordinary; no artwork adorned the stone walls, no ceremonial pottery was lying about.

It was just a dull gray chamber that was given a bit of life by the eerie glow that lit it up.

She stilled and concentrated hard, her senses flying from her as she sought any evidence of the enemy . . . or of her men. But there was nothing. Only the heavy weight of a silence that was somehow louder than a stadium full of football fans.

She stood up and nearly fell as another wave of dizziness came over her. She swallowed and winced. Slowly, her hands rubbed the raw flesh of her throat.

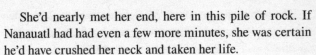

She'd nearly met her end, here in this pile of rock. If Nanauatl had had even a few more minutes, she was certain he'd have crushed her neck and taken her life.

Julian saved me.

The thought whispered through her mind as she turned back to the shifter, the intense need and longing that clutched at her heart was painful.

How could she feel this way? For a man who'd rejected her?

He groaned and flung his arm above his head, and her eyes fell to the scars etched into the flesh under his heart. They looked angry and raw.

Jaden knelt beside him and bit her lip as she glanced down his long form. He was completely naked, and as her eyes followed the hard, muscled lines of his body, heat began to build as her heart spiraled out of control.

He moved once more, his leg bending, and when his knee touched her, electric sparks of energy rippled across her flesh. Jaden whimpered as they shot across her body, and her nipples instantly hardened.

What the hell is wrong with me? The world was on the brink of disaster, she'd nearly been killed, she was trapped beneath Templo Mayor with a man she loathed more than anything, yet . . .

And yet her hand moved of its own volition and she found herself hovering over the marred flesh on his chest. The need to touch him burned heavy inside, it was an ache that settled between her legs, and she moaned as her jaguar shifted beneath her skin.

It wasn't her fault really. She knew she was at a delicate time in her cycle. That as a female jaguar, she was on the cusp, in heat, and the need to mate was strong.

Usually, she tried to sate the desire with whomever the hell she could, but it was never enough.

The only man who could complete her, who could temper the raging desire that simmered beneath her flesh, was Julian Castille.

How unfortunate.

For her.

She panted as images and pictures of their long-ago night flickered in her mind, and whimpered as she tried to force them away. But it was no use—her own erotic memories were burned forever into her brain.

She shook her head in denial, but the memories of Julian's body taking hers in every way imaginable, of an intense passion that rivaled hers . . . she knew many a night it was the only thing that had gotten her through.

How pathetic. Replayed fantasies and her handy-dandy vibrator.

Her skin itched and burned, and she threw her head back as a wave of heat suffused her entire body. A low, keening sound fell from her lips, and as it sliced through the silence, her hands fell to her chest, her fingers running over the aching nipples that strained against her T-shirt.

A throb pulsated between her legs, slow, heavy, and she ached inside.

She could smell herself, her desire and need, and even though shame scorched along her cheekbones, leaving a flush of red in its wake, she had no control.

"Oh God," she whispered, her vocal cords painfully bruised by the sun god's hands.

She moved slightly, but it only served to increase the friction between her inner thighs, and a sob escaped her lips as bolts of desire shot up from the hotness between them, to claw at her belly painfully.

Her hips began to move, and as she sat there, her body

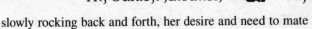

slowly rocking back and forth, her desire and need to mate killing her, she lost all desire to fight it.

Her hands continued to massage and caress her aching breasts, and she thought she was going to lose her mind when two male hands joined them.

Her eyes flew open, and she stared down into Julian's face. His eyes were intense, the deep golden depths reflected liquid honey, his long, dark lashes too sinful to belong on a man. She swallowed, and whispered, "I hate you."

His eyes held hers for several long moments. He moved slightly, positioning his legs so that she was ensconced between them. She was aware of his hardness, the straining length of him, but couldn't take her eyes from his.

His heart beat in time with her own, and she felt like crying, so high was the anticipation that rode her.

She wanted him. Badly.

He lowered his mouth and paused, only a whisper between their lips. She inhaled the air that fell from his lungs, and the yearning inside was painful. She growled, low and deep from her chest, then opened her mouth.

Screw the consequences.

When his lips met hers, she was ready, and her hands found their way to the thick hair at his nape. She pulled at him, groaning into his mouth as she took a taste and smiling against his flesh at the feeling that shot through her.

His tongue immediately plunged deep inside her mouth, and she suckled from him, the taste and feel of him hitting her hard in the gut. Each time his tongue passed over her lips, she felt the pull of it deep within the folds of her sex.

Sharp pangs of desire that left her damp and aching.

She kissed him long and hard, her jaguar raging with need as the minutes passed. When she broke away, she could barely breathe. Her skin burned, and her hair clung in damp waves to her neck and shoulders.

"I hate you," she said again, her hands falling to his shoulders and reveling in the strength that burned beneath his skin.

"You already said that," he answered roughly.

"You don't understand," she began, but his finger fell to her mouth, and she was silenced.

"Why don't you show me." His voice was barely above a whisper, rough, colored with an edge that screamed at her.

Molten heat rolled over her skin and slipped inside her, leaving her nerves quaking with need. She looked down at the erection between his legs and felt her mouth go dry.

Everything faded into the dull gray stone, leaving nothing behind but desire and painful need. In that moment, nothing else mattered except satisfying the urges that rode beneath her flesh with a ferocity she could barely manage.

She inched closer to him. The longing would never go away until she satisfied the cat.

Jaden rose onto her knees and pushed him so that his mouth was level with her aching breasts. She smiled down at Julian, loving the way the black of his irises bled into the gold of his eyes. The air shimmered around him, lighting up the taut muscles in a halo of energy.

Slowly, she reached for her waist, her fingers curling along the edge of her T-shirt, and she heard the breath hitch at the back of his throat as she carefully pulled it up and over her head.

His hands reached up once more, but she slapped them away, reaching around for the clasp of her bra and drawing out the moment into long seconds as she carefully let the slip of black fall from her skin.

She reveled in the cool air that swept across her breasts

and felt her nipples harden even more, the peaks turgid as they became engorged with a host of sensations.

His mouth was there before she had time to react, her hands fell to his thick hair as he teased and nipped at her. His tongue swept along the dark pink skin, which was now puckered, raw with desire, and a trail of fire followed in his wake.

She felt his hands creep up along her back, until she was held firm within his grasp and couldn't have moved if she'd wanted to.

He continued to tease, his tongue caressing her nipples until she thought she'd go mad. His mouth hovered above the soft flesh, and she whimpered once more as he blew over the wet skin.

And when she thought she could take no more, when the need between her legs was painful, his hot mouth enveloped the entire peak, and he pulled hard at her.

She moaned, loudly, as hot bolts of desire shot straight to the center of her core.

"Oh God," she whispered. "I can't . . . I've never . . ." She stopped abruptly as his teeth closed along the small hard bud, and held fast in anticipation as he continued to tease her mercilessly.

She felt her heat, the wetness that seeped from deep within, and she slowly gyrated her hips as he held her there.

"You taste like candy," he said, his voice vibrating against her skin in delicious waves that shot energy along her nerve endings.

Christ, what the man could do by only speaking.

"I like candy." The timbre of his voice changed, and she held her breath as he pulled away from her breasts and looked up at her. "It's been forever since I've had something sweet."

Jaden stared down at him, small pants of air escaping from between her teeth as she tried to get hold of her emotions.

The sight of his dark skin against the golden hue of hers was incredibly erotic. She cocked her head to the side and let her hand run along the clan tattoos that burned beneath her flesh.

And she smiled as his eyes followed the motion, the dark depths burning with a need that matched her own as her breasts swung in front of him. But it wasn't her nipples he was after.

He kept one hand at the small of her back, though he applied just enough pressure that she inched closer still, and when his other hand followed hers, intertwined with hers, she thought she would come apart.

His fingers caressed her clan tattoos gently, his eyes hooded and half-closed.

"They're beautiful." His words were simple, yet the emotion behind them was real. She could feel it.

It brought tears to her eyes. Did the man care about what they meant after all?

Did she care?

He continued to stroke them, and the tattoos pulsed beneath his touch, her eyes closing as she drifted off into a haze of sensations.

When his hand left her body abruptly, she couldn't help herself. "Don't . . ." she whispered but her voice died in her throat as she gazed upon a deadly, feral beast that both excited and scared the crap out of her.

Julian's eyes had morphed into large round balls of black. All of the gold vanished, and the vicious nature of his jaguar was reflected in the depths. He snarled softly, hissing as her hands fell to the scarred flesh of his chest.

He flinched, the lines of his face shifting like shadows, and she stilled as the energy around him darkened. When he flipped her onto her stomach, she didn't know if she was surprised or pissed, or just plain confused.

Something had just changed.

The cold earth was now at her breasts, hard against the softness of her flesh, and she began to protest but stopped abruptly when she felt his tongue at the base of her neck.

He kissed her along the ridge of her ear, and her entire body shuddered in reaction. All conscious thought fled. Any warning bells had died abruptly. His hands on her flesh calmed her beast, soothed her soul. And as much as she wished it was anyone other than Julian, she could not deny her animal. She could not deny that Julian Castille was her mate.

Everything melted away, save for his rough hands upon her flesh, and when she felt his fingers at the waistband of her jeans, she lifted her hips, smiled as he pulled them from her roughly.

She lay there beneath him, as naked as he, and groaned when his fingers sought the hot wetness between her legs.

"I see commando is your thing," he whispered close to her ear. "I'm not surprised at the easy access."

A twinge rippled through the haze of pleasure that she felt. There was something in his voice, but the animal inside her pushed it away, keen only on mating.

She felt his hardness at her ass, the warmth of his large frame as he slid over her. He held himself above her body with one hand, while the other continued to stroke the slick walls of her sex.

His long fingers had no problem finding the treasure he sought, and she spread her legs slightly, angling her hips up until she touched the hardness of his belly.

His breath quickened, short spurts of hot air against the back of her neck, and she groaned loudly as his long fingers plunged deep inside her aching walls.

"Christ but you're tight." His words were hoarse, and his teeth scraped along her shoulder as he sought the magic spot so deep inside her.

"Nico know how to do this?" he asked roughly, and the world went dark as he shifted, his thumb rubbing along her clitoris while his fingers applied just the right amount of pressure to kick-start an orgasm.

She felt the walls deep inside her body begin to convulse as a flood of cream fell from within.

"What?" she asked dazedly, not sure if he'd even spoken.

"Or this?" he said sharply, and warning bells clamoured deep within Jaden's sex-induced fog. He pulled her ass back toward him, spreading her legs wide as the tip of his cock rested against her swollen, exposed center.

"Does Nico satisfy you?" He continued to manipulate his fingers, creating all kinds of magic.

"Nico?" she asked dazedly as she shuddered with the strength of an orgasm that filled her body with liquid heat.

"When he fucks you, does he satisfy the animal like I can?"

Jaden's mouth fell open, her chest tightened, and she squirmed as anger rushed over her. This was wrong. All of it.

But then he was there, deep inside, and she bit her tongue instead.

He was large and filled her with ease. She heard him breathing behind her, felt the hard length of him swell until she thought she could take no more. And when he slowly began to move, she thought she would die from the sheer pleasure that rolled over her.

Shame colored her cheeks and ripped across her heart.

There were no more words, no tender encouragement. This was a joining that fed the darkest parts of their souls and filled a need long ignored.

Jaden pushed aside all thought and arched her back as he quickened his tempo, his long cock sliding in and out of her with torturous measured strokes. Each pass spread fire along the way, and the walls of her womb constricted and vibrated as he pounded against her flesh with a savage need that was answered deep inside her.

The tattoos along her neck burned, her chest felt like it might explode, and, deep within, a crushing orgasm was brewing. The sounds of flesh against flesh reverberated inside the chamber, and when Julian's teeth broke through the skin on her shoulder, when his hands cupped her breasts and massaged her aching nipples, a low, keening growl erupted from deep inside her throat.

She felt her jaguar shift beneath her skin, felt the ancient magick surround her as he slammed into her flesh. When her orgasm crashed through, and she felt him shudder against her skin, in that moment, clarity opened her eyes.

Slowly, her breathing returned to somewhat of a normal state, and she felt a rush of cool air against her heated flesh as he withdrew. There were no tender words, no soft lover's endearments.

There was nothing. She felt empty, and though her desire was sated, it was bittersweet and left her wanting.

It was a cold dose of reality.

Julian rolled away, and she wrapped her arms around her body, squeezing her eyes shut in an effort to force away the tears that pricked the corners. They infuriated her, and she clamped down her teeth tightly. She had no time to cry for things lost and those that would never be gained.

Julian Castille was her mate, and that would never change. But she'd never let him use her again, regardless of how much she needed the physical bond.

Not like this.

She would die before she'd let that happen.

Chapter 17

Julian turned from Jaden, needing some space between them. Though he knew he was acting like a total fucking asshole, he'd been unable to stop himself. Such was his curse, this need to hurt and punish. This disregard for feelings.

It was easy to do when you had none. His were long gone, torn in half and buried beneath layers of pain. He knew he was on the edge of crazy, and it was only a matter of time before he was lost forever. Each hour that he spent in the human realm destroyed a little bit more of what was left of his soul.

If he and Declan didn't find the portal and return it, they'd both be done within the week.

He ran his hands along the puckered flesh beneath his heart and hissed, his frustration nearly blinding him with rage. He felt like he was coming apart, and the loss of control was something that pissed him off. It was something he'd just taken back, and he'd be damned if he'd give it up so easily.

He heard Jaden move, felt the air stir as she gathered her clothes, and he turned to watch her in silence.

She'd pulled on her jeans and was about to don her bra and T-shirt when she looked up and paused. Long waves of silken hair slid across her skin, and she made no effort to hide her nakedness from him.

Her full breasts showed evidence of his passion. He saw small blemishes, love marks along the soft curves, and the nipples remained turgid, hard peaks under his gaze.

Her eyes shimmered as if unshed tears filled them, and for a second, as their eyes connected, something inside him twisted.

It soon passed, and he rolled his shoulders in an effort to alleviate the tension he felt.

"The answer is no, by the way."

Her voice was muted, no animation or emotion.

He remained silent, an eyebrow raised in question. What the hell was she talking about? She pulled the T-shirt over her head and shook out her hair.

She smiled though her eyes remained cold. "Nico."

She began to walk slowly, her head turned from him as she studied the chamber they were in. "I haven't had sex with him, so, no, he's never fucked my animal into submission."

A hint of bitterness entered her voice. "You win that award. Hands down."

Julian was surprised by her admission, and if he was truthful, there was a part of him that was pleased by her words.

"So now that you've satisfied my itch, we can put this behind us and forget it ever happened." She cocked her head and turned to him, cool as a cucumber. "Are we clear?" she asked softly, an edge to her voice.

Julian nodded, feeling the dead space inside him expand and pulsate. "I have no problem with that."

Liar.

"Good," she retorted sharply.

Something flashed across her face, a fleeting wrinkle of pain, but it was gone just as fast. The intimacy of the moment, if it had every truly existed, had all but disappeared.

"We need to get out of here," she said, her voice neutral, devoid of emotion, "and you need to get some clothes."

Julian glanced down at his nakedness. "Sorry if it offends, but there's nothing I can do about it at the moment."

"Whatever," she muttered. "Glad it's not my bits hanging out."

She turned once more and ran her hands along the stone wall. The damp chill of the earth at his feet slowly crept along his flesh, and he shivered slightly as it clung to him.

The smell down here was brutal, old and stale. He inhaled sharply, his nostrils flaring slightly as the lingering scents of their sexual encounter teased him.

He shook his head, cleared all thoughts from his mind except one, and that was getting the hell out from beneath the temple. Time was fleeting. If the portal wasn't retrieved, if Azaiel wasn't dealt with and Cormac destroyed, the consequences would be unimaginable.

"Why did you come here?" he asked abruptly as he walked toward the wall, his eyes traveling along the gray stone as he studied it closely. "What did you think you'd find?"

"Answers." Her tone was matter-of-fact. "Kragen said something to me that got me thinking about the whole situation, about Azaiel and the portal. I realized I don't know shit about the fallen, about his connection to us, and I need to know everything because when I find him, this ends."

Julian ran his fingers along the stone, and his hand caressed the rough surface. It pulled at something deep inside him, and, for a second, he felt humbled by the history it represented.

Hundreds of years before, someone had carved this from the earth. Some Aztec man who'd wanted a temple for his god. He shook his head. It still stood, had somehow survived the test of time. Amazing.

"Only he who created the portal can destroy it," Julian murmured, more to himself than anything.

"Or an eagle knight can seal it, I get that."

"Then what the hell are we doing here?" He felt anger tickle inside his mind. "We should be searching for Cormac and Azaiel, not fucking trapped beneath a temple." He snorted. "Hell, the sex was good, but we could have done that anywhere."

Jaden's mouth tightened, and the color of her cheeks darkened noticeably.

"I didn't ask you to follow me, so quit your bitching." Her eyes narrowed. "How did you know where I was anyway?"

"I figured out your password and hacked into your computer."

"My password?" Her cheeks flushed red, and he smiled. "I'm flattered."

"Get over yourself, Castille. I chose a password that no one would ever guess. There was no other reason."

He changed the subject. "Why have you not had sex with Nico? He follows you around like a pathetic pup."

"We will not discuss Nico again," she hissed, angry at his baiting. "I care about him, but his feelings are . . . misplaced."

"So you only screw men that you hate?" Julian was at her side in an instant, savoring the heat of her flesh as it caressed the bare skin of his body. He flashed a wicked smile down at her. "Good to know."

Her eyes looked like glass, deep reflections of the pain and anger that burned beneath her skin. He heard her heart beating strong inside her body, and though she would deny it, he knew that she was still aroused.

Her animal was ready. He could smell it.

Julian's smiled widened. He could take her again if he so chose. His eyes fell once more to the vibrant clan tattoos that shimmered along the side of her neck. They pulled at him, deep in his gut, and his hand rose, but her long fingers closed around his wrist and held him in place.

The two of them stared at each other for several long moments. Her chest rose and fell slowly as she stood there, her stance wide as if on the attack. She was strong, a warrior, and her fierce, passionate nature was something to behold.

He could snap her arm in two. She had no idea what he'd become, yet he let her dig her claws into his flesh and push him away.

"Let's get something straight. I'll never let you touch me again," she said hoarsely. "This here was a one-off. Maybe I was too close to death and needed that connection, I don't know." She pushed long ropes of hair away from her face, the strands sticking to her moist flesh.

"What I do know," she continued, "is that time is running out, and I've missed something. I can feel it, a piece of the puzzle . . . it's tied to the eagle knights and Azaiel." She looked at him, her face earnest. "He created the portal for

Toniella, but why? Why did she want it? Why was he cursed into hell, and what happened to her? It's like all mention of her has been wiped clean."

Julian shrugged. "The answers you seek will be found once we locate Cormac and Azaiel. There's nothing down here."

Jaden raised an eyebrow. "It's no coincidence that I came across a demon on the way inside. They're watching the temple, like they're waiting, and the dude I wasted said something that . . ."

Her voice trailed off, and Julian's radar began to pulse. He turned to her.

"What did he say?" he asked, trying his best to control the urges that were falling through the cracks with too much ease. There was too much at stake, and if she was going to get in the way, he might have to resort to drastic measures.

Jaden stilled, and she looked away as she bit her lip in concentration. Her brain was working overtime, calculating, wondering. She clenched her hands together, and he got the impression that the woman would love nothing more than to crack his skull open.

She looked at him and spoke softly, a deadly whisper. "He said it was *the others* they were gunning for." She paused. "What are you not telling me?"

Julian's mouth tightened into a thin line, but he remained quiet. It was obvious certain factions knew what he and Declan were up to. They'd stop at nothing to keep the fallen from being returned to the upper realm.

"What do you know? What did you learn down there?" Her anger flushed her face a dark crimson. "Did you make some kind of deal with the devil or something? Are you his bitch now?"

She was hitting a little too close to home.

"I answer to no one." *Liar.*

"Yeah"—Jaden eyed the mess beneath his heart—"sure." She snorted. "You spent six months underground and somehow miraculously escaped. A little dark and twisty, mind you, damaged for sure, but you're out."

"Lady, you have no idea," he spit out; his voice was rough.

"You keep saying that, but I think it's a little too convenient. Are you going to elaborate?" she asked, and shook her head. "Don't bother, I've a feeling anything you're willing to give up will be nothing more than a bunch of bull anyway."

Julian's gut tightened again, twisting harder. "Our agenda is the same. Find Azaiel and the portal."

"It better be." She turned from him and began to feel along the wall once more, her long, elegant fingers caressing every nook and cranny. "But if you and Declan are hiding something," she continued, her back to him, "you can bet your ass I'll find out what it is."

Julian clamped his mouth shut as an image of the woman from below flashed through his mind. She of the ethereal light—giver of unimaginable pain.

"Do you think this is part of The Temple of the Warriors? Because it looks like nothing but a pile of crap to me."

Deftly she changed the subject, but he knew she wouldn't give up. He chose to play along and was about to answer when a low-intensity rumbling began to build. Vibrations fingered their way out along the earthen floor, tingling up his legs, and he watched Jaden spring back from the wall in alarm.

"What the . . . ?" she said, glancing back to him quickly.

The entire section in front of her had caved in, most likely when they'd been sucked beneath the temple floor.

The limestone began to glow an eerie shade of green, and the entire pile pulsated as if it was being squeezed from the inside out.

The wall began to moan, and as the air shimmered around it, symbols appeared, then disappeared. Weird illuminations that were snatched from the air.

Julian grabbed her arm, and they both ducked as the wall exploded, and the entire chamber was filled with dust and debris.

He pushed her behind him, coughing, as his lungs filled with the ancient crap that floated in the air, and he gritted his teeth as a voice floated toward him.

"Jesus Christ, Castille, this ain't no nudist resort."

Declan stepped through an opening the size of a fridge and grinned at the two of them. "For God sakes man, I'd cover up if I were you." He cleared his throat and nodded. "It's a little cold in here, no?"

Julian glared at the sorcerer, ignoring the obvious taunt.

Declan reached around and pulled something from the satchel that hung across his shoulder. "Lucky for you I'm always prepared."

He threw a pair of jeans at him and winked at Jaden. "Damn shifters always losing their clothes."

Julian pulled the soft denim up over his legs and had just snapped the jeans closed when Nico and Finn slid through the opening.

"What the hell happened?"

Nico's nostrils flared, and Julian felt a keen sense of pleasure as the jaguar inhaled the remnants of his sexual encounter with Jaden. He watched as the shifter's gaze moved over Jaden, and a ghost of a smile slid across Julian's face as Nico turned to him.

"What the hell did you do to her?" he snarled. The jaguar

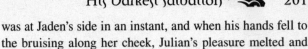

was at Jaden's side in an instant, and when his hands fell to the bruising along her cheek, Julian's pleasure melted and disappeared into a black hole of anger.

Jaden's hand fell to Nico's, and Julian clenched his teeth together so tightly, his jaw throbbed.

Nico's massive chest expanded and fell in rapid succession, and his anger was such that his voice shook when he spoke. "I will kill him."

"It's all right, Nico. It wasn't Julian, it was . . ."

An understanding passed between the two of them, one that spoke of a closeness, an intimacy Julian didn't much care for. It left a knot in his gut, but he backed away. He wanted no claim on the woman, and she could take what comfort she wanted from whomever.

"Your father," Nico finished.

Jaden nodded tightly and moved away from the shifter. "You know how he likes to play rough."

An uncomfortable silence fell between them all.

Julian rolled his head, trying unsuccessfully to alleviate the tension that hung on his shoulders.

"Where'd you get those?"

He glanced at Finn. The eagle knight was staring at the artwork etched into the flesh beneath his heart.

His teeth flashed white though the smile never reached his eyes. "You think this is interesting, you should see O'Hara's."

Declan made a face. "Unfortunately, the bitch was honing her skills on me. She perfected them by the time she got to you."

Julian remained silent and watched as the eagle knight ignored them both and moved to kneel in front of the far wall.

Jaden walked toward Finn. "What do you see? What is this place?"

Finn moved his hands over the stone, and Julian heard the eagle knight hiss softly. He followed Jaden to Finn's side, and, in seconds, they were all gathered around, but as far as he could see there was nothing but dull, gray wall.

Finn continued to run his hands over the wall. "This is amazing," he whispered. "This is one of the original chambers, a place of ceremony and great magick."

"And you can tell this how?" Declan asked casually, though he glanced at Julian, his eyes flat, his mouth thinned into a tight line.

"Symbols and etchings tell me everything." Finn's hands grazed over the stone in a slow, methodical gesture.

"I can't see shit," Declan said.

Jaden pushed Declan out of the way and knelt beside Finn. "Does it tell us anything about the portal? What do you see?"

Julian held his breath, and as Finn shook his head, he let it out slowly.

"These are more like ceremonial prayers." He looked up at them. "It was a chamber used to prepare and orientate the original eagle knights."

"And they did this, how?" Declan asked.

"By sacrifice," Finn answered quietly. "Human sacrifice."

"Nice ancestors you got there," the sorcerer said as he turned away. "Though I suppose we've all got skeletons."

"There has to be more," Jaden exploded. "What about Toniella? What happened to her? Who cursed Azaiel into hell? Was it Nanauatl? Or someone else?" Her chest heaved, and Julian could tell she was barely holding on. "Who or what the hell do I need to track down in order to find that son of a bitch?"

Jaden twirled around, her hair flying everywhere, and Julian found himself mesmerized by the sight. "We need to seal the portal, Finn." She shook her head, and whispered, "You know this . . . or we're totally screwed."

Finn sighed. "Sorry, Jaden, a lot of what happened is cloaked in mystery. What we do know is pretty bare-bones. The original eagle knights and jaguar warriors were created to protect the portal, among other things."

"Until several of the jaguar clans went rogue and wanted the portal for themselves," Julian inserted.

Finn stood, stretching out his long limbs. His features remained neutral, but Julian sensed the darkness that slid beneath his skin. "Until your people all but obliterated the eagle knights from the earth. It's a goddamn miracle we managed to keep the portal hidden for so long."

"Well thanks for the history lesson and all, but are we in agreement this has been a wild-goose chase?" Declan looked at them all. "Seriously, it's been fun watching you guys get your asses kicked, but it doesn't change the fact that we're stuck down here, and we need to be"—he pointed upward—"topside."

Julian glanced around. Declan was right. Cormac was out there with Azaiel and the portal.

"You got any suggestions?" he asked the sorcerer. "You brought us here. Can you open it up and get us out?"

"Sure, let's go party with the sun god and his band of seriously fucked-up phantom knights. They'll be happy for another chance at your ass."

Julian clenched his teeth together. He felt a myriad of strange sensations. They had him on edge and slid over him as he began to pace. "We need another way out."

"No shit," the sorcerer answered.

Nico had moved toward Jaden, and the sight of her surrounded by the jaguar and Finn totally screwed him the wrong way.

"She's something else," Declan said softly as he stood beside Julian.

Jaden turned toward him, and as their eyes connected, the anxiety and anger inside him vanished completely. It startled him, that moment of clarity. She looked away, put her hand on Finn's shoulder as the eagle spoke to her quietly, and the moment was gone.

"She's not for me," he answered roughly. "She can't . . . we can't . . ." His voice trailed off as his thoughts turned to the mission at hand.

"Dude, if we don't get to the portal first, we're both screwed, and you'll never know."

Julian looked at Declan and frowned. "Know what?"

The sorcerer looked away, and murmured softly, "Peace."

The tightness around his chest burned as the white noise in his head broke through. It was almost unbearable, and he had to concentrate hard in order to minimize it so that he could breathe again.

He knew what the edge of madness felt like. It had been his constant companion for the last six months, and, right now, it was knocking on his door hard.

Time was running out. He glanced at Declan.

For the both of them.

Something caught his attention then, a tingle of energy that didn't belong. His animal shifted, and he was immediately on edge. Someone was there.

A cough sounded from just outside the chamber. It was low, rumbling. He swung around and bared his teeth.

"What the hell you boys doing down here?"

Two long legs stepped through the opening, and Julian

relaxed as a tall, powerfully built man slipped inside. His eyes were a crazy shade of silver-gray, and they shimmered in the gloom. He spit to the side, and his mouth opened into a smile.

"Welcome back," Cracker said gruffly as he looked at Declan and Julian. "You both look like shit."

Chapter 18

Jaden watched as Cracker crossed to Julian and Declan.

"How the hell?" she asked, shocked to see him.

"Jaxon dispatched him to the area. If you'd checked in with us before leaving, you would have known that."

She ignored Nico's reprimand. "How did he get down here?"

Nico's eyes were fixed upon the ex-soldier. He shrugged his shoulders. "I have no idea"—he moved away from her—"but I'm going to find out."

Jaden watched as Julian shook the man's hand. Even with Cracker, an old friend of the Castilles, he was stiff, awkward. Her gaze fell to the scars on his chest.

Something twisted inside her as she studied them covertly. The skin looked raw, the edges of the scars red and tender. She could be mistaken, but it looked like there were more than before. Was it possible?

Julian stepped back as Declan and Cracker exchanged

greetings, his face was blank, devoid of any form of emotion. She studied him for a few moments, noticed the whiteness around his mouth, the lips clamped tight, and the stiff line of his shoulders.

He looked up, and, for a second, their eyes met, and she was taken aback by the pain that hung deep in their depths, however briefly. He looked haunted.

The moment passed just as quick, and the cold hard lines of his face returned once more.

She turned away from the men, and whispered to Finn, "You sure there's nothing here?"

Finn shrugged his shoulders. "Not that I can see, but I've not had time to explore yet."

Jaden bit her lip as her eyes wandered back to Cracker and the boys. Nico had moved toward them, and they were deep into conversation. She glanced back at the opening in the wall, then looked down at Finn.

She nodded and slipped through, the eagle knight right behind her.

This chamber was much larger, the air cool yet still thick with the damp stale odor of old earth. Again the walls appeared to be nothing more than bare, gray rock. She followed Finn as he passed his hands over the ancient limestone. Energy sizzled along his fingers, yet nothing was revealed to her.

"You see anything?"

"No." Finn sighed. "There's nothing here."

Jaden swore and paced in a circle. Her skin was slick, flushed with the sheen of sweat, and she shivered as cool air rushed over her body. Her teeth chattered, and the nervous energy in her gut was making her nauseous. Time was running out. Had she just wasted a precious amount of it?

She'd been so sure she'd find answers here. Instead, she'd found a crazy sun god and his band of freaky phantom knights.

She sighed in frustration. It was an emotion she was getting way too familiar with, and she gritted her teeth as her gaze followed Finn. He moved along the walls, his hands touching the surface carefully. She heard muted conversation coming from the small chamber they'd just exited.

"How did you find us?" she asked suddenly.

"We came from there." Finn pointed to a passage to the left of her. "It wraps around to just behind the chamber you and Julian were in."

Now that she took the time, she could see there were several offshoots from the chamber she was currently in.

"Oh." She was curious. "How did you know we were just beyond this wall?"

Finn cleared his throat and bent down to study the wall in front of him.

"Finn?"

"Uh, Nico knew you were . . . uh, in there with the Castille shifter."

"But how did he—"

"He could hear you."

She blushed. Heartily. Something she'd not done in years. Just fucking wonderful, she thought.

Finn stopped several feet from her, his arms outstretched, palms facing the wall and energy flying from them in small sparks. Several seconds later, he fell to his knees, and whispered, "I found something."

She was at his side in a second, watching again as his hands passed over the stone.

"What is it? What do you see?" she asked roughly. The

etchings and symbols embedded in the rock were only visible to an eagle knight.

Finn grinned up at her. "There is a small room." He turned and pointed to the far corner. A narrow opening could barely be discerned against the rough wall. It was nothing more than a shadow. "It should be through there. It was Toniella's."

"Toniella's? She lived here at the temple?"

Finn stood up, and she followed him to the opening. "Apparently so. If I'm reading these symbols correctly, she spent her entire life in the temple."

Jaden digested that bit of information and followed Finn as he slipped through the narrow passage. It was dark, claustrophobic, and Jaden was happy her nocturnal vision allowed her to see clearly. The walls were damp, and she thought she heard running water. The sound was dead and the oxygen thin.

The passage widened and eventually they found themselves in a small but impressive room. It was lit, eerily so, and the source seemed to be coming from within the huge pillars that fortified the four corners.

She stopped and stared in wonder at the ancient art on the walls. Here in this chamber they were abundant, beautiful, and vibrant. She had no problem whatsoever seeing them.

There were many drawings of eagles in flight, basking in the sun, of nature and the beauty of the Aztec culture. The sun figured prominently, and in the center of the far wall, a rendering of the sun god himself stared down at her.

It was an incredibly accurate drawing. Her hand rose to the tender flesh of her neck as she looked away. Nanauatl's hands had nearly done her in. Too bad the bastard wasn't trapped in the stone.

She crossed over to a low-lying bench and picked up a small object. It was an eagle, painstakingly crafted from clay. Again, it was intricately done, and she marveled at the talent it would have taken to reproduce such a gifted piece.

"Skye would love this," Finn murmured, and she crossed over to where he stood. He held up an impressive headdress made entirely of feathers.

"How has it survived all this time?" Jaden asked, her fingers reaching out to stroke the soft beauty of it.

"This is not a normal dwelling. There is heavy magick at play, strong wards. I can feel them, their subtle signatures."

Jaden exhaled and nodded. She felt it, too, the weight of history. "The only reason we broke though is because of Declan."

Finn shook his head in agreement. "Yeah, makes you wonder at the impressive nature of his magick." The eagle knight raised an eyebrow. "He's got some seriously jacked-up mojo going on."

Finn crossed over to a dais located beneath the huge drawing of Nanauatl. He bent over it, and she watched as he ran his hands over the top, inches from the limestone. He studied it, hands out. Jaden followed him and grabbed hold of his hands.

Finn paused and looked at her in surprise.

"I want to see," she whispered. "Jagger told me Skye showed him amazing things by doing this." She moved closer and slipped between Finn and the dais.

The eagle knight hesitated, and Jaden paused. Their energy was different. She knew on some level she made him uncomfortable. "I'm not going to bite you," she said lightly. "Let's do this."

Finn slid his hands over her forearms and she smiled in wonder at the sight beneath their fingers. Light danced upon the dais, golden showers of energy that appeared luminescent against the dull gray. As their hands passed over the limestone, images and symbols appeared.

"It's beautiful." Jaden was in awe. "What do they mean?"

"It's a story, a pictorial rendering of fact." He paused as their hands continued to glide over the stone. "It tells of Azaiel's fall and Toniella's betrayal of her people."

Long moments of silence passed as Jaden let Finn move her hands over the entire surface with exact precision. They passed over an etching of a tall man who was colored black and gold. "This is Azaiel," Finn said, and he pointed toward a rendering of a woman. She had long, flowing blond hair, and the sun was held in her hands. "This is Toniella . . ."

He stilled, his hands held in midair, and Jaden glanced to the side sharply. "What's wrong? What does it mean?"

"Everything makes so much more sense now," he murmured.

"What? What the hell are you talking about?" She glanced down at the weird-shaped symbols next to the picture of Tonialla.

"She was a true daughter of the sun. Nanauatl's daughter."

The sun god himself? Jaden's eyes widened as she continued to study the picture. She was shocked. Seriously surprised, and that was saying something. "Damn, that must have been like the best-kept secret ever. How could you not have known that?"

Finn shrugged his shoulders. "He's a powerful entity. A god. For whatever reason, he hid her origin." Finn studied the pictures for a few more seconds. "Maybe he was ashamed. I don't know."

"What happened to her?" Jaden was curious.

"They were both banished from this realm. It doesn't say

where, only that darkness would feed their souls for all eternity."

"Well, we know where Azaiel ended up," she murmured, her eyes not leaving the dais.

Finn pointed to another set of drawings. "Nanauatl is forever tied to this temple. I think there's something he wants to keep hidden."

"Toniella and her link to the portal," Jaden answered. "No one knew it was she who tempted Azaiel from above. If he'd not told Skye, we never would have known . . ."

The eagle shifter nodded in agreement. "That would be my guess." He continued to move their hands over the dais. Several more symbols followed in an intricate series, and Finn spoke quietly as he retraced their tragic story.

"Azaiel was of the highest order, one of the Seraphim, a powerful and true entity who served his god. And yet he was tempted by her beauty, by her charm, and he fell in love with her. He could not see what was inside her. He fled the upper realm to be with her and became one of the fallen. He brought his light to the people here, and he bestowed the power of the eagle on them, and when she asked him to create a portal that would . . ."

Finn stopped abruptly, and Jaden glanced back at him, her eyebrows furled in concern.

"What's wrong? She wanted him to make a portal that would open the gates to hell. We know this."

"No." Finn shook his head, and she shivered at the dead tone of his voice. "There's more."

Jaden went still and glanced up at him. The eagle shifter was solemn, and his eyes reflected a bleakness that she felt deep in her gut. Christ, could nothing go as planned? Be easy? Was their path always going to be littered with crap?

"More? I'm almost afraid to ask."

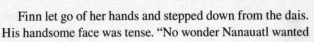

Finn let go of her hands and stepped down from the dais. His handsome face was tense. "No wonder Nanauatl wanted this place hidden."

"What are you talking about? What could be worse than his little whore of a daughter cajoling a freaking angel into constructing a portal that can open up the depths of hell?"

She grabbed his hands once more. "I need to see."

The symbols that were revealed beneath her fingers meant nothing to her. Frustrated, her voice rose. "Finn, what the hell does this shit mean?"

"It means the portal is the most powerful thing ever created."

Julian's voice drifted between them, and they both turned as he and Declan slipped into the chamber. His eyes were flat, the golden depths dark and somber. There was no expression, just a flicker of something she couldn't really describe as his gaze lingered on the two of them.

Jaden let go of Finn's hands and stepped away, suddenly uncomfortable and not really sure why. She looked back at Finn. The eagle knight avoided her eyes and looked away. Something major was going on.

"But what does that mean?" Her words exploded in a rush of air. "An explanation would be good right about now." She looked back at Finn. "What is Julian trying to say?"

Finn ran hands across his temple and exhaled. "Our world is made up of layers, the human realm being one of many. This portal has the ability to open several of them." Finn glanced toward Julian, and the look that passed between the two men set her teeth on edge. She clenched them together, ignored the pain that sliced its way along her jaw, and looked at the both of them.

"No talking in riddles. I need this laid out real precise."

Julian turned at her words, and again she was taken aback

by the utter lack of emotion in him. "It means the portal is not only a direct conduit to the demon realm, it can also be used as a path to the upper realm."

"The upper realm," she echoed. "Like heaven?"

"Bingo. That would be it, the penthouse suite," Declan answered.

Shocked silence followed his words, and Jaden didn't quite know what to say. The thought of someone like Cormac managing to rip open hell was bad enough. The human realm would suffer greatly, would in fact never recover.

But what would happen if he successfully opened a path to the upper realm? The battle would be unprecedented, their world forever altered.

"Sounds like one hell of a party, don't you think?" Though Declan grinned at all of them, she sensed his anger. The energy around him thickened as his eyes narrowed. "I can't wait."

She crossed to Julian and stood within inches of him. She heard his heart beating, saw the pulse at the base of his neck. Her gaze wandered to the scars under his pectoral before traveling back up to his face.

"Is this what you and Declan are hiding? Why didn't you tell me the other night?"

A muscle worked its way across his cheek, but he remained silent, his golden eyes narrowed on her.

Her animal reacted, and her fist flew out to thump him in the chest. Hard. "What the hell is wrong with you? You're acting like a fucking zombie."

Her gaze fell on Declan. "Seriously, why would you keep such crucial information to yourself? This situation has just gone from shit to worse."

The sorcerer's eyes glistened, and his teeth slashed white

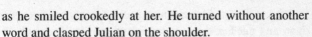

as he smiled crookedly at her. He turned without another word and clasped Julian on the shoulder.

"You wanna fill her in?" he murmured. "Secret's out, sport."

Jaden stared at the two of them, her chest heaving and a truckload of emotion threatening to break through.

"My reasons are none of your concern." Julian stared at her and bared his teeth, before glancing toward Finn. "This information must stay between us. You do understand the consequence if it gets into the wrong hands."

Finn nodded and remained silent. Julian turned to leave.

"Do not walk away from me," Jaden shouted at his back. She rolled her shoulders as she tried to contain the anger that was agitating her cat something fierce. She could not believe he would keep something so important from her.

The others slipped into the chamber and were greeted by Declan. "I think maybe we should leave them alone, it seems they have some issues to work out." Declan nodded to Finn and turned back toward the passage. "We'll give you five minutes. Then we need to vamoose."

Jaden bit the inside of her mouth and ignored the pain as she watched Cracker and Finn follow the sorcerer from the chamber. Nico, however, refused to follow and took several more steps until he was inches from her. He was angry, his hands clenched to his sides.

She knew he wouldn't leave unless she told him to. "Go, Nico, I'll be fine. Castille and I need to . . . come to an understanding of sorts."

The jaguar turned eyes that were as flat as obsidian on Julian, and Nico growled menacingly. "If you touch her, I will kill you."

"You could try, but it wouldn't end well for you."

Nico took a step toward him, but Jaden stepped between them and put her hand on his chest. "Nico, I'll only be a minute." She watched as conflicting emotions ran over his handsome face, and, in that moment, Jaden wished with all her heart that Nico belonged to her.

Her life would be so much easier.

Instead, she was forever linked to a man who disliked her as much as she did him.

"Go," she said softly. She felt Nico tense beneath her touch. He looked down at her and didn't bother to hide the need, the pain that lay there. She knew on some level he thought of her as his. That she was his responsibility.

She also knew it was a facade. The man had loved intensely and lost everything. He still belonged to Bella even though she no longer walked the earth.

How would it feel to have someone love you that way? She ached at the thought.

"Please," she whispered. He glanced at Julian once more. Her gaze followed Nico as he left the room. And then she was left in silence with the man who twisted her insides so badly that she felt ill.

"We need to tell Jaxon and the others." Her tone was matter-of-fact as she turned back to Julian.

"No." His one-word answer was simple, yet she sensed the intensity of his resolve.

"You're unbelievable," she snorted, and threw her hands in the air. "You think you're the Lone Ranger or something? Riding in to save the day? That's not how it works."

"No one can know. It's bad enough you are in possession of such knowledge." His eyes glittered, their depths like liquid honey. He moved quickly, gliding across the room with the sensuality and grace of his animal. "No one can be trusted."

"You think Jaxon would betray you? Jagger? Are you fucking nuts?" she huffed, impotent anger burning her insides. "I'm no fan of Jaxon. Hell, he's just as arrogant as you are, seems to be a Castille trait. But I do know he'd protect what's his with his life." She looked at him, her eyes wide. "You're his family."

Julian blew out hot air. She felt the caress of it against her cheek and shuddered as it fell across her skin. Goose bumps broke out along her arms, and she kept herself stiff, when all she wanted to do was wrap herself tight and gather a bit of warmth to her.

She was so cold and tired of it all.

"I know my brothers would give their lives for me," he answered harshly. "I can't vouch for anyone else in their organization. If word gets out about the true power of this portal, every sick and depraved son of a bitch is gonna want in on this game. Your enemies will be tenfold within hours."

She opened her mouth as anger lit her tongue, but nothing came out. He was right. As much as it killed her to admit it, he was. "I hate secrets," she whispered instead.

Julian smiled then, his even white teeth a contrast to the dark color of his skin. Her breath hitched in her chest, and an unfamiliar ache took hold.

"I'm surprised. Secrets seem to be second nature to you." His gaze moved to the clan tattoos that lay at her neck, and his hand followed them. She flinched as his fingers caressed the intricate design. "DaCosta jaguar, yet you belong to a Castille."

His eyes were no longer golden but flecked with specks of black. His voice was rough. "I wonder," he continued, but then stopped.

"What?" she mouthed softly, strangely entranced by the moment.

"If we'd met under different circumstance. If we didn't"—he exhaled—"have all this shit to deal with, would we still feel this way?"

Jaden gazed at him, her heart tight with emotion. "How do you feel?"

Julian frowned, his hand fell from her flesh. "Confused, empty, and filled with a craving for something that belongs to me but I'm not sure I want."

Her chest split into slices of hurt, yet she kept her face devoid of emotion. She would never let him know how much his cruel words tore at her.

"Just so you know, for future reference, it's *you* who belong to *me.*"

Calmly, she stepped away from him.

"Who pulled you from wherever the hell you were?"

Julian studied her in silence for several long moments.

"Look, if I'm going to keep this on the down low and work with you to recover this portal, I need to know everything. Bottom line, you come clean with me, and I'll consider all our options."

He exhaled harshly and she knew that he was struggling with something.

"Who was it? Who do you answer to?"

His right hand crept over the scars on his chest. "I don't know," he answered.

"What do you mean you don't know? How can that be?" She was incredulous and didn't believe a word he'd just spoken.

Julian cocked his head to the side and shrugged. "I know nothing of him other than his name, Bill."

"Bill," she repeated. He had to be joking. Yet why did the name tug at something inside her? What was she missing?

There was no time to figure it out at the moment. She filed it away.

"Bill," he said again, though she got the impression he was worlds away from her.

"So, this *Bill* released you from . . . where?"

He closed his eyes. "A place of darkness, despair, and constant pain."

"Why?" she asked as she watched him closely. She hated the sliver of compassion that she felt. The man was all kinds of wrong for her. He'd used her even though she apparently meant nothing to him.

You used him, too.

She banished her inner voice and focused on the reality. She had every reason on earth to hate the very sight of him, but . . . there was something that called to her, and it was more than just the fact she'd claimed him as a mate three years earlier.

Something pulled at the strings inside her until she was turned inside out with a need to touch him. *To comfort him.*

Julian's eyes flew open, and her heart turned over at the savage look that hung in them. He growled, low and deep, from his belly, and stepped away from her.

Her eyes fell to his hands. He clenched and unclenched them, and she knew he was close to the edge.

"Why?" He laughed harshly. "Simple, really. Declan and I have the motivation needed to do whatever it takes to get the job done."

"And I don't?" she asked incredulously. "I've given up the last several years of my life in order to find the fucking thing and make sure it's sealed forever."

Julian's eyes darkened until the gold was gone completely. The dangerous edge she'd sensed earlier rose to the fore and draped his powerful shoulders in a caress of darkness.

He smiled, a cold, calculated grin that did nothing to warm the lethal look in his eyes. "Lady, if we're not successful in finding the portal, I'm screwed for eternity. The pain, the darkness that eats at me every second of every day will win. It will never stop."

Her gaze fell once more to the scars on his chest, and he thumped them with the palm of his hand. She winced as he did so but couldn't look away.

"Pretty, aren't they? They're a constant reminder of what I've lost."

"And what's that?" she asked hesitantly, not sure that she really wanted to know.

"Half of my soul was ripped from me, taken in pieces. Tiny fucking pieces." His eyes bored into hers, and she swallowed thickly at the intensity of his gaze. "Every minute that I'm in the human realm, a little more of my soul dies. If we can't get to the portal and destroy it within seven days, we'll be lost forever. Hell on earth will be living inside me, and I'll never recover."

He would be like one of *them*. The shades that had wandered aimlessly in the underworld, feeding off the bottom like rabid dogs.

His fingers rubbed the raw edges of his scars. "Even now I can feel it, eating at me, destroying anything that is good and honorable." He drew in a long breath, his dark eyes steady on hers, his teeth bared. "I told you I was nothing like before. If you were smart, you'd stay far away. Who knows what the hell I'll be in a few days, or even tomorrow?"

Jaden was silent, and even if she wanted to say something, her vocal cords were frozen.

His mouth twisted into a feral grin. "I'll be neither

human, nor shifter . . . I'll be nothing more than a vessel of empty space and doomed to live that way for eternity."

He turned from her and moved toward the passage, leaving her to stare after him.

"So yeah, pretty damn good motivation, don't you think?"

Chapter 19

Jaden watched Julian disappear through the small passage, his tall frame barely able to clear the ceiling. A shiver rolled across her skin, and she hugged herself tightly. There was just way too much to process, and none of it was good.

Her mind was tired; hell, her body was pretty much done, yet there was still so far to go. Her fingers ran along her forearms, and an image of Julian's dark skin against hers planted itself in her brain.

Such sadness grabbed at her soul. It puzzled her that he could pull such intense emotions from her.

Angrily, she pushed them away and moved toward the passage. There was no time to linger; they had no such luxury.

Cracker glanced up as she swept inside and nodded, a smile tugging the corners of his mouth. "Hey, Rambo."

Her feet slid to a halt and the first genuine smile she'd felt in forever touched her lips. He'd been calling her Rambo since they'd first met in the jungle in Belize several months earlier. She'd been tracking a demon, intent on gathering intel, when she'd run headlong into Jaxon's soldier.

Literally. She knew firsthand that Cracker's head was hard as rock.

He was ex-military, and they all knew he wasn't human. His signatures were different than any she'd come across. She'd asked Jaxon once about Cracker's origins. The jaguar had shrugged his shoulders, said it wasn't important. The only thing that mattered was the fact that he trusted Cracker with his life.

It had been enough for Jaden, and she'd not dwelled on it again.

"Hey," she answered, as her gaze swept the room. She stopped as Julian's dark eyes regarded her from several feet away. Nico stood with Finn and Declan, and suddenly she felt hot, uncomfortable, as all eyes strayed to her.

She turned back to Cracker and shook her head, "Let me guess. You just happened to be in the neighborhood and thought you'd drop in? Are you going to share how it is you managed to get down here?"

Cracker's silvery eyes crinkled as his grin widened. "I got connections."

She laughed at that, relaxing a bit as she moved closer to him. "Really," she murmured. "How'd you slip past the sun god and his band of merry men?"

She arched an eyebrow as he spit to the side.

"Nanauatl owes me a few favors," he answered simply, his words dead serious as the light moment passed.

"He owes you a favor?" She looked from Cracker to Finn, then back to the soldier. Unbelievable.

"We should probably get out of here before the bastard

reconsiders. He's not the most stable." His eyes shifted to behind her. "He's also not terribly fond of jaguars or magicks."

Jaden stepped back. "No kidding."

Cracker nodded and turned. "Follow me."

Julian watched as Jaden disappeared down the passage behind Cracker, Finn and Nico following behind. He let out a long, painful breath, unaware he'd been holding it until he did so.

"You all right?" Declan asked quietly.

"Fucking wonderful." He glanced at the sorcerer. "We're no closer to finding the portal, my body feels like it's cracking into a million pieces, my brain won't stop, and that woman is driving me nuts." He shook out his limbs loosely. "I'm jonesing something fierce and not liking it one damn bit."

"You didn't tell her everything, I hope."

Julian sighed and shook his head. "No."

"Good. You need to hold it together, sport." Declan's face darkened. "We've got a date with my father, and I aim on keeping it."

He followed Declan and quickly climbed the ancient stairs that were revealed at the end of the passage.

He alighted within the temple chamber and felt a gentle woosh as the stone rippled behind him, and the passage was once more hidden. His eyes immediately sought Jaden. She stood stiffly beside Cracker, her head held proud as she gazed up at the sun god.

Nanauatl's phantom knights were several feet away, and he saw the soft beam of morning's kiss drifting into the darkness from outside. The entrance was once more free of debris. He ran his hands along his temples and up through the thick hair atop his head.

He couldn't remember ever being this weary. Not even after six months in hell had he felt so tired. It wasn't just his body. His mind and spirit were lagging. Dread sat low in his belly, and the noise that was a constant in his mind spiked as he let the weakness slide over him.

It stilled everything inside, but only for a moment, then he shrugged it off, like he'd crush a bug, and focused on the dark energy that was still heavy in the air. It energized him like a drug.

He felt like a fucking addict.

"The secrets held within these walls must stay," Nanauatl said harshly, ignoring them all and focusing solely on Cracker.

"I give you my word," the soldier answered.

"It's not you I am concerned with." The sun god nodded toward their group though his eyes remained on Jaden. His lack of respect and the intensity of his gaze rubbed Julian the wrong way.

He took a step closer to her, not realizing he'd done so until Nico shot him a dark look and stepped between Julian and Jaden. His anger was instant, harsh, and cutting, and his chest rumbled as he bared his teeth.

His control was eroding, faster than he'd like, and it pissed him off to no end that his instability was out there for everyone to see.

Nanauatl turned his attention toward Julian, and he clutched his hands at his sides tightly, holding himself rigid when all he wanted to do was hurt. Someone. Or something. It was irrational, this need to inflict pain. But then, how could someone who wasn't whole be rational?

"You will leave here, Jaguar, and never return. Find the portal, destroy it, and you might find peace. But before you go . . . a word."

"Ah, no. Whatever you want to say to him must be shared. The secrets have to stop," Jaden inserted, her chest heaving as she turned her stormy eyes his way.

"Do not defy me, Jaguar," the sun god thundered, his voice echoing crazily inside the confines of the temple. The energy darkened, and Julian took a step forward, ready to defend the woman who stared up at Nanauatl with so much defiance.

"My courtesy does not extend to you." The air shimmered around him as his phantom knights inched closer. Their eyes were lit from behind, small spools of gold, and they began to make low, keening noises, their excitement palpable as the violent energy in the room spiked.

Cracker rolled his shoulders and turned toward the entrance. "It's best we get going, Rambo. As much as I'd like to see you kick his royal ass, there's no time."

Jaden's dark eyes turned to the sun god, and her lips pinched together tightly.

"Screw you, asshole," she muttered under her breath as she turned to follow Cracker from the temple. Nico fell in behind her, and Finn left with them.

Declan arched an eyebrow. "Am I invited to this party?" he sneered, his hands held loosely at his sides. Julian saw the sparks that lit up the air around them; he felt the energy shifting in the room and knew that Declan was itching to fight.

It was seductive, the need to instigate chaos and cause pain, but Cracker was right. There was no time.

The sun god moved forward, his feet gliding across the earthen floor in a rush until he stood before them. The energy that sizzled along Nanauatl's body was intoxicating, powerful, and Julian felt the pull of it as he gazed into the eyes of a god.

The emotion held deep within them surprised the hell out of him. Nanauatl was struggling with something.

"Did you see her?" the sun god asked quickly, his voice low, his words rushed as if he were scared anyone should hear.

"Her?" Julian repeated, not really understanding.

The sun god's face darkened, and the earth began to tremble beneath them. "Toniella."

An ethereal face flashed before him, one with long, elegant lines, classic features, strong hands that gripped the special dagger. The dagger of pain.

Julian glanced at Declan. The sorcerer was studying the sun god, his cold eyes intense. Declan grinned wickedly as he spoke. "I heard she was hanging down in District three, which is about one step away from where the real nasty shit happens."

Nanauatl turned his attention from Julian and focused fiery eyes on Declan. "Do not toy with me. I will crush you."

Declan shrugged his shoulders. "You could try"—he winked—"but I was being serious. She's down there. Most popular whore there is, last I heard. Demons favorite tramp I think—Gang Bang Toni they call her."

Nanauatl bellowed his rage, and Julian readied himself for battle as the phantom knights roared along with their god. Time slowed as Nanauatl rushed toward Declan. The noise inside Julian's head deepened, and his animal shifted, eager to join in the fight.

A wall of energy flew up, a barrier of magick that was incredibly powerful. Julian looked at Declan in surprise, then back to the sun god, who stood inches from them, his visage comical as he tried to break through.

"You've been feeding on some heavy shit, O'Hara," Julian said quietly. He was barely able to contain the animal inside him. The darkness that he was inhaling agitated his animal something fierce, and he was trembling with excitement.

It was intoxicating, every last wretched shot of it.

He watched and relaxed as the sun god struggled with his inability to get to them. His rage and anger penetrated the barrier, but he wasn't able to break through.

"I will kill you, Sorcerer. Rip your entrails from your body and feed them to my knights."

"I'd like to see you try," Declan rasped as he turned. His dark eyes were empty, and the smile that graced his face was cold. "Let's go; I've spent far too much time in this pile of crap."

Julian started to follow Declan when Nanauatl spoke once more. The sun god's voice was rough and filled with emotion.

"Jaguar, stop."

Julian paused. He shrugged, his white teeth a slash through the gray. "It's not Club Med down here."

Julian quickly followed Declan from the temple and welcomed the rush of fresh air once they cleared the tunnel. The early-morning quiet was heavy on his ears, yet it did nothing to soothe his soul. Warmth could already be felt creeping over the horizon. He cracked his neck and looked up to the sky. It was going to be a bitch of a day.

He thought of the human populace, asleep and unaware of the evil that was fast approaching. Humanity was so fragile and at the mercy of an entire realm of existence most of them had no knowledge of.

Cracker nodded to him. He looked past the soldier, his

gaze resting on Jaden as she stood silent, her eyes hidden by the sweep of her lashes, her thoughts concealed.

He sniffed the air and felt his animal rouse as the unpleasant stench of demon lay on the breeze in subtle doses.

"They're still around," Cracker said. "I wasted a few on my way in, so watch where you step."

Julian glanced down to his feet and moved to the right, avoiding the patches of demon leftovers scattered about.

"Why are they here? What do they want? How did they know we'd be here?" Jaden asked, and she studied Cracker closely as the soldier spit into the dirt.

"The entire underworld is in chaos. They're gravitating toward anyplace where they think there might be clues that will help them find Cormac and the portal . . . or anyone else on their hit list."

Julian's eyes narrowed. What did the soldier know?

Cracker glanced at him, his tone matter-of-fact. "There are hot spots the world over right now. We've got teams dispatched everywhere."

"That's just great." Jaden shook her head. "The shit is about to hit the fan in a major way, and we've got our forces spread so thin, we'll be lucky if we can find our own asses." She glanced at Julian, and he felt his stomach muscles clench together tightly. "There's not a lot of time to get this done."

"No," Cracker agreed, "there's not, but there's no reason to give up hope." His eyes flashed, a weird silver-gray shining eerily in the early-morning light. "Jaxon wants us to rendezvous at PATU in Canada. He's got intel but wouldn't share, even over a secure channel."

"What kind of intel?" Julian asked as he glanced toward Declan.

Cracker shrugged. "Dunno, but it's got to be important

if he wants us all there." The soldier's eyes narrowed as they bored into Julian's. "And that includes the two of you by the way."

The thought of seeing his brothers again should have filled him with joy. Yet he was ambivalent, detached.

Julian looked away. There was nothing inside him except the constant raw pain that gnawed at his guts and the white noise that lingered in the background.

"The jet is waiting outside of town on a private airstrip. We need to leave asap."

Half an hour later, Julian found his large frame tucked into a soft leather seat as the plane thundered down the runway. As they lifted off and ascended into the sky, his eyes found the dark head he'd been trying to avoid.

Jaden was seated next to Nico, and he hated that the shifter was so close to her.

"Like I said before, you need to tap that." Declan's soft voice cut through the fog that had settled around his brain. The sorcerer was seated across from him, and Julian didn't much care for the sloppy grin that fell across his face. "Oh, sorry, guess you already did."

Julian snarled and lunged forward, his hand going for Declan's throat, his long fingers sliding across his neck with ease. Declan did nothing. The pounding in Julian's ears receded as he slowly let go.

He was aware that all eyes were focused on him and ignored them as he leaned back in his seat and stared out the window. His heart was still beating madly, and it took every ounce of control he had to calm himself.

Below him, the earth lay, dazzling in the face of a strong sun, but all he could think about was the impending doom. His gut was tight, heavy with the knowledge that they'd most likely be too late. It was a crapshoot, really, and one that would either win him his life or leave him to wallow in the depths of hell for eternity.

"You boys hungry?" Cracker nodded toward the galley. "There's plenty of food back there."

Declan stretched out his long legs and smiled. "Cool, I'm fucking starved. But the real question, my friend, is do we have a nice dark ale? I'm thirsty as all hell."

Jaden rose and walked past Julian, her head turned to the other side. She was doing everything in her power to ignore him. He knew the truth. He felt the pull as much as she did.

He groaned, slid deeper into the soft leather, and closed his eyes hoping that sleep would come. He couldn't remember the last time he'd actually slept.

Down below, sleep brought nightmares, the kind that you could feel, the kind that left you bloody and banged up when you awoke.

"A bitch, isn't it?"

He ignored Declan.

"You asleep?"

Julian exhaled loudly.

"Didn't think so."

"What is it that you want?" he asked roughly, his eyes still closed, though he knew any thought of sleep was nothing more than a far-fetched dream.

"I want . . ." Declan's voice trailed off, and Julian cracked an eye open. He was astounded at the raw display of emotion that blanketed the sorcerer's face. It was etched into the depths of his eyes.

Declan turned to him, and, in an instant, it vanished, leaving nothing but the cold, calculating man he'd become in its place.

"I want peace," he said simply, "and I'll get it." He turned away, his face half-hidden as he gazed out the window.

Julian saw his long fingers tremble as the sorcerer grimaced. "The moment I rip Cormac's heart from his body, that's when I'll have it."

Julian said nothing. He closed his eyes once more. For the sorcerer's sake, Julian hoped like hell Declan would be able to find his peace, that revenge would fuel his road to recovery.

His gut told him otherwise. He had a feeling that even when it was over, it would never end.

Chapter 20

They landed in Canada in the middle of a snowstorm. It was mid-December and to be expected, but after spending the last nine months in either the hot jungles of Belize or the burning fires of hell, the cold and snow were not really things Julian was excited to experience.

A blast of frigid air greeted him as he exited the plane and kept his head low, trudging through slippery snow as he followed Cracker and the others. Jaden was still avoiding him and kept close to Nico. Their whispered words had ticked him off the entire trip. He'd pretended sleep but in reality nearly lost the battle to smash his fist into Nico's cranium.

The thought alone brought a half smile to his face.

The wind was cutting, lashing at his skin with snowflakes that felt like bullets. His shoulders were wound so tight, he winced in pain as he stopped in front of a large SUV.

The door flew open, and he stepped back as a set of lean legs encased in skintight jeans and tucked into boots—

which were totally inappropriate for the weather—slid from
the truck. The small, trim woman who stared up at him was
something fierce to behold, her long, amber waves billowing
around her delicate face. Her pale skin was a dramatic contrast to the crimson shade of her lips, and a glimpse of fangs
could be seen as she smiled.

She squared her shoulders and nodded to him as her
focus shifted to the man at his side.

Julian glanced at Declan, then slipped past Ana before
disappearing into the truck. He slid into the far corner, his
eyes drawn to the driver. He didn't recognize him, but the
smell of otherworld clung to his frame.

Cracker slid into the passenger seat up front, and Julian
watched in silence as Jaden climbed in. Her dark eyes caught
his, and for that one brief moment, the craziness inside him
subsided, like the layers of noise and pain had suddenly been
peeled back.

She paused in the doorway, her body still, though he
could see her pulse beating fast against the crook of her
neck. He wasn't aware of anything but Jaden, her long hair,
the small tilt of her nose, and the generous curve to her lips.
Her dark eyes glistened eerily in the late-afternoon gloom,
and he focused on one solitary snowflake that lay against
her cheek.

It was perfect, the design brilliantly displayed against her
golden flesh, and he envisioned his tongue licking it from
her. The taste and smell of Jaden invaded his nostrils, and
they flared as his heart sped up, and his breaths came in
rapid spurts.

Slowly, her hand reached for her face, and she wiped
away the snowflake, as if she knew exactly what he was
thinking. Her eyes widened, ever so slightly, and she looked
away, cleared her throat.

"Jaden, I'm freezing my ass off, so it'd be great if you could get that pretty butt of yours moving." Declan's sarcastic voice ruined the moment, and Julian looked away as she slid into the seat behind him, Nico and Finn following suit.

Ana stepped in and sat next to him. "Damn, Julian, if your board of directors could see you now, they'd be crapping their pants for sure."

Julian glanced at Ana but remained silent.

He noticed the tense set to Declan's lips as he closed the door and sat on the other side of the vampire.

"Seriously," she murmured, "as much as I'm sure it totally sucked hanging in the demon realm, you gotta admit . . ."

"Admit?"

"It's made you one hell of a badass, and you weren't exactly pleasant before."

"More like asshole." Jaden's whisper surrounded him, and he saw Ana smile.

"Is Father running Blue Heaven?" he asked suddenly, his thoughts turning to the company that up until several months ago, had meant everything to him. Under his care, Blue Heaven Industries had tripled in growth. It was the premiere manufacturer of communication devices in the world, and he'd brokered several huge contracts with the military.

"Your father has made sure that the family business stays afloat. No worries. When this is all over, you can return to your old life."

Ana's words sank in, and he settled back into the seat, his eyes drawn to the window and out at the swirling snow. The wind continued to howl, pushing the flakes into a chaotic dance of white. It looked as confusing and frenetic as his life. Return to his old life?

What a fucking joke.

Julian closed his eyes and rested his head against the

seat. It would never happen. He was forever changed, and he knew it wasn't for the better. He was ruined, damaged beyond repair, with a hole inside him that even if he was able to patch, would never fully heal. How could it?

Bleakness sat heavy in his chest, and he felt the burn of his scars bleed through.

"Where are we?" he murmured, caring enough for the first time to ask.

"A few hours north of Toronto. Jaxon has set up his new headquarters near a town called Gravenhurst. It's a vacation hot spot for the Canucks in the summer. Lots of water, cottages, money."

"Lots of fucking snow," Declan observed dryly, and Julian felt a smile tug at his lips. The Irishman was bang on.

The rest of the ride continued in silence, all of them deep into their own thoughts. Twenty minutes later, they turned off of the main highway, and the truck plowed through a snow-covered road that was barely more than a path.

They passed several homes, all of them expensive, large. Some were lit up with colorful display of lights in honor of the impending Christian holiday, most were empty. Julian sat straighter in his seat and gazed ahead, his eyes fixed on the large structure that could barely be seen over the thick stand of trees that blanketed the entire area.

They were weaving along a twisted lane, the elevation dropping, and he assumed they were headed toward a large body of water. He could smell it in the air, the cool crispness of ice. Though the wind continued to howl and throw snow at them, making visibility nearly impossible, the driver had no problem navigating his way through. He was obviously familiar with the area.

A few minutes, later the truck slid to a slow crawl as they

made a left and approached a massive gate. They came to a full stop, and he watched with interest as they were approached by two guards.

The driver's window slid open and after a few words were exchanged, the gate retreated, and they were able to drive through. They took a sharp turn to the right, and several moments later, the trees thinned until they disappeared, and a large home came into view.

It was massive, and he saw several smaller buildings scattered on either side. Julian was impressed. Jaxon had managed to make his new headquarters both a home and a state-of-the-art base of operations.

They pulled in front of the main house, and, as he slid from the interior of the truck, he tried to ignore the nervous energy that pulled at his gut. He blew out a harsh breath, and was startled when he felt Jaden at his side.

"Guess it's been a while since you saw your family," she said simply, her voice husky and low.

She looked up at him, her dark eyes like pools of black licorice, and his hand moved before he even knew what he was doing. She flinched when his palm touched her cheek, and as her energy mixed with his, the biting wind and driving snow disappeared, and there was nothing but the two of them.

He stared down at her, hoping the intense need he felt wasn't reflected in his eyes. He wasn't used to this, these feelings of want. They confused the crap out of him.

"It's Jaxon." Nico's rough voice cut through whatever the hell it was that held him in his grip, and his hand fell away as he turned from Jaden and glanced up at the house.

Several silhouettes could be seen, their dark outlines eerie shadows against the light from within the house. The two tall ones in front were his brothers. This he knew, yet, there was nothing inside him. No joy. No anticipation. Just . . . *nothing*.

Julian frowned as he followed the rest of the group up the stairs until he was inches from Jaxon and Jagger. The two brothers stood shoulder to shoulder, united, linked on a level he couldn't understand anymore.

Jagger smiled, a wide sweeping grin that transformed his handsome face into that of the young boy Julian remembered. He was enveloped in an embrace that was rough, genuine, and still he felt nothing.

"Christ, it's good to see you again," Jagger whispered into his ear before letting go. The youngest Castille laughed at him as he pulled away. "Damn, Julian, don't be so serious."

Julian arched an eyebrow, his expression wooden. "Well, Armageddon is pretty fucking serious, don't you think?" He ignored Jagger and turned to Jaxon, nodding curtly before he spoke. "I hear you have intel. Time's running out, so I suggest you get us up to speed."

His abrupt manner, the harshness of his words, clearly shocked his brothers, yet he didn't give a shit. He had no need for hugs and well-wishes or deep conversations where he bared his soul.

He looked away from them, frustrated and pissed off. A blond woman caught his eye, her smile was tremulous, but it was the child at her side, staring up at him, that stopped him cold.

He knew instantly who it was: Logan. Jaxon and Libby's son.

The dark eyes looked at him with no fear, and he broke from his mother, ignoring her protest. Julian felt a spark of admiration for the child. The kid had spunk, he had to give him that. The youngster stopped in front of him, his dark eyes surrounded by the Castille eyebrows and high cheek-bones.

His hair was longish, dark waves that caressed baby-soft skin.

Julian sensed the energy that surrounded the boy, and it was surprisingly strong. His signatures were not wholly shifter. There was something else. Something powerful. Magick.

Julian frowned.

The little hand reached for him but hesitated in the air, inches from his own. Julian was aware of all eyes upon him. He knew that Jaden was close, inches from his back, and that Declan and Ana stood several feet away.

For a second, he nearly turned. The need to disappear was overwhelming, and he thought how easy it would be to lose himself in the cold and snow that surrounded the compound. How easy it would be to let his soul slowly break apart until there was nothing but darkness inside him.

He could give in, say fuck it, and let whatever happened lead him to wherever the hell that road would take him.

And yet as he gazed down upon the chubby cheeks of the small boy in front of him, he felt a glimmer of hope. A touch of heat inside him that was gone just as fast.

The little boy's hand moved, and Julian did nothing to stop him from clasping his large index finger. The child pulled at him gently.

"Come on," he said simply, his face breaking out into a shy smile. "I want to show you my doggie."

Julian let the boy lead him forward, and he nodded to Libby as he passed her.

"Hey," she said softly, the merest whisper of a smile gracing her face.

His throat felt tight, and he kept silent as he walked into

thc house, very much aware that everyone was still watching
him. It made him uncomfortable, the attention.

"Well, holy Christ, what about me? My ass was burned
just as bad if not worse down there, ya know. A little tender
lovin' would be much appreciated." Declan's sarcastic comment followed him inside.

Julian cracked a genuine smile and shook his head.

"And we should care about your ass because?" Ana interrupted.

"Baby, you know you care. I mean, it's one hell of a fine
specimen, don't you think?"

Their words faded away and so did his smile, as little
Logan tugged at him and squealed in delight. The clatter
of nails across tiles echoed into the room and he glanced
toward a bundle of golden fur that ran at him crazily.

The dog skidded to a halt, its feet sliding across the floor
until it nearly crashed into them. Logan let go of Julian's
finger and wrapped his small arms around the young dog's
neck, giggling the way small children do. The sound was
musical, notes of glee that fell from his lips.

The child looked up at him, his smile wide. "This is my
Shelby girlie; do you wants to pet her?"

Julian cleared his throat and shook his head.

Logan frowned. "She won't hurt you. I promise. She bit
Skye once, but that was an accident."

Awkward didn't begin to describe the energy in the room
as he stared down at the boy helplessly. His feet felt like they
were entrenched deep in cement. He wanted to act but was
frozen in place. It was frustrating, and he felt the hole inside
him widen.

"I don't like dogs." The words slipped from him, and the
boy's frown deepened.

"What's wrong with you?" he asked before his gaze settled on someone behind him. "Mama, why is the dark mist around Uncle Julian? I thought that was only for bad men."

He heard Jaden inhale sharply, then heard her whisper, "This child is how old?"

He turned away, scowling as he caught sight of his brother. "I didn't come here for a family reunion. I heard you had intel, so either we get to it, or I leave."

Jaxon's eyes narrowed. He nodded to Libby. "Have Mr. M get Logan for dinner."

Libby walked toward them, and though she smiled up at him, he sensed her wariness, a slight hesitation. The last time he'd seen her she'd been very thin, beaten down, having just been rescued from the clutches of the DaCosta jaguars. She was a different person today—happy, healthy.

Wearily, he ran his fingers through his hair. It seemed so long ago.

A lifetime, yet it had only been months.

Her hand strayed to the top of Logan's head. A healthy glow kissed her cheeks, and the love she felt for her men, the child and Jaxon, was easy to see.

"Julian," she said simply, and she rose onto her tiptoes as she slid her arms across his shoulders. She hugged him fiercely, and though he held himself stiff and kept his hands at his sides, a part of him welcomed the warmth, the touch. He closed his eyes as she whispered into his ear.

"The ghosts will go away. This I promise."

She let go and stood back. "Logan, why don't you take Shelby to the kitchen and feed her? Mr. M is in there waiting for you; we'll be along in a bit, okay?"

The small boy ran to his father and gave Jaxon a high five before calling the dog after him.

Julian felt detached from the domestic joy his brothers had found. Jaxon and Libby were screwed if they thought they could raise a child in this world and have a happy ever-after. The security they enjoyed was false. He knew what was coming.

He paused as his eyes fell upon Jaden. She stood a few inches away, and, as her eyes caught his, a calm blank facade slid into place, masking her feelings once more. But not before he saw the yearning and want she held inside her. *For a child.*

The two of them stared at each other in silence. He was aware of movement, of Cracker and his brothers having a muted conversation. Of Finn and the woman Skye, his sister, talking excitedly to each other. Of Declan and Ana standing stiff as boards, each trying like hell to ignore the other.

Of the child Logan and his mother Libby.

None of them touched anything inside him except the woman who stood directly before him. She held her head high, and though her lips trembled slightly, and her eyes reflected back at him like liquid glass, she was in control. He could feel it, her strength.

She deserved the life his brothers had managed to eke out of the chaos that had rained down upon them. She wanted it though she denied it.

Suddenly, Julian was filled with a need to make sure she got it, or at the very least had a chance at something half-normal. *How fucking crazy is that?* In the midst off the mess he'd found himself in, he, a Castille shifter, cared about a DaCosta.

No matter that she was his mate. He wouldn't be around to claim that legacy. Had no interest in it, but damn if he wouldn't try to make sure she started a new one. Was it possible for her to claim another?

The constant burn that fed upon his skin quickened, but

he ignored it and felt the white noise recede as he clenched his teeth together.

He turned from Jaden. Nico waited in the wings.

He'd find the fallen and return him to his maker. As much as he'd like nothing more than to kill the fucker himself, that was the deal.

No one but he and Declan knew the truth: Azaiel *was* the portal. They were to recover the fallen and return him to Bill. In return, they'd get back the shredded pieces of their souls—and the pleasure of serving Bill for the next thousand years.

Or fail and fall into darkness.

Yeah, he knew his future was pretty much fucked, but he would do whatever it took to make sure Jaden had a shot at hers.

Chapter 21

"Follow me."

Jaxon Castille's crisp voice cut through her thoughts, and Jaden jumped, her eyes falling from Julian as she glanced toward the other Castille brothers.

Jaxon nodded to the right, toward an imposing set of double doors, a polite smile gracing his features though the look in his eyes was frosty. It irritated her. She'd not expected open arms or anything, but hell, they'd been working on the same side for years.

Jaxon had never been comfortable working with a DaCosta. Had in fact protested when she'd been given her own unit though he'd relented somewhat when he'd become aware of her undercover activities. He knew she was on the right side and had thought they'd put his distrust behind them.

Apparently not.

Skye walked toward her, and Jaden felt a stab of jealousy

hit her hard. She watched Jagger, who was a few feet away. He couldn't take his eyes off her. They stalked the woman as she moved through the room. In spite of everything—she being an eagle knight and he being a jaguar—the two of them had found something special, something worth fighting for.

She was happy for Skye, *really,* yet it was bittersweet. She couldn't lie to herself. The woman had found something she'd never be able to claim—true love and everything that went with it. To have a man look at you with such raw need was something she could only imagine.

The problem with imagining such things was that it led to hope. Her gaze strayed to Julian once more. They belonged to each other, yet it was a divide that could never be crossed. *Hope* and *Julian Castille* shouldn't be in the same sentence.

"Damn, Jaden, you've got quite the entourage."

"Yeah," she answered, "not what you expected I suppose."

Skye's eyes regarded her closely, and Jaden shifted beneath the intensity of her gaze. "Julian Castille, back from the dead. Who would have thought?" The eagle shifter frowned and lowered her voice. "What's wrong with him? He seems . . . strange."

Jaden's heart constricted painfully as she studied him. He stood to the side, his back to everyone. Cold. Aloof . . . and so very alone.

"Can he be trusted?"

Skye frowned, and though Jaden sensed concern, the question did nothing but raise her hackles.

Can he be trusted? How could she ask such a thing? What gave Skye the right to question his integrity, his honor. It burned her ass big time to hear it.

None of them knew what he'd been through; hell, *she* could only guess.

"What kind of question is that?" Jaden's voice was sharp, and she bared her teeth as she turned on the eagle shifter. "Of course he can be trusted."

"He's not the same. His energy is dark, and it's strong."

Jaden's temper flared, and she clenched her hands so tightly she felt her nails rip through skin. "Of course he's not the same. How can he be? He just spent the last six months being tortured. *In hell.* You try a vacation like that and see if you come home with an attitude that's all sunshine and full of happy."

Skye took a step back. "Hey, I don't mean any disrespect. Trust me, I know a little about what went on down there. When I first woke up after the explosion, I had images in my mind that even now creep me out." Skye's eyes were wide, and Jaden knew she was speaking from the heart. "Of Julian and Declan and where they were. I get that he went through hell, but something is definitely wrong with him. Even little Logan can see that."

Jaden remained silent, aware that they were attracting attention.

"I just need to know if we can trust him. There are a lot of lives at stake, and I will do whatever it takes to make sure what's mine is protected."

The subtle challenge was thrown down, and Jaden's back bristled at her tone.

"You mean Jagger." She could barely get the words out as her jaw was clenched so tightly together.

"Yes, among other things." Skye arched an eyebrow and cocked her head. "It's interesting to me, the change in your attitude. I thought you hated Julian. If I recall correctly, you told me he was an asshole."

"He is," she retorted quickly.

He's my asshole. The thought whispered through her mind, and she stilled, her body and mind freezing as a realization hit her like a Mack truck going one hundred miles an hour.

Her eyes found him once more, and she drank in his profile, the stubborn bent to his chin and the lips that had haunted her for years.

Her world was a chaotic mess, with nothing to look forward to other than a looming battle of epic proportions that might save humanity . . . or might not. And yet she felt a glimmer of hope nestled in there somewhere. A small ray of light. She thought that maybe there could be redemption, that Julian might somehow find his salvation.

She licked her dry lips and looked away from him. The man had caused her all kinds of pain and given her untold pleasure. Their families hated each other. But he was her mate, and with that came a bond that was not so easily cast aside. She wanted him to have a future even if she was not in it.

"You coming?" Jagger held the door open.

Both women turned toward the shifter. The others had already disappeared, and she followed Skye, noticing the way the eagle shifter's hands caressed the tall jaguar as she walked by. She nodded to Jagger and disappeared through the doors.

She found herself in a smallish foyer with two large guards standing by what she assumed were elevator doors. Both were otherworld and looked mean as hell. The doors slid open, and she slipped in behind Skye, with Jagger not far on her heels.

He moved around her, and the low, muted tones of the other two grated on her nerves as the lift descended rapidly.

Their intimacy and obvious love for each other was sweet, but she was not in the mood to be around it. Too much sugar made her ill.

As soon as the lift doors opened, she bolted and stepped into a shiny, modern world that would make the geekiest techno wizard take notice. The main hub for intel was staffed by seven operatives, all of them busy tapping away on their computers while overhead flatscreens kept them abreast of the latest developments.

It was similar to her setup, and as she studied the huge monitors, it saddened her to see the red zones spreading to nearly every country and region on the planet.

Things were about as bad as they could get.

"It makes you wonder."

She didn't need to turn her head to know that Julian stood at her side. Her nostrils flared, and his subtle scents tingled along her nerves as she took him into her lungs.

She couldn't fight it anymore.

The man was her mate whether she wanted him or not. It didn't mean she had to like it, but it did mean she had a choice. She could give in to the crazy notions banging around inside her head, the ones that told her to take him once more, to claim him and use him for pleasure. Or she could deny the need and live in misery.

He didn't want her. Not for life. She knew that, but still . . .

Jaden gave herself a mental shake. She knew it was her animal making noise. She was on the edge and riding the cusp of heat. It would pass. She gritted her teeth. She'd just have to deal.

Christ, it would help if he didn't smell so damn good.

"Sorry?" she asked, glad that she sounded in control even if the butterflies were having a field day in her stomach.

Julian nodded toward the monitors. "It makes you wonder

how long it will take for the entire world to become one hot red zone."

A chill swept across her skin, and Jaden shivered. "It won't take long." She shook her head and looked up at him. "So we better get this right and get it done." Her gaze swung back to the monitors. "Or this will be nothing but a solid mass of crimson."

A few moments of silence passed. She cleared her throat. "Where are the others?"

Julian shrugged his shoulders. "I was waiting for you."

She tried not to show how surprised she was at his words but seriously doubted she'd been successful. Why would he wait for her? She felt a jolt of pleasure, which was silly, considering that it was, in reality, a small gesture.

But to Jaden it was huge.

"This way." Jagger nodded toward a corridor to their right. She and Julian followed, and they trekked down the hall until they came to a door that required extra security measures. She waited patiently as Jagger activated the mechanism, and once the door slid open, they all stepped through into yet another world entirely.

Jaden wrinkled her nose as the subtle stench of magick greeted her. It was tinged with a hint of darkness, and she was puzzled by the signature as she continued to follow Jagger through a series of checkpoints.

She wasn't familiar with it but recognized the potency of the energy in the air. Someone down here was practicing powerful magick, and it wasn't all good.

They stopped in front of a door, and it was opened almost immediately. Jagger and Skye entered, then Jaden followed suit, with Julian close behind.

Her eyes were immediately drawn to the far end of the large room. Inside a glass-encased prison a man stood. His arms and feet were bound to the post in the center, and his face grinned wickedly as he stared out at them all.

There was blood on the floor, and she could tell he'd been tortured, his body showed obvious signs.

"Who the hell is that?" she asked, striding forward.

"His name is Tom," Jaxon said.

"Tom?" she asked, her tone biting. "Who the hell is Tom?"

Julian was at Jaden's side, and they both walked the last few steps until they stood near the secured room.

The man on the inside continued to stare at them with a crazed expression gripping his features. His eyes seemed unfocused, and Jaden whispered, "Can he see us?"

"No." Jagger angled up alongside her. "He knows we're here, but he can't see anything other than his own stinking reflection."

"Who is he?" Julian asked.

"He's one of Cormac O'Hara's soldiers, otherworld and definitely demon influenced."

"He's one of O'Hara's inner circle," Jaxon interjected.

"And you know this because?" Jaden asked, curious.

"He carries the mark," Declan murmured.

Jaxon nodded. "Everyone in his inner circle does."

"So what's this intel?" Julian asked. His tone was clipped, and Jaden knew he was fast losing patience. They both were.

"I know you're out there."

Jaden glanced toward the prisoner. His eyes looked glassy, as if he were high. The man began to shudder, his chest heaving with the effort it took as he pulled air into his lungs. After a few seconds, he turned to them once more, his body bathed in sweat, and spit at them, as if he could see them, shouting furiously. "When the legions of darkness invade this realm, you will all be damned."

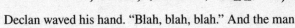

Declan waved his hand. "Blah, blah, blah." And the man was silenced once more.

"Not that I don't appreciate the show and all, but do you know where my fucking father is or not? I'm assuming that's why you hauled our asses clear across two countries." Declan looked to the Castille brothers.

Jaden stepped closer to Julian, not even realizing she'd done so until her foot nudged the hardness of his boots.

Julian paid her no mind, his focus entirely on his brothers. "Where is he?" His words were controlled, precise, yet Jaden felt the tremors that ran underneath his skin. They were reflected in the energy that shimmered in the air around them.

"Well, I hope you're all feelin' lucky, boys, because as soon as Jaxon gives the go-ahead, we leave for Vegas." Absolute silence greeted Jagger's words.

"Las Vegas?" Declan asked incredulously. After a few moments, a wide smile cracked the tense set of his face, and he turned to Julian. "Un-fucking-believable, yet so perfect." His dark eyes glittered though his voice was devoid of emotion.

The two men looked at each other, and Jaden saw their torment clear as day.

Declan nodded and looked past them to the prisoner inside. "Well, hello, Sin City," he said softly, and, with one twist of Declan's wrist, the prisoner stopped moving.

Permanently.

Deep in the bowels of Black Magick, Las Vegas's newest casino, the air was bitter cold. It was a massive space befitting the large casino overhead, and was used for two things—storage and torture.

At the very back, tucked away and camouflaged behind a shield of magick, was a room. Inside, a lone male exhaled a mist of air that lingered for several seconds before evaporating into nothing. He was bare of clothing save for a tattered pair of jeans that hung low on his lean hips, and he shivered constantly. His feet were wet, and the harsh light that shone down on him was relentless.

It was a miserable, painful existence but one the man had grown accustomed to.

For six long months he'd been held captive, tortured beyond what any human would ever be able to endure, and even most who claimed the mantle otherworld. And he would survive. He had to. There was so much left to do.

The door slid open, and the voice he hated above all others slid into the space, echoing eerily against the iron-infused walls.

"Well, my old friend, are you going to make me happy today?"

His eyes opened slowly, the long lashes sweeping upward as black bled into the gold around his irises. He watched, careful to keep all expression from his face, as Cormac O'Hara stepped inside.

The silver of the man's hair glistened against the never-ending light from above, and the skin of his face was smooth, free from wrinkles. He looked good, for an old son of a bitch. Cormac smiled then and walked forward to within an inch of his face. O'Hara was so close he could see the tiny blood vessels in his eyes.

He could smell the depravity that Cormac had ingested for lunch.

He tensed, though it took great pains to remain still. He was frozen, a macabre marionette with no will of his own other than what is locked deep inside his mind. His arms were spread wide as if they were wings, which was sadly ironic.

Considering his origin.

"I am running out of patience, my friend." O'Hara smiled then, his tone soft, cajoling. "Are you not tired of this game? Tell me where the portal is, and I can end it."

His muscles bunched and he gritted his teeth as his mind closed.

Cormac shook his head. "Very well, Azaiel, let's dance."

The sorcerer raised his hands and grinned wickedly as energy flew from his fingers. It hit the fallen's flesh and sizzled along his frame in a shower of light.

There was no sound to be heard other than the scream that ripped through Azaiel's mind, to echo inside his skull.

It was the first of many, and they would last for hours to come.

Chapter 22

Snow continued to fall though the intensity of the storm had subsided. Julian watched the flakes drift through the night sky, like tiny jewels in the air. He sat alone in the great room located at the back of his brother's home. The entire wall was glass and allowed him an unobstructed view of Lake Muskoka.

His first thought was that the compound was vulnerable to attack, being on the water. Jaxon had assured him measures had been taken, and strong protection wards were in place.

He sighed and stretched back into the leather sofa. To his right, a fireplace burned, casting an arc of heat. He welcomed it, felt his body relax.

He was finally alone, and the solitude was exactly what he needed. Tomorrow, they headed to Sin City, and he was ready. The crack inside him was getting larger, and he knew there wasn't much time.

His brothers had attempted to reconnect with him, but he'd not been interested. He'd tried. The white noise that pounded inside his head had made listening difficult, and he didn't think he'd been entirely successful in hiding his disinterest.

After a while, they'd given up and retreated with their women to wherever the hell they slept. Jagger apparently still had the cabin in Jersey and was only here because of the crisis.

Their attempt at a family reunion had been awkward. He wasn't going to take it personally. Some things were meant to remain broken.

Even little Logan had steered clear of him, happy to fool around with Finn and Nico while Julian watched from the sidelines. Jaden had disappeared soon after, and within an hour, he was alone.

Yeah, he was the life of the fucking party.

He saw lights twinkling across the lake, small beacons tucked in amongst the thick forest that blanketed the shoreline, and he imagined families grouped together for the holidays. Christmas was still several days away, yet the house looked like a bloody elf had exploded green and red everywhere.

Decorations filled every nook available, and a magnificent tree glittered in the corner, decorated, and quite thoroughly, with a host of different things, including many that were handmade.

There was an entire series of jaguars and eagles sprinkled along the branches, and they'd obviously been made by a young hand. It brought a rare smile to his face. Logan.

His family had always been fractured—his father and mother barely tolerated each other—and he had no real memory of togetherness at holiday time. Long before he walked the earth, the jaguars honored their god of war, Huitzilopochtli, but as time marched on, Christmas had slowly been integrated with their traditions.

His thoughts strayed back to his family, such as it was. His brothers were worlds away from where he was. They'd both found their mates and were looking forward to a life that included domestic bliss.

And he, well, he was just trying to get through, to make it to the other side and hopefully save the world while he was at it. His belly tightened at the thought of what still needed to be done. He sank deeper into the leather and closed his eyes as he listened to the quiet.

It was hard, sometimes, to hear such a thing, to have the quiet become louder than the chaos that lived inside his head. After a while, he adjusted and felt himself relax.

He must have dozed off and come awake with a start, the smell of her already inside him. He knew she was there. Jaden.

He sat up and wiped sandman from his eyes, thinking for the first time there'd been no nightmares. No visions of terror.

"Hey," she said softly. She was perched on the edge of the sofa, her hair loose and falling over her shoulders like ripples of licorice. Her dark eyes were overlarge in a face that was somber.

"How long you been here?" he asked sharply.

Her face changed, the softness disappearing, and she straightened her body. "A couple of hours," she answered, her eyes staring down at him intently.

A couple of hours? She'd been watching him for a couple of hours? He didn't know what to say.

"I couldn't sleep," she said again as she got up from the sofa and crossed over to the still-twinkling Christmas tree.

The wash of color amongst the green glowed in the near-dark room, and he watched as she touched several of the decorations.

"It's nice," she said.

"It's pine, I think."

She snorted. "The tree is lovely, but that's not what I was talking about."

"What then?"

"It's nice that Libby and Jaxon were reunited with their son. That all the pain and shit they went through was worth it."

He studied her profile and saw the emotion that was there. Something inside him broke loose, and he nearly stood, so great was his desire to go to her. And yet he held back. Some cold piece of reality had clicked into place and kept him still.

"I used to love Christmas," she murmured so quietly he had to strain his ears in order to hear properly. She grabbed a small paper jaguar and studied it closely. "He's good." She looked back at him, "Your nephew. An artist in the making."

Julian nodded, his eyes narrowing as he spoke. "When did you start hating Christmas?"

Jaden stilled, her gaze dropping to the floor, and she shrugged her shoulders. "Things changed for my family when I was nine. Something happened to my father." She turned away from him and walked over to the glass wall and placed her hand upon it as she stared off into the darkness.

"What?" He was up before he could command his body otherwise and across the room before she took another breath. Their eyes met in the window, her reflection painful to see.

His hand rose as if to touch her, then, slowly fell back to his sides. She looked away.

"Jakobi was touched by evil. I have no other explanation. Was it demon? Magick? I don't know. I can't pinpoint one moment in time. It was a gradual thing. He became convinced my mother was having an affair, they fought constantly, and in the end, she left." Jaden slowly shook her head, her voice was tremulous. "Took me with her, and we went to live with her family."

Long moments of silence passed, and he sensed the struggle she was having as she relived her memories.

"He used to be wonderful; he used to love me," she whispered. "I know it's hard to believe after what you saw, but he did."

Julian thought of the photo he'd found in her room, she'd looked happy, relaxed, and secure with her family.

"Sometimes I wish I could grab hold of what I had in the past and fix it. Keep it pure and real, but I've realized there are some things that you can't change." Their eyes met once more in the window. He saw the anger that was there. "There are things that are unforgivable."

He knew the DaCosta history. He was well aware that Jakobi was a bastard of the highest order. What had he done to cause the hatred his daughter held for him?

"What did he do?" Julian asked as he stepped closer. She turned to him, and his eyes fell to the single tear that slowly weaved its way from the corner of her eye. It glistened like a diamond against her skin and his hand—rising of its own volition—carefully wiped it from her.

She rested her cheek into his palm, and her own crept up to hold his there. The simple gesture tugged at him.

Jaden exhaled a ragged breath, and he felt the shudder that swept over her frame. "He murdered my mother."

Shocked silence followed her words, and Julian truly

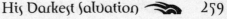

had no clue what to do or say. As dysfunctional as his own family was, murder was incomprehensible. This was the stuff of nightmares. "How . . ." He began to speak, but she nodded quickly, and he was quiet.

"I found her in the jungle, not far from the resort. She'd been shot." Her eyes swept upward, and he stilled at the pain that lay there. "Her body was left out in the open because he knew I'd find her. Her paw had been cut off, her canines removed." She was shaking, and Julian pulled her close, not knowing what else to do. The sensation was strange—the need to comfort—yet he welcomed it. It told him that he wasn't dead inside. Not yet anyway.

"It was a sign. One meant to scare me back into the fold, to make me into the good girl, the obedient daughter. I'd been living with my mother since they separated. He thought I'd cower and do his bidding." She laughed harshly. "He was wrong, just as my brothers were."

He felt her breath against his neck and became aware that the air had changed. It was charged with an energy that pulled at him hard.

"Instead, I focused on bringing him and his organization down. They thought I was the perfect doll who only knew one word: yes. They're fools."

He felt the heat of her continue to grow against his skin, and his animal reacted instantly. His flesh became feverish, and his canines ached as his need to claim her rose within.

"Business deals he lost out on, contracts that were broken, all of it was because of me. He knew someone on the inside was involved in the sabotage, but always looked to his men. Never once did he think to look closer to home, to the daughter who saw her dead mother every time she looked at him."

He listened to the frantic beat of her heart, and his own ached at the pain that laced her words. She exhaled shakily, and continued, "Then Father got deeper into the real heavy shit, and my job became harder. His security was unparalleled, and my brothers went crazy with power—all of them, from Degas the oldest down to Tomas the youngest. I couldn't believe how thoroughly Jakobi's darkness bled into them. Sometimes I think I could have intervened, done something to influence them, but my brothers lived to please Father." She looked up at him then, and her voice broke. "Tomas was so young, four years younger than I. He was killed in a raid organized by PATU, after I'd joined forces with them. That is something I must live with."

Julian held her and whispered near her ear, "We can only do so much with family. In the end, our siblings will choose their own paths. You must know there's nothing you could have done."

Jaden hung her head. "I'd already assembled a team of sorts, men and women who shared the same goals as I, when I was contacted by PATU. I jumped at the chance to work with them. It was the perfect opportunity to get the job done and have all the added resources I'd need. That's what I was doing that night . . ."

He was breathing heavily and barely heard her words. "That night?"

"The night we met." She pulled away from him and stared up into his eyes. A long strand of hair tickled its way across her face, and she blew it away impatiently. She looked earnest, her brows furled in concentration, and he fought the urge to touch her sweetly. To sweep the hair from her face and kiss her lips.

"I didn't seduce you, Julian. I had no clue you were a Castille. I'd been sent to The Grand Hacienda to meet with a contact." She paused, and his eyes flew open at the catch in her voice. "I should have left instead of staying for that last drink. Something kept me there. Fate? I don't know; you were a complication I so did not want."

"I pulled you away from the bar," he said huskily, his eyes fixed on her lips.

Her tongue darted out, and he watched, fascinated, as it swept across the plump redness, leaving a sheen of moisture in its wake.

"Onto the dance floor," she finished, and smiled, poking him in the chest. "You moved with such grace, your energy was unique. I knew right away"—she paused, and the way her breath caught in her throat made him ache—"that you were shifter," she whispered.

His hands crept up to her shoulders, and he pulled her into the crook of his arms. There was no resistance, and he groaned softly as her body slid against him.

Slowly, they moved together. There was no music, no sound except the breaths that fell from their lips. He had no idea what was going on in Jaden's head, but in his mind's eye, he was back at The Grand Hacienda, the air was flush with the Caribbean, and heat was all around them.

He felt his cock swell and shifted his body in an attempt to alleviate the discomfort, but all it did was spread a host of sensations along nerve endings that left his skin on fire. His body was suddenly tense with need.

Her arms went around his waist, and when she ground herself against him, it felt as if he were coming apart. "I wanted you so badly that night. I don't give a damn what you remember, it wasn't just me. You felt the same way, and I thought . . ." Her whispered words echoed into the quiet.

"What did you think?" he asked.

Her gaze swept upward, and, for several long moments,

they stared at each other in silence. After a bit, she moistened her lips, and spoke. "I knew you were a shifter, I could sense it, and I'd never felt such a connection before. My jaguar wanted you in a way that hurt."

"Why did I not recognize you as such?"

"I wear a cloaking charm when on assignment." She looked away. "It's not always stable in times of great . . . emotion. It slipped from me the moment I claimed you."

Julian stilled at her words. The raw honesty that he sensed grabbed the little bit of his soul that still existed. Her pain was huge, and he felt every bit of it.

He asked the question that he wanted most answered. "Why did you claim me as your mate?"

She bit her lip, and he could see her confusion, her pain. "I've thought about it a lot. Why would I screw with my future and mate with a man I knew nothing about?" Her eyes widened. "I don't have an answer other than it felt right. In that moment, I knew you were the one to complete me. It was like I had no control. I was weak and let my body lead me down a path that has been filled with nothing but pain. When you saw what I was." She bowed her head, and he felt her shame as her voice dropped to just above a whisper, "When you rejected me . . . I can't even describe how that made me feel."

Julian didn't know what to say. Everything was true. All of it. That night . . . he'd had the best sex of his life, several times over in fact. Something about her had been different; he was a fool not to have noticed earlier.

For the longest time, he'd avoided anything that was otherworld, especially the shifters. He was a refined CEO of a major conglomerate known the world over, and a shapeshifting jaguar had no place in that world. Not with him, anyway.

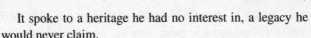

It spoke to a heritage he had no interest in, a legacy he would never claim.

Julian grimaced. Fuck, Mr. Cosmic Mojo had kicked his ass thoroughly.

He remembered coming down from the heady release of an overwhelming orgasm and knowing that something had changed. He'd seen the air move around her body, shimmering as it played along the soft golden skin that he'd just tasted. Her eyes glowed, and he'd sensed the animal that lay just beneath her flesh.

She was wild, untamed, and, to his horror, represented everything he did not want to recognize in himself.

Julian groaned and closed his eyes, wishing the memories would fade. He still saw the hurt and disbelief in her eyes when he'd tossed ten one-hundred-dollar bills onto the bed and asked that she leave immediately.

That was the last time he'd seen Jaden until that night in Belize before the portal had gone AWOL, along with him.

She exhaled raggedly. "I watched you from afar like a pathetic loser. I knew your every move, who you slept with, who you dated."

She turned to him, and the silence in the room fell heavy on his ears. Her eyes glittered dangerously, and he saw her shame. What it cost her to confess to him.

"It killed me because you belonged to me even though you had no clue. I was the one-night stand of regret. A mistake to forget about. A dirty shifter." She shrugged and ran her hands through the long bands of hair that fell about her shoulders. "And here we are, and everything still sucks."

"I am one dumb-ass son of a bitch."

"Yeah, you are." He sensed her anger, mingled with pain, and realized that he felt the same.

He shook his head. "I have no words, Jaden, other than sorry." He pushed her away. "It's too late to make things right. I would if I could."

Julian dragged great gulps of air into his lungs and tried to focus his mind. It was hard when her scent was everywhere. He wanted her. Badly. He thought of the night before and how he'd taken her in the temple, and he knew he could not use her again. Not like that.

He might be a grade-A bastard, but he was drawing the line.

"You say it's too late," she whispered. Julian tensed when her hands slid along his arm and across his abs as she stood in front of him.

"You may be right, but we only have a few hours left before we leave for Vegas. I have no clue what's going to happen when we get there." She rubbed his chest and surprised him when she ripped his T-shirt from neck to hem, her long nails exposing the damaged flesh beneath.

He hissed as her fingers gently traced the scars that were there. "My control isn't what it should be," he managed to get out from between clenched teeth.

"Good," she said, her voice thick, "because right now my control is gone, and what I want is standing in front of me." She bent, and he saw red as her tongue gently traced the symmetrical scars on his chest. "And that would be you."

She pushed away, turned, and his gaze immediately fell to her ass. The jeans that she wore should be fucking illegal. His mouth watered, and he felt the beast stir within.

"I have a surprise. You coming?" she tossed over her shoulder before disappearing from view.

Julian was stunned. A few minutes before, he'd pushed her away, yet he couldn't deny the part of him that ached for

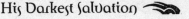

her. For her touch and scent and taste. For the calm that he felt when she was near.

The echo of her steps faded, and, suddenly, it was as if a fire had been lit under his ass. He moved quickly to follow.

Hell yeah, I'm coming.

Chapter 23

Julian followed her scent down the hall until it connected to a long corridor that ran perpendicular to the main house. He heard her ahead, her soft footfalls, and he quickened his pace, enjoying the game as his animal reveled in the hunt.

The light in the corridor was muted, and he caught trace signatures of his brothers and their women. They'd all been this way within the last several hours. When he reached the end, he paused in front of a door. It was open several inches, and a whisper of heat caressed his face.

His nostrils flared, and the scents that he pulled into his lungs were entirely out of place here in the land of snow and ice. He inhaled the warmth of jungle, cool water, and abundant greenery. It ignited such a need in him that he growled loudly as he pulled back the door and stepped inside.

His white teeth slashed through the charcoal darkness in a feral smile as he looked around, surprised to hear the call of a wailer monkey and the cry of a toucan. He'd heard about Jaxon's jungle room back at his former headquarters for PATU and wasn't surprised he'd replicated it here in the Canadian wilderness.

A splash sounded to his right, and he started to pant as he carefully picked his way through the vines and earth at his feet. Jaxon had spared no expense, and Julian marveled at how rich the room felt. A soft glow fell from above, and he realized the entire ceiling was glass, enabling him to look out onto an arctic sky and yet he was toasty warm inside a jungle.

Unbelievable.

He felt layers of darkness slip from his skin as Jaden's subtle scent settled inside him. She calmed the beast and allowed some sense of peace. His eyes narrowed as his heartbeat increased, and he focused on one thing—Jaden.

He slid through a mass of vines, discarding his torn shirt as he did so, and flexed his powerful muscles as he shook out his limbs. He held himself loose and continued along silently, stalking his prey with savage glee.

Up ahead he heard a waterfall and was just able to make it out through the abundance of trees that stood like silent soldiers. When he parted the leaves and stepped into a small clearing, he felt a rush of emotion pummel him.

Before him was a large basin of water. It glowed softly, as if lit from within, and the gentle sounds of the waterfall were like a symphony. It was beautiful, yet it was the woman who floated like an angel that pulled at his gut.

Jaden lay upon the water, her arms spread out to the sides, moving slowly as she kept herself afloat. Her hair rippled outward, riding the liquid and encircling her head like a halo. She was naked, her skin glistening in the soft light. His groin tightened, and his mouth went dry.

Her full breasts were pert, the nipples hard, and he ached

to touch them. His mouth watered, and his nostrils flared in excitement as he envisioned his lips upon them. His gaze traveled slowly over her body, taking in the translucent tattoos that moved against her neck, down past the taut belly, until they settled on the patch of hair between her legs.

Christ, he was sure her legs were parted, just so, to drive him crazy. The secrets that lay there, hidden between the folds of her sex, were tantalizingly exposed, and he felt his cock swell painfully as his eyes fixed on her.

He could look nowhere else. He wanted her. All of her.

With a low growl, he quickly shed his pants and stood at the edge of the water as Jaden turned over. Her gaze swept the length of him, and a smile drifted over her lips as she stopped at his straining cock. It was hard, aching for her softness.

"Aren't you coming in?" she asked, her voice was breathless, and the catch in it drove him crazy. "The water is sheer heaven."

She began to drift away, the round globes of her ass taunting him. "Catch me if you can."

She disappeared from view, and Julian slid into the water, hissing at the sensation of the warm liquid against his aching appendage. His eyes scoured the smooth glass surface, and he pushed off, long, powerful strokes carrying him forward as he searched for Jaden. The little minx was playing a game, and he laughed as he dove under.

He immediately spied a flash of leg and took off with a powerful kick, only to come up empty when he reached the other side. Julian surfaced, shedding the water from his eyes as he turned.

Where the hell is she? He growled in frustration and tried to calm the animal inside.

He floated for a bit, his eyes scouring the water and the bank where he'd just been. He felt the edges of darkness creep into his mind once more as his frustration grew.

"Whatcha looking for?" The soft words hit him, and he turned around, nearly choking as his eyes ate up the beautiful creature who stood before him.

She dipped her toe in the water and sent a spray arcing toward him, laughing as she did so. He let the water fall over his head though it did nothing to cool the heat of his desire.

He wanted to say something, but the words weren't there, so he stared up at her, helpless and hungry. Her laughter slowly died as she returned his gaze, her head cocked to the side, her legs spread in such a way he once more caught a glimpse of the wetness inside. Her fragrant arousal assaulted him, and his skin burned as everything inside him tightened.

It was painful, but it was a good pain, the kind he'd not experienced in years. Three, to be exact. She was the most erotic thing he'd ever seen.

"I can't play this game," he said roughly, and began to pant once more as her eyes darkened and she swept her tongue across her lips. Her hands crept up to her breasts and he watched as she pulled on her hard nipples, her slender fingers massaging them aggressively. Her tongue was caught between her teeth, and as her chest heaved, she pinned him with a direct stare.

"Then you better get up here because I feel like I'm coming apart." Her voice was hoarse, heavy with desire, and she'd barely got the words out before he was at her side. The speed of his jaguar propelled him out of the water, and he was a blur of hard-assed muscle.

They stood together with only a whisper of air between

them. Julian looked down into her dark eyes and felt something break inside him, like a balloon had just been ruptured.

There was a well of emotion inside, a need to have her that pounded hard. But not just to claim her body. A soft growl escaped. He wanted her soul. Her mind . . . her heart.

How fucking crazy is that?

Her tattoos shimmered, their vibrant colors luminescent against her skin, and his hand fell to them. When he touched her, energy tingled along his fingers and spread like fire up his body.

Slowly, he bent and his mouth claimed them, his tongue sliding across the intricate markings as he felt her tremble beneath him. When she groaned, he smiled against her skin, liking the fact that he affected her so.

"Only you," she whispered, her voice nearly breaking, and he stilled.

Julian's hands crept to her shoulders, and he held her tightly as he straightened and looked directly into her eyes.

She trembled still, and he wasn't so sure it was from the heat of passion anymore. Her eyes glistened like liquid onyx, and it killed him to think she was about to cry.

Something was going on that he didn't understand. *Have I fucked up so badly already?*

"I don't . . ." he began, and had to take a few seconds to compose himself before he could continue. Inside his mind and body, a war was raging. The constant voices and pain were slowly receding, and he realized, in that moment, that when he was with Jaden, the madness that lived inside him was diminished. It wasn't gone completely, but it was bearable.

She made his life worthwhile, if only for a moment. It was like a fucking lightbulb had exploded suddenly, and he panicked. He needed to make her understand.

He began again. "I don't . . . I can't promise you anything, Jaden. There are things . . . my future is . . ." He inhaled a ragged breath and tried to temper the emotion that was suddenly wide open inside him. It was fucking confusing.

"It's okay," she whispered.

"No, it's not." He spoke harshly, and she winced at his tone. He hissed and shook his head. He was totally fucking things up and groaned as he shook his head. "Three years ago, I was a total asshole."

She nodded, a hint of a smile playing up the corners of her mouth. "Agreed."

"I can't take it back, but what I can do . . ." His voice lowered and ended on a growl as his body was once more suffused with heat. He felt his cock twitch painfully as she moved closer to him, her body now flush against his hard frame. He held her tightly and nuzzled the hair at her neck. "What I can do," he repeated hoarsely, "is honor the bond between us tonight. As for tomorrow . . ."

Pain lashed through him as her hands crept up to his shoulders. He turned from the crook of her neck and stared down into her beautiful eyes.

"It's okay, Julian. Tonight is for us. Let's forget about the damn mess waiting in Vegas." She rubbed her breasts against his chest, and as she did so, her soft belly slid against his hardness. It was without a doubt exquisite torture, unlike anything he'd ever endured before. "And give ourselves something to remember."

"Amen to that," he whispered, and bent down to claim her lips.

Jaden opened wide for him, and she reveled in the feel of his hardness beneath her fingers as she pulled him against her. His tongue slid inside her mouth, attacking her softness with an aggression that teased the animal inside her to a feverish high.

The sounds that he made, small animalistic groans of need, drove her crazy.

He tasted like sin, and she moved against him, her sensitive nipples scraping along his chest. She was on fire with need and groaned loudly as his lips rained sweetness across her face, tasting every inch before finding the sweet spot between her ear and her neck.

He growled softly and suckled her there, his hands roaming across her shoulders and down to her hips before he grabbed her roughly and pulled her against his straining hardness.

She felt his cock, its long, pulsating length slide along her belly, and she lifted her right leg, encircling his hips as she tried to get as close to him as possible.

She slid her wetness against him, her swollen clitoris aching as it rubbed along his flesh.

"Oh God," she whispered, "I've never . . . not even that first night." She couldn't finish her thoughts as his hands gripped her tightly, and he pulled her upward, coaxing her left knee up until she gripped him with both legs.

She felt his arms at the small of her back, anchoring her, and when he bent his head and took a hard, turgid nipple deep into his mouth, she cried out. He suckled from her there, pulling long and hard, his tongue doing crazy things to her as he licked and sucked. Each draw hit her hard, and she felt her sex cream as her desire grew to a feverish pitch.

"Christ, Julian, I don't know how much I can take."

His mouth fell from her nipple, and he blew air upon the wet skin, smiling up at her wickedly as she looked down at him.

Her animal was scratching hard, wanting to mate, *needing* to have him buried deep within her body. She was on the cusp and could feel the edge of ecstasy teasing from the inside out.

"I want you now," she said hoarsely, grinding against him, small whimpers falling from her lips as she did so.

He smiled and looked up at her, murmuring, "Not yet."

His arms slipped up her back to rest against her shoulders, and he pulled her flush to his body as he inhaled the air in a great gulp. "You smell like candy," he murmured. "I think you've forgotten how much I like the taste." He growled, and it was nearly her undoing.

Her head fell to his shoulder, and she shuddered as he slowly lowered her to the ground. The soft earth welcomed her body, and she fell back, arms splayed above her head and legs spread wide.

The look on his face as his gaze fell to the glistening apex between her legs made her weak, and her hands fell to her breasts. He looked feral, animalistic. Fucking hot.

She massaged her swollen flesh, ever so slowly, hissing as exquisite fingers of delight spread across her breasts.

With a groan, he bent over her, his powerful shoulders holding him several inches from her body though she ached to feel him pressed against her. Their eyes locked, and she marveled at the golden hue of his as they began to glow with a fire that fed her own.

"You're so beautiful," she whispered fiercely. "And you're mine."

His mouth caressed hers once more with the merest of kisses, and it only served to heighten the need inside her to a feverish pitch. Her hips were moving slowly, in time to an ancient rhythm, yet without him inside her frustration began to build.

"Please," she gasped as she squeezed her eyes shut. "I can't take much more."

"Look at me," he commanded.

Something in his voice was different; the words fell from his lips in several layers. Her eyes flew open, and the raw need that lay deep within his touched a place inside her that was sacred.

She felt as is she were ripping apart with need. It wasn't just for sex. It wasn't just to answer the call of her animal and mate. It was for the man above her . . . for his soul and *his heart*? All of him.

Was it possible? Were her feelings that strong?

He was a Castille, yes, but he was also her mate. Were her feelings a by-product of the bond? Were they real?

All thoughts vanished from her mind as she felt his fingers slide through the slick folds between her legs, and she bit her tongue. His eyes held hers captive, and she couldn't look away even if she had wanted to. When he began to massage her clitoris, she knew he saw the pleasure he gave her, and when he plunged two fingers deep inside, he heard her groan.

She was laid bare and wouldn't have had it any other way.

There was no sound. It was like the world had faded away, and everything had been sucked into a black hole save for the two of them.

His fingers continued their assault, and she angled her hips in such a way that he was there, right where the pressure was hot, and she whimpered as he coaxed the orgasm that was building.

She groaned and threw her head back as she arched her breasts.

"Don't you dare close your fucking eyes," he said roughly. "I want to see them when you come."

He began to massage her in earnest, and her right hand clung to his powerful forearm while the other joined his down below. She felt the pressure continue to build like liquid fire, and it spread quickly as her hips danced along in jerky movements that she had no control over.

"Keep your eyes on me," he commanded as he slowly slid down her body. She watched him grin wickedly, bit her tongue, but couldn't keep the scream from escaping as his fingers withdrew and his mouth claimed her sweetness.

"Oh God," she whispered. His eyes never left hers, and she spread her legs wider, allowing him as much access as he needed. His tongue was doing wicked-crazy things to her, teasing her swollen clitoris mercilessly, and when he suckled her there, hard, it was her undoing.

His hands held her ass tightly so that she couldn't move, and when her orgasm came crashing down, she literally felt like she was being ripped apart. It was the most painfully exquisite moment she'd ever had. The tattoos burned along her body, and the sensation only added to her pleasure.

"Do not look away," he growled against her thigh, and he began to trail a fiery line of kisses along her body. She was weak, satiated, yet his feral gaze did weird things to her.

She felt her animal shift and her canines sharpen as his golden eyes bled into black.

She never took her eyes from his and felt the fever begin to build once more as he passed over her trembling belly, up along the side of her rib cage, until he licked the undersides of her breasts.

Julian was poised above her, his skin glistening with sweat, his hair damp from the water. He was feral, he was wild, and he was all hers.

"I'll never want anyone else," he said. "You've ruined me."

His mouth crashed down upon hers as his cock slid deep within the welcoming wetness between her legs. She groaned into his mouth, and he ate her passion as his hardness filled her completely.

He was large, and he moved his body slowly, scraping along every single nerve ending inside her, spreading electric fires along the way. Their tongues danced together, and still their eyes remained focused on each other.

Her legs gripped him as she arched her hips and began to move with him in perfect harmony.

"You're so tight," he groaned against her lips. "So wet."

The walls of her vagina clenched against him, and he nearly withdrew before plunging into her again, with slow precision. It was torture, and the pressure that was building inside was making her crazy.

She needed more.

"Faster," she said hoarsely. "Harder."

He ignored her, and her animal reacted in anger. She snarled and pushed against him, her strength gaining her the advantage. She flipped his large frame until he was on his back and immediately she was astride, sliding his cock deep within as she began to ride him hard.

"Holy Christ." Julian's words excited her. "I've died and gone to heaven," he whispered.

Jaden bared her teeth and bent low, biting him on his shoulder as she continued to pump her hips. "You ain't seen nothing yet."

She righted herself, and they began to dance. His cock slid in and out of her, each pass igniting more fire as they quickened their pace. Her hands slid to her breasts, and she watched him, her mouth open slightly, as his fingers joined hers.

The only sounds she could hear was flesh against flesh, and as the tempo increased, she felt her walls constrict against him, pulling at him in such a way that he groaned loudly.

"I can't hold off, babe," he said, his eyes half-closed.

"Good," she answered. "Keep your eyes open . . ." She clenched her teeth as her insides exploded into molten fire. "And watch me come."

His hands fell to her hips, the fingers gripping her hard as he pulled her up and down. She felt him expand, felt his cock straining deep inside, and when they both came together, she screamed loudly and welcomed his answering cry.

His eyes burned, and he snarled as she continued to move against him. For several long moments, the two of them moved slowly, until she collapsed upon him. She felt his heart beating fast and furious against her cheek and closed her eyes as his arms slid up her back to cradle her tight to his chest.

Three years ago, he'd sent her packing. Three years ago, she'd let him.

Jaden clenched her teeth together. That was a lifetime ago. Things had changed. She'd never give up so easily now.

He had changed.

I love you.

The words were a whisper in her mind, slipping from her subconscious like a secret she couldn't share, and they surprised the crap out of her. She stilled, her breath held at the back of her throat as her mind processed what her heart was saying.

She smiled tremulously and released a long breath as she relaxed and let his warmth melt into her.

She wasn't giving him up, and she had to believe that one

day he'd return her feelings. Whatever tomorrow brought, she'd be there by his side, and damned if she was going to let Cormac and *the fallen* ruin everything.

They'd save the world, and she'd save his soul, whether Julian wanted her to or not.

There was no other option.

Chapter 24

Hours later they both awoke warm, still tucked into the other's embrace. A new day dawned, filled with the promise of violence and the possibility of death. Kind of sucked the joy out of fresh beginnings.

They made love one more time. It was a feverish joining, fueled by longing and fear.

Fear of the unknown and of losing everything before it had even been gained. Words were not spoken, feelings were not discussed. It was as if they each needed to connect once more on a level that was primal, real. That by joining their bodies together in the most basic way a man and a woman could, they were grabbing hold of something they could control.

Their passion.

Julian watched Jaden from hooded eyes as she quickly dressed. Her clothes were damp, and he tried not to stare, but the T-shirt clung to her breasts in all the right ways, which for him was *all wrong*.

He could not afford distraction. Not when there was so much at stake. Saving the world and all that.

He turned from her and grimaced as he scooped up his jeans and slid them over his hips. The energy that burned beneath his flesh was frenetic, and it kept his heart beating fast and hard.

Kept his mind alert. He felt good.

He slipped his feet into his boots. "You ready?"

Jaden was quiet; when she glanced up at him, her eyes shimmered. "Last night . . ." she began, and paused.

"Shh, you don't have to say anything."

"I do." She shuddered and looked at him. "Last night I realized something. I know things aren't perfect between us, but there is something more than just sex and mating and all that crap." Her eyes fell from his. "At least for me."

Julian's throat tightened, clogged with emotions he wasn't capable of handling well. "I think you're an amazing woman, and if things were different . . ." He didn't know what to say. He had no future.

"But we can try, can't we?"

Her lip trembled, and he swept his mouth across her softness. His forehead rested against hers, and he murmured, "We can try." It was an empty lie but one he was willing to believe in.

"Let's do this." Jaden pulled away from him, suddenly all business. She cracked a smile. "I want it ended, tonight."

Her long hair fell in tangles down her back, and he found his hands reaching for bits of debris stuck within the silken waves. "We look like shit," he murmured.

"Speak for yourself, Castille, I think you look damn hot." She smiled up at him, and her fingers fell to the scars on his chest. He hissed at her touch, and her eyebrows furled slightly.

She was quiet for several seconds.

"Who did this to you?" Her words were soft, and when she raised her head once more, the tears that glittered deep within the depths of her eyes pulled at him fiercely.

"I don't remember," he answered.

"You lie."

Julian frowned, not caring for the challenge. "Why does it matter? What will change if you know?"

Jaden's eyes darkened, the whites nearly receding as she narrowed them angrily. "If I know who the bastard is, I can tell him exactly *why* I'll be cutting his balls off in the most painful way possible after I hunt his sorry ass down," she snarled, and he was taken aback by the rage he sensed. "That someone would mark you in such a way is unacceptable."

She turned from him, and he knew her control was rapidly fading. "We will destroy the portal. I will kill Azaiel myself, or anyone who stands in my way."

She started to walk, and he had no choice but to follow the woman who would protect him as if he were nothing more than a child.

"And then I'm going to make whoever did that to you *pay*."

A smile slipped into place and he shook his head, awed at the power and determination the woman possessed. She would protect him. How fucking bizarre. A DaCosta.

My DaCosta. The thought was bittersweet considering he had no clue what the hell was coming down the pike.

They slipped from the jungle refuge and quickly made their way back to the great room. It was near dawn, darkness still hung in the sky, and, through the windows, stars could be seen twinkling like diamonds.

The smell of food wafted toward them, and his belly rumbled. He turned immediately and followed Jaden across the foyer and into an extremely large, modern kitchen.

It was full. His gaze traveled across the room, taking in the shocked faces as everyone stared back at him and Jaden.

"Julian, what the hell happened to you?"

The harsh voice belonged to Jagger, and Julian squared his shoulders angrily, not liking the focus of so many. His brother's eyes stared at the scars exposed on his chest, and they burned beneath Jagger's gaze. He felt like a damned bug under a microscope.

The edges of his mind condensed and expanded as darkness seeped into the cracks. It was always there, the blackness. The rage.

"Do you want a detailed play-by-play or the condensed version? It's not like we have a whole lot of time," he asked, frowning darkly as he stared at his brothers.

He fought the urge to cover himself, ashamed of the scars and what they represented. Weakness. Helplessness. He saw the horror on Skye's face before their eyes connected, and she looked away.

It was Libby that pulled at his heartstrings.

Her eyes were huge as she rose from her seat and crossed to him, her hand reaching for his even though he flinched at her touch. He knew of the scars she carried. Of how the DaCostas had carved her flesh and left their own unique brand of tattoo behind.

She'd suffered as well, and he respected how far she'd come.

"Julian, Mr. M has made pretty much every breakfast item you can think of. Please help yourself." Her eyes strayed to the scars on his chest, and he tried not to show his aversion as she rested her hand against them. He was unsuccessful. She ignored his discomfort, and whispered, "They'll fade, and, eventually, the memories will as well." She looked at Jaden, her eyes sad. "Life goes on, and we learn to deal." She squeezed his hand. "You're not alone, Julian, even if it feels like that. Your family loves you."

He shook his head politely and withdrew his hand, murmuring, "I'm gonna grab a coffee."

Jaden followed him to the side table, and they both poured themselves a strong cup of brew. Her dark eyes never left him, and he was starting to feel confined, like he needed to shift and run.

Declan joined them, his face grim.

"You look like crap," Julian said as he studied the sorcerer. The man looked like he'd not slept in days, which Julian knew from personal experience was most likely the case.

"Beggin' pardon, but not everyone got laid last night." Declan winked and laughed softly as his gaze moved to Jaden. "Lucky son of a bitch."

Julian's chest rumbled, and his nostrils flared. "Move away from her."

Declan paid him no mind and continued on, his tone light, though the fire that lit his eyes was anything but. Julian sensed the darkness inside the Irishman and thought that maybe the sorcerer was closer to the edge than he realized.

"I think your woman can more than take care of herself, and if I'm guessing right, won't take too kindly to having you decide who gets to stand next to her." He flashed a grin. "Besides, she smells really good."

Julian's animal shifted, and his skin burned as he bared his teeth.

"Julian, it's okay." Jaden put her hand on his arm, and his anger receded. She turned to Declan, and her voice was curt. "You will stop antagonizing him. Do not cross me on this. Everybody needs to be on top of their game. I don't have to remind you how high the stakes are today and what will happen if we fail."

"No, you don't." Declan backed away and grabbed himself a cup of coffee. "It's all I can think about."

"If you guys are done with the drama, we need to get organized." Ana's dry voice cut between them, and they all turned to the vampire. She stood a few feet away, her lips pursed tightly, a look of annoyance pinching the delicate features of her face. She looked pale, even for a vampire, and Julian knew that there was something heavy going on between her and Declan. It was in the way her eyes never strayed far from him.

It was in the way Declan tried to avoid her at all costs.

"Ana's right." Jaxon rose from the table and nodded toward the foyer. "We'll meet downstairs in ten minutes." His dark gaze settled on Julian. "Can I have a word with you two?" He nodded toward the sorcerer.

Julian watched as everyone else cleared out. They were off to their corners to get ready for whatever the hell was coming their way. Finn's golden complexion was pale, and his eyes looked haunted as he nodded before slipping away. Nico lingered, his eyes claiming Jaden even as he turned to leave.

It bothered Julian to see the want reflected in the warrior's eyes, but he knew that Nico would give his life to protect Jaden—that he'd claim her if he could. Julian didn't like it, but he needed to be cool with it. She deserved so much more than he'd ever be able to give.

He watched the jaguar leave and unclenched his jaw.

"Jaden, you remember how to get to the hub? This isn't official business, more of a family issue," Jaxon said politely.

"I'm not going anywhere."

"She stays." Julian spoke quickly, surprising even him-

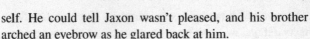

self. He could tell Jaxon wasn't pleased, and his brother arched an eyebrow as he glared back at him.

"Fine," Jaxon answered, his tone clipped, though he could tell his brother was perplexed.

Jaden moved closer to him, and just the presence of her body, the feel of her warmth, did wonders for him. He was fast losing control, yet, with her at his side, the slide wasn't so slippery. He was able to hold his ground.

"What are the two of you not telling me?" Jaxon asked, looking at the both of them, ignoring the chuckle that fell from Declan's mouth.

The sorcerer snorted and stood with his arms crossed. "This should be good."

Julian ignored him and faced his brother, not liking his tone or the way he was looking at Jaden.

"She is mine."

Julian heard the words, and as they echoed inside his skull, he looked down at the woman beside him. *She is mine.* It felt . . . right to vocalize it. He glanced into Jaxon's shocked face and smiled wickedly, liking the fact that his brother was off center. "We are mated."

"He is your mate?" Jaxon asked Jaden, his tone incredulous. "And you never thought I might like to know this?"

"It was none of your business, Castille," she said softly. "Hell, Julian didn't even find out until a few days ago."

"When? How?" Jaxon asked, his questions fragmented.

"Well, I'm guessing they did the nasty at some point," Declan inserted, his face alight with a devilish grin. "It's usually how it works isn't it? I mean with you shifters. Christ, is there no other way? Some cultures jump over a rock or sing to the moon. Easy and it's done, but you guys . . . it's all about the sex."

The sorcerer sighed and ran his fingers through his hair.

"And while I'll be the first to admit I'd love to hear all the tasty details, we don't have time for this shit." His eyes narrowed, and the energy in the room changed slightly. "What the fuck do you want to know, Jaxon? Just ask the question."

Silence fell between them for several long seconds. Julian could tell that his brother was struggling with something. Join the fucking club, he thought.

Jaxon glared at the three of them, his dark eyes narrowed, his lips thinned. His broad shoulders were square, and the power that clung to him would scare the shit out of most men.

"You're hiding something. I can tell. I need to know everything before we head to Vegas." His brows furled together into a grimace. "There's no room for mistakes." Jaxon looked at each of them, and there was no doubt as to the seriousness of the situation. "There's too much at stake. I won't jeopardize my son's future."

"There's nothing that you need to know." The lie slipped easily off Julian's tongue, and his face remained blank as he faced his brother. They were way too close to his objective to fuck things up now.

Jaxon's eyes narrowed, and they glittered, a dangerous, dark color. He took a few steps forward but stopped as a growl erupted from Julian.

The two brothers stared at each other, while the energy in the room darkened.

"Where have you been for the last six months?" Jaxon spit out, and it was obvious he was furious. "Why did you not contact us as soon as you could?" His eye turned to Declan, full of accusation. "You were part of my team, Dec. What the hell is going on?"

"Why do you care?" Julian asked. "Isn't it enough that

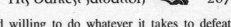

we're here and willing to do whatever it takes to defeat Cormac? Why the interrogation?"

"I care because someone let you out from wherever the hell it is you were." Jaxon's face was fierce. "Nothing is coincidence. I'm assuming that *someone* wants *something* from you in exchange for your freedom."

Julian's gut clenched. His brother was a smart son of a bitch. He narrowed his eyes and the anger inside of him burned hard.

"And you!" Jaxon's furious eyes leveled a dark look onto Jaden. "You are part of PATU. We've worked together. What's your role in all of this? Can we really trust you? Or does the DaCosta blood that I can smell from here taint you the same way it's painted your family in darkness."

The animal inside Julian bellowed in rage, and he snarled, his body a blur, as he reached for his brother. His vision narrowed until he saw red, so great was the anger inside of him.

She was there, her body slipping into the space between them, preventing him from getting to Jaxon. His canines erupted painfully, and the darkness that always circled the edges of his mind expanded until he began to pant loudly. He was riding the edge, and, for the moment, it looked inviting as all hell.

His eyes looked deep into his brother's, and he knew that in that moment, if not for Jaden, he would have done everything in his power to rip Jaxon's throat out. He envisioned it, clear as day, and smiled wickedly at the thought.

He felt the animal beneath his skin shift, felt the claws that had erupted. A growl rumbled, low, from his belly, and he heard Declan swearing, inventing new words as he tried to calm the animal.

His energy changed and he turned his head, pinning the

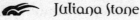

sorcerer with a furious look. "Stand back and don't try your fucking mojo on me."

Declan's face was tight, but he nodded and fell back.

It was then that he smelled the blood, and, instantly, the madness faded as he looked down at Jaden. In his rush to get to Jaxon, she'd stepped in the way of his claws. Even though he'd not shifted, the tips of his fingers had become razor-sharp, and he'd pierced the flesh of her shoulder.

"I'm fine," she whispered. "It's nothing Julian, really."

He felt like the worst kind of bastard ever and snarled at his brother once more though he knew there was no one to blame but himself. His control was leaving fast, and if he didn't get it together . . .

She grabbed his chin and forced him to look into her eyes. They were huge, intense. He noticed for the first time small golden flecks that surrounded the irises. Funny he'd not noticed before, but then again, it's not like they'd had a normal relationship.

There'd been no romance. No courting. Declan was right—it had all been about the sex. For a second, he thought it would be nice to romance the woman in front of him.

"Are you okay?" The words fell from her lips like soft whispers, and the concern in her eyes couldn't be hidden. "I need for you to be okay. I need to know that you're not gonna go all ape-shit on me before we get this done." She moistened her lips and tried to smile. "We can do this, Julian, but not by fighting amongst ourselves."

She gently pushed him away, and he let her, watched as she turned to his brother and flicked a long piece of hair behind her shoulder. He focused on the silky strand, feeling the wash of madness leave him as he did so, and his heart slowed, beating in a more normal manner.

Jaden squared her shoulders and faced his brother like

the fierce warrior she was. Something melted inside of him, a piece of ice that broke from the darkness.

"I will not have you question my loyalty, Jaxon." She paused, and Julian's gaze settled onto Jaxon's intense features. He knew what his brother had lost. What the DaCostas had done to Libby.

When had the world become so twisted and dark?

"I'll forgive your harsh words. I know that my family has done much to deserve your hatred and disgust. So you can imagine how I feel." He heard her blow out a long breath. "Because you're right." She shook her head, and her hands waved wildly in the air. "We do share the same blood. I am a DaCosta. Jakobi is my father, I can't change that." Her voice dropped to just above a whisper. "But I'm also DeCruz, and my mother's blood is pure and strong, and I'm filled with the power of her people."

Julian stepped forward until he was beside Jaden. He was calm, the beast had been beaten back, his resolve was firm.

"You will show her the respect she deserves." He spoke sharply and arched an eyebrow as he stared into his brother's eyes.

Jaxon frowned and opened his mouth to speak, but Declan cut him off.

"Christ, we all agree Jaden's one of the good guys. We trust her. Now can we get the hell out of here? Are we not wheels up in less than an hour?"

Jaxon nodded and turned to the sorcerer. "If anything happens that jeopardizes my team, *my family*, I will hold you personally responsible, O'Hara. Understood?"

Declan flashed a smile and turned away. "Yeah, no worries, my friend."

Jaxon's gaze fell to Jaden. "I meant no disrespect. I know you've sacrificed a lot, I just . . ." He paused for several seconds. "I have a son now, and I can't risk his future or the future of every single human on this planet. What we do will affect all of them. I need to know we're on the same page."

Jaden nodded. "We are."

His eyes narrowed, and he looked to his brother. "Okay." Jaxon held out his hand, and Julian slowly grasped it tightly. His brother's grip was strong. "Don't make me regret trusting you," Jaxon said.

Jaxon released his hand and turned to follow in Declan's footsteps. The thrum of energy that surrounded him was powerful. "We leave for the airstrip in twenty minutes."

Jaden's hand crept to Julian's arm. He ignored it as he felt his emotions tighten. He sensed the quiet strength that she possessed, and nearly turned into her embrace, but something stopped him. A need to separate, to acknowledge a future that could never be.

Yet through the confusion, something shone through, gripped him hard. *Love. I love this woman.*

He opened his mouth, but the words died before he could speak them. What was the point? In the end, it would only hurt her more.

They stood there, each listening to the other's breaths, then she tugged on him, and whispered, "I know things are complicated, but I won't play this game, Julian. After this is all over, we'll figure things out. But in the meantime"—her eyes flashed—"let's go kick Cormac's ass."

Chapter 25

They boarded the jet an hour later. It was a large crew, consisting of his brothers, Cracker, Libby, and Skye, as well as Ana, Declan, Finn, and Nico. An eclectic but deadly bunch.

Jaxon had just boarded when the pilot messaged that Drake was on the line and needed to speak to him urgently. Julian watched a muscle ripple across Jaxon's jaw sharply as he went to answer the summons.

Drake was Jaxon's direct commander and technically the person in charge of PATU. *Technically* because Jaxon had always run his unit without outside interference. His success rate was high, and, from what Julian understood, Drake usually gave him free rein.

Things had changed over the last few months, and Jaxon had kept Drake in the loop on a need-to-know basis only. The stakes were too high, and at this point there was no way to know who could be trusted. Anyone could be compromised.

As of now, Jaxon and his branch of PATU were basically working dark. No contact with anyone outside the people in the jet.

Julian kept to himself, sitting near the back and avoiding eye contact. It was the only way to keep conversation to a minimum. He had nothing to say really. The end of his journey was near, and he'd either fail or succeed. It was that simple.

Jaden sat across from him, her face tense as she stared out the window. Her long, elegant fingers kneaded her thigh, and she kept biting her bottom lip. It was a nervous gesture, and the weight of the coming hours was something she'd have to work through on her own.

And she would, of that he had no doubt. She was a warrior, after all, tough as nails.

He watched Nico from beneath hooded eyes. The shifter was quiet, his features blank. He couldn't hide the hunger and need that reflected in his eyes each time he glanced toward Jaden.

Julian sighed and settled back into the soft leather. What a sorry-ass fucking bunch they were. Each of them had scars. Some were visible, all were deep, the kind that cut into hearts and souls.

The kind not easily fixed.

He had a chance to do just that, to put back together the part of himself that was broken. Though it meant leaving everything behind to serve the mysterious *Bill*. And now he was left with regret for what could have been. Jaden represented a life that he hadn't even known he wanted.

Until last night.

She looked at him then, and his breath hitched as their eyes met. He felt her like a physical punch to the gut. He saw the thin sheen of moisture that lay upon her skin, the flushed heat of her cheeks. She smiled warily, but he could not reciprocate. The cold part of him was locked into place. That was how it had to be.

He looked away and ignored her soft sigh.

Within twenty-four hours, he'd either be dead or tied to a new life that could have nothing to do with the old. Things were better this way. Luckily. he played the part of bastard well.

"All right, listen up." Jaxon's calm voice drew everyone's attention, and Julian sat a little straighter in his seat. The energy in the room intensified, and he saw the dead seriousness on each of their faces. The past year had led to this. His gaze fell to Libby's tense features.

Hell, the past three years had led to this.

He was surprised she'd come. That she'd leave her child. But the woman was determined to see Cormac pay for his sins, and Logan would be fine. Mr. M was in charge, and an elite team of guards was there to protect them.

"We'll be landing on a private strip in Nevada about an hour outside of Las Vegas. A team will meet us there and escort us to a safe facility, where we'll prepare."

Jaxon took the time to look at each and every one of them. "I don't need to tell you how important it is that this plan goes off without a hitch. We can't afford any fuck-ups. The consequences are too great. Cormac must be stopped. The portal must be retrieved." He paused for a second as his gaze fell on Libby. "There is no other objective other than that, and I'll do whatever it takes to get it done."

The engine rumbled beneath them, and Julian glanced out the window. Snow continued to whirl in thick bands of white, obscuring everything within its grasp.

"We'll land in just under five hours. Once in Nevada, I'll brief you." He nodded to them all. "I'm finalizing our plan now, so I suggest you get as much rest as possible. I need all of you on your game. Once we hit the dry heat, there's no turning back."

Jaxon slid into the seat beside Libby and his arm went around her shoulders almost immediately. Julian watched the way she rested her head on his chest, the way his brother pulled her into his embrace like she was a breakable.

The power of the engine accelerated, and the plane took off down the runway, leading them toward an uncertain future and a date with evil. Declan turned around and nailed him with a half smile, his eyes icy cold. "Been a slice, but glad the ride is almost over."

Julian nodded ever so slightly, then pushed it all from his mind as he closed his eyes and pretended to sleep.

Jaden leaned back and forced her body to relax. She wasn't tired, but her muscles ached with tension. She was wound so tight, it was a wonder she could even breathe.

That wasn't a great way to start a mission. She needed to conserve her energy, not waste it fretting and freaking out. She had to keep her mind alert and free from distractions.

Though she wished Julian would move his ass to the other end of the plane. That would make it easier. His raw energy was intoxicating. He called to her on such a primal level that everything inside of her was aware of him. Of each breath he took. Of the long-as-sin lashes that fringed his eyes, the aristocratic nose and square chin.

She ached inside at the thought of him and her animal moved restlessly. The night she'd shared with Julian had been breathtaking. But the magic hadn't lasted. He was already pulling away from her. Her jaguar was in turmoil, sensing the mixed signals Castille was swimming in and the coming battle. For so long her life had been about revenge and hatred, and, now that the end was near, what did that mean for her? What did she have to show for her efforts?

She had a family that was fractured—*screwed up* and *dysfunctional* didn't even come close to describing her situation. Her father was an evil son of a bitch, and, sadly, her brothers were more than ready to fill his shoes. Never mind that they'd already lost the youngest DaCosta to battle.

She'd never had an adult relationship that was anything beyond fulfilling her body's needs. Hell, her longest relationship had been with a cockatoo. Even that had failed. She was gone more than she was home, and eventually her maid had claimed the poor thing.

No strings . . . that had always been her motto.

Her gaze strayed to Julian. Until he came along. Boy, had she screwed up with him. What she wouldn't give to turn back the clock and have that moment over. The one where she refused another drink and left the bar. Alone.

Choices. It was all about the choices. Unfortunately, when you fucked up, the consequences tended to bite you in the ass. Like being mated to a man who would never want to be with you, not in the way you wanted.

Sex wasn't everything.

She gazed out into the bright sun and winced. It reflected off the stark, clear morning. Down below, the earth was covered in a white dream, and soon it would fade, give way to green and blue, then to the heat of the desert.

Las Vegas. Cormac had been hiding in plain sight for months. How in the hell had the bastard managed to keep that on the down low? Not just from PATU but from her father? He'd placed a huge bounty on O'Hara's head months ago. Truthfully, nothing Cormac did surprised her. He was one hell of a slippery son of a bitch.

Jaden felt a tingle of *something* ripple across her skin.

Apprehension? Fear? They said it was called Black Magick, *Las Vegas's newest casino.* A fitting place, really, for the final battle.

She sank farther into her seat and stretched out her legs, taking care not to touch Julian's. Though his eyes were closed, she knew he was awake. All around her, she heard muted voices, whispered words of love.

She supposed in times of crisis that was what you did, reached out for the one who mattered most. Seriously, she wished everyone would can the love crap and shut the hell up. It did nothing but leave her empty inside, aching, as she did everything in her power to ignore the man who sat across from her.

"You feel it."

She turned her head slightly and arched an eyebrow at Nico. He looked tired, somewhat resigned.

"Feel what?" she asked, sitting a little straighter.

"The end," he answered softly before turning toward his window.

Jaden shivered at the finality of his tone and once more sunk into her seat. She wrapped her arms around herself, trying to find what comfort she could.

She had a bad feeling about the coming hours, and she'd always learned to trust her instincts. Her tummy rolled beneath her fingers, and she closed her eyes as she broke out in a cold sweat.

A bad feeling indeed.

It was early afternoon when they deplaned. The airstrip they'd landed on was out in the middle of nowhere; however, there were two large SUVs waiting for them.

After the chill of the Canadian north, Jaden welcomed the warmth of the sun and took a few moments to drink in some vitamin D before following the others. She slipped in beside Julian, and though he nodded politely, there was no conversation. No touch or lingering glance.

His face was dark, and the tightness around his mouth spoke volumes. If she were a girl with issues, the cold shoulder would be a definite blow to the ego. As it was, it just fed the ball of nerves in her belly until her entire body was humming from the force of it.

Her teeth chattered, and she clamped her mouth shut. It was odd. She was in the middle of the freaking desert, and, still, she was trembling. No one spoke as the SUV started off, and though she'd wished for silence on the plane, here, now, it was heavy. Uncomfortable.

Her eyes followed the distant skyline, glancing past the sparse vegetation and brown earth as they sped down the highway. The desert was an unforgiving space, so different from the lush jungles of her home.

She was suddenly filled with such longing for home that it brought tears to her eyes. The jungle had always been the place she ran to when she needed to escape the shit reality of her life. This time was no different. She felt as if she was on the precipice. That the darkness she'd been chasing for years was no longer on the horizon but had bled into the here and now.

She closed her eyes and let her mind wander. *You're not in Kansas anymore.*

They drove for over an hour in silence, and when they finally stopped, Jaden jumped out quickly, needing to be away from Julian. His dark eyes had flattened to a dull opaque, and she felt his power coiled tightly around him. His energy was dark and agitated her cat something fierce.

Her jaguar was scratching hard, the burn was uncomfortable, and she walked a bit, shaking out her limbs in an effort to calm her nerves. They'd driven underground, into what appeared to be a bunker at first, but instead led to a secure facility controlled by PATU.

She stretched in quick, precise motions and felt a sense of pride as she eyed her crew. They'd all been touched by the evil of Cormac and had vowed to end his reign. It would happen. Tonight.

"You all right?"

Nico stood a few feet from her, his shoulders held stiffly, his hands clenched at his sides.

"Not really," she answered, a smile tugging the corners of her mouth as his dark gaze rested on her. She raised an eyebrow. "You?"

The shifter stared at her, his handsome face devoid of emotion. He loosened his body and rotated his powerful shoulders. He ignored her question and answered with one of his own. "You and Castille . . . has he acknowledged your claim?"

Jaden felt her cheeks burn hot under the warrior's intense glare.

"Will he not honor you as his mate?"

Christ, like she had time for this shit. Irritation colored her words in sarcasm. "My God, Nico, don't confuse me with Jane and go all Tarzan on me. That's not the way it works."

He frowned. "Actually, that's exactly how it works."

Jaden blew out an exasperated breath and closed the space between them. Sometimes the jaguar warrior's Neanderthal outlook irritated the crap out of her. She supposed they couldn't help it, really. It was part of the genetic code. "It doesn't matter, Nico, do you understand? Whatever happens between me and Julian *should not matter* to you."

Nico hissed, and she sensed his anger but pushed forward, knowing it was not the time to dance around his feelings. Besides, he'd started it.

"There will never be anything between us, not the way you want. You need to listen and understand, Nico. I don't love you. I don't want you as a mate." *I already have one.*

She thumped him in the chest. "You think you have these feelings for me, but you've never gotten over Bella." She grabbed his hand, hating the way he held himself so stiffly. Hating the way her words hurt him. "You still love Bella, and until you come to terms with what happened, with how she died, you'll never be able to move forward." She had to make him see. "You say that Julian is using me? How is that any different from you wanting me as a replacement for a dead woman?"

He wrenched his hand from her and took a step back. "You would preach to me about moving forward when you're fucking the man who threw you away like nothing more than a piece of garbage three years ago?"

His voice echoed against the concrete, and Jaden was aware that she and Nico were the focus of everyone.

They'd heard his words. *Julian must have heard his words.* Jaden swallowed thickly. She couldn't deny the fact that the man was right.

Nico's face was thunderous as he plunged on. "It is unacceptable to me that you'd settle for him." He tossed a dark look toward Julian and growled before his voice fell to a whisper. "I would give you everything."

Jaden felt defeated as she looked up into Nico's eyes.

Defeated, hurt, and humiliated. "When a warrior mates, the bond is something that is not easily broken. You, more than anyone, know that." She stepped back, and her voice hardened. "My personal life is none of your business. Who

I *screw* is none of your business. This isn't a reality show, Nico, it's the real deal. Life and death. Understood?"

His lips pulled back in a snarl. "I will do whatever it takes to make sure we are successful tonight. Once this is over, I'm gone." He looked away, his nostrils flared as his face once more resumed its blank look. "The jungle calls. I should never have left."

He walked away and left her there, alone with the weight of all their stares at her back.

Her cheeks burned, she felt the sting as they flushed red. Nothing like starting a mission on the heels of chaos.

Jaden inhaled quickly and shook out her long hair before turning toward Julian. His eyes were averted though he faced her from several feet way with Declan and Finn. She crossed to them, quickly aware that the vampire Ana's eyes followed her as she did so.

"Let's do this," she said to Declan.

The sorcerer cocked his head as he looked behind her. "You better keep that kitty leashed."

"Nico will be fine." Jaden pushed past them, ignoring Julian, who stood in silence, his hands clenched, his face dark.

They followed Jaxon through two high-level checkpoints, each of them thorough. Jaden was impressed with the security. She'd heard of Desert Hole, as the facility was called, but had never had the opportunity to visit. It was manned by a mixture of otherworld and human, and run by the legendary Ethan Crane.

He was a shapeshifter, a wolf, who'd fought in both world wars, Vietnam, and had apparently been in Afghanistan as well. She'd never met him in person, but his reputation was legendary. A lethal killer with insane tracking capabilities.

He was also, apparently, quite the ladies' man.

A few minutes later, she could appreciate the latter.

Crane didn't walk so much as glide into the briefing room. His age was pegged at over one hundred human years, but he had the appearance of a man in his prime.

The tall American smiled though the glint of his eyes remained frosty as he quickly scanned the room. His build, though muscular, was lean in the hips and long-legged. His movements were those of a predator.

He was very much like her men, and she found her eyes drawn to Julian. As always.

He stood on the fringe of the group, his lips set in a tight line. The pent-up energy that thrummed through his body could easily be felt. She saw his nostrils flare, and when he suddenly turned and met her gaze, she stopped breathing.

His golden eyes glittered in a strange way, a wild look hung in their depths. He looked like a man on the edge. She wanted to do something. To say anything to calm him.

"Okay, let's make this quick."

Jaxon's voice cut through their moment, slicing it away as they both turned their attention to the warrior.

"We've been able to determine that Cormac is keeping Azaiel underground, beneath Black Magick. Here is a schematic of the building. Luckily for us, our prisoner was one of Cormac's inner circle, and his mind held many details that will help us."

They all looked up at a large screen that had noiselessly slid from the ceiling. The impressive casino's secrets were laid bare. To the east was a large amphitheater, where the main attraction, magic shows, were held. Apparently Cormac had quite the apprentice, and it was the hottest ticket in town.

The main casino was large, with nearly two hundred thousand feet of gaming room, and there were nearly six thousand rooms, located in towers at each of the four corners, including four luxurious penthouse suites. As was the trend in Vegas, there was an additional theme park where you could bring the entire family and let them feed on the dark energy that surrounded Black Magick.

Nice.

"We need to get to the lower level, and there are only two ways that we feel we can successfully penetrate." Jaxon pointed toward the south end of the casino. "There is a service entrance near the kitchen that allows access below." He then pointed toward the amphitheater. "And there is another access point located behind the main stage."

He looked up at all of them. "This is where we'll get in. Azaiel is being contained in a room. At this moment, we're not quite sure where."

"I didn't think basements existed in Vegas," Declan observed.

Jaxon grimaced. "This will be no ordinary space, of that we can be sure." Jaxon paused as he took a few moments to look at each and every one of them. Jaden felt his strength, his worry, and as his eyes passed over his woman, Libby, she felt his love.

She clenched her hands together tightly as a wave of emotion ran over her. They could do this. She felt Julian at her side. They *would* do this.

"Our mission is twofold: The main objective is Azaiel. We need to retrieve the portal. Second to that is Cormac." Jaxon literally spit his name. "That son of a bitch will not live to see another day."

"How can you be sure the fallen will cooperate? That he even knows where the portal is?" Nico cut in. "Seems to me Cormac has had him for months; if he couldn't extract the information, what makes you think we can?"

"If Azaiel refuses to cooperate, he will be eliminated." Jaxon was firm in his answer. "The portal shall remain hidden, and for now I'm okay with that as long as Cormac is dealt with."

"What the hell do we do if, miraculously, he gives it up?" Skye asked.

"He will be eliminated either way." Jaxon again was curt and to the point.

"How do you suggest killing something that is supposedly celestial?" A hint of sarcasm tinged Declan's words, and Jaden looked at him sharply. He was pushing the boundaries. Not good. The darkness that threatened both him and Julian was digging in deep.

She knew they were running out of time.

"You get close enough and cut its fucking head off," Cracker answered as he spit to the side. "Even then it's a crapshoot."

"Okay then," Declan retorted, as a smile crept over her features.

Cracker's eyes narrowed as he stared at both Declan and Julian.

"We'll split into two teams," Jaxon continued. "I'll take Jagger, Cracker, Skye, and Libby. Our objective will be to penetrate the kitchen entrance." Julian nodded toward Ethan. "Crane will lead the second team and come in through the amphitheater. This way, we attack from two ends and hopefully one of us can get to Azaiel."

His gaze swung to Jaden. "No disrespect, but Ethan is the unit leader in this area."

Jaden nodded. She wasn't going to get into a pissing contest over who led the team. She didn't care. She just wanted the job done.

The room had suddenly gone deathly quiet.

"We've got operatives inside, and early intel indicates that the place is crawling with otherworld." Jaxon's eyes focused on Jaden. "The DaCostas have been spotted in Las Vegas. Jakobi and Degas have entered the game."

Jaden felt the weight of his words and a sliver of fear rifled through her body at the mention of her father's name. It was fitting, really. That he would be involved right to the very end.

Her hand strayed to the bruise along the side of her face. It was still there, courtesy of her father. She winced as her fingers passed over it. The pain was good. It was a reminder. Maybe it was time for her to deal with all of her nightmares. Finish it, once and for all.

She returned Jaxon's hard gaze and cocked her head to the side in challenge. If he thought she'd run away like a coward, he was sadly mistaken.

"You need to stay away from the line of sight targeted by the security cameras. They'll definitely have facial-recognition programs in place, and they are immune to cloaking charms. There will be guards everywhere, otherworld, human, demon, you name it. It's not going to be easy to accomplish our task. We must succeed. If we don't . . ." He paused, and his words softened. "I have every faith in all of you, and when this is over, I will see each and every one of you back here. Nothing less is acceptable."

His dark gaze swept over them, pausing as he rested on Julian.

"We clear?"

Jaden felt the air leave her lungs in a whoosh. She was more than ready. She felt like every single thing she'd ever done had brought her to this moment. It was time to make things right.

She glanced at Julian and was startled to catch his

dark eyes staring at her intently. His lips moved, and, for a second, she thought he was going to speak to her. Something flashed across his face but was gone just as quick. What was he thinking?

He turned abruptly and left. Guess she'd never know. Jaden felt something loosen inside of her and slide away until all that was left was a big hole.

"Sin City awaits, boys. Who's feeling lucky?" Ethan cracked a smile though it did nothing to thaw the cold glint in his eyes.

Declan winked at her as he turned to follow Julian, and she heard him laugh. "Giddy up."

"He seems like a crazy son of a bitch," Ethan observed.

Jaden started forward.

"You have no idea."

Chapter 26

The dark interior of the amphitheater did nothing to hide the sinister taint that lingered in the air.

Jaden smoothed the blood red silk over her hips as she slid in beside Julian, her arm linking through his as she did so. They'd just entered the cavernous room and looked every inch a successful, wealthy couple out to enjoy an evening in one of Vegas's finest.

She glanced down at the heavy necklace that lay between her breasts. It was ornate and, though delicate in appearance, built to withstand a shift. The piece was charmed, heavily so, and for the moment hid their trace signatures from Cormac and his minions. Hopefully, they wouldn't be recognized. She felt the gentle touch of magick that slid over her skin. How long it would last was anyone's guess.

Center stage was occupied though the sounds of the band that entertained the crowd grated on her nerves. It felt like the notes were off-key, only by a fraction, causing them to distort. Her feline ears, supersensitive as they were, protested, and she fought the urge to cover them.

She glanced around. No one else seemed to notice. In fact, from what she could tell, everyone was paying rapt attention like it was freaking U2 up there.

They looked like zombies.

Her eyes narrowed. Something was definitely off. Dark energy was heavy in the air. The place was rancid with its sick, sweetly scent.

She felt like gagging.

"There are two entrances that lead to the storage areas in the lower level. One is stage left. The one we'll have most success with is stage right near the dressing rooms." Crane had found his way to their side in silence. "There will be more traffic, people and noise. A lot easier to blend in." His eyes were calculating as he looked at Ana and Jaden. "My guess is the two of you will be our best bet to get close enough to the guards in order for us to take them out with minimum exposure."

Jaden nodded and turned to the vampire. The petite woman held herself stiffly, as if she were afraid to touch the man beside her. It irritated her, how much the vampire acted as if the sorcerer were nothing more than an acquaintance, yet her need for him, her *desire* for him, was palpable.

It was bizarre since the worst-kept secret in PATU was the longing Declan O'Hara had for Ana.

For the first time, Jaden realized she knew nothing about the vampire. Not even her last name.

"Okay, you ladies ready?" Ethan smiled as an usher nudged him out of the way.

"Sir, you must take your seats. It's dangerous in the aisles."

"We're on it," he said good-naturedly, the smile fading fast as the usher went about his business.

"Finn, Nico, you're with me, we'll hang close to the women. You two"—he nodded to Julian and Declan—"keep to the shadows and watch our backs. We'll give the ladies exactly two minutes, then we'll go in." Ethan's tone was serious, his eyes hard as ice as he turned back to the girls. "You need to act fast. Cormac is an arrogant bastard, and he'll not be expecting an attack here on his home turf. We're heavily outnumbered, so surprise is our friend. Understood?"

Nervous excitement rushed through Jaden and she exhaled slowly in an effort to calm her nerves. She nodded and squared her shoulders.

"Be careful." Julian's breath was at her neck, and she stilled, hearing only the mad beating of her heart.

"You too," she answered, but kept her eyes trained on the stage, afraid to look up into his eyes and not really sure why.

She turned and followed Ana into the waiting darkness, missing his hand as it froze in the air, inches from her back.

Julian's eyes adjusted quickly to the dimly lit room as he followed Jaden's progress. He had no issue with the dark; in fact, he relished it.

He stretched his fingers and slowly let his hand fall back to his side. She'd been so close. He'd just wanted one final touch. Instead, he was left grasping nothing but air.

Nico's dark eyes regarded him for several seconds before he turned and followed Jaden.

His nostrils flared as her scent faded away, the sweetness of it stolen from him much too fast, and he felt empty. The darkness that lingered around the edges of his mind seeped through, and he clenched his teeth as it washed over him.

"Sucks, doesn't it?"

He arched an eyebrow though he kept his gaze centered

on Jaden and Ana as he observed their progress. They'd made it to the far side and were near stage right.

"What's that?"

Crane moved out of earshot, and Declan lowered his voice. "That you've finally found a woman worth fighting for. After tonight, you're either dead or on a goddamn road trip to bum fuck *wherever* with Bill the elf."

Julian scowled. "Jaden and I would never have had a future together."

"Yeah, the hot sex and superhero-babe thing she's got going on is so not working."

Julian turned to the sorcerer abruptly and nailed him with a dark look. "Bill the elf?"

Declan rotated his neck slowly. "Ya gotta admit, Castille, the fucker is under five feet and round as a bouncing ball. Dip the dude in green and red and toss him toward the North Pole." He smiled wickedly. "You'd see. Santa would sign him up for sure."

Julian ignored Declan and dragged his gaze back toward the stage. The music left much to be desired, but then he'd always been more of a blues man.

Jaden had disappeared, and his animal shifted beneath his skin. The scars that laced his flesh pulsated, and the burn was becoming more of an issue. If would surely drive a lesser man mad.

He just had to hold on a little bit longer, and he'd finally be freed from the constant darkness, the noise in his head, and the need that gnawed at him.

"Let's do this," he said abruptly. "You ready?"

"A walk in the park, my friend." Declan's voice was light but Julian glimpsed the torment that battered the sorcerer. He knew it well. He'd been eating it for breakfast, lunch, and supper for months.

He nodded. It was time to end this.

Declan indicated they head to the left, the opposite direction from the rest of the team.

Julian called the shadows to his body as he slipped into the darkness. The charm that hung from his neck was powerful, full of Declan's mojo. A little extra protection wouldn't hurt. He was confident no one could see them.

At least not the humans.

They slid through the crowd, with none the wiser, and adrenaline pumped through his body as they neared the stage area. It was a rush that he welcomed.

The music that pounded into the air was dark, seductive, and wrong. He glanced into the faces of the humans he passed and frowned at the rapt look in their eyes, as if they were in a trance.

He knew there was dark magick blended between the notes, he felt them, and the pull was strong. Sorry bastards. They were so vulnerable to the forces of the dark. If the demon realm did manage to break through, they'd be screwed. It would be a bloodbath.

His eyes scanned the room and rested on the two large men who stood stage left. They blocked the path to the door and were definitely otherworld. Even without the smell that drifted from them, the pimped-out clothes would have been a dead giveaway.

A smile cracked his face as a growl hung low in his belly.

Silently, he and Declan approached them. The band was in a frenzy, pounding out notes as the singer wailed into the microphone. The sound echoed around the room, a cacophony of noise.

It somehow was appropriate and fed the rage that built inside him. Darkness preyed on darkness, and, in this instance, he was working it.

His animal burned beneath his skin, and the power of his jaguar flooded his veins. Both men were vampires, and he withdrew the deadly dagger from beneath his jacket.

Their presence wasn't felt until they were almost upon the two men. By then, it was too late.

To the observer, a lone human whose attention might have been drawn from the music, all that was seen was a blur, a slight whisper in the air as if the shadows had moved.

They blitzed the vamps, Declan throwing two sharp and penetrating energy bursts at them, while Julian followed up with clean and precise swipes to the neck.

He watched dispassionately as their heads separated from their bodies, then grabbed the lifeless forms, dragging the remains along behind him. The entire attack lasted less than five seconds, and as he slipped through the door, he turned, his eye quickly scanning the immediate area.

No one had witnessed their advance.

Declan was just ahead and put a finger to his mouth, indicating there was more filth to deal with. The frenetic, heavy chugging of the guitars was somewhat muffled in here, yet the aggressive nature of the music fed his mind, excited his jaguar.

Julian sensed a third body several feet away. This one was different and he held back a snarl as its demon scent slowly drifted toward them. The large man was tapping his foot, moving his neck to the rhythm, totally digging the music.

Declan cleared his throat and smiled as the demon turned toward them. Its eyes were blood red and glowed eerily in the dark.

"Damn, you need to invest in some shades, boy, your freaky laser eyes are fucking ugly."

The demon snarled at Declan and immediately began making a series of clicking noises from deep in his throat.

Julian clenched his hands together. He knew the demon was calling on his true form, and it wouldn't take long for it to transform.

He'd been itching to hit something for a while now. He might as well start with a nasty-ass demon from hell.

He took a step forward. Declan held a hand out, and he stopped. "This one's mine," he whispered. The air shimmered around him as Declan slowly walked toward the demon.

A loud hiss escaped from between its teeth, followed by a moan that was abruptly cut short as Declan came to within an inch of it. He twisted his hand in a gentle arc, yet the dark energy that flowed from him to the demon was anything but. It was a harsh, grinding burst of power, and the demon sank to his knees as it fought for air.

Julian stood back, watched closely, and though he might be mistaken, it looked as if energy was flowing both ways. As if Declan was feeding on the filth that lived inside the demon.

Several long moments passed, the demon's eyes dimming as it eventually lost the battle. Declan grunted from the effort it took but held firm and relaxed as the demon fell to the floor.

Julian was surprised. He held the dagger loosely at his side and stared down at the corpse. It had been much too easy for Declan to destroy the demon.

The sorcerer ran his hands across the back of his neck and loosened his shoulders. A long, shuddering breath fell from between his lips. When he turned to Julian, the smile that hung there seemed out of place.

No matter. He knew they were both riding way too close to the edge, and the crevice that separated them from the filth of the underworld was getting smaller as time marched on.

"Let's go." The urgency to get to the fallen sat heavy in his chest. He wanted it to be done.

"My father is here somewhere. I can feel him, which means if he doesn't already know I've returned from the dead"—Declan nodded toward the crumpled form at his feet—"he will now." Declan's eyes narrowed. "He'll be coming after me full on. Do not touch him, he's mine."

Julian snorted. He didn't give a rat's ass who snuffed the life out of Cormac O'Hara. His business was with Azaiel.

With stealth, they carefully picked their way across the back staging area, noiselessly moving amongst the massive snakes of electrical cables and cases of equipment. There were several staff, some human, some otherworld. None paid them any mind.

It was not what he expected, and he was beginning to suspect it wasn't so much the cloaking charm that covered his body, but the music. The hypnotic pull was unnatural.

They found themselves in a long corridor that ran perpendicular to the stage. It headed in the direction Jaden had gone, and, for a second, Julian hesitated. Had she made it past the guards with no problems?

"There it is." Declan pointed toward a nondescript door that was tucked in amongst a pile of boxes and large road cases. It looked easy enough.

He pushed Jaden from his mind. She was a warrior, after all, and could look after herself.

As they approached the door, he felt a change in the air. It was heavy, full of the weight of darkness, and he narrowed his eyes, noticing for the first time the film of gray that slithered slowly around the frame.

"I'll need a few minutes," Declan whispered, his face intense as he studied the magick that surrounded the door.

Julian stepped back and watched the sorcerer work.

Declan had become an extremely powerful mage over the last few years. His time in hell had increased his strength exponentially.

He was packing some seriously dark mojo and had no qualms about using it.

The energy that flew from his fingers was quick, precise as he drew his own personal charms into the air. It was amazing really, what the man could accomplish.

It didn't take him long.

"Ready?" Declan asked, not bothering to wait for an answer. He disappeared through the door, and Jaxon quickly followed suit.

The door swung shut automatically, the locking device clicking into place and leaving the two of them surrounded by total darkness.

Julian was immediately assaulted by the taint of evil, of demon and otherworld. It slithered across his skin like a lover's caress. He should find it repulsive, but he didn't. He *liked* it. In fact, he liked it . . . a lot.

A feral smile touched his face, changing the handsome features to menacing as he followed Declan into the bowels of Black Magick.

Chapter 27

Jaden felt like she could eat the darkness. It was that thick.

Her crew had managed to gain entrance to the lower level, not without a few casualties, but luckily they'd all been team Cormac.

Quickly, her eyes adjusted to the gloom. They'd taken a service elevator down and had just spilled out of it into a large, cavernous space. The cold hit her immediately. It was biting, harsh. The air that rushed into her lungs seemed thick and made it hard to breathe.

Down here everything was wrong. Up seemed like down, the air was rank with confusion and pain. She stilled her fast-beating heart, or at least tried to.

"This place is haunted. Things are not right," Ana whispered.

The magick that slithered across Jaden's skin was cold, like the underbelly of a snake, and she shivered from the weight of it. The bad feeling she'd been carrying for several hours pressed into her gut, *hard*. Damn, but she wanted to be wrong.

Ethan was pissed.

"Where the fuck did Castille and O'Hara get to?" he asked her pointedly.

She felt Ana's interest—though the vampire tried to hide it—as Nico slid into view. His face was blank, his eyes flat and cold. She hated the way he looked at her. Like she'd betrayed him.

Finn's gaze was hard, but he remained silent, a muscle working its way across his cheek.

Where *were* they? If anything, she thought they'd fight like hell to get down here before anyone else. Her belly rolled over. None of this made any sense.

"They're as committed as we are, if not more so," she answered roughly, though the doubt weasels were burrowing in fast and hard.

"What the hell does that mean?" Ethan asked shrewdly. His face was tight, his eyes cold. She saw the controlled anger that burned beneath the surface, and an answering flush built inside of her. Who the hell was he to question Julian's integrity?

She looked at him boldly. "It means we don't have time to debate their whereabouts. They're good, so let's move on."

"I don't trust either one of them," Nico said harshly.

Crane's grimace spoke volumes. "And you're telling me this now?"

The warrior remained silent, obviously tense.

"What the hell kind of outfit you running?" Crane said, his dark gaze trained on Jaden. "I have no idea how your unit's success rate is so high. You've got too many people involved with each other, and when that happens, mistakes occur," he snarled. "Lives are lost."

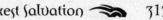

"Get over it, Crane." Jaden's eyes flashed. "When you care about people, *really* care about them, you're willing to do whatever it takes to get the job done. Julian would never do anything to jeopardize the recovery of the portal." She tried to control her emotions but was finding it increasingly hard. "So I suggest we move on and find the damned thing."

Crane was silent, his mouth pursed into a tight line. "We split up," he said abruptly. "The space down here is massive, and I'm sure you've all noticed that O'Hara has some serious shit going on. The wards are like none I've ever seen." He looked at all of them. "Mind-warping shit, so be on guard. Not everything will be as it seems. Jaxon and the others are coming down from the west end. We need to do a grid search and cover every inch of this place."

"Our com units have been activated. I don't know how well they'll work down here, but let's stay in touch." Finn nodded to them, his voice quiet, controlled as always. "Understood?"

Jaden felt the small device nestled in her ear and shook her head. A shadow passed behind Crane, a deviation in the light, and she was instantly on guard. This place gave her the creeps. She just wanted out. She slid the charmed dagger from its sheath against her thigh and squared her shoulders.

Time to dance with the devil.

"Let's do this."

"You, Ana, and Nico take the left side and we'll"—Crane nodded to Finn—"cover the right. Our objective is Azaiel, there is nothing else. Once we have him, we can worry about Cormac." His face was shrouded in shadow, casting a macabre expression over his features. Ethan Crane was one hell of a dangerous man, and she knew he'd stop at nothing to reach their objective.

At the moment, it was the only thing she liked about him.

"Stay safe," he said harshly, then indicated Finn follow him.

Jaden watched as the inky black swallowed them whole and a shudder passed over her as the shadows started to move, like they were pulsating from within.

"I don't like this." Ana's words were hard to understand. Her fangs were fully distended, and her eyes glowed fiery red. She turned to Jaden and for a second Jaden caught a glimpse of such torment, such pain, that she was stunned. "Where are they?" Ana whispered, as her cool facade slowly slid back into place.

Jaden knew *they* really meant Declan. "They're here somewhere, Ana, and the sooner we get to Azaiel, the sooner we'll find them." She nodded to Nico. "Let's go."

She cleared her mind of all thoughts save, one—Azaiel—and they moved toward the far left. Within moments, Jaden cursed silently and tossed her heels, though the cold, wet concrete at her feet was uncomfortable. Ana did the same, and, for a second, she felt laughter bubble up inside her.

She looked like a damn cocktail waitress, nothing like a trained operative and certainly not like a jaguar warrior. No matter, it could only work to their advantage.

Nico tossed her a modified Glock, and she looked at him in surprise. "How the hell did you manage to sneak this in past security?"

"Declan." His one-word answer was terse as he tossed one to Ana. "They're charmed, though since we don't know how well they'll work against demons, best to use your dagger and cut them down." He gave what passed as a smile. "Shifters and magicks, however, are gonna feel the burn."

"Where are they?" Ana asked, clearly puzzled. "O'Hara's security? I thought for sure we'd be in the middle of a blood-bath as soon as we gained entrance."

Jaden peered into the darkness and shivered as her body

reacted to the cold. A dark and malevolent presence was felt, and her jaguar shifted beneath her skin as unease slid over her.

"I think he's got it covered. We just can't see it yet," Jaden whispered. She turned to Nico. "Check out those storage rooms over there; Ana and I will do a sweep of the immediate perimeter." There were rows of shelving units holding large containers.

Nico nodded, opened his mouth as if to say something, then melted into the dark.

"This way." She nodded to Ana.

The two of them slowly made their way toward the rows of shelving. They were made of steel, looked sturdy, and rose into the air nearly ten feet. They were jam-packed with containers and, if toppled, would surely kill.

She tapped the com in her ear, heard Crane though his voice was cutting out, and tapped it off. The com units were necessary, but most of the time she found them annoying as all hell.

The steady drip of water could be heard, like a sad echo bouncing against the concrete. *When did Cormac develop an obsession with water?* The hem of her dress was dragging through puddles of it, and, with a curse she extended her long nails and let their razor-sharp ends slice through the fabric until her legs were bare.

"You should do the same, Ana, it's much easier to maneuver . . ." Jaden's words fell into nothing as she looked up to empty space. "What the hell?"

Ana was gone.

She whirled around, her hair flying and water spraying out from her feet. There was nothing there. It was as if the shadows had swallowed the vampire. She stilled as her senses expanded, and she scented the air. There were no trace signatures, no scent . . . nothing. It was if she'd never even been there.

Jaden tapped her com unit, and whispered hoarsely, "Ana?" She waited a few seconds and then cautiously moved forward. Again she whispered, "Ana?" There was nothing but static.

She tried again, "Nico." Again, nothing but silence.

Jaden gritted her teeth together and exhaled slowly as she focused all her senses and tried to read past the never-ending darkness. Something slithered across the floor, near her feet, and she jumped to the side, her arm arcing forward with the dagger held ready, and the Glock aimed as well.

The beady eyes of a rat stared up at her, and she resisted the urge to kick the bloody thing, hissing, instead, as her jaguar bled through. The rodent froze, as if it knew something dangerous was in sight, and scurried away.

She took a second to center herself and started forward. Something was there, just ahead.

Her eyes narrowed, and adrenaline rushed through her body, feeding her jaguar into a state of excitement. The mission was dangerous, but there was a part of her that craved the danger. It made her feel alive. It made her remember her purpose.

The shadows swirled and parted, the gray becoming mixed with light, and as the energy manifested fully, she was ready.

A loud hiss and clacking noise began in earnest, definitely a demon, and she rushed forward, her arm extended in a deadly arc, and faltered at the last second. It was Julian's face, *his* eyes and lips that snarled down at her.

What the hell?

Jaden's hesitation cost her, and she felt a burn as the demon's fist knocked into her chest and sent her flying backward. She landed, hard, and pain radiated out as her head connected with the concrete.

Confusion threatened and, for a dazed second, nearly won, but her jaguar roared to life, and a snarl erupted from between her teeth as she rolled to the side and pushed herself up.

Jaden held the dagger loose in her grip, welcoming the burn beneath her flesh as her jaguar made noise. The power of her animal was exhilarating, and she smiled at the demon as it hissed down at her.

It no longer looked like Julian, and she knew it had been the dark magick at work. She'd not make that mistake again.

The demon was in its true form, standing nearly seven feet high. Thick scales covered its flesh, and they glowed with a luminescence that was beautiful. A total contrast to the nasty evil that lived within.

Its eyes burned fire, and, as it snarled, the teeth dripped poisonous saliva. She remembered the pain of a demon's bite as she stared up at the thing. There was no way she was letting it get close enough to break skin.

She began to make quick calculations as it smiled and rotated its head, the clicking of its teeth still riding the air. She needed to get close enough to it to cut its head from its body without letting it take a bite out of her. In the confined space, she knew it would be difficult.

"You should run, little kitten, make the game that much more enjoyable." The demon's voice was multilayered and fell from its mouth in waves. It took a step toward her and swiped its long arm. She jumped back and gritted her teeth as it began to laugh. "I'm hungry, and it's been too long since I've had fresh meat."

The fucker was playing with her like she was a goddamn mouse.

Jaden gripped the Glock tightly in her other hand and arched an eyebrow as she looked up at it. At that point, she had nothing to lose.

"Eat this, asshole."

The demon stopped and opened its mouth to speak, but Jaden aimed and fired the Glock point-blank into its mouth. The force of the hit spun the beast around, and its entire head glowed green as dark liquid spewed from every orifice.

She jumped back as the demon toppled, and the poison arced outward. An awful keening sounded from deep within its chest, and, as it fell forward, she jumped through the air, her arm going wide, and she separated its head from its neck easily.

Jaden landed on the other side and turned back to the demon's body. It was twitching, a small burst of energy that slowly died to nothing. She looked down at the Glock and smiled.

Declan's charm worked on demons. Good to know.

She didn't bother looking back, kept moving forward as the dark shadows continued to swirl. She reached the end of the row and turned up the next, her gaze studying everything, her ears listening for any sound.

"Julian?" She tried her com again, but the static was too loud, and she switched it off. Whatever weird mojo was going on made the device pretty much useless. She was on her own.

The silence was heavy, weighing on her. Her heart beat against her chest, and the adrenaline that rushed through her body made every nerve ending sizzle with power.

She carefully made her way down the long row and stopped when a noise crept through the silence. At first she didn't know what it was, it was soft, feminine. It took a few seconds, then she realized it was the sound of a woman weeping.

Sweat rolled down the back of Jaden's neck. Her body was heated, and mist rose from her skin to halo her frame. She exhaled softly and moved forward, her dagger at the ready and the Glock held firmly in her right hand.

She rounded the corner cautiously, at first seeing nothing but mist and shadow, then it all fell away.

And she felt her heart break at the sight before her. She knew it was wrong, impossible, but the hope that sprang from her gut was nearly crushing.

Her mother knelt amongst the filth and wet of the floor, her body twisted as if in pain. She was sobbing quietly, her gentle profile so familiar.

Jaden took a step closer. *This place is haunted.* Ana's words echoed in her head, and she paused.

Her mother turned to her then, the eyes empty and rotting with maggots as she held her arm aloft. The hand was gone, leaving a bloody stump in place, and Jaden bit her lip in horror at the sight.

Her mother opened her mouth to speak, yet no words came forth. Black liquid spilled from the corners, the stench was nearly overwhelming, and she heard her mother speak, inside her mind.

Help me.

Jaden took a step backward, confused and angry. She knew the head games were part of Cormac's dark magick, they were built into the wards, but the sight of her mother tugged at the most painful night of her life.

Help me.

Again, her mother's voice whispered through her mind.

"You're not real," she said hoarsely, wanting to look away but not able to.

Her mother's head lolled to the side, and Jaden wiped away the tears that sprang to her eyes as she watched. She needed to move on, needed to get to the portal, yet her feet felt like they were encased in cement.

"You're not real," she said again, this time louder as she forced her feet to move forward, the cold and damp making her feet numb. Her teeth were chattering loudly as her body shivered in earnest.

She gripped the dagger so tightly that her fingers ached. She raised the weapon, knowing that whatever was there, just in front of her, was not her mother. It needed to be destroyed.

The air changed then, the shadows rushing around the woman, and as the darkness parted once more, Jaden cried out. Gone were the maggots, and blood and darkness.

Her mother smiled up at her, her body no longer broken. She was returned once more to her former self, beautiful, serene, and strong. The air sparkled, glowed and encircled her in a soft light.

She looked ethereal. She looked *real*.

Hope flared, however briefly, but Jaden tucked it away and welcomed the anger that burned inside her once more. She'd not let Cormac win using the demons of her past.

She took a step forward and raised the dagger, hating the way her mother smiled up at her as she did so.

"Fuck you, O'Hara," she whispered, then rushed forward. She jumped into the air and, at the last minute, closed her eyes, not wanting to see her mother's face as she attacked.

And yet when she landed, crouched along the floor, the dagger held firm, there was nothing there.

She looked to the side, her heart nearly beating out of her chest, but the space was empty.

"It seems you were right, Degas. My little pet has betrayed her family."

Dread rolled over in her belly, and slowly Jaden straightened. She turned around, and though her face gave nothing away, inside, fear clawed at her gut.

Her father Jakobi, brother Degas, and their guard Benicio stood several feet away. Her brother looked at her, a smug smile gracing his handsome face, while Benicio looked nothing if not bored.

But it was Jakobi who had her full attention. His dark eyes blazed with anger, and his teeth flashed through the gloom as he smiled at her and shook his head.

She knew in that moment they were not visions. They were very real. Her past had finally caught up with her, and she could no longer run from it.

"It's time to teach you a lesson." Her father moved toward her, and the rage that he felt sliced through the air, reaching for her.

It hit her hard, and she knew the end was near. There was no way she could defeat three jaguar warriors.

Jaden loosened her grip on the Glock, her fingers soft on the trigger. They could beat her down, but she'd not give up without a fight. She owed her mother that much.

She owed Julian as well.

She snarled, aimed the gun, and fired.

Chapter 28

The madness that hung in the air fed the black hole inside him. Julian inhaled deeply, welcoming the energy that flowed through him as he and Declan slipped through the shadows.

His nostrils flared. Dark Magick smelled different from any other. It was heavy, sweet, and intoxicating.

Cool flowing air caressed his skin, sliding over his body. It soothed him somewhat, as his skin was hot, his mind chaotic. One thing was constant.

Azaiel. There was nothing else.

The com unit in his ear sparked, and he thought he heard a voice, something soft, feminine, but then it was gone.

"This way," Declan whispered. "There's a thread of energy that's overpowering everything else." The sorcerer stared up into what appeared to Julian to be nothing more than inky black space, yet Declan smiled and shook his head. "It's fucking beautiful."

Julian frowned. "I don't see anything."

"I thought you pussycats had night vision." Declan started forward. "Trust me, it's this way."

The two men slid through the shadows, their tall frames splitting the night as mist swept the path in front of them. A gunshot ripped through the air, and Julian stilled. He held his Glock at the ready and unsheathed his dagger.

Declan nodded to the right, and Julian fell in behind him as they made their way forward. He felt a presence watching them, the weight of it heavy on his shoulders. The fine hair along the back of his neck rose, and his animal growled, sensing danger, as the beast began to scratch the surface.

At the last second, he whirled around and snarled ferociously as a face parted from the shadows, followed by two more. They were neither human nor otherworld, and shock grabbed him hard as he narrowly avoided a clawlike hand that swiped downward.

He glanced back at Declan and saw the same reaction.

How in the hell had shades from the underworld gained access topside? It made no sense. As far as he understood, they couldn't survive anywhere other than hell.

The one closest to him moaned, its mouth gaping as the sound magnified and became louder until Julian wanted to crush the bastard's larynx. He lunged and swiped his dagger across its throat and felt a burning pain rip across his flesh as his arm passed through the shade. Like fire enveloped inside ice.

His momentum carried him forward. He compensated and rolled, whirling around and ducking just in time as a second shade rushed him.

The air that followed in its wake was fetid, and he grimaced, snarling at Declan. "How the hell do we kill them?" he yelled. His voice was thick and dead-sounding. There was no echo, and he shook his head as a weird sensation pressed

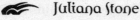

against his ears. Like a box of cotton had been stuffed inside his cranium.

Dread sat heavy as a stone in his belly. He'd taken every lick of pain that the bitch with the dagger had doled out. He'd inhaled confusion, dined on fear and depravity below, yet nothing terrified him more than the shades.

Julian wasn't ashamed to admit it, either. It was the reason he pressed on, was willing to sacrifice all to complete his task. He would not end up as one of them. Souls condemned to an existence that was neither dead nor alive. They were cursed to roam eternity in the hell realm as nothing more than an imprint of their former lives.

Declan's face was lit with a feral fire, his eyes luminous as they shone through the gloom. He held his hands out at the sides, his Glock and dagger on the floor beside him. His fingers glowed in earnest as the three shades moved toward Declan, their disembodied forms gliding across the floor rapidly.

"Come on, you bastards," Declan snarled and he rushed to meet them head-on. Energy sizzled from his fingers, electrical conduits of death that sparked into a shower of light as they encased the three forms.

Instantly, the shades rose into the air, twisting as their mouths opened into a noiseless scream that somehow echoed deep inside Julian's head. The pain that ripped along his skull was instant, and he closed his eyes, staggering back from the force of it.

When he was able to focus again, the air was rank with dark energy. It sizzled as he pulled in gulps of air, and it fed the beast, which answered in kind. He felt it stir, that part of him that he'd been fighting for days. The empty space inside him expanded, and he knew that, before long, it would eat the last bit of his soul until there was nothing left.

The rage that pounded in his chest erupted into an ominous growl as he crouched low, ready to battle. Three forms lay at Declan's feet. Their energy seemed to fluctuate, as if they were holographs gone crazy. Light still danced around them as they twitched, and their true forms bled through intermittently.

Julian stood quickly and crossed to where they lay in pathetic ruin. Their huge eyes gazed up at him, their mouths open in a macabre grimace. Declan was breathing hard and held his hands aloft. His face was devoid of emotion as he blasted the shades once more.

They writhed along the wet concrete, and Julian could again hear their screams inside his head, though they were now faint and more of an annoyance than anything.

He didn't have time for this shit and knelt beside them. Waiting for the moment when their true forms pulsated through, he made quick work of them with his dagger.

He felt nothing as he did so. No joy, victory, or satisfaction . . . just a big empty pile of *nothing*. He was losing his last shred of decency faster than he'd like. The darkness that surrounded him was destroying any positive energy that he had.

He looked up at Declan. "Your father is more powerful than I thought. Shades?"

Declan grabbed his Glock and dagger. "He's a slimy son of a bitch, I'll give him that, but the bastard's diet hasn't been as varied as mine." Declan grimaced. "He's not fed from true, pure darkness, and it's the only thing I've eaten for months."

The two men looked at each other, and an understanding passed. This was the end of the line, and they would make the most of it.

"Let's go." Julian was on the move before Declan had

a chance to react. The burn beneath his skin pushed him forward, and sweat ran down his bare chest in rivulets. The scars that lay there were raw, and he passed a hand over them, wincing as he did so.

"Mine hurt like hell," Declan said.

Julian ignored the comment. "Where we headed?" he asked roughly.

Declan smiled and nodded into the ever-swirling shadow and mist. "Follow me."

They began to jog, their footsteps muffled, though Julian heard the steady drip of water. It was a constant in the otherwise bizarre and random space. He couldn't see clearly. It was obvious the basement was large, and if the casino above it was any indication, they had a lot of ground to cover.

The farther they penetrated, the darker, more malicious the shadows became. Every sense Julian possessed was on high alert.

His com unit began to make noise, and he paused, growling as the static began in earnest. He was just about to rip it from his head when a voice slipped through. Clear, precise, and feminine.

Jaden.

"Julian?" Her voice echoed in his ear, teasing him with its warmth, and he stopped cold. She sounded tense. He tapped the unit, but there was nothing, only static, and he wondered if he'd imagined the entire thing.

"Did you hear that?" he asked roughly, as Declan turned back to him.

"What?"

"Jaden. I thought I heard her."

"Dude, we're so close to the prize, you need to forget about Jaden DaCosta. She's a warrior and can look after herself. Trust me." The sorcerer cracked a smile. "Besides, she's got crazy Nico watching her ass. Literally."

Julian snarled at his words. Energy flooded his limbs, and he felt the darkness knocking hard.

Declan's eyes narrowed. "That's good, Castille. You need to hold on to that anger. Feed from the rage that's inside you. It's our only chance." The sorcerer paused, his face harsh. "We're close."

Julian felt like his insides were ripping in two. His blood was boiling, churning through his veins, and he rotated his neck as he tried to alleviate the pressure. He closed his eyes and concentrated, opening up his senses, using every bit of power he possessed to breach the unforgiving shadow that surrounded him.

In spite of the chaotic darkness, she still called to him.

His body stilled, and he heard the beating of his heart and his lungs expanding as he dragged air deep into them. Something soft and feminine slid over him and teased his nostrils. His jaguar erupted painfully as it recognized the smell.

Jaden. She was near.

And she was in trouble. Her scent was filled with fear, pain, and rage.

"It's right there," Declan murmured.

Julian's eyes flew open, and he glanced toward the far corner. Declan started forward, then turned to him. "You coming?"

Julian was so close, he couldn't believe he was contemplating abandoning his endgame. For Jaden DaCosta. "I can't leave her. She's in trouble."

Declan's face was fierce. "I'll hold him off as long as I can, but there are no guarantees. If we fuck this up, you know what happens."

Julian was stunned at the direction he wanted to take. It was then that he realized an absolute truth. He loved Jaden. Her snarkiness, mind, strength, stubbornness, and beauty. Everything about her. To think he'd find such a connection when his world was about to end was ironic.

The burning desire to get to her, to make sure she was safe, couldn't be denied. He would leave this world, honor his bargain, but he needed to see her one more time.

"I'll be back." Julian whirled around and disappeared into the shadows.

Pain ripped along Jaden's forearm as Benicio knocked the Glock from her hand. The warrior had rushed forward and attacked as she'd fired off a shot. The bullet had gone wide. She heard the *clang* as it hit one of the containers above them.

And then there was nothing. No sound. Only the fast beating of her heart and the breaths that fell in puffs of mist from between her lips.

Her right hand still held the dagger, and she dropped to the floor in a defensive crouch as Benicio shifted into his animal. The large jaguar eyed her intently, its canines dripping with saliva as it panted and waited.

For several long seconds, no one moved.

And then Jakobi walked toward her. Slowly she stood, her mind whirling in several directions at once, but there was no way out. She knew that now.

He stopped a few inches from her, and she swallowed as her eyes focused on the slight flare of his nostrils. He sneered, and she was shocked at the hatred that lit his eyes.

"You disgusting whore." His voice was controlled, measured, and each word sank like a stone into the pit of her stomach. She wanted so much to feel nothing, but the raw

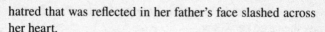

hatred that was reflected in her father's face slashed across her heart.

"Name-calling doesn't become you," she answered softly.

His fist flew out, a blur of air, and pain exploded along her cheek as he landed a blow. Her head snapped back, and she felt blood flood her mouth as her teeth cut through flesh.

She staggered backward, and the dagger clattered to the concrete as she struggled to maintain her balance. And he was there again, another blow to her chest, then another, as he pummeled her to the ground.

"You would mate with a Castille? And flaunt your indecent act in front of me?" Jakobi's voice was like crushed glass, fury shadowing his words in layers of darkness.

He grabbed her hair and pulled hard until she was forced to stand once more. Her lungs ached as she tried to drag air into them, and blood dripped into her eye from a cut on her forehead.

"How . . ." she began, then fell into silence. It didn't matter. Jakobi DaCosta's reach was long and tenacious. She'd been on borrowed time for months. It was surprising he'd not discovered her secrets sooner.

"I can smell *him* on you. Julian Castille." He spit the words at her. Though the entire side of her face ached, and her skull was on fire, she held her chin up and squared her shoulders.

His eyes narrowed into slits of dark liquid, and a feral smile gripped his mouth. Jaden swallowed, and the sadness that fell over her heart was as harsh as the pain he'd inflicted.

This man was her father. He'd loved her, cherished her at one time. The memories were real, weren't they?

"If only you'd been on the hunt with your mother that day—"

That got her attention. Jaden yanked her hair from his

grasp. "You would have killed me, too?" Her chest heaved as she faced her father.

"Gladly," he whispered. "I knew then you'd be no different than her. Traitorous bitch that she was." He smiled, a cold, calculating turn that raised the hair on the back of her neck. "I told her as she was taking her last breaths that I would cut out your heart one day."

She heard Degas snicker, but her father had all of her attention. His handsome features were cloaked in shadow. He was evil. The darkness inside of him coated his features in a macabre caricature that was nothing like the memories of her youth.

"What happened to you?" she whispered. Her soul cried out as pain lanced across her chest, the sorrow inside of her was enormous. So much lost and for what?

Jakobi's hands snaked toward her, and though she tried to duck, to maneuver away from him, he was too quick. She yelped as his long fingers encircled her neck.

He pushed her back and slammed her body against the steel shelving behind her. A sharp edge dug into her back, and a strangled, gurgling sound escaped from her lips as his claws elongated and dug into her tender flesh.

The roaring in her ears subsided until all she heard was the heavy silence that surrounded them. Her father cocked his head as he continued to apply more pressure, cutting off her airway as he did so. She was a specimen to be studied as he choked the life out of her.

A tingling along her flesh began in earnest, and a spark of energy rushed through her veins. Her eyelids fluttered, and one thought crept into her head.

Juilan.

The edge of her mind railed against the darkness, and her vision began to blur as she struggled to breathe. Her hands gripped his shoulders in an effort to push him off her. He was too strong, too filled with hate-fueled adrenaline.

Her clan tattoos burned in earnest, and she struggled to hold on, a guttural cry escaping from between her lips as her frustration spilled out.

Jakobi lowered his head until he was inches away, and his whisper caressed her flesh as he smiled. "I haven't had this much fun since the last time I saw your mother . . . alive." He pressed his thumb into her esophagus, and she closed her eyes against his madness.

"And we've only just started."

The pressure increased, her mind filled with crimson, then suddenly, his hands loosened and fell away. She clawed at him as her lungs expanded painfully, and she drew in great gulps of air.

Surprise was mirrored in her father's eyes, and she pushed him away, not understanding until she was able to slide from beneath him.

Her brother, Degas, stood inches from her, a malicious smile resting upon his face as Jakobi leaned against the shelves in an effort to hold himself erect. Jaden staggered away, her mind confused as she took in the scene before her.

Her dagger was embedded deep within Jakobi's back, put there by her brother's hand. She knew by the position, the charmed blade had cut through to his lungs, maybe even nicked his heart if he still had one.

It was a fatal blow.

Her father slowly turned though he fell to one knee as he looked up at Degas, cold fury etched upon his features. He opened his mouth to speak. Blood was already pooling at the corners, and nothing but a wheezing sound escaped.

"You taught me well, Father. I've been waiting patiently for the right time to take my place at the head of this family,"

Degas said calmly. He used his foot to push Jakobi to the ground, then he turned to Jaden, his tone flat. "And then there were two." Laughter slid from between his thin lips as a smile lifted the corners. "But not for long."

Jaden eyed her brother carefully as her father's lifeless body toppled over inches from her. She had seconds.

Shadows played hide-and-seek around them, and the ominous evil that she'd sensed earlier was fully awake, feeding from the madness that surrounded her.

It was now or never.

She exploded into action, ripping the blade from her father's flesh, ignoring the thick feel of it as it slid from his body. Anticipation was her friend, and fresh adrenaline fueled her limbs as she rose into the air and kicked outward, her heel connecting with Degas's chest in a vicious blow.

She knew that Benicio was on the move and whirled around, her dagger at the ready as the large cat rushed toward her. A guttural roar erupted from the darkness, and Benicio stumbled as a new player entered the game.

A flash of gold cleared her vision. It was a jaguar.

Julian.

She had no time to process any of it.

Degas slammed into her, his large frame taking her to the ground with him. Jaden's only thought was to hold on to the dagger, her fingers aching with the effort it took to achieve that, and still, it slid from her grasp.

They rolled along the concrete, a mess of limbs, curses, and determination.

Jaden squirmed beneath her brother, her claws ripping into his chest. She knew only one of them would survive. Degas outweighed her by over a hundred pounds, most of it muscle, and tears pricked her eyes as she continued to struggle. Even with her warrior strength, he was too strong.

His head crashed into hers, and a dull whack sounded as her skull connected with the hard floor. Stars floated in front of her eyes, and she blinked rapidly in an effort to clear her vision. She saw the dagger, it lay just out of reach. *Fuck!*

His hands slid up the side of her skull, and he bent down so that his eyes were inches from hers.

"Ready to join Father?" he asked.

Jaden's heart broke in that moment as she lay beneath a brother she once loved. A brother who'd taught her to ride a bike and had stood up to Alphonso, the neighborhood bully.

So many things had been lost as the fragile thread that made up her life lay in tatters.

She bucked wildly, and her body slid a few inches. She was close. Her fingers clawed along the wet pavement until she found the prize. She would not give in. Degas had made his choices, and now she must as well.

Ready to join Father?

She prayed for strength, and hissed, "Are you?"

Her fingers grasped the edge of the blade and she attacked with all her might. She screamed, venting her pain, frustration, and rage as she heaved forward and swiped the dagger across Degas's neck. She felt it cut through flesh and bone. She felt the warm spray of blood as it splattered against her flesh. He thrashed against her, and still she held, not relaxing until his body stilled.

She turned from him, feeling the cold wet concrete at her back, and stared into the lifeless eyes of her father. A roaring echoed inside her head, gripping her painfully.

And then she felt nothing.

Chapter 29

Julian leapt away from the dead jaguar, leaving its broken body to fall to the ground. His only thought was to get to Jaden, and her scream penetrated the black wall of rage that clouded his eyes.

The ancient magick of his people slid over his limbs as he shifted back into human form. He was at her side in an instant and gripped the body on top of her, throwing Degas aside in his effort to get to her.

Blood was everywhere, agitating his jaguar, and for a second his heart stopped cold.

Was she dead?

Pain the likes of which he'd not yet experienced rushed through him, gripping his heart and pulling every string available. Not even when he was ensconced deep within the armpit of hell, had he felt such anguish.

Gently, he gathered her close, and when he heard her heart beating, felt the air in her lungs, something akin to peace settled over him. He shuddered from the strength of it.

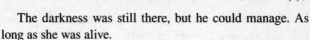

The darkness was still there, but he could manage. As long as she was alive.

Her eyes flew open, stared up into his, and she shifted in his embrace, her arms encircling his chest with a strength that was surprising. He closed his eyes, relishing her touch, wanting her to crawl inside him.

"Julian." Her whispered word, the sound of her voice, was like a soothing balm that slid across his flesh.

She trembled in his arms, and he pulled her away from the carnage that was her family. He buried his face within the silken length of her hair and inhaled her scent. He knew it was something he'd never lose. Her smell. The memory of her touch.

Wherever the hell he ended up, at least he'd have that.

He could have stayed like that for hours, simply drinking in the warmth of her flesh and the feel of her in his arms. There was no time.

"Where is the rest of the team?" he asked.

She shook her head. "I don't know. Nico, Ana, and I were doing a grid search, but the shadows, they . . ." She paused, and he felt her gather her strength. "They're full of dark magick, and we became separated."

"We need to get to Declan." His tone was urgent, and Jaden nodded in understanding.

"Let's do this," she answered.

His hand rose to gently remove the solitary tear she'd allowed to fall. She rested her cheek in his palm, her soft skin like velvet against his rough hand. Such need gripped him that he gritted his teeth until his jaw ached.

She pulled away and turned without another look back. "Come on, Castille. We've a date with the devil."

His warrior woman had returned, sliding back into her skin with ease.

Julian snarled as he scooped up the remnants of his trousers and followed her into the dark.

Declan felt dead eyes watching him from the shadows. He paid them no mind. The shades were there in abundance, but they held back, wary of the power that clung to him.

The bastards were smart to stay away.

Small puffs of mist evaporated as he exhaled slowly. Just ahead, he saw the outline of a large contained area. Above it, the thread of energy that called to him writhed and shimmered in a chaotic blend of mist and magick. It coated the room in a protective shield, and he felt the power of it hanging in the air.

It really was stunning. He'd have to compliment Cormac on it.

His dark eyes narrowed, and his mouth thinned as he cautiously made his way forward. Noises slid out from the dark, whispers and howls of pain. He ignored them all, his focus concentrated on the room.

Azaiel was inside, as was his father. He could *feel* it. The fallen might be Julian's priority, but it wasn't his. Bill the elf could go screw himself. The driving need to see his father pay for his sins was what had gotten him through his darkest hours in hell.

He'd imagined so many ways. *Christ, it was the only bright spot.*

His chest burned, and he hissed, as his hand automatically passed over the scarred flesh. It had been killing him for hours, the clean precise lines a constant reminder of the emptiness inside him.

It told him that the end was near. He was cool with that.

He tapped into the well of power that was inside him, the one that had fed from the purest fountain of evil. *Lilith.* He let it expand and soak into his cells as he moved his hands in the air, weaving an intricate spell as the energy flowed through him.

He would break the protection ward and destroy his father. It was the only reason he'd come back. The only reason he'd danced with Lilith.

You came back for Ana. He pushed the thought aside. It didn't matter anymore.

Darkness pulled at him hard, and he panted from the force of it. It was a delicate balance, the line between good and evil. He just needed to hold on a bit longer. There was no other option.

Minutes passed as he worked feverishly to break through the wards his father had constructed. The shades disappeared altogether; he felt their presence lessen as he worked and knew they were part of the intricate pattern his father had created.

"Declan."

He stilled, his gut tightening as his frame tensed. He gave no indication he'd heard anything, though her voice, low and rough, like she'd inhaled a bottle of whiskey, touched a chord inside of him that stretched painfully.

She'd always had that effect on him. From the first moment he'd laid eyes on her, he'd been done for.

Ana.

She was the one woman on the planet who could literally have him by the balls and didn't give a damn either way.

She stepped into his line of sight, and the two of them stared at each other in silence. The world faded into gray swirling mist and white noise. Her long amber waves hung in tangles, dampness curling the ends wildly. Her dress had been ripped off well above the knee, leaving a vast expanse of bare leg, and her eyes shone like round pools of licorice.

He saw the edges of her fangs; they were distended, and he could tell by the way her chest rose and fell rapidly that the vampire was on edge.

She should be. The night was rancid with the scent of evil. He should know. He'd been inhaling a steady diet of it for months.

"Where are the others?" he asked, not pleased to see her. Ana owned the damaged, ripped pieces of his soul, yet she didn't care. He didn't have the time or energy to waste worrying about her.

He wanted to deal with Cormac on his own.

"I don't know where Jaden got to . . . we became separated," she hissed, and shook her head. "This place is not for the living. It's haunted."

Declan arched a brow. "Well, technically you're already dead, so I suppose you feel right at home then."

Her face froze, the eyes huge, as her features shifted, and the cold facade he'd come to know so well slid into place, nice and easy. The woman would never change, and he was through playing games.

He started forward as the flame of anger inside him erupted, begging to ignite into an inferno. Ana squared her shoulders and stood her ground, meeting him like the warrior that she was.

He stood within an inch of her, his nostrils flaring as her scent rose in the air, teasing him with its exotic signature. This woman represented everything that he'd ever wanted and a future that he'd never gain.

The fact that *finally* he didn't give a damn was liberating.

"The fallen is in there, and so is Cormac. Wait for the others."

Something inside him broke loose, bringing with it a sense of freedom he'd not felt in ages.

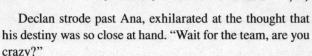

Declan strode past Ana, exhilarated at the thought that his destiny was so close at hand. "Wait for the team, are you crazy?"

Her hand grabbed his arm and yanked hard, stopping him instantly. The petite vampire packed three hundred years of power in her grip. She was strong. He stared down into her eyes. Normally, they were blue but at the moment were solid black balls of fury.

She was pissed. He could see that.

A wicked grin slid across his face, and suddenly he bent low. A gasp escaped from between her lips, and he felt her stiffen beneath his hand, as his mouth grazed her softness. It was nothing more than a whisper of touch. A good-bye.

He lifted his head and removed her hand from his arm. "Crazy doesn't come close to describing what I am."

Declan felt her gaze upon his back as he turned from her and strode purposefully toward the room. Energy sizzled against his flesh as his hand fell upon the door. Cormac's ward was faltering.

His hand tightened upon the handle, and Declan felt it give way as he pushed the door open.

Jaxon felt the shift in the air at the same time as Jagger. He frowned and stared into the darkness. They were surrounded by creatures the likes of which he'd never seen before though he'd read reports about them. They were shades, beings that hovered between the living and the dead. Their existence was a permanent state of chaos . . . of pain.

Shades were forever trapped in their own hellish form of purgatory.

Silence filled his ears. It pressed down upon him, and he stilled. His senses sharpened, and his jaguar stirred, agitated, as the shades slowly evaporated into nothing.

He glanced back at Libby, saw the confusion on her face, and winked at her. Her eyes widened, and a quick smile claimed her mouth. She was good. He wished that she was home with Logan, but knew Libby had the skills to take care of herself.

A low-grade keening erupted from the shadows as if the walls themselves were alive. The energy thinned, and he felt it begin to pulsate as the darkness moaned, like the world was tipping, and the edges were ripping away.

And, always, the sound of dripping water echoed in the distance.

Cracker moved in close to his side. The hardened soldier spit on the ground, his movements steady and precise as he did so. He sniffled and smiled fiercely. "The shit's going to hit the fan any—"

The moaning wavered, amplified into layers, splitting the dark with a hard thrust as the shadows parted violently. Wind came at them from all directions, bringing with it bone-chilling cold.

Jaxon heard Libby gasp as an impressive array of bodies stepped forward, solidifying within seconds. There had to be forty or more demons, and every single one of them began to make a strange series of clicking noises.

Cracker gripped his Glock in his right hand and held his impressive machete in front of him with his left. Jaxon heard him murmur, "Time to rock and roll, boys and girls."

Jaxon knew they needed to act quickly. Within minutes, the demons would transform into their true selves.

He gritted his teeth, and his eyes flattened into a cold black stare. "Stay safe and shoot to kill. Aim for their heads," he yelled at his team. He turned quickly to Libby and nailed her with an intense look. "You stay close to me and don't take any chances. We need to blast a hole through their formation."

She waved her dagger as she stood loose on the balls of her feet. "Don't worry about me. I'll stay close. Someone needs to make sure you don't get your ass kicked."

Jaxon arched an eyebrow, his face dark, though his heart swelled at her words. The woman never failed to surprise him.

The clacking reached a crescendo. Jaxon was about to give the order to move out and attack when, suddenly, it stopped. There was no sound other than the steady drip of water and a constant moaning that was slowly fading away.

A roar sliced through night, and his jaguar reacted painfully. At the same moment, one of the demons pitched forward, smoke rising from the back of its head as it fell into a lifeless heap at his feet.

Dark liquid spewed everywhere, and a rancid odor erupted into the air.

"Someone told me there was a party down here. Good to know they were right." Ethan Crane stood several feet behind the line of demons, at his side was a large black jaguar. *Nico.*

Julian was nowhere to be seen. Neither was Declan. Not good.

Ethan snarled, his eyes glowing with a fierce light as he nodded to Jaxon. "Seems a little tame for my liking."

Jaxon looked to Cracker. "Now." At the same time, Ethan double-fisted a pair of deadly Glocks and opened fire.

All hell broke loose.

Chapter 30

Julian heard the sounds of battle well before they could see anything. He and Jaden slipped between the long rows of shelving as they rushed forward.

The entire building seemed to be moving, as if the earth beneath the concrete was heaving, protesting the darkness that slithered along the surface. The constant cold was relentless, yet his flesh was heated, and mist rose from his skin.

"Holy Christ," Jaden whispered, and he paused, his eyes following her line of sight. Above them, a thin ribbon of energy pulsated in the air. Its strength fluctuated as it continued to weave amidst the darkness, shimmering one second, dulling to near invisible the next.

"It's Cormac," he said.

Jaden nodded in agreement. "I can smell him. His scent is evil." Her teeth flashed in the gloom, and her breath was ragged. "We need to end this." She turned to him. "It *has* to end tonight."

"Agreed."

She turned to leave, but Julian grabbed her to him, relishing the feel of her heat against his bare chest. There were no words for the intensity of what he was feeling.

He stared down at her, took note of every nuance that made her features unique. Her soft lips parted as agitated breaths escaped . . . the curve of her cheek, the tilt of her nose. She'd brought him a certain peace, and he knew the image of her as she was right now, in his arms, was one he'd carry to the grave.

"Jaden, know that . . ." he began, and faltered.

"It's okay, Julian," she whispered.

Loud bursts of gunfire echoed through the dull, thick air. He cupped her chin. "Know that in another lifetime, you would have been all I needed."

"Why wait for another lifetime? Why can't we have our happy ending right now?" She was angry, the tone of her words sharp.

He didn't answer. The joy of the moment was gone, and he turned from her. It could never happen. His deal was done. "Let's go."

The pulsing energy above them was like a beacon that cut through the darkness, and he knew they were close. As they neared the target, he glanced back at Jaden and indicated silence.

The air was thick with the smell of death, of demon and of black magick. He caught trace signatures of both Declan and Ana and knew that they were near.

Sporadic bursts of light rippled across the ceiling, casting macabre shadows in their wake. He heard shouts, screams, and moans of pain and rage.

Julian centered himself, and his senses exploded from

within, traveling along an invisible conduit as he searched the immediate area for anything that didn't belong.

The hairs along the back of his neck stood on end, and he snarled softly, relishing the power that flooded his cells as he whirled around, a dagger held in his hand, a vicious growl escaping from between his lips.

There was no need.

Jaden was already wiping the blood that dripped from her knife. The crimson liquid stood sharply against the never-ending dull of gray and black. His eyes settled upon the body on the ground. It lay at a weird angle, and he marveled at the strength of his woman.

It was a young male, and Cormac's mark was clear against his pale skin. The sorry bastard never had a chance. He was much too young to resist O'Hara's pull. His lifeless eyes stared up at Julian, and he shook his head. *What a fucking waste.*

A fiery scream ripped through the layers of thick air, and his nostrils quivered as the pain continued to pour out into the night. It was a long, drawn-out cry, and it rode the cool thread of air with such sharp madness that he fought the urge to cover his ears.

Jaden took off running before he had a chance to react. He was fast on her heels, adrenaline pumping hard, fueling his muscles into a blur of speed. The two of them covered several hundred yards in seconds. Above them, the gray gave way to light, and suddenly they were in the thick of it.

He saw a large room to the left. The energy thread that hovered overhead surrounded the entire circumference, caressing the walls in a shower of sparks.

Before him was madness.

He pulled up short, his hand on Jaden's shoulder as they quickly scouted out the scene. The blackness inside of him reveled in the violence in the air, and he felt it expand. All around him was chaos.

His brothers, their women . . . the rest of the team . . . all of them were fighting for their lives. A snarl ripped from his throat as he jumped forward, deep into the fray.

No sense in letting them have all the fun.

"Stay close to me," he shouted at Jaden, his teeth slashing white as he smiled at her reaction. She flashed him her middle finger before cleanly severing the head of a demon that rushed her from behind.

The woman could clearly look after herself.

"We need to get inside." His brother Jaxon had his attention, and Julian nodded, slicing his way through the demon wall as he and Jaden fought their way toward the door.

They were the closest.

The demons were desperately trying to prevent them from gaining entrance, yet they were losing the battle. Jaxon and his crew had taken care of all but a few of them. It only confirmed the obvious.

Cormac was inside, and that meant that the fallen was as well.

Jaden leapt over several dead bodies, her gun firing as she did so. Julian followed in her wake, his dagger dripping dark with the foul poison of demon blood as he secured their path.

His chest heaved as he reached the door, and he snarled madly as his fingers gripped the handle. It was painfully hot, a vibrant conduit of energy that shot up his forearm.

His need to get to Azaiel was riding him hard. Everything was so close to being completed.

"Fuck," he yelled, hissing as he gripped it harder and pushed it open.

Behind him, the noise evaporated into nothing but a mess

that was easily ignored. How could it not? The sight before him was sobering.

He felt Jaden at his back, felt her warmth against his skin and the horror in her voice as she ducked around him.

"Oh my God," she whispered hoarsely.

"God has nothing to do with this."

An eerie howl whistled through the room, accompanied by a phantom wind that came from nowhere. The corners were in complete darkness, shrouded in mist and fog. The only light was centered in the middle.

Above them, suspended high in the air, was a man, his body bathed in a soft glow that should have been comforting but, instead, was sinister. His arms were spread wide, held aloft by invisible threads as he slowly turned in a circle. His upper body was bare, the lean, muscled lines, however, awash in crimson.

Blood flowed from his hands and dripped from his feet. His head hung low, as if he were unconscious, and as he made a full turn, Julian noticed the large wings that were tattooed upon his shoulders.

His eyes narrowed, and he realized they were not tattoos but an intricate marking that had been carved into his skin with perfect precision.

This was without a doubt Azaiel. The fallen.

The room was encased in iron walls that bled with never-ending water. It was in every miserable corner, the constant cold and wetness.

"Azaiel doesn't look like he's loving Vegas so much," Jaden whispered.

Julian didn't answer but stepped into the room.

Where the hell were Declan and Ana? He'd expected Cormac to be here as well.

Behind him, all sound ceased. There was no more fighting,

no grunts of pain or screams of rage. He glanced back and saw the shock on every single face that filed into the room.

His brothers, their women, Nico, Finn, and Cracker . . . all of them were silent. Ethan Crane seemed a little unsettled at the sight of Azaiel suspended high in the air.

Julian smelled the evil in the air and knew that the shadows hid something dark.

Jagger pushed through and aimed his weapon into the air, but Julian grabbed it. "You will not shoot," he snapped.

Jagger studied him for several long seconds. "You got a better idea how to get him down from there?"

"Where's Declan?" Jaden asked, stepping between the two brothers.

"He's there. Beyond."

The words were hoarse and fell at them from above. Julian glanced up at Azaiel. The fallen's eyes were open. They shimmered, their black roundness shot through with gold. It was fucking freaky, and if he had a spare pair of glasses, he'd toss them up pronto.

"And just when I thought this evening couldn't get any more interesting."

Cormac O'Hara appeared from the shadows, the invisible cloak of dark slipping from his body as he emerged into the light. His hand was gripped tight around Ana's neck. Foam fell from the corners of her mouth, and her eyes were dull. Crisp white fangs peeked from between her pale lips, and the sorrow in the depths of her eyes seemed inconsolable.

"Step forward, son. Don't be shy."

Julian held Jaden still as Declan slid from between sheets of mist. His face was blank, though Julian felt his anger. His hands were clenched into fists, the lines around his mouth white with tension.

Cormac glanced up at the fallen and smiled wickedly. "Azaiel, are you willing?"

Silence greeted his words. Julian looked sharply at Declan. The sorcerer was staring straight ahead, his eyes not focused on any of them.

Julian was uneasy, not understanding the game. They had the bastard surrounded. He was about to charge forward when Nico snarled.

He was still in his animal form and barked loudly, his challenge unmistakable.

Cormac didn't look at the animal. In fact, his eyes never left the body suspended in the air. He flicked his free hand, as if it was an afterthought, and Nico went down. Hard.

The howl that erupted from within the jaguar was bone-chilling, and Jaden fell to Nico's side.

Cormac continued to stare up at the fallen, the predatory smile never leaving his face. "Azaiel, will you not at least answer me?"

Julian gritted his teeth, letting the anger inside of him burn hard and fast. He chanced a glance at Jaxon. His brother was studying the sorcerer intently, his body shielding Libby. The look on his face was pure hatred.

He wanted to grab the bastard by the throat and squeeze his last breath from him, but he had to be smart. He could feel the seductive shield of magic against Cormac's flesh, and he knew it was deadly. Cormac had a protection ward in place that was ironclad.

His mind continued to whirl as the drama unfolded in front of him.

He watched as Azaiel gazed down upon Cormac and felt the surge of power that lay within the fallen. It was suppressed somehow, as if it were a capped geyser.

Julian's eyes fell to the floor and swept over an intricate

series of designs. He frowned. They could have been fucking Chinese for all he cared. He needed to figure out how to get to Azaiel.

Cormac suddenly looked away from the fallen and directly at Jaxon. "Libby, why must you hide behind that beast? Will you not show your face?"

A kiss of winter lived in his eyes as Cormac smiled widely and glanced back at Declan. Libby stepped forward, but Julian could tell it was not her own doing. She was being compelled, and Jaxon cursed as she slipped in front of him.

"Your brother won't cooperate. Declan knows where the portal is or, at the very least, how Azaiel is tied to it." Cormac grimaced and dug his fingers into Ana's neck, sliding his hand along the skin that was now slick with her blood, as he pushed her to the floor. "He thinks that as long as he plays his game and keeps this from me, I won't hurt the vampire." He laughed softly. "That he can stretch time and somehow defeat me."

"I hate you," Libby whispered.

Cormac cocked his head to the side and sighed. "I know." He spoke slowly, as if lecturing a small child. He dragged Ana along the ground, and Julian growled loudly as he rushed forward, only to be knocked back by the shimmering protection ward that hung in front of them.

Energy sizzled along his skin, burning into Julian's flesh as he snarled. Declan's eyes were now completely black, and the air around him began to blur. Cormac couldn't see it. His focus was on Libby and the vampire.

"Guess I won't win Father of the Year." He sighed and shook his head. "Though I do keep my promises. You know this, Libby."

He winked at Libby, a ghost of a smile playing around the corners of his mouth, and stretched out his fingers as a long, dangerous stake flew from nowhere into his welcoming hand.

Declan's face was dark and twisted, guttural sounds fell from his lips. His entire body shook.

"I told Declan the vampire would die if he didn't bow to my wishes." The sorcerer stilled. "He didn't believe me."

All motion ceased. Julian was aware that Jaden was at his side once more, her arm on his as a scream erupted from her throat. All of it echoed in his head as a film of black crept into his vision.

Declan struggled to speak. His face was mottled red, filled with rage. It was obvious he was not in control, but he managed to snarl, "Do not touch her."

Cormac's face twisted into a grimace, his voice lowered and fell from his mouth in layers. "Your time is up."

He pushed Ana down as if she were nothing more than a puppet and, without pausing, plunged the stake directly into her heart.

There was no dramatic ending, no smoke. Her body didn't dissolve into mist or ash. She just stopped moving.

Julian stared at the vampire in shock as time stilled. The silence in his ears was deafening.

The floor beneath his feet trembled, and the protection ward in front of him shimmered erratically, as cracks began to infiltrate the magick. Cormac leapt from Ana's body and turned to Declan.

"You would think to challenge me? You're nothing more than a pathetic shadow of your mother." He gestured toward Libby. "Both of my offspring have sorely disappointed me. It is a sad truth that the child Logan shows the most promise."

"You'll never get near him again," Jaxon said, his anger barely contained in his words.

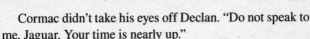

Cormac didn't take his eyes off Declan. "Do not speak to me, Jaguar. Your time is nearly up."

Cormac held his hands aloft and gently arced his fingers, motioning to the shadows. Loud growls that sounded like crushed glass sliding across chalkboard slid out at them.

Julian pushed Jaden behind him. He recognized the sound.

Azaiel continued to spin in the air, his body picking up speed as he twisted crazily.

The wards that separated them pulsated as Declan's hands slowly rose. His eyes were now deep crimson. He didn't say a word as his limbs moved slowly, and he stepped out of Cormac's compulsion.

The hatred and anger that had lived inside Declan for six months erupted into a cry of pain that echoed inside the room, but it was soon drowned out by the madness that ran at them from the shadows.

The protection wards vanished, and there was nothing between them and four hellhounds.

Chapter 31

J aden exploded into action, her only thought to protect her mate, but Julian shoved her out of the way. The men rushed forward, ready to form a line of defense.

She had no time to curse their chauvinistic behavior. Skye stood off to the side, her Glock aimed dead center on Azaiel.

"No!" she screamed, and ran toward the eagle knight, knocking the gun from her hand as it discharged, and the round went wild.

Jaden barely missed the fist that flew out at her as the blonde cursed loudly. "What the fuck are you doing? I had him!"

She didn't have time to explain. "You will not kill him. We need him alive."

Skye's eyes flashed, and she spit her words out angrily. "That bastard, you don't know what he's done."

Jaden whirled around. "I understand, trust me, but it's not gonna happen."

Everywhere, chaos rained down upon them. Cormac and Declan were locked in a deadly battle, and the men were fighting off the four rabid hellhounds.

The patrons in Black Magick thought they were seeing cutting-edge entertainment. If only they knew. Down here, it was like Buffy had exploded into reality. Who the hell needed late-night cable?

"I think your plan is about to fail." Skye shoved past her, as Jaden eyed the fallen closely. He was still spinning madly, his arms spread wide. Blood flew from his body as he teetered in the air.

He jerked and fell several feet until he hovered in the air like a grotesque marionette.

Jaden's eyes fell to the markings on the floor. She had no clue what they meant but knew they'd harm the fallen if he touched them.

She heard Cormac screech in pain, heard Skye curse and Julian shout in rage. She ignored all of it. Crane was off to the side, his cold face set as he aimed his gun.

Azaiel began to free-fall, and she rushed forward, and leapt into the air. The energy that lay upon the markings burned her skin as she sailed over them, and she grabbed Aziel, taking him with her as they tumbled to the ground on the other side.

Pain exploded in her shoulder, fiery hot, and it shot across her body as she landed on top of the fallen.

She'd been hit.

She pushed herself up. Goddamn, but the pain was bad.

Azaiel stared directly at her, the bicolored swirls in his eyes hypnotic. "I will not harm you." The words echoed inside her head though he'd not opened his mouth to speak.

She felt the world falling away and clung to him desperately. She knew she needed to protect the fallen until Julian

could complete his mission. She had to protect her mate at all costs, even if it meant giving her life.

"Move away from him." She turned to the side and looked up at Ethan Crane. His face was grim, and a deadly machete was held firm in his hand.

"I will not," Jaden hissed, barely able to get the words out. "You will not harm him."

The wolf eyed her as the madness continued all around them. "We came here to take him out, and I'll put another one of these special bullets through your other shoulder if you don't get your ass off him."

Ethan Crane was a singularly focused operative. He meant what he said.

Crimson bled into her line of vision, and she shook her head, feeling the world tip once more. An edge of panic threatened and knew she needed to focus.

She looked across the room and locked eyes with Julian. The rage she saw in the depths of his was startling, and he yelled as he leapt over the dead carcass of one of the hounds, his dagger swinging wide as he cut the head off another.

His mouth was moving, the words were there, but she couldn't hear a thing.

He charged Crane and slammed into him before the wolf had time to react. The two men rolled across the concrete, and Crane cursed loudly as his foot touched the edge of the etching that lay there.

It was enough. Julian flipped him over and pinned him, his hands going around Crane's neck, the fingers digging deep.

Her head rolled back, and it was Azaiel who caught her against his chest, held her carefully as the poison circulated through her system. She saw Cormac and Declan locked into a fight to the death, and her soul cried out at all the violence.

She shuddered, and whispered, *"Why?"*

Because I was weak. Azaiel's words slipped into her mind, and she heard the world of pain that colored them. With her last bit of strength, she pushed herself up, leaning heavily against Azaiel's body for support as she looked to the right.

Declan was crouched over a body. He stood, but a deadly dagger remained behind, embedded deep within Cormac's chest.

Libby was at his side as they stared down at the writhing man who was their father.

"You are pathetic. I will not let you win." He spit up at them, his voice hoarse, filled with hatred.

Libby looked down at Cormac and pointed the Glock she held in her hand. "Beat this, asshole."

And then she emptied the entire magazine into his body.

Cormac's body spun over as the force of the shots hit him hard. The floor still shook, and an unearthly scream fell from his mouth as he crawled several feet away. Blood spewed from his wounds, trickled from his nose and mouth. He clutched his chest, ripped the dagger from within and tossed it aside.

"I will not end here . . . at your hand." Cormac's voice was raspy, vibrating thickly.

Declan took two steps, his hands turning in the air as he spoke. "That would be the wrong answer."

Cormac's body rose in the air, a grating scream falling from his mouth as his body trembled. His form stretched and twisted in a macabre dance, and Jaden, turned away, horrified.

Silence fell, and when she chanced a look, Cormac was no more.

Julian's warmth was around her, his hands cupping her

face as his dark eyes bored into hers. He pulled her from Azaiel, deep into his embrace as he cuddled her against his chest.

"Why did you . . ." He couldn't finish his sentence.

"It's not that bad," she whispered and smiled, though the lie was blatant. She knew the wound wasn't fatal. Not for her, but, still, the pain was killer. "I couldn't let him die. He's your only chance at finding the portal."

She rested her head against his shoulder, wanting to drink in his smell, his warmth. "I'm so tired."

"I say we separate the bastard's head from his body and be done with it. He dies, and the location of the portal goes with him." Ethan was breathing heavily, his eyes filled with anger as he challenged Julian.

You will not touch him.

A blinding light pierced the darkness, illuminating the entire room. It laid bare the carnage and the loss. Julian tightened his arms around Jaden as she struggled to sit up in his embrace, to stay conscious.

The center of the far wall liquefied, the gray swirling into diamonds as the light continued to evolve into a hole. Out of it stepped a man. He was small, round, and less than ordinary.

"Bill." Julian spoke quietly.

The little bastard elf was right on time.

"Who the hell are you?" Ethan glowered and moved forward. Bill held out his hand, and the wolf froze.

"Seraphiel," Azaiel whispered, and struggled to gain his feet. His abused, bloodied body was weak, but he pressed on.

"Surely you knew we'd find you one day?" Bill said, a jovial smile gracing his features. "It took two half-broken men to get it done, and I'm not certain anyone really believed they could do it, but I'm very pleased."

He winked at them all as if he were sharing a secret. "Once Azaiel was liberated from the hell realm, we lost touch. We are limited in our abilities to track each other, the original seven."

"We?" Jaxon asked, though his eyes never strayed from Libby. She was bent over Ana, her face wet with tears.

"The Seraphim."

"Angels," Skye whispered as she moved closer to Jagger.

Bill smiled and walked around the hellhounds, who lay in grotesque shapes upon the floor. He was careful where he placed his feet, and Julian held tightly to the woman in his arms as he approached.

"Stay back," Jaxon warned.

Guess my time is up. Julian glanced back at his brothers and shook his head, telling them it was all right.

And yet it wasn't. He didn't want to leave her.

Bill bent over. "She's beautiful, your lady."

Julian nodded but didn't speak. What the hell was there to say?

Bill righted himself, his hand scratching his head as if he were slightly confused. "Too bad she'll be left incomplete for the remainder of her days."

"What the hell does that mean?" Nico had shifted back to his human form and clutched his midsection, several large bruises already forming to join the older scars.

"Well, Nikolai, it means that Mr. Castille and Mr. O'Hara made a deal with me. We needed to get our hands on the portal, but with no way of tracking Azaiel, we had to outsource."

Bill paused and looked back to Declan, but the sorcerer's eyes were held by Ana's still form. "They had the motivation we needed. A man cannot live with only half of his soul. Without light to give him salvation, he will fall into the abyss. It's only a question of time. In exchange for handing Azaiel back to us, we agreed to return the missing bits and pieces of their souls that were left behind, and, well, they'll have to serve our organization for the next little while."

Julian snorted. *Next little while? A thousand fucking years?*

Jaden's eyes flew open, and he couldn't bear the look that lay there.

"You were never coming back?"

"No."

"Oh," she whispered, then took a deep breath. "It wouldn't have worked anyway. I was never a white-picket-fence kinda girl. Besides, Castilles and DaCostas don't mix." She sounded flip, but he knew her pain.

Her bottom lip trembled, and, in that moment, he knew that if he could he'd change everything, he'd live with only half a soul. It hit him then.

Jaden DaCosta was his light. *She* was his salvation.

"You have to know you are everything to me. Your strength and courage, your passion . . . I'll never forget one second of the time we've spent together." Her dark eyes glistened, and his heart cracked as a single tear fell from the corner. "I love you, Jaden. I always will no matter where I end up."

She touched him, a gentle caress full of sadness. "Ditto," she whispered.

The bitterness of regret and the weight of his mistakes punched him in the gut. He looked away from her and into the hard eyes of Nico.

"Take me instead," the warrior whispered.

"It's not that simple, my friend," Bill said, his tone still jovial, though his eyes narrowed as he studied the other jaguar.

Nico glared at the small man, his teeth exposed as he snarled in anger. "Let's make it that simple. I'll do whatever you ask. Something good has to come out of this entire mess."

Bill puckered his mouth. "I suppose—as long as I return with the two bodies I promised." He glanced down at Julian. "Are you willing to live in limbo?" he asked, and nodded to the woman in his arms. "She is your true path to salvation and is the only thing that will keep the darkness from claiming you whole."

Julian didn't speak. He looked at Nico, saw the determination, and knew his sacrifice was for Jaden. Nico's dark eyes were focused, clear. He knew what he was doing.

He turned his attention to Bill, tried to be strong, but his voice broke as he spoke. "I will never leave her."

Bill glanced up at his brothers. "If he strays, the darkness will corrupt. I will destroy him." The small man's true face was revealed, only for a second, but there was no doubt his stature hid great power.

Jaden stirred in Julian's embrace, and he knew she was weak from her wound. "Let me . . ." He let her go and stood as she stumbled toward Nico. She wrapped her arms around the warrior, but Nico hesitated, before pulling her close. She cupped his face and kissed him softly, whispering words not meant for anyone other than the jaguar.

"All right, Azaiel. It's been a long time, old friend. Lots to catch up on."

Azaiel stretched out his long limbs. The blood had finally stopped flowing, and his features were sharp as he nodded at Bill.

"I'm ready."

"Where the hell is the portal?" Crane exploded.

"I am the portal." Azaiel turned to them, his golden eyes

clear of the darkness that had bled into them earlier. "It is inside me."

Bill clapped his hands together. "This is good. We've taken care of some nasty business, recovered a fallen. Good times, my friends, but it's time to go."

Julian looked at Nico and nodded, unable to articulate his thanks.

"I'm not doing this for you," Nico said roughly. "Take care of her. She tends to run first without looking."

Julian nodded and welcomed Jaden back into his embrace. Inside, the cat that had long hungered for a mate was finally at rest.

"Mr. O'Hara?" Bill nodded toward the sorcerer. "You ready?"

The sorcerer knelt by Ana's still form. His hand grazed her pale cheek, traced the lines of her mouth, then he stood. He cracked his neck and rolled his shoulders. His eyes were still fully black, and, when he looked at Julian, he was shocked at their dead countenance.

"There's nothing for me here."

Bill winked at Julian, as if they were sharing a beer or a joke, then a blinding light swallowed them whole.

For several long seconds, there were no words, and Julian was content to cradle Jaden as she breathed against him. Her heart was beating like mad, and he found the rhythm intoxicating. It meant that she was alive, and, after so many months of darkness, so was he.

"You gave up peace to be with me?"

"I gave up nothing," he replied. "In fact, I gained more than I deserve." His mouth lowered, and he caressed her lips softly. "Nothing will part us. That's my promise to you."

Jaden snuggled against his chest. "That man, Bill. I've met him before. He was the drunk at the bar who said I'd find something of value in your penthouse. It's why I went there, or I might never have . . ." She shook her head. "I thought he was a shifter, but he was a freaking angel."

She looked up at him, and his heart constricted painfully. "I mean, isn't it a sin for them to booze it up?"

Julian snorted. "I think the Seraphim have their own rules and don't give a damn about anything else."

"So that's it? We done here?" Ethan Crane arched a brow.

Jagger glanced around. "Our objective was to destroy the portal. With Azaiel returning to the upper realm, I think we're good." He slipped his arms around Skye's midsection and pulled her in close. "We're headed back to Jersey. As for the rest of you, I really don't give a damn."

Crane nodded toward Julian. "No hard feelings. I wasn't aiming for your lady."

"Let's take Ana home." Libby's soft voice drew their attention.

"I can't believe she's dead," Jaden whispered. "And Declan, did you see his face? How can he recover from that? He loved her. I hope she knew."

Julian watched as Jaxon scooped up the vampire's lifeless form and turned toward the door.

"Will Declan be all right? Will we ever see him again?" Jaden murmured.

Julian shook his head. "I have no idea."

"Let's go. I've got operatives near the kitchen entrance. We can make our way out with the least amount of visibility." Jaxon's voice was wooden. Ana had been a member of his team for years. He'd just lost family. "Good work, everyone. We're done here."

Julian nodded. "Jaden needs a doctor."

"You coming back to base?" Jaxon asked.

"For now, but once Jaden's been looked after . . ."

"We'll head home . . . to Mexico," she finished.

"You've still got brothers out there, members of the DaCosta organization who will be gunning for your ass." Jaxon frowned. "I think the compound in Canada will be safer."

"No," Jaden said firmly, "my home is in the jungle. They will not defeat me." Her voice shook, and Julian's heart turned over.

"We'll be fine," Julian said. "And if needed, I know you've got our backs."

Jaxon nodded. "Always."

He watched as Jaxon disappeared. *Home.* Funny that thought, one that wasn't solitary but included the lady in his arms.

The jungle. Hot nights and a woman who completed him.

It was so simple . . . and it was all he needed.

Epilogue

The darkness pressed down on her. She felt it, along the edges of her mind and didn't want to open her eyes. But the hunger inside was near consuming and, in the end, forced her awake.

Layers of blackness had to be dealt with, and she worked feverishly to tear them down. Satin, wood, concrete, then the cool touch of earth.

Within minutes, moonbeams caressed her face, and she inhaled great gulps of air deep into her lungs. Which hurt, as if ill used.

In fact, her entire body ached.

And there was the thirst. It was constant and pushed her on until she clawed her way out and fell upon the cold, frozen ground.

"Hello, Ana."

She jerked up, her head twisting to the side as she sought the voice that slid from the darkness.

"Who'?" she croaked, her vocal cords sore.

"Ah, I'm not surprised you don't remember, but do try . . ."

She peered into the dark and her eyes widened as a small form fell from shadow.

"Bill." She answered, confused and afraid at the same time. She knew him. As fuzzy as her brain was, she knew him and she knew *what he was.* "I'm . . . I don't . . ."

She shook her head and closed her mouth. She couldn't articulate the madness inside her mind. It was overshadowed by the hunger.

He sat down on the ground beside her and smiled. "You were dead." He tapped her on the shoulder. "And now you're not."

"First things first." He motioned toward the shadows, and she watched silently as a young man walked toward her. He was so very pale. Moonbeams emphasized the thin blue veins that carried what she so desperately wanted.

The man stopped and sat beside Bill, who promptly withdrew a sharp knife and plunged it into his jugular. Blood spurted everywhere, and her fangs exploded painfully as her world of darkness became drenched in crimson.

Bill wiped his hands, a look of distaste crossing his face. He nodded toward the dying human. "Feed." And then he turned away though his voice drifted back toward her as the night enveloped him.

"I'll be back. We have lots to discuss."

Ana was awash in fire and consumed with need. She hissed, and everything faded away until there was nothing but pain.

A groan fell from the young man. His life was leaving him. Ana pulled him close and fed.

*For millennia the struggle between light and dark
has been policed by a secret group of warriors
culled from every fabric of existence. Their pledge:
to protect the line between the two realms and
ensure neither side grows too powerful. If they fall,
so shall the earth, the heavens and hell. The cov-
enant shall break apart and there will be no more.*

Wicked Road to Hell

THE FIRST BOOK IN

The League of Guardians

JULIANA STONE'S BRAND NEW SERIES
DESCENDS SUMMER 2012
FROM AVON BOOKS.

DON'T MISS THE PREQUEL
NOVELLA COMING FROM
AVON IMPULSE, FEBRUARY 2012.

78-0-06-200304-1

978-0-06-173508-0

978-0-06-204508-9

978-0-06-199079-3

978-0-06-203368-0

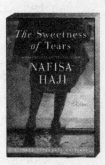

978-0-06-178010-3

At Avon Books, we know your passion for romance—once you finish one of our novels, you find yourself wanting more.

May we tempt you with . . .

- **Excerpts** from our upcoming releases.

- Entertaining **extras**, including authors' personal photo albums and book lists.

- Behind-the-scenes **scoop** on your favorite characters and series.

- **Sweepstakes** for the chance to win free books, romantic getaways, and other fun prizes.

- Writing **tips** from our authors and editors.

- **Blog** with our authors and find out why they love to write romance.

- **Exclusive content** that's not contained within the pages of our novels.

Join us at
www.avonbooks.com

AVON

An Imprint of HarperCollins*Publishers*
www.avonromance.com

Available wherever books are sold or please call 1-800-331-3761 to order.

FTH 0700